PRAISE FOR IM

An Unwanted Inheritance

'Brimful of emotion – a wonderful plot and characters that you are rooting for, even when you know you shouldn't. *An Unwanted Inheritance* is that gem of a thing: a story to truly lose yourself in. I LOVED IT!'

—Faith Hogan, bestselling author of
The Ladies' Midnight Swimming Club

'What happens when you drop a bag of cash right in the middle of three siblings and their families? A whole lot of good fun and drama. *An Unwanted Inheritance* delightfully explores the flaws that come with being human as Clark plunges us into a story about what is right and wrong and what it means to be a family. She ratchets up the tension as the story races to its surprising and oh-so-satisfying conclusion.'

—Boo Walker, bestselling author of *The Singing Trees*

'A gripping tale about money, greed, and what really matters.'

—Anstey Harris, bestselling author of
The Truths and Triumphs of Grace Atherton

'Imogen Clark deftly peels back the layers of loyalty, family secrets and moral dilemma to examine a family that must make a choice between need, greed and integrity. Pacey, thought provoking, and with characters that test the ties of blood, marriage and friendship to the limit, *An Unwanted Inheritance* will have you wondering how far you'd go to uphold your own principles – and how much, or how little, it would take to betray them.'

—Julietta Henderson, author of
The Funny Thing about Norman Forman

'Lovingly crafted, with flawed and nuanced characters, this riveting story will stay with readers long after the last page is turned.'

—Christine Nolfi, bestselling author of *A Brighter Flame*

Reluctantly Home

'Connected by loss, a friendship blooms across the generations in this compassionate and nuanced story of endings and new beginnings.'

—Fiona Valpy, bestselling author of *The Skylark's Secret*

'Imogen Clark is a master at creating flawed, real, lovable characters and exploring their emotions. This novel cleverly weaves together the past and present, and will leave you thinking about the story long after you finish the final page.'

—Soraya M. Lane, bestselling author of
Wives of War and *The Last Correspondent*

The Last Piece

'This is a wonderful novel about the secrets we keep from the ones we love the most. Imogen Clark has a real talent for shining a light on the idiosyncrasies of family life and revealing past traumas, present hurts and future hopes.'

—ictoria Connelly, author of *The Rose Girls* and
Love in an English Garden

'*The Last Piece* is a beautifully crafted, insightful tale about family and the cracks below the surface of seemingly perfect lives. Clark's characters, with their various secrets and flaws, leap off the page. A most enjoyable and riveting read.'

—S.D. Robertson, author of *My Sister's Lies* and
Time to Say Goodbye

'I couldn't resist going on this journey with the Nightingale family. With emotion on every page and mystery swirling around each character, *The Last Piece* explores how the past can be as unpredictable as the future. I raced through this life-affirming book, which left me buoyed with the promise of second chances.'

—Jo Furniss, author of *The Last to Know*

Where the Story Starts

'Once again . . . Imogen Clark urges readers to turn the pages as the delightfully pleasant facade of her characters' lives begins to crack when the mysteries of the past come to call. Both soothing and riveting, *Where the Story Starts* asks: what if your greatest secret is the one you don't even know exists?'

—Amber Cowie, author of *Rapid Falls* and *Raven Lane*

The Thing About Clare

'Warm and emotionally complex . . . A family drama that's hard to disentangle yourself from.'
—Nick Alexander, bestselling author of *Things We Never Said*

In a
Single
Moment

ALSO BY IMOGEN CLARK

Postcards from a Stranger

The Thing About Clare

Postcards at Christmas (a novella)

Where the Story Starts

The Last Piece

Reluctantly Home

Impossible to Forget

An Unwanted Inheritance

In a Single Moment

IMOGEN CLARK

LAKE UNION PUBLISHING

Text copyright © 2023 by Blue Lizard Books Ltd
All rights reserved.

Published by Lake Union Publishing, Seattle

www.apub.com

Amazon, the Amazon logo, and Lake Union Publishing are trademarks of Amazon.com, Inc., or its affiliates.

ISBN-13: 9781542034562
eISBN: 9781542034579

Cover design by The Brewster Project
Cover images: © Quang Vinh Tran © wilkastok / Shutterstock

Printed in the United States of America

In a
Single
Moment

1976

1

It was the heat. It bore down on her, forcing its way into her already burgeoning body. Sweat trickled from her hairline and across her face. She could feel it pooling in the hollows at her collarbones.

She longed to fill her lungs with cool, crisp air but there was only the stale sort that felt as if it had already been breathed in and out a hundred times. She tried to visualise a mountainside, fresh green grass sparkling with dew, a crystal-clear brook babbling its way down to a deep lake where the water was so icy cold it would take your breath away.

But then the image was snatched away from her, and the oppressive, heavy atmosphere filled her nostrils again. She could smell the sharp tang of antiseptic and beneath that hot bodies, no doubt washed less frequently than usual due to the effort of collecting water from the emergency standpipes along the street.

And then another wave crashed over her, and all thoughts were washed away as she focused entirely on the pain of the contraction.

'That's it, Michelle,' she heard the midwife say. The voice sounded distant, as if the woman was speaking to her from another room. 'Try to keep your breathing nice and steady. It won't be long now.'

Michelle wanted to scream at her that she was doing her best but this was as steady as she could manage. It was her fourth baby and she'd got the measure of her labours, so she knew the midwife was right. It would be over soon, but the awful, overwhelming heat was shifting all the goalposts. She really wasn't sure she had the strength to keep going. One minute she felt as insubstantial and limp as a damp rag and the next a rigid poker of pain seared through her, making every muscle in her body as solid as steel. The rhythm of it was relentless.

The pain subsided again, and Michelle felt her aching muscles sag. Dean would be in the pub now, celebrating the birth of his child before he even knew it had happened. She pictured him, pint in hand, laughing with his mates without a care in the world whilst she . . .

The thought of the pub made her realise just how thirsty she was. Her tongue was sticking to the roof of her mouth and her lips felt as if they might crack if she smiled, not that there was any danger of that.

'Water,' she croaked.

It came out more dramatically than she'd intended, like something from *Lawrence of Arabia*. The midwife passed her a half-filled tumbler and Michelle craned her head up and took a gulp. The water was tepid and unsatisfying but it would have to do.

And then the pains were at her again and this time she knew it was nearly all over. She gritted her teeth and pressed on.

Michelle and Dean had first got together at school where neither of them had been convinced about the importance of a solid education. They had married in haste to avoid scandal, Michelle's bouquet hiding what it could, and Carl had come along four months later. After that Tina and Damien had followed in quick succession and then there had been a merciful hiatus before Michelle unexpectedly found herself once again pregnant at twenty-five.

She had been horrified at first. What would they do with another child? Where would it sleep, for a start? The house was already rammed full. And then there were food, clothes, all the other stuff kids needed. Dean brought in a decent wage from the garage, but without what she earned at the engineering works she knew they'd struggle to make ends meet. But how could she hold down a job and bring up four kids? It was impossible.

But as the baby began to grow inside her, Michelle had known that they would muddle through somehow. Even though they might never have got married but for the accidental first child, she and Dean made a strong team. He wouldn't let her down. And he hadn't. When she'd told him that five were soon to become six, the fear on his face had been fleeting, and swiftly replaced by a not-unconvincing grin.

'Well, there you go,' he'd said, with a lascivious raise of an eyebrow. 'There's plenty of lead left in my pencil!'

She'd swung her handbag at him, bashing him gently on the side of his head and he'd swept her off her feet and squeezed her tightly. She'd known then that she truly loved him and always would.

But right now, she could cheerfully saw off his head with a plastic knife and feed it to the seagulls on the Brayford. And why was it so hot? Did they not have fans in these places? How could she possibly be expected to give birth when she couldn't actually breathe? The window was open but its pale green curtain dangled limply with no hint of a breeze to move it. The air felt stifling, cloying, sticky on her already sticky skin. She needed to get this baby out just so that she could have a shower. They had water in hospitals, she assumed. No standpipes here.

And then the pain changed again and the primal need to push overtook her.

2

Michelle leaned back in the bed. Her dark hair, darkened further by sweat, was plastered to her head and her body ached from the rigours of the past few hours, but she was otherwise bathed in a glow of contentment. Her newborn baby lay in her arms, sated and sleeping.

Michelle ran a finger over the silky-smooth skin of the baby's brand-new cheek, let the tiny dark eyelashes brush her own fingernail. It was a miracle. She thought that every time, but it really was true. How had she created someone so tiny and so perfect?

The baby's plump fists were curled tight like snail shells, and Michelle tried to slide her little finger inside without waking her. The tiny fingers unfurled a little to accommodate her and then renewed their grip. Michelle felt their connection bloom in her heart. It was as if some part of her were channelling directly into her child and vice versa.

A moment later, the baby opened her eyes and met Michelle's gaze. They contemplated one another, a silent introduction of sorts.

'Hello there, gorgeous,' whispered Michelle. 'I'm your mummy.'

The baby seemed to trace the features of her face, finally settling on her eyes and then, secure and content, she fell back asleep. She was smaller than the others had been, just over seven pounds to their seven and a half, but she had the same dark hair that they had all had. She had Dean's nose and chin and maybe something about the eyebrows too. He would be pleased about that. Someone had once told Michelle that all babies looked like their fathers. It was nature's way of building a bond between a man and his child, so there could be no doubt as to paternity. Well, that was certainly true in her case. All four of her children had come out looking the spit of their dad, their features only altering after a few weeks, until eventually she could see her own features reflected back at her. This little one was no exception.

It was quiet in the room, the other three beds currently unoccupied. Two were freshly made but the one next to her had a body-shaped dint in the bedding, and there were some belongings scattered around. Michelle tutted to herself. This was a public space. You couldn't just take it over because you were in labour. She looked at what there was, trying to form an idea of the woman who had left them there. A patchwork tote bag was spilling its contents over the floor. There was a paperback novel and a notebook of some kind with a pencil jammed into the spine as well as an expensive-looking jumper – in this heat? – and a hairbrush. She couldn't see what else was inside but from the bulge of it there was clearly more.

The bed was strewn with discarded clothing as if the occupant of the space had performed a striptease. A cheesecloth dress in a pale lemon and a white T-shirt, the straps of a cotton maternity bra just peeping out beneath. Maybe whoever it was had been in a hurry to get to the delivery room and there hadn't been time to tidy up their belongings, Michelle thought charitably. There was no room for mess in her own life. Five, no, wait, six people in a compact three-bedroom terraced house made sure of that.

There were voices in the corridor outside. She recognised Dean's, getting louder as he approached. She didn't catch what he was saying but she could tell from the tone that he was flirting. She pictured the younger nurses blushing prettily as he complimented them. It was entertaining to watch Dean at work with other women from the security of her place in his heart. He was your natural charmer – how else had she ended up with a baby at seventeen?

'That's your daddy,' she whispered to the baby. 'He's coming to meet you and then we can give you a name.'

She lifted the baby and placed a gentle kiss on her forehead. The baby stirred but didn't open her eyes.

'Hello, hello. And where is my beautiful baby?' Dean asked as he came through the door, making no allowance for the hushed surroundings.

'Shhh,' urged Michelle. 'You'll wake her.'

Dean pulled a face. 'Sorry.'

He was carrying a pink teddy bear that was bigger than the baby and he placed it on top of her.

'There you go, darling,' he said. 'A present from your dad.'

Michelle snatched the bear away.

'You'll smother her,' she said, tutting. 'And what are you doing buying her that? She's less than a day old. She doesn't need toys.'

Dean looked crestfallen and Michelle instantly regretted her tone.

'I just thought . . . I got it on the market. It wasn't much. And all babies need a teddy bear, don't they?' he said.

Michelle smiled at him, trying to make up for her sharpness.

'They do,' she said kindly. 'But no more, eh? We've got enough on without you . . .' She wanted to say wasting money on stupid soft toys, but instead she said, 'buying lovely presents.'

Dean shrugged. 'She might be the fourth, but she's just as precious to me as our Carl was when he arrived,' he said.

Michelle took the bear and tried to get it to sit up on the bed next to her, but it wouldn't bend at the middle and so it either had to stand erect or lie flat and stare at the ceiling.

'Before bears, we need to give her a name,' she said.

'Fair enough,' he replied. 'Any thoughts?'

Michelle had had hundreds of thoughts during the nine long months of her pregnancy, but one name had kept coming back to her. She had practised saying it out loud when no one was listening, not wanting to tempt fate, but at the same time needing to feel the shape of it in her mouth.

'I wondered about Donna,' she said.

She had suggested the name before but Dean would never concentrate on names until the babies actually arrived. He nodded thoughtfully, trying it on for size.

'Donna. Donna,' he mused. 'Like Donna Summer?'

No. Not like Donna Summer, Michelle thought. Donna in her own right and not like anyone else, but if that helped to sell the name to Dean then she was happy to go ahead with it.

'Yes,' she said.

Dean stuck out his bottom lip as he considered the suggestion. 'Donna White,' he said after a moment or two. 'It's got a nice ring to it. Carl, Tina, Damien and Donna. Sounds good with the others too. Yeah. I can go for that.'

Michelle smiled.

'Good. Donna it is then,' she said.

Donna gave a little snuffle as if to say that she approved.

3

It was dark outside when the mysterious woman from the next bed came back into the room. A porter was pushing her in a hospital wheelchair and there was an inordinate amount of fuss as they manoeuvred her from the chair to the bed. Michelle wondered if the woman had had a C-section but decided against. It was probably just stitches. If the poor cow thinks she's sore now, Michelle speculated to herself, then just wait until the anaesthetic wears off.

No one took any notice of her, so she closed her eyes again and lay still, just listening.

'There you go, love,' said a male voice, the porter no doubt. 'Good luck.'

'Thank you so much.'

That must be the mother, Michelle thought. Her voice was ribbon-thin and posh-sounding, slightly higher than an adult's. A child's voice, a slightly frightened child.

And then, 'Where's . . . Leonora?' The tone of the mother's voice suggested that she wasn't actually that interested, that she was asking because she knew she ought to.

Leonora?! That was one hell of a name. Michelle fought the urge to open her eyes and see exactly what kind of people had named their child that, but if they knew she was awake she would miss the chance to spy on them and so she resisted the temptation.

'She's right here, my love,' said a second woman's voice, older, gentle.

The sound of a crib being trundled into the room.

'Shall I pass her to you? You need to get those lovely mummy and baby bonds building.'

That must be the midwife. They were forever banging on about maternal bonding, as if any mother wouldn't immediately connect with her own child.

There was a whimper. An actual whimper. Michelle couldn't resist peeping through her half-shut eyes to see. The woman was a wisp of a thing, but much older than Michelle would have guessed at going by her voice. It was almost impossible to believe that she had been nine months pregnant just hours before. She flopped back against the bed, her eyes closed. She had wild chestnut hair that fanned out on the pillow around her head in such a way that it looked as if it had been carefully placed like that. And she was pale. She reminded Michelle of those consumptive women you saw in old films.

The midwife was gathering the baby out of the crib but the woman, the mother, put her hand up to stop her.

'I can't. Not now. Jeremy. You take her.'

He must be the father, but he wasn't in Michelle's rather limited line of sight.

The baby was fussing now. Michelle recognised that plaintiff newborn mewl. If they didn't comfort it then the fuss would quickly build to a full-blown cry. But the midwife knew this. Michelle could hear her crooning to the child and imagined her rocking it gently to settle it.

'Somebody wants their mummy,' she said in a sing-song voice.

The baby must have been handed over then because there was much rustling of bedclothes and several 'ouch'es from the woman.

'There,' said the midwife. 'Isn't that lovely?'

The man spoke then.

'Oh, for a camera,' he said, 'to capture the two most perfect creatures in the world in repose.'

'I'm not sure a camera would be quite the thing just now,' the midwife said hurriedly. 'Let's wait until Mum and Baby have had a good night's sleep.'

'I could sketch you,' he said. 'Preserve the moment. What do you say, Sylvie? Shall I draw you as you sleep?'

Who was this clown? thought Michelle. What kind of idiot drew pictures in the middle of the night? Unable to resist any longer, she opened her eyes fully now to see. The room was dim, lit only by the light from the corridor outside. The woman, Sylvie, was lying on top of the bed – it was still far too hot to climb under the blankets – with the baby placed on her chest. She was wearing a white cotton nightdress with lace round the collar and cuffs. It was like something you'd see in a low-budget horror movie, chosen to portray innocence. Totally impractical to give birth in. Michelle thought of the long T-shirt that she used for the purpose, bleach-stained and with a hole where next door's dog had chewed through it, but far more serviceable than pure white cotton.

The man had his back to her and his hair stuck up from his head in a halo of frizz. He was wearing flared cords and a long-sleeved burgundy shirt, making no concessions to the searing heat of the day just gone. Michelle wondered if they were aliens who had just dropped in from another planet. They certainly didn't belong in the world she occupied.

Their baby was no longer just mewling. It was building up a proper head of steam. Michelle felt herself tense. If they weren't careful, they were going to wake Donna, currently sleeping quietly in the crib at the side of her own bed. A wave of exhaustion washed over Michelle as she thought of all the broken nights that lay ahead of her. She really needed to sleep through this one, when her baby was full and exhausted from the very stressful business of being born. Once she got home she would be thrown straight back into the rigours of family life. No one would remember to make any allowances for the fact that she had just had a baby. Michelle began to curse the woman internally. Just settle the baby and let us all get some sleep.

But the woman was still objecting.

'I can't,' she whined again, holding the baby out at arm's length and looking in horror at her husband. 'What's wrong with her anyway? I've only just fed her. She can't be hungry. Not so soon.'

The midwife took the dangling baby and pulled her tightly into her ample chest.

'She just wants to hear your heartbeat, love,' said the midwife, her kind tone slipping a little. 'You give her a nice cuddle, and I bet she falls straight back to sleep in your arms.'

But Sylvie was having none of it. She closed her eyes and turned her head away from the baby.

'I just need to sleep.'

Michelle bit her tongue. It was all she could do not to tell the woman to stop being so ridiculous and just take her child. This was motherhood, which involved making sacrifices. It started right now and Sylvie needed to step up.

The husband, Jeremy was it, was no better, dancing around the bed, about as much use as a chocolate teapot. The baby's cries were becoming steadily more anguished and the midwife was bouncing her with more and more vigour.

'I tell you what,' she said. 'How about I take Baby to the nursery for tonight? Let you get some sleep. I'm sure tomorrow you'll feel a whole lot better.'

Sylvie gave her a look that radiated gratitude.

'Oh, that would be perfect,' she said in her tiny voice. 'Thank you.'

And then Donna woke up. She took a deep breath of hot stuffy air into her tiny lungs and let out a yell that Michelle would have been proud of had it not been the middle of the night. She was at breaking point too. She just needed to sleep.

She reached over and tried to stroke her baby back to sleep, her insides aching at the awkward movement.

'Now then, Donna,' she said pointedly. 'It's rubbish being woken up, isn't it? I know, lovely, I know. But there's no need to make all that noise.'

The midwife looked over.

'Are you okay there, Michelle?' she asked.

'I was,' replied Michelle, glaring at Sylvie. 'If you're going to take her baby to the nursery then could you take Donna too and then we can all get some sleep?'

'Of course. When did she last feed?'

Time had started to do strange things in Michelle's head. She looked at the clock on the wall and tried to work out how long she had been asleep. Had it really only been forty minutes?

'Less than an hour ago,' she said vaguely. 'And it was a good long one. She's full to the gunwales.'

'Then that's fine. I'll take them both and bring them back to you when they need feeding or we'll give them a bottle depending on the time.' She placed the complaining Leonora back into her crib carefully. 'Could you push Baby, please, Daddy?' she said to the man.

Then she put her sturdy hands on to the sides of Donna's crib and the two of them left the room in convoy.

The other woman let out a noise that sounded between a sigh and a whimper, and dropped deeper into the pillows. Michelle was expecting an apology or some thanks at the very least, but the woman didn't address her at all and within seconds appeared to have fallen asleep. And a minute after that, so had Michelle.

4

When Michelle woke up, she had no idea where she was and it took a moment or two for the world to resettle itself into some order around her. The temperature had dropped a little, mercifully, but the air was still cloying and over-warm. The low ache in her abdomen reminded her of what was no longer safe inside her, and in a panic, her eyes darted to the side of the bed. Where was Donna? Where was her baby?

Then she remembered. The scene in the night with the woman in the next bed, the babies being taken to the nursery. She looked over to see if her neighbour was still asleep but the bed was empty. She must have gone to the bathroom. There was no sign of her baby either.

Michelle felt perkier than she had done for a while. It was amazing what one decent night's sleep could do. She loved her family to pieces, but there was usually some form of nocturnal kerfuffle that required her to get up. Dean seemed to become deaf after dark.

In the corridor outside her room she could hear the hustle and bustle of the ward already wide awake. It must be late. The clock on the wall told her that it was almost nine. Michelle's chest tightened. Donna couldn't possibly have gone that long without a feed. It must be – she struggled to do the calculations in her head – at least six hours since she'd last fed her.

She sat up gingerly and edged her way to standing. The coppery tang of blood filled her nostrils. She had forgotten that the maternity ward smelled like this. So many women all bleeding in harmony. She suppressed a little shudder.

Now she was upright she felt relatively normal, just hot and thirsty, but then that was normal these days. She poured herself a glass of lukewarm water from the plastic jug on her side table and drank it in one. Then she set off to find Donna.

As she stepped out of her room a familiar voice rang out.

'Mum!'

Michelle turned awkwardly towards the door to see Carl, Tina and Damien heading towards her. Eight, seven and five years old, they made a proper little gang, taking up most of the available space as they barrelled down the corridor.

'We saw Donna,' said Tina before she was close enough to tell her without shouting the information. 'She's so diddy. I wanted to pick her up, but Dad said we had to leave her to sleep.'

'Never wake a sleeping baby,' said Carl, her eldest child and already with plenty of baby-care experience in his short life.

Michelle gave him a fond smile. 'That's right, Carl,' she said. 'Although she must have been asleep for ages. I've only just woken up.' Her hand went to her hair, which felt as though it had dried sticking up at comical angles.

'The nurse lady said that they gave her a bottle in the night because you were sparked out,' said Tina, proud that she had news to give her mother.

Michelle's heart sank a little. She had been planning to feed this last one herself to try and create some special bonding time, but it was probably easier if Donna was bottle-fed like the others. At least it appeared she would take either happily. That's what Michelle needed this time – a nice easy baby. Such a thing would be a first, though: none of her children had been without their challenges so far. Still, maybe this would be fourth time lucky.

'We've come to take you home,' said little Damien, his expression so earnest that it made Michelle smile.

She went to scoop him up as she would usually do, but next to the tininess of Donna he looked lumpen and far too big to be her child. She stopped shy of lifting him up but he still launched himself at her and then recoiled when his hands met the soft flab of her babyless stomach.

'Errr, yuk,' he said. 'Your belly's all soggy.'

Michelle rolled her eyes.

'Thanks for that, Day,' she said. 'Where's your dad?'

Tina turned and pointed to the nurses' station where Dean was chatting animatedly to a midwife with steely grey hair and a face to match, but even she appeared to be succumbing to his charms, a smile both on her lips and in her eyes.

Dean seemed to sense that they were talking about him and turned round.

'Morning, love,' he said and gave her the kind of grin that had always melted her heart. 'The lovely Betty here says that you can go home. Just need to sign a couple of forms.'

This wasn't what Michelle had had in mind. She had planned to stay at least three nights in the hospital, more if she could swing it, a mini holiday from the chaos of home. Didn't she deserve that at the very least?

But she knew that Dean struggled with the kids on his own. She'd arranged for Sharon next door to watch them before and after school, but Sharon had three herself. Seven children under eight was a lot for anyone to take on. It was probably for the best if she just went home and stepped up. After all, four kids was her lot now; she might as well start getting used to it.

'Well, give me ten minutes to have a bath,' she said. 'I can't go out in this state. What's the weather like out there today?'

'Hot!' they all chorused.

◆　◆　◆

It took longer than ten minutes to get herself ready. She lay in the cool bathwater pressing at her tender womb and marvelling that it had, until so recently, contained a baby. They said it took nine months to grow a baby and nine months to get your body back to normal, but Michelle had never had any difficulty on that score. The first three pregnancies had barely left a mark and she had no reason to imagine that this last one would be any different.

And this would be the last baby. Of that she was absolutely certain. Donna had been an accident, or a surprise as she had now decided to refer to her. She would make sure that there were no more of those. Life was tough enough as it was.

Eventually, with her damp hair pulled back into a ponytail and her empty maternity dress billowing as she walked, she was ready to leave.

In the room where she'd had just one blissful night's sleep her family were waiting for her. Carl was playing with the pedal that raised the bed up and down. He had tipped it up like a dumper truck and Damien was clinging on to the headboard and pretending that he was on a cliff face. Tina had taken a rose out of a forgotten vase of flowers and was plucking each petal off in turn and discarding them in a trail across the floor. Dean was reading the paper, the bare breasts of that day's Page Three girl creased beneath his hands.

The baby, Donna, was in her crib still sound asleep. She was dressed in nothing more than a vest and a nappy, but then it was so very hot that was maybe all she needed. Michelle wondered what had happened to the little all-in-one she had been wearing the night before. It was nothing special, but all three of her children had worn it and she didn't want to lose it.

'Have you got that little towelling Babygro that I put her in yesterday?' she asked. 'The green one with the frogs on it?'

Dean merely shrugged.

'They just handed her over like that,' he said. 'Her nappy's clean,' he added with a gleeful smile.

'Newborn nappies are no problem,' replied Michelle. 'It's when they start on solids that the fun begins.' She held her nose and stretched her mouth into a grimace for the children's benefit.

'Poooey!' said Damien, as he slid down the upraised bed, taking the bedding with him.

'I'll just go and ask about the Babygro,' she said. 'Carl, can you put that bed back, please.'

Michelle made her way to the nurses' station. There was no sign of the midwife that had delivered her, or the one from the middle of the night adventures with the pointless woman in the next bed. Michelle had almost forgotten about her. The midwife who was on duty looked up expectantly as she approached.

'Hi,' she said. 'My baby was in the nursery last night and she's come back without her Babygro. It's green with frogs on it. It's as old as the hills but I'd still like it back.'

Michelle was suddenly aware of how silly she must seem, making a fuss about such a tatty garment, but baby clothes were expensive and they grew out of them so fast. Plus she was very fond of the little thing for sentimental reasons.

'Hang on,' said the midwife. 'I'll go and check.'

Michelle nodded and leaned against the counter, letting it take as much of her body weight as she could. The temperature inside was building steadily already. She dreaded to think how hot it was outside. At least she would no longer have to endure it as a heavily pregnant woman.

Further up the corridor she saw a ghostly shape in a white nightdress hobbling towards her. That was her – Sylvie. Seeing her now, Michelle could tell that she was in fact older than herself. Much older. Maybe as old as forty, although Michelle wasn't very good at estimating ages. Sylvie looked almost as old as Michelle's own mother and she was forty-one. Michelle's mum was a grandmother four times over, but something told Michelle that this baby was Sylvie's first. What had they named it? Something ridiculous. Michelle struggled to concentrate through her brain fog and finally landed on the name – Leonora. That was it. Poor kid.

She was just going to wander over and introduce herself as the woman in the next bed when the midwife reappeared clutching a little green rag.

'Is this the one?' she asked, holding the Babygro by its shoulders so it hung in mid-air, oddly empty.

Michelle smiled. 'Yes! That's the one. It's a scruffy old thing, but all four of my kids have worn it so . . .' She let her voice drift to a stop, hoping that what she was trying to say was apparent.

The midwife gave her a tight little smile and then went back to her more pressing duties.

'Thanks,' added Michelle lamely.

She turned to head back to her room. She could hear her children bickering and blew out a sigh. Maybe she would have a quick word with that woman, Sylvie was it? Just to be polite and to eke out the time before she had to slip back into her own reality. But when she turned round to where Sylvie had been, the corridor was empty.

5

Dean's car was in the car park and as soon as she saw it Michelle perceived a problem that hadn't occurred to her previously.

'How are we all going to get in there?' she said.

She didn't mean just then. Donna was tiny and so could sit on her knee in the passenger seat with the other three sliding about in the back as normal. But as the baby grew, transporting them all around was going to be a problem that would need addressing.

Dean either didn't hear her, or more likely chose to ignore her. He would tolerate no criticism, overt or implied, of his beloved flame-orange Mark III Cortina. The car was his pride and joy. Michelle sometimes thought he loved it more than he loved her, although the green sun visor with 'Dean' and 'Michelle' emblazoned on it in bold white lettering told another story.

'Right then, kids,' he was saying. 'It's going to be hot in there so let's open the windows for a bit.'

He sat in the driver's seat, swearing under his breath at the temperature, and leaned over to open Michelle's door. The heat hit her before she had even tried to get in, and she knew that the vinyl seat covers would be hot enough to blister the backs of legs. She would be just about all right in her dress, but Carl and Damien had football shorts on.

'Hold Donna,' she said to Tina, passing her the baby. Tina held Donna tightly into her shoulder, proud to have been given the responsibility over Carl, who was older than her. Michelle dug a towel out of her hospital bag and passed it to the boys. 'You lot sit on this,' she said.

Tina gave her the baby back and there was some fussing as the kids got the towel into place underneath all their legs, but eventually they were ready. Dean revved the engine unnecessarily, and then they were off.

It was only a ten-minute drive back to their street and as home got closer Michelle could feel her heart starting to get heavy. She wasn't sure she could do this. If someone had told her younger self that by the time she was twenty-five she would have four children, she would have hoped they'd got the wrong woman. She'd never had much to offer the world, with no formal qualifications to speak of, but she'd always wanted to amount to more than the people she had grown up with. It wasn't that she felt superior to them in any way. It was just that she had always expected more of herself.

But maybe she'd been wrong. As things had turned out, she'd ended up exactly the same as everyone else; living in the same block of streets she'd grown up in, with more kids than was sensible and not enough money. She needed to stop daydreaming about impossible might-have-beens and get on with the day-to-day job of living as best as she could.

The Cortina pulled into their road. It was long and as straight as a poker with the city's football stadium at one end and a clear view of the cathedral at the other. Their house was about halfway up. Michelle was no gardener, but she liked to keep the front looking neat and always made the kids pick up their toys when they'd finished with them. Her net curtains were old and a little bit ragged in places, but she bleached them regularly and they were as white as she could get them.

Sharon next door's house had less kerb appeal. The patch of lawn at the front, more weed than grass and parched brown from the drought, was strewn with bikes, buckets, a doll with no head, a rusted pogo stick and the outside of a television set, the tube having long been smashed. There was also a mattress on the pavement outside her front door that the council was supposed to be taking away but which the local youths had adopted during the heatwave for their nightly gatherings. Michelle was no snob, but she wished that Sharon could be just a little bit more house-proud.

Dean pulled the car up and the children all fell out, clearly relieved to be in the fresh air once again.

'Can we play out, Mum?' asked Tina, looking longingly at a gaggle of children about her size who were hanging around a little further down the road. Michelle nodded.

'But don't leave the street,' she said. 'And keep an eye on Damien.'

As the eldest, responsibility for younger siblings should have fallen to Carl, but he was too much like his father to be trusted with something as important as his baby brother. He was quite likely to get carried away with some game or other and forget about Damien entirely. Tina, by contrast, was her mother's daughter and even at seven was sensible enough to be trusted with the task.

Michelle swung her legs round so that she could stand up without relinquishing her grip on Donna. The sky was the cobalt blue that had become so familiar, not broken by a single cloud. The sun blazed down, and it was hard to remember a time when the weather had ever been anything but searing hot.

A little further along the road a huddle of neighbours had gathered, no doubt to bemoan the heat. They waved at her as she got out and she smiled and waved back. These were Michelle's people. She had known them all her life, growing up two streets down in the house where her mum still lived. They knew everything about each other from their middle names to what colour pants they wore, as they saw them hanging on washing lines week in and out. It was a community. Michelle sometimes wished things were different, but she knew that she had a lot to be grateful for as well.

At the sound of the car, Sharon came out into her garden. Dean's was one of only a handful of cars on the street and so their arrival home from anywhere was always noted.

'Where is she, where is she?' called Sharon as she came towards them, arms thrown wide. 'Where is that gorgeous baby girl? Seven pounds! Such a good weight. And Donna. What a pretty name.'

Dean must have given her all the details already, leaving nothing for Michelle herself to share. Sharon plucked the baby from Michelle's arms and rocked her in her arms. Donna gave a half-hearted cry but didn't have any real objections to being passed around. Michelle objected though. She had only just given birth. All she wanted was to get inside her house, put her feet up with a nice cup of tea and admire her new baby.

She was realistic enough to know that she had to get through this welcoming committee first. The arrival of a new baby on the street was hardly a rare event, but it still made a change from the tedium of the day-to-day.

Sharon rubbed her nose against Donna's face. Michelle could feel the heat radiating off her friend, together with the slightly sweet smell of dried sweat. She resisted the desire to pull away and stood her ground.

'There she is, there she is,' Sharon said in the kind of sing-songy voice that was specially reserved for infants and dogs. 'She's the spit of the others,' she said, talking to Michelle now. 'Dark hair just like them. She's got something of her own though,' she added, looking more carefully at Donna's squashed little face. 'You're your own woman, aren't you, darling?' she said to Donna, who yawned in response and then puckered up her little face as if she might cry in earnest.

Michelle took her baby back, cradling Donna against her breastbone.

'She's probably hungry,' she said. 'I'm just going to get her inside and out of this sun.'

She took a couple of steps towards her own garden.

'Yeah,' said Sharon. 'Good idea. But I'll pop round later for a cuppa. Yeah?'

Michelle gave her a weak smile.

'That'd be nice,' she lied, and then felt bad. It would be nice to see Sharon. She just needed a little bit of peace and quiet to get herself straight first.

'You go get sorted and I'll be round in a bit,' said Sharon. 'Hey, Dean!'

Dean looked up from where he was locking the car.

'You've got a proper little belter there. Congrats and all that.'

Dean raised an arm in acknowledgement.

'All my own work,' he laughed.

◆ ◆ ◆

It was cooler inside the house, and Dean had left the windows open so there was at least a breeze of sorts. Michelle could feel the sweat gathering under her arms and at her hairline. A bead was trickling down the side of her face and she swiped at it, imagining that it was an insect before she realised.

'God, this heat!' she said to no one in particular.

Dean followed her in, dropping her hospital bag on the sofa. He'd stripped off his T-shirt and his muscled torso was tanned and glistening, but Michelle couldn't muster the energy for a single lewd thought. She flopped on to the sofa, cradling Donna's head from the impact.

'Right, you settle yourself down,' Dean said. 'I'll make you a nice cuppa. I didn't know what you wanted to make for tea so I didn't get anything in but I can send Carl to the corner shop. Just say the word.'

'We need to make some bottles up,' said Michelle, weary at the thought of everything that needed doing. 'I was going to feed her myself but . . .'

'Nah,' replied Dean with a wink. 'You need to save those beauties for me.'

He nodded at her cleavage and she rolled her eyes. She wanted to point out that she had only given birth the day before and sex was very far from her mind, but what would be the point?

'I'll do the bottles today,' said Dean. 'Let you get some rest. You'll have to remind me what to do, though.'

Michelle talked him through how to sterilise them with Milton and make up the formula and soon there were enough chilling in the fridge to get them through the rest of the day and that night. She had a cup of tea at her side together with a bottle for Donna and could finally relax. She sank back into the sofa and let her eyes close for just a second.

'I thought I'd pop to the Mason's Arms,' Dean said from the doorway and Michelle looked up. His tone was breezy as if this was no big deal, but Michelle could tell from the sidelong glance he threw her way that he was nervous about the response he might get. Michelle didn't have the strength for a fight, however. On a different day, she might have pointed out that he must have done a fair bit of head-wetting the night before, but now she just nodded.

'Don't be late back,' she called after him as she heard the front door open, even though what constituted 'late' was something they never seemed to agree on.

She picked up the bottle for Donna, tested the temperature of the milk on the pale skin on the inside of her wrist, and offered the teat to her daughter who latched on to it straight away and began to suck as if her life depended on it, which it did really, Michelle thought.

As she sucked, Michelle looked at Donna's tiny face, drinking in each feature one by one. She thought she could see something of Carl about the nose, maybe Tina's eyes. What little hair she had had a definite kink in it like Damien's. That wouldn't be much fun for a girl, Michelle thought regretfully. She couldn't see anything of Dean in her now, though. Maybe nature only provided a trace of the father at birth, letting it fade once paternity had been established. As mother and daughter drifted off, Michelle hoped Dean had seen the fleeting resemblance for himself.

6

It had been a week already and Sylvie was still waiting, but it hadn't arrived. She had assumed it would crash over her like a tidal wave, or creep up on her at the very least, catching her unawares. But thus far nothing had happened. The celebrated maternal instinct that everyone had told her was as natural to a woman as breathing had not yet put in an appearance.

Each morning Sylvie plucked Leonora from her crib and held her aloft.

'Good morning, daughter,' she would say. 'How are you? Did you sleep well? Well, I know you didn't because you woke me five times. Shall we change your nappy? I imagine it must be quite wet by now. And then would you like some breakfast?'

It sounded peculiar, talking to a newborn baby as if it were an adult, but Sylvie found that she had no other way of doing it. What was she supposed to say anyway? It wasn't as if the child could understand. It all felt so silly to her, like talking to the television or to a houseplant, both of which she had been known to do in the past but only once in a while when she was lonely, and definitely not every day.

She had tried to affect the kind of voice she had heard other mothers use when speaking to their children. The tone should be light, she thought, with lots of smiles and upward inflections. But when she spoke to Leonora like that she just felt ridiculous. It was something real mothers did, not imposters like her.

So, she had gone back to talking to her daughter as if she were an overnight house guest that she didn't know very well, in a tone that was polite but slightly aloof. And with no upward inflections.

By contrast, Leonora seemed to have read all the baby books. She did everything that was expected of her, eating, sleeping and filling her nappy with alarming regularity.

And she cried. Oh, how she cried. Morning, noon and night: she wasn't fussy about when. In fact, Sylvie was beginning to suspect that the only time her daughter didn't cry was when she was eating or asleep.

Each time she started to wail, Sylvie would pick her up and pat her awkwardly on her back, saying, 'There, there,' to no avail. The words 'There, there' seemed to have magical qualities on the tongues of other women, but Sylvie might just as well have been saying 'garden shears' for all the effect it had on Leonora.

But she persisted, because it would come. Eventually. Her mother-in-law had told her so and she was never wrong, apparently. Yes, Sylvie would find what it meant to be a mother soon enough. And until then she would fake it. The trouble was her fake was just so very, well, fake.

She had Leonora in a clinch on the changing mat when Jeremy put his head round the nursery door. Holding the baby up by both ankles, Sylvie was attempting to wipe her bottom clean but was simply succeeding in smearing the yellow dhal-like poo over previously clean patches of skin. All the while, Leonora wriggled and howled. It was undignified, Sylvie would give her that, but was there really any need to make all this fuss?

'How's it going?' Jeremy asked before quickly deducing the answer for himself. 'Ah,' he added. 'Need a hand?'

He didn't venture any further into the room, however, but continued to loiter on its threshold. He was already dressed for work, and a tiny spike of resentment stabbed at Sylvie, who hadn't yet made it out of her nightdress. She wanted to be working too, not going ten rounds with this tiny tormenter.

'I'm fine,' she said as brightly as she could over the sounds of Leonora's objections. 'I'll just do this and then I thought we would go for a little walk. She seems to settle a bit when we're on the move. You could come with us,' she added optimistically, but Jeremy shook his head.

'I have to finish the Maxwell piece and this damned heat is making everything twice as hard as it needs to be.'

'It has to break soon, though,' she said confidently. This was England. The sun never shone for more than a week at a time. It went against the way of things.

'Well, let's hope so,' replied Jeremy, 'Or I might have to throw the whole thing out and start again.'

This wasn't true, Sylvie knew. Jeremy was prone to the dramatic from time to time. It was his artistic temperament. The painting would be fine in the heat. If there was to be any starting again it would be nothing to do with the weather.

'So, I'll just crack on then,' he added. 'As you have everything here under control.'

'Excellent,' said Sylvie, her voice now bright to the point of brittle. 'I'll bring you a cup of coffee when we've just got this little rear end cleaned up.'

'Thanks,' called Jeremy and she heard him bounding up the stairs to his studio, which ran across the whole top floor of the house. Her own studio was, in keeping with Sylvie's style, far smaller and self-contained but with fabulous views over the castle. Sylvie thought with longing of her little space, its pots of pencils and charcoal all standing alert and ready to be called into action, the piles of creamy linen-textured paper neatly stacked on the shelves. What she wouldn't give to be in there now, losing her morning to some tiny but accurately rendered sketch.

But there was no point thinking like that. This was her life now, for the time being at least. She and Leonora were going to have to find some kind of level between them. And at the moment, the world seemed to be tipping precariously in Leonora's favour.

7

Donna was a dream baby.

With the others, the endless round of feeding, changing and trying to get everything done in the few hours when the baby slept, whilst functioning on next to no sleep herself, had hammered Michelle into the ground.

But with Donna it was different. Donna had already slept through the night and she was only two weeks old. Michelle had woken of her own accord one morning feeling more refreshed than she had done in months, only to have the cold shroud of fear fall over her as she realised why she had slept so well. Donna had not made a sound.

With her heart in her mouth, she had peered over the side of her bed and into Donna's carry cot, hardly daring to look but knowing that she had to. She braced herself for what she feared she might see, but little Donna was sleeping soundly, her arms held aloft framing her head and her mouth opened slightly into a tiny little 'o'.

Michelle leaned over and nudged Dean.

'She slept through, Dean. She slept all night. Isn't that ace?'

She could hear the note of triumph in her voice even though it really wasn't anything that she could take credit for. Dean grunted in reply but didn't open his eyes. Sleeping through was a relative term and it wasn't yet six a.m.

Donna barely cried during the day either. Even the prodding and poking that she got at the hands of her siblings seemed to make no difference to her equilibrium. She stared at them with her dark eyes, more curious than anything else, but rarely objected to being played with like a living doll.

It was amazing, Michelle thought, how you could have four children, each created from the same basic raw materials and yet they could all turn out so differently.

In many respects, however, this was no bad thing. It was to be hoped that Donna didn't end up like her eldest brother. At eight and a half years old, Carl was already proving to be a proper handful. If there was trouble to be had then Carl would sniff it out and was often to be found slap bang in the middle of it.

And so here they were again. She and Dean had been summoned to the school that morning. Dean had objected to missing work for something he considered so trivial, but Michelle, who thought that Carl's behaviour was due in no small part to Dean's influence, had arranged the meeting before school started so that Dean could go with her on his way to work. She had no idea what Carl had done, however. When she asked her son why he was in trouble this time he just shrugged and kicked at the table leg without looking up.

With Donna still sleeping, Michelle decided to take advantage of the moment and have a quick bath before she got dressed. It was still so hot that she felt wrung out every morning, as if most of her had seeped into the sheets overnight.

There was no sign of the heat abating either and, according to the news, water supplies were becoming increasingly short as demand soared. There was talk of the taps running dry in just eighty days, although Michelle was sceptical. This was England. It never stopped raining most years. Things surely wouldn't get that bad. The newspapers joked that they should all 'bath with a friend', but there was no way that Michelle would be showing her body to anyone but Dean, not until she'd shifted the baby weight at least. Dean said he liked it when there was more of her to grab hold of, but she felt he was probably lying.

By eight fifteen the family was ready to go and meet whatever was waiting for them at school. The children had objected to turning up half an hour early but had been persuaded by the lure of having the swings in the playground to themselves for a while.

'So, mate, why are we heading into the lion's den today, eh?' Dean asked Carl as Michelle locked the front door behind them. 'What have you done this time?'

Carl met his father's eye but didn't open his mouth. Dean ruffled his hair and grinned at him proudly, as if being summoned to see the headmistress was an achievement. Meanwhile, Michelle's sense of dread grew.

They made a raggle-taggle crew as they headed along the road, Michelle with Donna in the pram, Dean in his overalls and the other three children, dressed for the heat in shorts and T-shirts, pushing and shoving each other off the kerb and into the road. It had been so hot that the road surface had melted and little puddles of shiny black tar glistened in the gutter like jewels. The tar had already stained most of the children's clothes. It didn't matter how many times Michelle told them to leave it alone – it was evidently irresistible, even to Michelle herself who had poked a tentative finger into one little black circle only to regret it the moment the warm treacly goo stuck to her skin.

Carl and Damien had gone a beautiful golden colour like Dean whereas Tina, whose skin was more English rose than Grecian olive, had burned the tops of her shoulders, and they were now peeling, revealing yet more pale skin underneath. It was hard to tell which way Donna would go when her skin was so new, but Michelle hoped for her sake that she had her father's genes, at least as far as her skin was concerned.

It wasn't far to the school, and soon Michelle and Dean were waiting outside the headmistress's office with Carl. They were still there ten minutes later.

'Does she think her time's more important than ours?' chuntered Dean, not quite under his breath. 'I need to get to work. I don't want Mr Wallace docking my pay.'

Michelle shushed him and rocked Donna back and forth in the pram, a movement that she did without even thinking about it, but she too wished they could get this over and done with.

Finally, the office door opened and the headmistress ushered them in.

'Good morning, Mr and Mrs White. Good morning, Carl.'

Carl looked at his feet and Michelle gave him a hefty nudge.

'Carl,' she hissed. 'Say good morning to Mrs Simpson.'

'Morning,' muttered Carl under his breath, but without raising his face.

'Please sit down,' Mrs Simpson said, and her tone took Michelle right back to her own school days. She had also spent more time than she ought to have done in the head's office, but unlike Dean, who hadn't given two hoots, an ache of disappointment in herself had tugged deep inside. She'd kept this to herself, though. It wasn't cool to care about stuff like that. Not then, and not now, or so it appeared.

Mrs Simpson drew in a deep breath and began.

'I'm sorry to have to call you into school like this, but there has been a serious incident to which I must draw your attention.'

Michelle's heart was beating faster in her chest. Next to her she felt Dean stiffen as if he was readying himself for a fight.

'Yesterday,' continued Mrs Simpson, 'Carl managed to get into the kitchens . . .' She gave a little shake of her head as if building herself up to share the hideous details. 'Once there, he relieved himself into a bucket that was being used to store water for the cooks . . .'

Dean sniggered.

'Helping with the water shortage, eh Carl?' he asked with a wink, and Carl looked up at his father and gave him a wide grin, clearly interpreting this as praise.

Mrs Simpson looked less impressed. 'He then tipped the contents of the bucket all over the kitchen floor,' she continued.

Dean snorted.

'It's no joking matter,' she said, giving Dean a look that ought to have had him quaking in his seat but which actually just dripped from him like oil from Teflon. 'The entire kitchen had to be cleaned again, which meant unnecessary water usage and a lot of extra work for the dinner ladies.'

'That's terrible,' said Michelle, anxious to contain what she could see might get out of hand at any moment. 'Carl is very sorry, aren't you, Carl?' She nudged Carl, who was still exchanging looks of delight with Dean. 'Carl! Tell Mrs Simpson that you're sorry.'

'Much as I would be gratified to receive an apology from Carl,' said the headmistress, 'I think we are beyond that point.'

Michelle sagged in her seat, resigned. It would be a week of detentions again and it would be her job to try and get Carl to go to them.

'As you know,' Mrs Simpson continued sternly, 'this is not the first incident we've had with Carl. Such reckless disobedience cannot and will not be tolerated. I am left with no option but to suspend Carl until the end of term.'

Carl punched the air and let out a muffled 'Yes.'

'But he's only eight!' objected Michelle.

'Which is quite old enough to know how to behave,' replied Mrs Simpson. 'Now, you have the right to appeal against my decision, but I wouldn't recommend it. I doubt the governors will see things any differently to me. The best thing for Carl is that he spends the time at home thinking about what he has done and comes back next year with a better attitude. Can you do that, Carl?'

Carl's head was hanging again.

'Answer Mrs Simpson, Carl,' said Michelle.

'Yes, Carl,' added Dean. 'Tell Mrs Simpson that you'll sort your attitude out.'

Dean was grinning as if he found the whole situation hilarious. Michelle wanted to punch him, but it seemed more important to show Mrs Simpson that at least one of them was taking the situation seriously.

'Yes, miss,' muttered Carl.

'I'm so sorry, Mrs Simpson,' said Michelle. 'I'll talk to Carl and make sure that nothing like this ever happens again.'

'Good,' said Mrs Simpson simply, but something about her expression suggested that she was finding that hard to believe. 'Please take Carl back home now,' she continued. 'He can return to school in September. His teacher has prepared some work for him to do whilst he's away and remember that he must not leave your home during school hours.'

She handed Michelle a cardboard folder, which Michelle took. There was more chance of hell freezing over than Carl even looking at what was inside, but she should at least show willing.

Mrs Simpson eyed Carl, who, as if he could tell he was being stared at, seemed compelled to lift his head.

'You are at the very start of your educational journey, young man,' she said. 'You can just about afford a slip-up now, but it's important that you don't do anything like this again. The consequences will only get more severe the older you get.'

Michelle wanted to say that her son was highly unlikely to see the best part of two weeks off school as a severe consequence of his actions, but it wouldn't be helpful to say so. She was relieved that Carl had the good sense to nod and at least try to appear contrite. Dean was tutting to himself, and looking around the room, clearly anxious to get out.

'All right,' concluded Mrs Simpson. 'Thank you both for coming. I find that it helps to set the tone to these meetings if the child knows that the school has full parental backing for its actions.' She gave Dean a steely stare and Dean nodded sagely which, if Michelle hadn't been so angry with both him and Carl, would have made her laugh. 'Off you go, young man. I'll see you in September. And stay out of trouble between now and then.'

Carl, finally released, pinged out of the room like a cork from a bottle, followed almost as quickly by Dean. Michelle let them go so that she had room to manoeuvre the pram out of the little room.

As she was leaving, she said, 'I'm sorry, Mrs Simpson. I truly am. But I'll get him to do that work and I'll talk to him about what he's done. Try to make him see.'

'Thank you, Mrs White,' replied Mrs Simpson.

There was an expression on her face that Michelle couldn't quite grasp, but she had a horrible suspicion that it was pity.

As Carl and Dean pushed open the double doors and burst out into sunlight she could hear them both laughing.

'You shouldn't have done that, Carl,' Dean said, mock serious. 'It was very bad.'

'Funny though, Dad, wasn't it?' replied Carl, looking up at his father.

'Bloody funny,' replied Dean, and then they both broke into laughter again.

8

Jeremy's mother was coming to stay. Just the idea of Jeremy's mother made Sylvie's heart pound. In the ten years since they were married this state of affairs hadn't improved at all. In fact, now it was worse than ever.

The damage had been done, Sylvie believed, the very first time she had met Jeremy's family at their rather grand house somewhere in Surrey. That weekend had definitely set the tone for their ongoing relationship, although now, with the arrival of Leonora, things had taken a different turn that she was finding equally difficult to manage.

Jeremy's mother was keener to be involved with her new granddaughter than Sylvie was comfortable with. There was little point in resisting, however, given the circumstances surrounding the baby's conception and birth, and so she had agreed to the visit even though Leonora was only three weeks old and still very much a challenge.

A challenge was also how she would have described her very first meeting with the Fotherby-Smythes ten years earlier. Jeremy had announced that they were invited to visit his family for the weekend, and Sylvie, consumed by curiosity, had agreed straight away. They had bundled themselves on to a train, Jeremy sporting his monogrammed leather suitcase whilst Sylvie's belongings were stuffed into a cloth bag.

'You won't need much,' Jeremy had said, incorrectly as it turned out. 'We don't bother dressing for dinner at home any more unless we have guests. And anyway, they'll love you just the way you are.'

He had wrapped his arms around her and squeezed her, leaving her to wonder what she was if not a guest, and whether not dressing for dinner meant eating in her pyjamas.

She had taken him at his word and packed very little. After all, she told herself, it was only a weekend, not even that, as they would be arriving at lunchtime on Saturday and leaving after breakfast on Sunday. This flying visit hardly felt worth the effort of paying the train fare to Sylvie, but Jeremy seemed sure that it would be long enough.

She had come to be grateful to Jeremy for his foresight. It turned out that twenty-four hours in the company of the Fotherby-Smythes was about as much as Sylvie could tolerate.

They caught a cab to the house from the station and all the way she had quizzed him about who would be there, aware of but trying to ignore the anxious tightening in her gut.

'Ma and Pa, of course. Ma can be a bit of a dragon, but she has a heart of gold really. Just try to agree with her if she asks you anything. Her bark's worse than her bite, and she loves the sound of her own voice so if you let her talk you'll be fine.'

Sylvie swallowed nervously. The woman sounded terrifying.

'If Pa says more than three words to you all weekend then you'll be doing well,' Jeremy continued. 'And you'll love Jo. She's an absolute sweetheart.'

Jo was Jeremy's little sister and was eight years younger than him. Sylvie was never sure whether her birth had been a surprise or just a long time in the coming and she hadn't liked to ask. Either way, it was clear that Jo was adored by one and all. Jeremy had lengthy phone calls with her often, sometimes not even waiting until after six o'clock when it was cheaper to talk. He would come back into the studio full of the things that Jo had said, and for hours afterwards he would spontaneously burst into laughter, only shaking his head when Sylvie asked what had amused him.

'Oh, you know,' he'd say. 'Just something Jo said. She's such a hoot.'

The cab pulled up outside a grand-looking house on a road dotted with other grand-looking houses. The Fotherby-Smythes' residence was an elegant Arts and Crafts villa built in crimson brick with a sweeping roof line that rose and fell across the gables. It was a beautiful house and the artist in her couldn't fail to be moved by its style and proportions. She had known that Jeremy's family was well-to-do, but this confirmed it.

Jeremy leapt up to pay the cab driver and to retrieve their bags from the boot whilst Sylvie tried to control her nerves. It was foolish, she knew, to be so anxious. There was no test to be passed here. It was 1966 and she could be with Jeremy without needing his family's approval, but in her heart she really wanted them to like her. She had an idea that she and Jo would become firm friends, despite the age gap, maybe becoming the sister that neither of them had. And whilst Jeremy's mother sounded like a trial, Sylvie could win her round, she was sure.

The cab drove away and Jeremy strode towards the house, but Sylvie hung back, her stomach turning somersaults.

'Come on, Sylph,' he called to her as he pushed open the shiny front door. 'Let's go and see who's around.'

The door opened on to a large hallway with black and white chequered tiles on the floor and huge paintings on the walls, all with heavy gilt frames. The paintings were old-fashioned landscapes in dark shades of dun and olive, very different from the work that

Jeremy was producing. Her own pictures were so tiny that it was impossible to make any kind of comparison.

'Ma,' bellowed Jeremy into the space.

An old golden retriever appeared first. It shambled in, spine bowed and hips clearly arthritic, but with its tail wagging enthusiastically.

'Hello, old boy,' said Jeremy, dropping to his knees and fussing the dog's ears. 'This is Rembrandt,' he said. 'He's as old as the hills but still plodding on, aren't you, my dear friend?'

The dog's tail continued to wag but it was clearly becoming more of an effort with each passing second and soon it hung limply, exhausted.

'Is that you, Jeremy?' came a shrill voice, and then Jeremy's mother, Margery, appeared. She was a big woman, tall and broad of shoulder and girth and she towered over Sylvie. 'Ah, there you are. I had no idea you were going to be so late. When you said you were coming on Saturday I imagined that would mean by lunchtime at the very least. It's already gone three. Really, Jeremy, you are hopeless.'

And then, as if noticing Sylvie for the first time, she turned the full beam of her attention on her. It felt like standing in a wind tunnel as Margery traced her watery blue eyes over every part of Sylvie, starting at her head and then scanning all the way down to her shoes. Sylvie wished that she could just melt into the walls.

'And you must be Sylvia,' Margery said. Her face was smiling but her voice was not.

'It's Sylvie, Ma,' interjected Jeremy. 'I don't know how many times I've told her,' he added to Sylvie with an apologetic shrug.

'Delighted to meet you,' said Sylvie, holding out her hand to Margery, who ignored the gesture and turned back to Jeremy.

'Well, you've missed lunch. I'm sure there will be some leftovers if you're peckish.'

'We ate on the train,' said Jeremy. 'What time's dinner?'

'Seven thirty. Joanna has a recital this afternoon and so we're waiting for her.'

Sylvie, anxious to make a better impression than she appeared to have done thus far, said, 'How lovely. Where is she playing?'

But this also seemed to be wrong and Margery didn't reply, leaving Jeremy to fill in the gaps.

'This is the sticks,' he said. 'There are barely any decent concert halls, so I imagine she's in the town hall, right, Ma?'

'Yes. Now, Sylvia. I've put you in the back bedroom on the top floor. It can get a little chilly in there so if you need the fire lighting just say, although we usually find that there's not much that an extra blanket or two can't remedy.'

'Thank you,' replied Sylvie, wishing she had the nerve to correct the woman about her name. But the moment had gone. Margery bustled off, talking to Jeremy about their journey, and she was left standing with Rembrandt in the hall. His tail had taken up wagging again and she stroked his velvety ears tenderly.

'Well, at least you seem pleased to see me,' she whispered.

9

The afternoon at the Fotherby-Smythes' passed in a blur of china teacups and awkward conversation. Most of the time Margery ignored Sylvie, speaking only to Jeremy, quizzing him about how his work was going, who he had seen in town, which galleries were worth visiting. Jeremy replied with his customary enthusiasm and as the conversation sallied back and forth, Sylvie realised how many people he knew, which just went to emphasise how small her own social circle was.

Every so often, Margery seemed to remember that Sylvie was there and fired a random question at her, which Sylvie had to field like an outlying cricketer who has lost interest in the game. She heard herself tripping up over her words as she struggled to sound both intelligent and interesting, and wondered what kind of impression she was making. Far from favourable, she suspected.

And then, just as she thought she could bear it no longer, the front door banged shut and a shrill voice called out.

'It's me! I'm back. Where are you JJ, you old fraud?'

And then Jo appeared. She was tall like her mother but more willowy than statuesque, with limbs that seemed to go on forever and appeared to be only just in her control. Her hands, Sylvie noticed, were slender and elegant with remarkably long fingers, as one might expect for a pianist, and her dark hair was caught up in a chaotic chignon from which tails were escaping.

Jeremy stood up, crossing the room in two bounds, and enveloped his sister in his arms. For a moment they stood there, just being in each other's space, and then he pushed her out to arm's length to look at her.

'I'm great,' he said. 'How was the recital?'

Jo screwed her nose up. 'Fine. The Rachmaninov was a bit stodgy, but I'm not sure anyone noticed.'

'Of course it wasn't,' snapped Margery. 'Don't be so hard on yourself.'

Jo tossed her head as if she didn't care one way or the other and turned to look at Sylvie.

'And you must be Sylvie! I've heard so much about you. All good, of course. I'm so pleased to finally meet you.'

In a moment Jo was at Sylvie's side and holding out her hand. Sylvie took it in her own and shook it, surprised by how strong Jo's grip was, given how fragile her hand looked. Then Jo dropped her hand and threw her arms around her instead, squeezing tightly as if they were long-lost friends meeting for the first time in years.

'Sylvie, meet Jo,' said Jeremy. 'An auspicious moment as the two most important women in my life finally meet.'

Margery harrumphed.

'And you of course, Ma,' said Jeremy. 'That goes without saying.'

Margery looked as if it very much needed saying, but Jeremy didn't seem to notice, his attention now entirely absorbed by his sister.

'Let's go out for a walk,' he suggested enthusiastically.

'But it's raining,' said Jo, waving an arm towards the leaded windows. Outside the January day was a deep, steely grey that looked less than appealing.

'A game then,' suggested Jeremy. 'Monopoly. What do you say you, Jo? Shall I set the board up?'

Sylvie didn't recognise this version of her boyfriend. In their circles in London he was the coolest of cool cats, but here he seemed to have regressed into a childhood that she was struggling to imagine.

'Oh, JJ,' sighed Jo. 'Can't I just sit and talk to the lovely Sylvie? You don't want to play a stupid board game, do you, Sylvie?'

Sylvie would struggle to think of anything she'd like to do less, and so offered Jo a grateful smile.

'See, JJ. She doesn't. Let's rustle up another pot of tea and then we can have a proper chat. We don't need you if you want to go out.'

'If you're going out you can take Rembrandt with you,' added Margery. She stood up slowly, letting out a heavy huff of air. 'And if you two intend to chatter inanely, I shall go and get on.'

Margery strode out of the room and Jo turned to Sylvie.

'Tell me everything about living in London. I need every detail. I can't wait to get away from here but Mummy says I can't go until I'm twenty-one and that's ages away. But I'm so desperate to start my life proper. I'm just mouldering away down here. Every day that I'm not in town is like torture. I can tell just by looking at you that you know exactly what I mean. You do, don't you, Sylvie?'

Sylvie, buffeted by the storm that was Jo, didn't know where to start, but before she had opened her mouth Jo spoke again. Excitement bubbled from her and Sylvie couldn't help but smile. It was infectious.

'So, tell me where you live and all about your art and where you go out and who you see. I suppose you see famous people all the time, don't you? JJ told me that he spoke to Francis Bacon last week. That's so cool.'

They had been at a party that Francis Bacon had been rumoured to have been at, but she hadn't seen him with her own eyes and she wasn't sure that Jeremy had actually spoken to him. In fact, her London life was very far from the version that Jo seemed to be expecting. Sylvie wondered what Jeremy had told his little sister. Perhaps he had exaggerated things a little in order to make it sound more exciting. Would she trip herself up if she tried to keep up, or worse still, expose him?

But Jo was sitting looking at her with eyes wide and expectant. She was going to have to make a stab at it at least.

'Well,' she began. 'I live in a tiny bedsit in Shepherd's Bush with my friend Christine . . .'

10

Michelle couldn't pinpoint the exact moment when she started to suspect that something was wrong, but once the idea had crossed her mind she couldn't get it out of her head. She would lose hours just staring at her youngest child trying to make sense of her face. She'd scrutinise Donna from every angle, sometimes squinting to see if using her eyes half-opened would reveal any otherwise hidden secrets, but it didn't and her sense of unease remained. Something wasn't right, but try as she might, she couldn't put her finger on what it was.

Or rather, she didn't want to.

Anyway, there was so much else going on. She trudged through her days, the monotonous routine of four small children her jailer, but also her saviour because it stopped her having time to think. And she really didn't want to think. She was too busy with just living. She simply didn't have room in her head for contemplation and certainly not for the kind of thoughts she was having.

In the end, it was Sharon who crystallised matters for her. They were having a cup of tea on the front doorstep. They always sat on Michelle's front step because Michelle couldn't bring herself to be associated with the junk yard that was Sharon's front garden. It was ridiculous, she knew. All the neighbours were aware that the mess was Sharon's responsibility, and she wasn't likely to be tarred with the same brush just by sitting in it. Yet despite this Michelle always made the tea, although sometimes Sharon brought some milk with her to even things up a little.

Donna was sleeping in the pram, a cat net stretched over the top to protect her from the infernal ladybirds that were everywhere that summer. Sharon put her hand under the net and started to stroke the baby's tiny foot. Donna stirred at the touch but didn't wake up.

'She's a dream, this one, Chelle,' Sharon said. 'I don't know how you do it. I swear my three came out screaming and have never stopped.'

She cocked her head in the direction of her own patch of burned grass where her two younger children were arguing over a one-armed Tiny Tears doll with a buzzcut hairstyle, its original blonde locks all having been hacked away at some point.

Michelle shrugged. 'Just lucky, I guess,' she said.

Sharon looked in at Donna as she slept, absent-mindedly swatting away ladybirds as she spoke.

'She don't look much like the others, does she?' she continued. 'She don't look much like you or Dean neither, come to that.'

And in that moment, Michelle knew it was true and that this was what she had been subconsciously grappling with ever since they'd brought the baby home.

Donna didn't look like any of them.

'She did, though,' said Michelle. 'When she was first born she looked just like Dean. It was so obvious. It just shouted out at you that he was her dad. But then the resemblance kind of faded away.'

Sharon peered at Donna harder.

'Can't see anything of him in her now,' she said, her eyes narrowing as she stared. 'Still, they change so fast at this age, don't they?'

That was true enough, but Michelle couldn't shake the feeling that there was more to it. She needed to talk it through with someone, but she was scared that once she'd uttered what was in her head it would start a ball rolling downhill and she would never be able to catch up with it.

'They do,' she agreed without much conviction.

She paused. Sharon's kids were now trying to gouge the doll's eye out with a tent peg, working together and egging each other on.

'Cut that out,' shouted Sharon over the fence. 'That doll cost good money.' She lowered her voice. 'It didn't actually. It fell off the back of Stunty's van but they don't know that. Bloody vandals.'

Michelle drew breath to speak, changed her mind, and then tried again.

'Do you think they ever mix the babies up?' she asked. 'At the hospital, I mean.'

Sharon took a drag on her cigarette and blew the smoke out, angling it away from Donna before she spoke.

'I dunno. I suppose they might,' she said. She studied the baby again. 'So, do you think she's not yours, then?' she asked, the corners of her mouth turned down. The idea didn't seem to have shocked her.

'Oh, I don't know,' replied Michelle, trying to sound as if she hadn't been serious. 'I just wondered, that's all. She doesn't look much like the rest of us either. I thought she did to start with, but maybe I just wanted to see it. But now she's growing a bit I don't think it's there. I really don't.'

Sharon stood up and stared directly at Donna, who, seeming to sense the scrutiny, opened her eyes and stared back.

'I think it might be,' Sharon said, tipping her head to one side as she spoke. 'There's something about her eyes that looks like you. Maybe. I wouldn't like to swear to it, though. It's really hard to tell. Do babies always look like their parents? I've never really thought about it. I suppose the important thing is how it *feels*, Chelle? Does she *feel* like your baby?'

'I don't know,' replied Michelle desperately. 'I don't know what I think any more. It's horrible, doubting her like this. I mean, what if she is mine and I'm just not feeling it? What does that say about me as a mum?'

'You're a great mum,' objected Sharon. 'Your kids are a proper credit to you.'

Michelle thought of Carl, currently suspended from school, and gave Sharon a wan smile.

'But I just don't feel a connection with her like I did with the others.' Michelle was whispering now, as if she didn't want to hurt Donna's feelings. 'I don't know. I'm just not sure.'

Sharon sat back down on the step.

'What does Dean think?' she asked.

'I haven't told him. I wanted to get it straight in my own head first.'

'You need to, though,' said Sharon. 'You have to tell him what you're thinking. She's his kid too. Or not.'

Sharon raised her eyebrows and Michelle nodded.

'I know,' she said.

'And then what will you do?'

Michelle let her eyes settle on the watchful Donna. She was a beautiful child, there was no denying it. But was she hers?

'I have no idea,' she said.

11

Michelle really wasn't sure what to do. Who should she talk to first – the hospital or Dean? Her instincts told her to approach the hospital first because they could set her mind at rest that the babies couldn't possibly have been mixed up, and then she would never need to tell Dean that she'd had any doubts and the whole thing could be forgotten about.

But the more she thought about it, the more certain she became that Donna wasn't her child and that meant that she should talk to Dean before she did anything else. It would feel all kinds of wrong to go storming off to the hospital demanding her real baby back if she hadn't even told her own husband.

Yet, what if she was putting two and two together and coming up with five? Sharon was spot on when she said that babies changed all the time. Donna could just be going through a stage. Next week she might be the image of Dean again and Michelle would have made all this fuss for nothing.

Still, though, she couldn't get the idea out of her head. It followed her all day, dogging her steps and preventing her from concentrating on anything else. She was short-tempered with the children, particularly Carl, who had refused to even look at the schoolwork that he'd been set for the period of his suspension. She tried to blame her mood on the heat, which blasted down on them all relentlessly, day after day, but in her heart she knew that it was neither Carl's lack of cooperation nor the temperature that was the cause.

It didn't help that she was so dog-tired. It was hard enough deciding what to make for tea. She didn't have enough drive left for anything more complicated than that. So, she tried to ignore her growing doubts, but it got harder and harder with each passing day.

Eventually even Dean noticed that she was not her usual self when a bottle of milk, fresh from the fridge and slick with condensation, slipped from her hand and smashed spectacularly all over the kitchen floor. The shards of glass went everywhere and, rather than racing to pick them up to prevent them getting embedded in the children's feet, Michelle just stood and stared at the mess. She couldn't even summon the energy to cry.

Dean, drawn to the sound of the crash, came in to find her standing there, motionless. He bent down to start picking up the larger pieces and, when she still didn't move, looked up at her.

'Are you okay, Chelle?' he asked, concern written all over his face.

The question brought her back to herself and she shook her head as if she was just coming out of a hypnotist's trance.

'Yes. Sorry. God, what a mess. I'm sorry. It just slipped out of my hand. Here. Give me that. I'll get some newspaper to soak it up.'

They worked together until all trace of the smashed bottle was gone. Then Dean led her into the tiny sitting room and sat her on the sofa. He sank down next to her and put his arm round her shoulders. She flinched. It wasn't intentional and probably more to do with the heat and the proximity of another hot body to hers, but Dean noticed. He pulled away from her slightly.

'What's going on, Chelle?' he asked her. 'You've been acting weird for a few days now. Is something up? Are you ill?'

Michelle shook her head.

53

'I'm fine,' she said doggedly.

'Well, you're obviously not,' returned Dean. 'You're snappy with the kids for no reason, and when you're not giving us all a hard time you're away with the fairies. What was that with the milk just now? Were you just going to stare at it until it cleared itself up? I didn't know we had a fairy godmother living here.'

She gave him a weak smile and leaned into him and he put his arm back round her shoulders and squeezed. He smelled of engine oil and sweat and a hint of the Old Spice aftershave he wore to go out. He smelled like Dean. It was comforting and reassuring. Whatever was going on in her head it had no place getting in the way of this.

But then the doubts crashed over her again. She knew Dean almost as well as she knew herself. She would recognise his scent blindfolded. So why couldn't she do the same with Donna? The more she thought about her, the less familiar her supposed child became. The others had all had a distinctive smell when they were babies. It had been there when they'd woken from sleep, their baby-fine curls tousled and damp. Michelle had buried her nose into their hair, trying to breathe it so far into her lungs that it would never come out, her child's scent forever part of her.

But Donna didn't share that with them. Yes, she had a fresh-from-sleep smell of her own, but it wasn't familiar to Michelle. She wasn't driven to preserve it in the primal way that had come over her with the others. That meant something, surely.

Dean tried again.

'Come on, love,' he cajoled. 'Just tell me.'

Michelle took a deep breath. This was her moment.

'It's Donna,' she began.

And then she stopped.

'What about her?' asked Dean, concern in his voice. 'Is there something wrong with her?'

Michelle paused, gave what she was about to say a second's more consideration, and then let it out.

'I don't think she's ours,' she said. 'I think they gave us the wrong baby at the hospital.'

She sat perfectly still and waited for Dean to respond.

'Eh?' he said after a moment. 'What?'

Michelle tried again. 'I think somehow our baby got muddled up with another and we've come home with the wrong one. I don't think Donna is really ours.'

She felt Dean move away from her so that he could look at her properly.

'Of course she's ours,' he said. 'Whose else would she be?'

Michelle shook her head. 'I don't know. It's just that she doesn't feel like she's ours. She never cries, for a start. That's weird.'

Relief crossed Dean's face and he gave her a grin.

'Well, you can't say she's not ours just because she doesn't cry,' he said. 'Not all babies cry, or so I hear. Maybe we've finally fallen lucky with this one. It's about time.'

He was mocking her gently, Michelle could tell, but he wasn't understanding her.

'It's not just that,' she said. 'She doesn't look like any of them either.'

'Well, Ricky looks nothing like me, but that doesn't mean we're not brothers,' replied Dean. 'And you said she was the spit of me when she was born,' he added.

'She was,' Michelle said, leaping on this as if it were the proof she needed. 'But she isn't now.'

Dean shook his head. 'She looks just the same to me, love. Bit bigger, that's all.'

'And remember,' Michelle continued as a new idea occurred to her. 'Remember when she came back from the nursery the morning we were bringing her home? She didn't have her Babygro on any more, the green one with the frogs on. Well, what if the reason why she wasn't wearing it was because she wasn't our baby at all?'

'They'd just have taken it off because she was too hot. It was roasting in that hospital. You know it was.'

'And thinking about it, she didn't have a band, did she? Around her ankle. The others all had bands when they were born.'

Michelle searched Dean's face for a reaction to this and saw that for a second it pulled him up short. But then he seemed to dismiss it.

'That doesn't mean that she wasn't the right baby,' he said. 'It probably just got missed in all the excitement. Or maybe it fell off. I bet that happens sometimes. And if there was a problem, surely the other family would have reported it. We'd have heard something. But we haven't, have we?'

Michelle hadn't thought of this and she had to concede that he was right. If the other parents had been having the same doubts then they would have told someone and the hospital would have been in touch. A warm wave of relief washed over her. It was okay. There was nothing wrong. She needed to hold on to that thought.

'Listen, Chelle,' Dean said, holding her at arm's length and looking deep into her eyes. 'You need to get this idea right out of your head. It'll be one of those funny notions that women get after childbirth. You know how my cousin Louise went a bit ga-ga when little Steven was born? Well, this'll be the same. Hospitals don't muddle babies up. Stop thinking that. You're just dead tired. Your mind's playing tricks on you, that's all. There's nothing to worry about. Absolutely nothing.'

12

Sylvie's relationship with her in-laws had improved a little since those early days, but they had never reached anything approaching close. This wasn't for lack of trying, on her part at least, but Sylvie firmly believed that the fault lay on her mother-in-law's side. Margery came from those upper middle classes where any demonstration of emotion was frowned upon, and her initial coolness towards Sylvie had never really warmed. Sylvie still didn't know if Margery objected to her personally, or if the stand-offishness that she felt each time they met was just her way, but she chose to think that it was the latter.

It had helped a little that Sylvie and Jeremy had married. The formality of that had brought a kind of legitimacy to Sylvie's presence at family gatherings, although the Fotherby-Smythes still had a tendency to close ranks in the face of a challenge, leaving her out in the cold. And Margery had never quite managed to drop the 'a' from the end of Sylvie's name. Sylvie wondered if she did it on purpose, exerting what little authority she had left in the only way she knew how. Over the years, Sylvie had almost stopped noticing, although she would never stop minding.

Sometimes she saw the name thing as an indication of just how low down she came in her mother-in-law's pecking list, after Jeremy and Jo, and now Leonora; not important enough to even bother getting her name right. On bad days, this thought would leave Sylvie in a dark, brooding mood. Even now, and after everything that she had sacrificed for the family, it seemed she could never quite be fully accepted. However, most of the time she didn't give the Fotherby-Smythes any thought whatsoever.

Margery and Gerald were due to arrive around two thirty. Sylvie had been careful over the timings, wanting to be certain that she wasn't obliged to provide any more meals for her in-laws than was entirely necessary. Three was more than enough for this early visit. Leonora was only a few weeks old and they were all finding their feet. So, there would be dinner that day and breakfast and lunch the next. A tiny part of Sylvie's brain, a part she wasn't terribly proud of, thought that if Margery had been hoping to spend more time with her precious granddaughter then she should have taken more care of her daughter-in-law. She knew this was ridiculous though. There would have been no point in having the blessed baby in the first place if she limited Margery's access to her.

Sylvie caught a glimpse of herself in the bedroom mirror. Her hair was lank and in need of a cut and the skin around her eyes was a fetching shade of plum that contrasted starkly with her pale complexion. She did look truly dreadful, but she wasn't concerned about her own appearance. Leonora was the star of the show today, and Sylvie wanted to take extra care with how she was dressed, not wanting to give Margery any opportunity to criticise.

She had bought her the sweetest little pink gingham frock especially for that day. It had ruching around the chest with tiny puff sleeves and a long, trailing skirt that would be totally impractical once Leonora started to crawl, but now just hung around her like a summer tablecloth.

Leonora didn't look pretty, though, in her pretty dress. Her face, almost perpetually screwed into a grimace, was quite red from the effort of crying and her eyes were squeezed so tightly shut that it was impossible to see their colour or shape. She wasn't an attractive child. Sylvie knew this and used the fact that she recognised it as yet more evidence of her failings as a mother. Surely all parents thought that their own children were beautiful. Wasn't that something that nature arranged, an inability to look objectively at one's own offspring?

Sylvie sat in the nursery in the rocking chair that Jeremy had insisted they buy, Leonora in her arms. The child did at least stop crying long enough to take on board sustenance, which meant that Sylvie looked forward to the four-hourly feeds very much. Now she chatted to her daughter as she sucked, in the odd adult way that she had with her.

'Your grandparents are coming to see you today, Leonora,' she began. 'Perhaps you remember them from their last visit. Can you remember things like that, I wonder? No matter. Your grandmother is a very forceful woman but quite delighted to have you here. Your grandfather rarely speaks but that doesn't mean that he thinks any the less of you. I'm not sure he thinks much of me, mind you, but I can live with that. I have had you, so I have fulfilled my purpose. But don't ever say that to your father. He won't understand. Now, you're to be on your best behaviour, please. If you scream the house down then no doubt it will all be my fault and your grandmother will have yet more reason to complain. I think that's rich, personally, given what I've done for her, for all of them, but a leopard never can change its spots.'

Leonora showed very little sign of having been listening. She sucked hard on the teat as if fearful that it would be snatched away if she did as much as draw breath. If she could just stay quiet as their guests were arriving, thought Sylvie. That would be perfect. After that Leonora could let rip to her heart's content. It would be entertaining to see her mother-in-law fail at the perpetual and impossible task of settling her. Or maybe she wouldn't fail and they might all get a few hours of peace. Sylvie thought that she could live with any comments about her incompetence as a mother if she could just hear herself think.

There was a knock at the front door, the loud confident rap of a person who expected to be attended to quickly, and Sylvie started and then stiffened. Leonora, just getting to the end of her feed, was starting to look milk-drunk, her eyes rolling back in her head. The timing was perfect, although Sylvie had known it would be, had arranged things just so this would happen. Delicately, she inched the teat out of Leonora's mouth in tiny incremental movements. Leonora looked as if she might object but then was too exhausted to do so.

Downstairs, Sylvie could hear Jeremy opening the front door, greeting his parents enthusiastically with the usual questions about their journey up from Surrey. She took a deep breath, stood up gently so as not to wake the baby in her arms, and made her way, in as serene a manner as she could manage, along the landing and down the stairs.

The three Fotherby-Smythes were standing in the hall and all looked up as they heard her descending.

'And here she is,' said Margery in a stage whisper, the closest her voice came to being quiet. 'My darling granddaughter.'

Sylvie reached the bottom step and then stood there, smiling beatifically at them all.

'Margery,' she said, without her smile slipping for an instant, 'Gerald. How lovely to see you both. Do come through.'

She led the way into their sitting room, tidied early that day so that there was space for four people to sit, Jeremy's books and magazines piled into tottering towers against the walls. She could almost feel Margery draw breath behind her, but the complaint didn't make it from her head into her mouth. Things really were improving. What a difference it made, having this child, the only grandchild. It gave Sylvie a kind of power that she almost relished, although being entirely honest she would have preferred no power and no baby.

But it was pointless thinking like that. She had made her bed and now she had to lie in it. With Leonora.

Margery had seated herself in a rather threadbare armchair that she herself had donated when Sylvie and Jeremy moved into the Lincoln house, choosing it as if this one familiar thing would give her comfort in an alien environment.

No sooner had she sat down than Sylvie approached her and placed the sleeping Leonora in her arms. Margery immediately bent over the child, running the pad of an index finger over her tiny features and seeming to melt just a little.

'Now, who's for a cup of tea?' Sylvie asked.

She had made it almost into the kitchen when she heard Leonora open her lungs and begin to scream. She couldn't help the little smile that played on her lips as she boiled the kettle.

13

By the time Sylvie went back into the sitting room, carefully carrying a tray piled high with the tea service and a plate of chocolate biscuits, Margery had got to her feet and was bouncing the complaining Leonora so vigorously that Sylvie wondered if the baby might actually fly out of her arms and on to the parquet floor. It appeared that a gauntlet had been thrown down in the settling of her grandchild, one that Margery was fully committed to. She had locked eyes with the baby and stared at her as if that alone could make her cease, whilst Leonora stared back wilfully and continued to scream.

'Here we are,' said Sylvie, raising her voice a little to be heard over the noise. She set the tea tray down on the coffee table. 'Shall I be mother?'

The impact of her words struck her just as it was too late to recover them and she saw Jeremy throw her a warning sidelong glance, but she sallied forth as if there was nothing untoward in what she had just said. As it was, Margery was so focused on her task that she didn't notice, and a marching band could parade through the room before Gerald spotted anything awry.

'She certainly is a wilful little thing,' said Margery through gritted teeth. She was holding Leonora's torso and rushed her through the air as if she were an aeroplane. 'Demanding now, but that kind of spirit all bodes well for the future. Imagine how she could use it if it's properly channelled.'

'That's exactly what I've been saying, Ma,' agreed Jeremy. 'She's taking after her namesake already.'

They had named the baby after the surrealist artist Leonora Carrington. At the time Sylvie, who really didn't have an opinion on the child's name one way or the other, had agreed with Jeremy's suggestion as it seemed important to him that their baby had a name that resonated with his vocation. It had only been when Leonora had started to throw her tiny weight around that he had made a comparison with the headstrong and uncompromising artist and their newborn child. Leonora Carrington, the artist, had apparently been expelled from her school not once but twice, had refused to follow the path her well-to-do parents had chosen for her and was currently in Mexico spearheading their women's lib movement. Jeremy had told Sylvie this with a sense of delight, as if it alone could explain their baby's temperament. Sylvie had thought the whole thing terribly far-fetched, but was happy to go along with Jeremy's theories. It was no skin off her nose and she had got quite used to the name now, even quite liked it.

And now here was his mother reaching much the same conclusion, not about the name but that the baby's fury could be used in later life to achieve some kind of greatness. And perhaps they were right. Maybe the perpetually angry Leonora would turn into a strong, determined young woman with something valuable to offer the world. Sylvie had never watched the progress of a person from baby to adulthood and so had no idea what to expect.

And then, without warning, Leonora fell asleep and the room was suddenly silent. They all cast anxious glances at one another, not quite believing the relief that the lull brought with it. Sylvie could see their previously tensed shoulders begin to relax. Of course, she knew that it would be a mistake to get too comfortable, that this would only be a brief respite, but when she glanced at Margery the look of triumph on her face was hard to miss.

'There,' she said with an air of finality. 'That's much better. I knew she'd settle in the end. She just needs a firm hand, do you see, Sylvia.'

It was on the tip of Sylvie's tongue to say that Margery would be perfectly welcome to take the baby away with her and adopt her firm-hand method to her heart's content. But then she remembered Jeremy and her promise to him. This was, after all, what she had signed up for. She could hardly change her mind now.

'I do like Lincoln,' said Gerald, apropos of nothing at all. 'Do you remember when we used to bring you here as children to visit your aunt and uncle, Jeremy?'

Jeremy nodded. He let his teeth scrape over his top lip, something he only did when he was nervous. Now it was the mention of the past that he was wary of. It only took a couple of wrong turns and they might all find themselves knee-deep in a quagmire that they could take the rest of the weekend to dig themselves out of.

But Jeremy began at once to steer them away from danger.

'Yes, Dad,' he said. 'Maybe we'll go for a little wander after we've had the tea and I can show you around. There's not much new up here, of course. Nothing's changed in this part of Lincoln for hundreds of years. But down in the town proper there are some nice developments that are worth a gander.'

Gerald had been an architect before he'd retired and always enjoyed looking at the built environment.

'Capital,' he said in a way that made it sound like 1930, not 1976.

Relief rushed through Sylvie. The weekend would be difficult enough without anyone looking back at what had been lost. They needed to look forward at what was to come.

14

Michelle stood outside the maternity unit at Lincoln County Hospital and looked up. The building was only a decade or so old and modern-looking, with taupe-coloured bricks and large plate-glass windows. Michelle tried to work out which room she and the weird woman had shared by trying to recognise the view they'd had, but concluded that it could have been any of them. She wasn't even certain which floor she'd been on, other than it hadn't been the ground.

Now she was here, she was unsure what her next move should be and she hung back as she considered. When she'd spoken to Dean, he had made everything seem so straightforward. She was wrong. It was as simple as that. It was just her exhaustion that was tying her mind in knots. Dean had reassured her that the problem with Donna wasn't real, was only in her head, and she had believed him.

But then her doubts started to creep back. With each passing week, Donna grew bigger and stronger and Michelle's fear that she was bringing up someone else's child grew with her. Yet at the same time, her suspicions were becoming harder and harder to hold on to as Donna changed. She was growing into a little personality in her own right. Instead of looking like her parents or her siblings, she was starting to look like herself, which was making it more difficult for Michelle to see anyone else in her face at all.

Sometimes a whole morning would pass without her once thinking that Donna might not be her baby. But then the uneasiness would start popping up again and she would be back where she started. She searched for patterns. Did it happen when she was especially tired, or if the other kids were playing up? If that were the case then maybe her concerns weren't real and easy to explain away.

But there were no patterns. At some point in every day her doubts would surface no matter how tired she got or how unhinged the older kids made her feel.

And so here she was at the hospital to ask some questions. Surely that couldn't do any harm.

There were plenty of people milling about at the entrance to the maternity wing. A man dressed in a shirt and tie was sitting on a bench with his head in his hands. He looked as if he had been up all night and probably had been. As Michelle drew near, however, his head lifted and the tiredness fell from his features.

'We had a boy,' he said, clearly delighted. 'I've got a son.'

He said this as if it was the biggest surprise he had ever had, even though there weren't many options when it came to babies.

Michelle smiled back at him warmly.

'Congratulations!' she said. 'That's great news.'

The man's head dropped back into his hands, overwhelmed by the enormity of his statement.

There were a couple of women wearing ballooning pastel nightdresses standing on the concrete paving outside chatting and smoking. They ignored her. A woman with a baby was nothing worthy of note here.

Michelle parked the pram, scooped Donna up into her arms and headed inside. Through the large double doors there was a wide reception area. On one side was a little shop selling sweets, magazines and flowers and next to that was the reception desk. Michelle hovered in the middle of the space, Donna in her arms, until the woman on the desk called over to her.

'Are you all right, there, pet? Are you looking for somewhere? Can I help?'

Michelle had no idea what or who she was looking for. Her intention had been to get back to the hospital, but she hadn't really thought any further than that. Who did she need to talk to and what would she say when she found them?

She took a couple of steps towards the reception desk, stopped and then took a couple more.

'I was wondering who's in charge?' she said.

The woman's eyebrows, plucked into two sharp arches and drawn on in a harsh line, pulled together tightly.

'In charge?' she asked.

'Yes,' said Michelle uncertainly. 'In charge of, well, the babies and that.'

The woman pulled a face as she considered this.

'What exactly is the problem, pet?' she asked, answering Michelle's question with a question.

Michelle hesitated.

'Is there something wrong with Baby?' the receptionist pressed on. 'I can get a midwife out here to see you.'

'No, no. She's fine,' replied Michelle quickly. 'It's just . . .'

As she tried to formulate what she wanted to say, it dawned on Michelle just how unstable it was going to make her sound. Even Dean hadn't believed her, had thought that it was a figment of an overactive imagination rather than a genuine concern.

'I'm worried that this isn't my baby,' she blurted, her words tumbling out on top of one another.

The woman's face went from confusion to concern in a heartbeat.

'Oh, my love,' she said, as if Michelle had just dissolved into tears in front of her. 'Let me get someone down to talk to you. You and Baby sit down over there' – she gestured to some chairs by the shop – 'and I'll just ring up to the ward.'

Michelle wasn't sure what was going to happen next, but speaking to someone was a start at least, even if they weren't in charge.

She waited for over half an hour, sometimes sitting, sometimes pacing backwards and forwards, jiggling Donna and pointing things out to her around the reception to keep her entertained.

Finally, a nurse arrived. She spoke to the receptionist, who nodded her head in Michelle's direction, and then came towards her, her face set in a sympathetic smile. They all think I'm mad, Michelle thought, and her resolve hardened a little.

'Now then,' said the nurse, taking the seat next to Michelle's. 'What can I do for you?'

Michelle straightened her spine and jutted her chin out to show she meant business.

'This isn't my baby,' she began.

She hadn't meant to start like that, so boldly, but there it was. It was out now.

'What do you mean, exactly?' asked the nurse kindly.

'I came in to have a baby last month,' Michelle began. 'And I had a baby girl. And then, when it was night-time, the woman in the next bed was having trouble with her baby and it wouldn't stop crying and it woke my baby. Hers was a girl too. And so the midwife said she'd take them both to the nursery so we could get some sleep. And the next day I went home. But my baby didn't have her Babygro. And then when I got her home it wasn't my baby. She didn't look like my husband. She did when she was born. And now she doesn't look like any of us. And she doesn't cry. All my babies cry. And I'm sure . . . no, I'm certain that she's not mine. She got swapped. And we need to swap them back before it's too late.'

Her words gushed out like water over a weir, but when she'd finished she knew she'd said everything that was important. The nurse sat back a little, nodding at her and smiling the kind of smile reserved for people who make no sense but need to be humoured.

'It's true!' Michelle added desperately. 'I can bring my other three kids and you'll see. This one doesn't fit in. She's not mine. I know it. I can feel it. And she had no tag when she came home. The others all did. On their ankles. That must mean something. The missing tag.'

The nurse put out a hand and placed it gently on Michelle's thigh.

'Oh, is that it?' she said. 'Don't let that worry you. I know there's supposed to be a system, but between you and me it can be a bit hit and miss on a busy night. Tags get missed off all the time. But it doesn't mean that we muddle the babies up.'

Michelle saw the hint of a blush on the nurse's cheeks. They did muddle the babies up sometimes then, she thought. She could see it written on the nurse's face.

'But what is quite common,' the nurse continued, '. . . sorry. What's your name, love?'

'Michelle.'

'What is quite common, Michelle love, is for new mums to take a while to bond with their babies, and sometimes they do think that their baby isn't theirs. It's to do with the shock of giving birth, part of the baby blues, but it will pass, believe me—'

Michelle was neither in shock nor suffering from the baby blues. She put a hand up to stop the nurse from continuing.

'It's not that,' she said. 'I've got three kids already. I know how it goes. But this one's not mine. I just feel it.'

The nurse nodded patiently. 'I think you're getting things out of proportion, Michelle, love. Babies go to the nursery every night and in the morning the right baby is returned to the right mother.

It's very unlikely that something went wrong. This supposed mix-up is far more likely to be in your head. Honestly.'

Her smile had switched from concerned to patronising and Michelle scowled back. This was no smiling matter.

'Well, if you won't believe me,' she said, her voice cracking as she fought to hold back her tears, 'can you give me the address of the woman in my room. Her name was Sylvie and her baby was called Leonora. It's unusual, that. Someone must remember her even if I don't know her surname. Just give me her address and I can go and talk to her. We can sort this all out between us.'

The nurse gave a slow blink.

'I can't do that, Michelle, love. That information is confidential. And anyway, you can't go around accusing other couples of having your baby. It's not fair.'

Michelle could feel her heart pumping hard in her chest.

'What's not fair is that I'm stuck with someone else's kid when mine is out there somewhere doing God knows what. That's what's not fair.' Her voice was starting to rise and the few people who were passing through turned to see what was going on.

'Please can you keep your voice down,' said the nurse. 'You'll upset Baby. Let me make an appointment for you to talk to one of our doctors. You can chat through all your worries with him and then I'm sure you'll feel better.'

Michelle stood up abruptly and Donna started at the sudden movement, her eyes opening wide.

'I don't want to talk to a doctor,' Michelle said. 'I want my baby back. And if you can't help me then I'll just have to find this Sylvie person on my own.'

She started walking briskly towards the door. The nurse followed her.

'I tell you what, love,' she said. 'I'll get in touch with your GP. They can send someone round to talk to you. It'll all be okay,

Michelle. I know it will. Just come with me and I can just take a few details.'

But Michelle had reached the double doors and pushed back out into the bright sunshine beyond. She didn't want an appointment with a doctor or to talk to anyone. There was nothing wrong with her and she didn't want them all telling her that there was. This was a simple mix-up. She had that Sylvie woman's baby and she must have Michelle's. It would be easy enough to sort it out now when both girls were so young. Neither of them need ever know that there had ever been anything wrong. And if the hospital wouldn't help her then she would just have to do it herself.

15

But despite how certain she had felt when she stormed from the maternity wing, Michelle didn't do anything to find Sylvie. Life was busy and chaotic and the weeks all ran into one another. The long summer holidays arrived and, with the kids all at home, there just wasn't time to go on wild goose chases looking for Sylvie and her baby. After all, she could be anywhere. Lincoln was a city and the hospital's catchment area also included dozens of surrounding villages. Sylvie could live miles away and Michelle had no car. Wherever she looked, it would need to be on foot, pushing the pram and with the older three in tow. The mere idea made her scoff. And anyway, where would she start? She couldn't just scour every street on the off-chance of bumping into her.

No. It was a hopeless mission. And because it was so hopeless Michelle tried really hard to push it from her mind. If she wasn't careful, her doubts would sour everything, like a mould that spoiled all it touched. Really she was very lucky. She had Dean and the kids and their life was pretty good. And Donna was a lovely baby, easy to manage and fitting into family life without difficulty. Michelle knew that everything would be much simpler if she could just accept that Donna was hers, and so that's what she tried to do. When she felt the familiar concerns start to eat away at her insides, she busied herself with something else. There was never any shortage of things that needed doing, and life was hard enough without inventing more hurdles for herself.

The heat made everything impossibly difficult too. By day she couldn't find the energy for the simplest tasks and by night, even with the windows open, there was no cool refreshing air circulating to give any respite.

With water so precious, there were still standpipes in the street. Getting it into the house when the supply was off, which had been a novelty at first, was becoming a massive chore. There were full buckets all over her kitchen, some filled with steeping nappies, others with Milton tablets dissolving to sterilise Donna's bottles. The kitchen was a tiny space as it was, little more than a corridor off the back room, but now she was tripping up at every turn. It was exhausting.

Michelle put Donna down for her sleep and went outside to see what was happening there. Carl and Damien were playing football with a gang of other boys in the street. Just seeing them running around in the heat made Michelle wilt. Tina was nowhere to be seen but Michelle could hear her voice floating out from next door where she was apparently in charge of the game they were playing. It sounded unnecessarily complicated.

As ever there was a queue of people waiting at the standpipe. Mr Smith, the old bloke who lived in number 48, was brandishing a kettle and the woman from number 26 had a washing-up bowl, a bucket and a child in tow to help her carry them both. It wasn't her child, Michelle noted, but one of the twins from number 24 who must have done something bad and was helping out as penance.

In the distance she could hear another siren. Apparently, there were fires in the fields that surrounded the city every day now, as what was left of the crops burned in the heat. Sometimes the acrid smell wafted around in the sultry air and the atmosphere was hazy, making everything look slightly out of focus. It was such a strange summer. The heatwave was a novelty, but also ever so slightly menacing.

Whilst Michelle stood and observed the business of the street, she had the peculiar sensation of eyes on her and turned to see who was watching. Linda who lived next door but one was standing in her front yard having just pegged out her washing, clothes that had once been white but were now varying shades of grey. Michelle bleached her whites until they gleamed and couldn't help but feel smug about her superior laundry skills. With anyone else she wouldn't have been bothered, but she liked to get one up on Linda, even if it was only in her head.

Linda dropped the rest of her pegs into an old Coronation tea caddy and then raised her hand in greeting.

'Turned out nice again,' she said sarcastically, looking up at the cloudless blue of the sky. 'I've had enough of it now, haven't you? I don't care if it rains till Christmas.'

'Yeah,' replied Michelle. 'Me too.'

'And these bloody ladybirds,' Linda continued. 'I didn't know ladybirds could bite. Nasty little buggers.' She waved her arms, swiping the insects away.

'I know,' said Michelle. 'I'm trying to keep them away from the baby but they get everywhere.'

'How is she?' Linda asked, coming out on to the pavement and walking the few steps to Michelle's house so that they could talk without shouting. 'Donna, isn't it?'

'Yeah. That's right. She's great, thanks.'

Michelle folded her arms across her chest and took a step towards her door. She didn't want to get into conversation with Linda. There was no love lost between the pair of them, old childhood rivalries never really fading away.

'Let's have a look then,' said Linda, stepping on to the concrete path that ran from the pavement to Michelle's front door.

'She's asleep just now,' replied Michelle. 'Inside. Trying to keep her cool.'

Linda raised her head in a single nod but something about the gesture suggested that she didn't believe Michelle, although why she would be lying about something like that Michelle had no idea.

'That's probably best,' she said.

To the casual observer it would have sounded as if Linda was talking about the heat, but something about her tone made Michelle wonder if she was getting at something else.

'Yeah,' Michelle replied vaguely.

There was a pause. Michelle examined her untidy cuticles. She wished Linda would leave, but she knew from experience that it was best just to ride the wave with her. She was like a circling shark, but she would lose interest and swim away when she realised there wasn't anything there for her.

'Not seen Dean around much,' Linda continued.

'He's been working,' replied Michelle as the hairs on the back of her neck bristled. 'They've a lot on. Engines don't like the heat either, apparently.'

Linda nodded again, taking this in. Michelle could sense there was something else she wanted to say. It hung in the air between them like a raincloud just waiting to burst. Linda narrowed her eyes, sucked her inner lip, but didn't speak.

Then there was a howl from the street. Damien had fallen chasing the football and was sitting in the middle of the road clutching his leg with tears running down his face and blood running down his shin. Michelle set off to tend to him and Linda was forced to retreat, leaving whatever it was unsaid.

16

And then, finally, it rained.

It was the last week of August with the new school term just around the corner. Michelle was giving Donna a bottle when the light in the room suddenly faded as if someone had flicked a switch. A refreshing cool breeze blew through the open windows and on to her cheeks, as welcome as a lover's kiss. A storm was coming.

Michelle stood up, with the feeding Donna balanced in the crook of her arm, and went outside. The flawless blue sky was gone, blotted by inky clouds that were gathering low in the west. The heat had fallen away and in its place an oppressive humidity sat heavily.

Everyone else had been drawn outside by the change in light and the street was littered with her neighbours, all standing and staring up at the heavens. It was as if they were gathering for a party. Some were laughing and someone else swore at the sudden drop in temperature. Mr Smith from number 48, dressed in a grubby string vest and a pair of brown pin-striped trousers, was calling out to anyone who would listen.

'Here it comes. I told you. Didn't I tell you it was going to break this week?'

Michael Fish the weatherman had told Michelle as well, and she had been more minded to believe him, but she gave Mr Smith a kind smile.

Then large drops of rain began to fall, plopping on to the pavement and splashing back up. Within minutes the grey, stained tarmac had turned to slick black and the smell of ozone filled the air. Then the heavy rumbles of thunder reverberated around them, and the heatwave was over.

◆　◆　◆

Once it started, it didn't stop raining for two months, by the end of which Michelle couldn't remember what it felt like to be too hot. The children went back to school, Carl promising to behave and not get into any more trouble. Michelle tapped him on his head as he trudged away, muttering something about him being a good boy from now on, but she didn't really believe he would be. He had too much of his dad in him to follow the rules.

Donna continued to grow. At three months old, the dark wispy hair that she had been born with was starting to thicken a little and the blue eyes had muddied into a rich russet brown with flecks of gold. When Michelle went to pick her up in the morning, she tried not to let her thoughts linger over who the child was. She was just Donna. The baby.

Dean didn't mention her baby swap theory again, and Michelle knew that it was best to let sleeping dogs lie with him, but one evening she wandered into Donna's room to check on her and found Dean already there. He was leaning over her cot, his face close to Donna's, scrutinising it inch by inch. Because he wasn't smiling at her she didn't smile back, content to just watch him watching her.

When he heard Michelle come in, Dean drew back quickly and stepped over to the window, fiddling unnecessarily with the curtains.

'What are you doing?' Michelle asked him, leaning over the cot herself to check that Donna was all right. She smiled at the baby who smiled back and held out her arms to be picked up.

'She made a funny noise,' muttered Dean. 'I was just making sure she was okay.'

Then he left the room without another word and Michelle heard him going down the stairs and out of the house. Had he really been checking on her? Or was he, despite refusing to take her concerns seriously to her face, contemplating them behind her back?

Michelle stroked Donna's cheek with the back of her finger. She was a pretty little thing, far prettier than the other three had been. And today she looked quite a lot like a younger Tina, her dark hair framing her face just as her sister's had done. Sometimes Michelle was almost certain there had been no mistake and it had all been a figment of her post-natal imagination.

The following week Michelle was at the corner shop picking up a tin of Spam and some eggs for the kids' tea. She had left Donna in her pram outside and when she came back out she found Linda, her head under the pram's canopy, peering at Donna. When Michelle appeared, Linda pulled away, but not in a way that suggested she'd been caught out.

'I see what Dean means,' she said, nodding in the direction of the pram. 'She doesn't have much of a look of him, does she?'

Michelle was thrown both by the comment itself but also by the fact that Dean seemed to have been sharing their personal business with all and sundry. Immediately, she felt her hackles rising and her face tightening as she stepped up to defend Donna.

'She looks like herself,' Michelle said. 'There's nothing says that they all have to look the same. Just look at Dean and his brother Ricky,' she added, falling back on Dean's own example. 'They don't look anything alike.'

Linda shrugged, conceding the point. They had all been at school together and Linda had had a bit of a thing with Ricky, Michelle remembered, when she couldn't get her claws into Dean.

'Still, seems a bit strange,' Linda said, giving Michelle a knowing look out of the tail of her eye. 'Might make a person wonder, when a baby looks nothing like the person who's supposed to be her dad.'

Michelle's heart jolted and anger rose up in her immediately.

'I don't know what you think you've heard,' she snapped, thrusting her shopping under the pram and spinning it round smartly on its back wheels so it was facing the way she'd come. 'But it's complete crap. Of course I'm sure she's Dean's. Whose else would she be?'

Linda shrugged nonchalantly, making Michelle want to slap her.

'Just saying what I heard,' she said.

'Well, you heard wrong. And I'd thank you to keep your nose out of my family's business.'

Linda raised an eyebrow. 'If you say so. But there's no smoke without fire, that's what I always think,' she added. 'Funny kind of thing to hear if it's not true.'

Michelle pulled her mouth tight and set off down the pavement at speed before she said anything she would regret to Linda. The whole incident would be the talk of the street by the end of the afternoon as it was. There was no need to pour petrol on the flames.

As she got closer to home and her heart rate had returned to something approaching normal, Michelle started to wonder who might have been talking to Linda. There were only two candidates. Dean or Sharon. Michelle would have trusted both of them not to gossip, Dean because it was his family in the firing line and Sharon because she was her friend.

But it appeared she was wrong – about one of them at least.

17

Michelle decided she would ask Dean about the rumour first. She would do it gently. There was no point causing a row if it hadn't been him talking out of turn. But at the same time, he needed to understand, if he didn't already, that this was their private business and not to be discussed in front of all and sundry in the pub.

That evening, after Michelle had put Donna down and the kids were watching *Top of the Pops*, she caught Dean's eye and nodded her head towards the staircase. Dean, clearly thinking that he was on a promise, gave her a grin, looked at the kids sitting in a row on the sofa, and then stood up.

'Just popping upstairs,' he said to them. 'Your mum wants a word with me.'

He emphasised the 'word' in a way that Michelle felt was totally inappropriate, but the kids didn't tear their eyes from the screen. Jimmy Savile, gold bracelets jangling, was just introducing the dance troop Legs & Co in their next number and Dean's eyes strayed to the television too as the dancers, dressed in gold bikinis with plumes of feathers sprouting from their shoulders and hips, began to gyrate. Michelle gave him an irritated nudge and he refocused his attention away and followed her up the steep staircase to the first floor.

Once upstairs she led him into their bedroom and shut the door decisively. His hands were on her waist and travelling down to her hips before she'd had the chance to say a word. Part of her wanted to let him continue. Opportunities to be alone had been thin on the ground since the summer and she would have liked to share a few intimate minutes now that they were undisturbed, but she couldn't relax into the moment with this question hanging over her, so she wriggled free and took a couple of steps away from him. His face fell into a look of disappointment.

'I thought you meant . . .' he began.

'No. Well, maybe. But first there's something I need to ask you.'

Michelle sat down on the side of the bed and patted the blankets to get him to sit next to her. Dean sat down close enough that she could feel the warmth of his body through his jeans.

'I saw Linda today,' she began. This was hardly surprising as they all lived in the same street. 'I caught her staring at Donna. She said she'd heard that Donna wasn't yours.'

She paused, looking up at Dean to read his expression, and knew in an instant that it had been him who had told Linda.

'Why would she say that?' he asked with a little shake of his head. He raised his eyebrows as if he couldn't possibly imagine how it might have happened.

'I don't know,' replied Michelle, 'and the thing is, it's not right. I know I said that I wasn't sure that Donna was our baby, but that's not the same as her not being *yours* . . .'

She let the difference between the two scenarios settle in his mind before she carried on.

'So, when Linda comes up to me saying that Donna doesn't look like you, you can imagine how that made me feel. You can see what she was getting at.'

Dean chewed at the inside of his cheek for a moment as he thought. His large hand, engine oil engrained around the nails and into the creases of his knuckles, rubbed at the back of his head.

'Yeah,' he said.

'And not only is that not fair,' Michelle continued, 'but it's also our private business and not for sharing with every Tom, Dick and Harry in the pub.'

'Right,' he said.

Michelle couldn't work out whether he was being contrite or just planning what he wanted to say next. He hadn't actually admitted that it had been him who'd said something to Linda yet, but it seemed pretty clear that it was. And he hadn't denied it.

There was a pause. Michelle looked at Dean. Dean looked at his hands. The bouncy rhythm of Billy Ocean's song 'Stop Me' came up through the thin walls. Tina was singing along, her little voice surprising strong, and Michelle thought how strange the lyrics sounded in the mouth of her seven-year-old daughter.

'The thing is, Chelle,' Dean said, without looking at her. 'She doesn't look like me. Donna, I mean. So . . .' He let the thought hang in the air.

'I know! I told you this before. She doesn't look like me either,' Michelle countered, her voice tight with frustration. 'That's the point. She's not our baby. Or at least, I'm not sure she's ours. But that's not the same as people thinking that she's mine but not yours. That would mean that I had a thing with some other bloke and I didn't. I wouldn't.'

She put her hands on his and looked straight into his eyes. When she had first raised her concerns about Donna, it had never occurred to her that they might end up on this square, and she wasn't sure how they had. She and Dean were rock solid. Okay, they had been thrown together very young, but that had turned out to be one of the best things that had ever happened to her. They had defied the naysayers by not only staying together but going on to have another three children, building a happy and successful life together. The idea that she'd cheated on him was unthinkable.

'You don't honestly believe . . .' she began, but found that she couldn't actually say the words out loud.

Dean shook his head.

'No,' he said. 'No! Of course not. And I'm sorry that Linda got the wrong end of the stick. I'll set her straight next time I see her.'

But it was Michelle's turn to shake her head.

'No. Don't do that. Definitely not.' She pointed a finger to emphasise her point. 'Just let it drop. They'll forget in time, especially if we don't make a fuss. We can't do anything about what's happened, or might have happened, so we just have to get on with things. We have to treat Donna just like the others. It's not her fault, the little lamb. And it might all be nothing. We might wake up in a year's time and find that she looks more like us than the rest of them put together.'

Dean nodded, giving her half a smile.

'But please let's just keep it all to ourselves,' Michelle added in a gentle voice. 'It's nobody's business but ours.'

'Okay,' agreed Dean. 'So, now can we . . .' He gave her a nudge. 'You know.'

Michelle rolled her eyes but let herself be pushed backwards on to the bed. From downstairs the week's number one hit accompanied them. It was Chicago's 'If You Leave Me Now', but Michelle wasn't really listening.

1981

18

Michelle opened her eyes and realised that she had woken naturally, and not been hauled from sleep by arguments ricocheting around the walls of the house. Next to her, Dean slept on, his breathing steady and rhythmic with just the hint of a snore. He never used to make noises in his sleep, she thought. Or maybe he had and she had just been too tired to notice.

She reached for her watch and squinted at the face. It was just gone seven thirty. No wonder the kids were still asleep. They had all been out in the street until past eleven the night before. It was impossible to maintain a reasonable bedtime when they could hear their friends still roaming around outside, so Michelle had abandoned trying. Even little Donna, just turned five, had fallen asleep in a little heap in the hallway and Michelle had had to scoop her up in her arms and carry her upstairs to the room she shared with Tina.

A light breeze was wafting in from the open window and the light being filtered through the curtains was bright. It looked like it was going to be a nice day.

Michelle got out of bed as carefully as she could, keen not to wake Dean so that she could enjoy this rare moment of solitude, and pulled on yesterday's clothes for ease. Then she padded down the steep stairs to the kitchen where she flicked on the kettle and made herself a cup of tea.

She took the tea outside to enjoy on the doorstep, savouring the crisp fresh air of a new day beginning. The street was still, with no one around so early on a Saturday morning. Somewhere in the distance she could hear the electric motor of the milkman's van but he had already been to them. Their pints were standing like little white soldiers next to her. In moments like this her body still craved a cigarette. She had given them up when she'd been pregnant with Carl. Everyone else she knew smoked right through their pregnancies, but something had told Michelle that that couldn't be right. Nicotine was a drug, after all, and babies were so tiny and defenceless. She still missed it, though, that first fag of the day.

She drained her tea but sat on for a moment, allowing herself a rare space for contemplation about her life and settled on somewhere between adequate and satisfactory. Thirty years old, four kids, a good-ish husband, a nice-ish house. She was doing okay. Michelle White was never going to set the world alight, but things could be a whole lot worse.

A dog barking further up the street made her turn her head. There was the cathedral, sitting proudly at the top of the hill a couple of miles away, looking down over the city. The early morning light was hazy, and the tips of the cathedral's towers looked as if they had been painted on in watercolour.

How long had it been since Michelle had ventured up to the top end of town? She couldn't remember. She was sure she hadn't been this year, maybe not even last. What reason did she have to go up there anyway, with its little shops selling expensive crap and pubs where the beer was almost twice as much as it was down near them? The High Street, which led all the way to the cathedral, was dissected by a railway line and she rarely got beyond it, all the shops that she needed being down on her side of the tracks. She would occasionally wander as far as Woolworths and she did go to the market when the kids needed new shoes, but that was about it.

But suddenly Michelle wanted to go. Why should only the posh people get to enjoy that part of town? Where was it written that the working class like her should stay on their side of the divide?

She put her mug down on the doorstep and went inside to pull on her sandals and then, locking the door behind her, she set off, leaving her family sleeping on.

She walked to the end of the road heading in the direction of the cathedral, over the level crossing and up the High Street towards the Stonebow. Her teacher in primary school had told her class that the Stonebow was an ancient gateway to the city.

'Does that mean we don't live in Lincoln, then, sir?' she had asked, confused, as everyone she knew lived on what appeared to be the wrong side of the imposing stone archway.

The teacher had muttered something about the city boundaries extending over time to include the streets where his pupils lived, but Michelle had known that he'd really meant they were somehow excluded, cast out. She hadn't thought about that for years, but now, as she passed underneath the arch, she remembered how she had felt as a child, concluding as she had done then, that she was somehow inferior to those who lived on the other side.

Once beyond the Stonebow, the street started to wend its way upwards, becoming increasingly narrow and steep the closer she got to the top. She had to stop a couple of times to catch her breath. She really should do more exercise. Maybe she would go with Sharon to that keep-fit class she kept going on about.

Finally, with more panting than there should have been, she reached the Bailgate, a cobbled area with the cathedral on one side and the castle on the other. There was an empty bench and she collapsed on it whilst she waited for her breathing to return to normal. It was coming up to nine o'clock now and the streets were starting to get busy.

Michelle considered whether her family would have woken up yet, and if they would be wondering where she had gone. She should probably have left a note, but it was too late now. And she would be back soon enough.

It would do them good, anyway, to wonder. She was always there, always at their beck and call. Just for once, she was doing something for her, even if it was walking up the steepest hill in the county for no reason other than because she could.

A man wearing a black clerical frock appeared, his dog collar a brilliant white against the dark fabric of the rest of his clothing. She couldn't see his feet beneath his gown and so it looked like he was moving on wheels across the square. His expression was so very earnest that it made Michelle want to giggle. What could possibly be so important that it required such a very serious face?

Michelle had never really been to church. Her parents hadn't been that way inclined and she and Dean had got married in the registry office because of her quite apparent bump. She'd only been in the cathedral once, on the same school trip when she learned about the Stonebow. She'd lived in this city for thirty years and had only been inside its most iconic building once.

The cleric glided past her and disappeared through the archway towards the cathedral. Not really knowing why, Michelle stood up and followed him. He made his way towards the huge wooden doors and disappeared inside. Without really thinking about it, Michelle went in too.

It was obvious that the cathedral was a vast building from the outside, but you really didn't get any idea of the size of it until you were in it. It was definitely the largest place Michelle had ever stepped foot in. It seemed to stretch on forever. She wasn't even sure that she could see all the way down to the far end. And then there was the height. Stone arches were cut into the walls down either side, each of them twice as tall as she was but completely dwarfed by the huge archways above them, which in turn were made small by the vaulted arches of the ceiling above. Michelle craned her neck to look up but it was so high that it made her feel dizzy.

Despite its size, the cathedral was warm and the air was full of the scent of candles and another sweet, heavy smell that she couldn't place. It was also so very light. From the outside, she'd have expected it to be dark inside, but it was quite the opposite. The pale stone, the white paintwork and the huge stained-glass windows all contributed to an overwhelming sense of light and space.

For a moment, Michelle was dazzled by it all, her brain not knowing how to process the grandeur of what her eyes were seeing. She swore quietly under her breath and shook her head. It was almost enough to make her believe in God.

There were a couple of the men in long black robes at the far end and she saw them notice her. Was she supposed to be in here? The cathedral was for everyone, right? Anyone could walk into a church for sanctuary or whatever, and this was just a church. A bloody big one, but still just a church. Then one of the men started to walk towards her, and assuming that she was about to get into trouble for being in a place that she had no business being in, she turned on her heel and went out the way she came, only stopping when she reached her bench again.

Michelle smiled to herself. Dean would never believe her when she told him what she'd been up to. In the cathedral? Her! Funny.

The cathedral bells sounded the half-hour and Michelle stood up. She really should be getting back. They would definitely all be up by now and wondering where she could possibly be. She took a few steps to take one last look at the cathedral, its incredible facade glowing in the early morning light.

Then a woman caught her eye. She was wearing a long leather coat in a dark forest green despite the warmth of the day, and her chestnut hair shone in the sunshine. Michelle's breath stuck in her chest and her jaw dropped open. It was the woman, the woman from the hospital.

The woman who had her baby.

19

Sylvie always enjoyed her morning circuit of the cathedral. On school days she tended to sally forth around midday after she'd had an hour at the housework and a couple in the studio. At the weekends, however, she could go when she liked as Jeremy didn't work then and could be relied on to entertain Leo. Sylvie would slip out of the house, calling to tell them where she was going only as the door was closing so that no one could summon her back. Or if they did she wouldn't hear them, which amounted to the same thing.

Sometimes on a Saturday, she would do the loop four or five times before she felt ready to return. When Jeremy asked her how her walk had been, she didn't confess that she had never been more than a few hundred yards from the house. For her, the purpose of the exercise was not to get anywhere or see anything but simply to be somewhere else.

It was an average July day, not cold but not especially hot. She was wearing her green leather coat, and whilst she felt a little overdressed next to the lightweight jackets of those around her, she wasn't too warm. That was the joy of leather – it was rarely wrong. She let the coat hang open though, no need to deploy the buttons today.

She'd had her green leather coat for years. She and Christine had bought it on Carnaby Street in '62. It had been a rash and extravagant purchase. They barely had the money to pay the rent and a large, one-off purchase could wobble their precarious little boat quite dangerously. But the coat had spoken to her. When she shrugged it on and twirled in front of the mirror Sylvie had known that she would be prepared to suffer to own it. If that meant turning off the heat and not eating meat for a few weeks to pay for it then that was what she was prepared to do. And Christine, she knew, would come along for the ride. If anyone understood the price of looking fabulous then it was Christine.

They had been such a team, she and Christine. They first met in Woolworths where they both worked, Sylvie to pay for her art (not everyone had family money like Jeremy) and Christine to fund the party lifestyle that she had come to London to enjoy. The pair had hit it off immediately, both laughing at inappropriate jokes made at their supervisor's expense. Within weeks they had found a flat in Shepherd's Bush with a space by the draughty window in the living room that was light enough for Sylvie to work in. She arranged her drawing board and her pots of pens, and Christine stuck up pictures cut from magazines on the walls to cover the damp patches. The images she picked were all female film icons: Marilyn Monroe, Brigitte Bardot, Natalie Wood.

'Well, a girl needs to aim high,' she told Sylvie when she asked about the selection.

That was Christine all over. When she discovered that Sylvie had studied at the Royal College of Art her eyes sparkled.

'Those artists' parties are supposed to be wild,' she said. 'Do you get invited?'

Sylvie shrugged. 'To some of them, I suppose. I don't go, though. Parties aren't really my scene.'

Christine raised an eyebrow. 'Parties are everybody's scene,' she said. 'The very next time you get even a whiff of a party you tell me and I'll make sure we get invited to every one from then on.'

Sylvie wasn't sure how Christine intended to achieve that, although she could take a guess. She hadn't really bothered with the parties at art school because she had always felt awkward and gauche in front of all the beautiful, cool people who were there. She had enjoyed the people-watching though. Being in the presence of such vibrancy and innovation was inspiring even if she didn't want to be front and centre. Maybe if she introduced Christine to a few people then she could just follow along in her wake without having to cause any ripples of her own.

It didn't take long. There had been a boy in her year at art school, Jeremy Something-posh-sounding. She had noticed him because he had that confident air that being born into money often brought with it. He wasn't arrogant, just comfortable in his own skin, a quality Sylvie admired. His work was very modern – a mixture of brash paintwork in strong colours and images cut from magazines. In his pictures a decapitated head might appear in the heart of a blowsy rose, or the corner of a cornflakes packet stuck on to the canvas and then painted over with exploding missiles. It was a far cry from Sylvie's own work and she wasn't sure she understood it, but there was something about its boldness that spoke to her.

Since they had graduated, however, she hadn't seen much of her fellow artists. She had just got herself a job to pay the rent and continued to draw when time allowed. So when Jeremy wandered into Woolworths one day, she screwed up her courage and spoke to him.

'Hi Jeremy. How are you? Have you had a good summer?' She smiled broadly but for a moment she feared that he hadn't recognised her out of context.

'It's Sylvie, isn't it? Sylvie with the miniatures.'

Sylvie nodded. In contrast to Jeremy's style, her own work was tiny; minute sketches rendered with photographic realism.

'Did you know we called you Sylph behind your back? Because you're so tiny, like a little fairy.'

Sylvie hadn't known, but it gave her a thrill to know that the cool crowd had not only noticed her but had bothered to come up with a nickname.

'And you're working here now?' he continued, his tone suggesting disappointment but not criticism.

Sylvie shrugged. 'Got to pay the rent, just until I get my big break,' she said ironically.

Jeremy dropped his eyes for a moment, his expression sheepish, and she realised at once that he didn't need to find a job to keep the wolf from the door.

'Have you kept in touch with the others?' he asked, and before Sylvie had a chance to shake her head he added, 'Listen, there's a party on Saturday. It's at The Green Room, downstairs, you know. You should come along. Catch up with everyone.'

'I will,' Sylvie replied, surprising herself with her confidence. 'Can I bring someone?'

Something flickered across his face at the mention of a possible partner, causing her to blurt, 'A girlfriend, I mean. My flatmate Christine.'

He flashed his open smile. Was it in relief? Sylvie wasn't sure, but something told her that it might have been.

'I don't see why not. Starts at eight.'

Then he lifted the black leather cap that he liked to wear and then went off to find whatever he had come in for, leaving Sylvie with a fizzing in the pit of her stomach.

20

Christine was quite beside herself at the thought of an arty party and started buzzing the moment Sylvie mentioned it. Now it was the day itself, and they were getting ready. Christine stood in front of the ancient mirror, almost more spots than glass, backcombing her long blonde hair.

'Tell me again, who will be there?' she said as she teased up the hair on the crown of her head and secured it with a clip.

'I'm not sure,' Sylvie confessed.

She was painting thick black lines in kohl over her lash line. One side always went much better than the other and she tutted as she examined her handiwork.

'Here,' said Christine, coming across and taking the kohl from her hand. 'Let me.'

Christine evened up her cat's eye flicks as Sylvie ran through a list of names of people that she thought might be there.

'Any of them famous?' Christine asked.

'Not quite yet,' replied Sylvie. 'But there's this one chap from Bradford who might be one day.'

Christine shivered. 'I'm so excited. A decent party. At last! How do I look?'

She stepped back so that Sylvie could admire her. She was wearing a knee-length black shift dress in a shiny taffeta that clung to her curves. Her blonde hair fell about her shoulders in heavy curls and her make-up was applied with a precision that any of Sylvie's fellow art students would have been proud of.

'Gorgeous!' said Sylvie, blowing her a kiss.

She herself had opted for a far more understated pair of black cigarette pants and a black turtleneck, her uniform. Her chestnut hair was bobbed and her fringe hung down over her dark eyes. Next to Christine she looked tiny and insignificant, but she was happy with that.

The Green Room was a club off Tottenham Court Road. On the ground floor, they often had jazz acts playing and the rooms downstairs, a series of interconnecting cellars, were used for drinking and dancing.

Christine and Sylvie caught the bus to Oxford Circus and walked the last part, arriving at the club just after eight thirty. They hesitated at the door. Sylvie would have liked someone she recognised to come along and take her in, but Christine had no such qualms.

'Come on,' she said, tucking her arm into Sylvie's, her hand sliding easily along the smooth green leather of Sylvie's coat. 'The secret is to look as if you belong.'

They made their way past the main bar and Christine steered Sylvie towards the back stairs that led to the basement. As they approached, they could hear dance music, something by Buddy Holly, and the sound of people talking and laughing. Sylvie might have held back a little if she had been on her own but Christine headed straight for the bar. She bought them each a glass of red wine, lit herself a cigarette and then leaned back to get the lay of the land.

The room was filled with people around their age, chatting and laughing, all looking as they had just strolled off the pages of *ArtReview* magazine.

'This,' said Christine, with an expansive gesture that took in the room, 'is why I came to London.' She threw her drink back in one gulp. 'Let's dance!' she said, grabbing Sylvie by the arm.

As Sylvie looked for somewhere to put her glass down the music changed to 'The Twist', and at once everyone thronged to the centre of the room to the makeshift dance floor. Unable to find a suitable ledge, Sylvie took her drink with her, making sure that she had drunk enough of it that it didn't spill, no mean feat bearing in mind Christine's enthusiastic twisting. There was nothing for it, Sylvie decided after a moment or two, than to just follow her flatmate's lead and throw herself into it and so she did, the tails of her coat swinging from side to side as she danced.

They stayed on the dance floor for over an hour, carried away by the music. Christine was drawing a lot of attention. She moved well, entirely aware of how to use her body so that she displayed it to its best. As she danced, her hair falling over first one shoulder and then the other, she was one moment seemingly unaware of the men watching her and the next making direct eye contact with them and yet at the same time, Sylvie felt as if her friend was entirely focused on her. It was very impressive.

Eventually, however, Sylvie needed another drink.

'Just going to the bar,' she mouthed at Christine and stepped away from the dancers.

As she stood waiting to be served, she became aware of someone at her elbow. It was Jeremy, dressed all in black and with his cap still in place despite the warmth of the room. She had shed her coat quite some time before.

'Hi,' he said. 'Having fun?'

Sylvie nodded.

'Your friend certainly is,' he added, turning to look at Christine who was now dancing with the boy from Bradford. They were leaping around, quite out of time with the music but without a care, his blond hair matching hers almost perfectly. 'She's a hit with David, I see,' he added, and Sylvie nodded.

'How's the work?' she asked him. 'Are you still working on similar pieces?'

'I am but I can't seem to get what I want to say across. I'm thinking of trying something new.'

Sylvie, who had thought that Jeremy's work very much resembled that of some of the more avant-garde students, nodded.

'It's always good to be able to take off in a new direction,' she agreed.

'You're very pretty,' he said, and the sudden change in subject matter threw her off balance.

'Thank you,' she muttered without looking at him. She could feel her cheeks start to burn. They had studied together for three years and he had barely paid her any attention in all that time.

'Have you seen what Warhol is doing over in New York? And Lichtenstein?' he continued as if he hadn't made the previous comment.

Sylvie hadn't. Pop art didn't interest her. It was large and loud and, with her background in fine art, she didn't really understand what they were trying to say, but she nodded, not wanting to discourage him. He was handsome in a conventional kind of way with even, symmetrical features, but it was his confidence that she found attractive.

'They are very exciting,' she said, hoping that she was right.

His face lit up and he moved a step closer to her.

'Aren't they?' he said, his voice higher than it had been. 'I think they're incredible. Listen, do you want to go out for a drink sometime? We can talk somewhere where it's a bit quieter.'

They had been at college together for three years, Sylvie wanted to say. He'd had plenty of opportunities to get to know her and had ignored her, but she found herself agreeing.

'And would it be all right if I kissed you?'

This she really wasn't expecting, and she was just gathering herself to respond when he leaned across and brushed his lips against hers, gently at first and then with more pressure. They were still kissing when Christine came over to find out what had happened to her drink.

21

And that had been the start, Sylvie thought to herself. The beginning of her and Jeremy. They had quickly become a couple, but they were rarely alone. Jeremy liked to hang out with other artists he knew and Sylvie was happy to go along. It gave her a way into their lives that she had never managed to find for herself and she enjoyed sitting quietly in a corner absorbing the energy of the others.

Much of their spare time was spent in scruffy studios and draughty bedsits, drinking coffee from chipped mugs and having animated discussions about the Cuban Missile Crisis, the death of Sylvia Plath and whether Harold Wilson would be the saviour of the nation. The studio walls would be covered with the work of whichever artist lived there. Most were very modern and all were totally different to the small, precise pieces that Sylvie was producing.

But Sylvie's work was selling. She had already held a small exhibition in a gallery off Shaftesbury Avenue, arranged for her by one of her tutors, and she had been thrilled when almost all her pieces had been graced with a red dot by the end.

Jeremy had been genuinely delighted for her, but she knew that a part of him was wishing for his own success. His art wasn't selling. 'Yet,' she said to him. 'It's not selling yet.' And he gave her one of his confident smiles and said, 'That's right, Sylph. I just need my big break.'

Sylvie continued working at Woolworths with Christine, though. A few sales were no guarantee of any more in the future, and anyway, she didn't mind working when the pair of them had such good fun. The days at Woolworths flew by and the nights were spent hanging out in studios talking art (which Christine was becoming increasingly good at – 'I just tell them what they want to hear,' she had confessed to Sylvie with a wink). And life had been good – everything, in fact, that Sylvie could have wished for.

One day, they'd been in someone's flat when a woman she didn't recognise turned up. This was nothing unusual in itself, but what was unusual was that she had a baby with her. Sylvie didn't notice at first. The baby was swaddled against her body so tightly that it just looked like layers of clothing. But then the woman, Ali, released the baby and her breast from the bindings and began to feed the child right there in front of everyone. Sylvie was very surprised. She had never seen a baby being breastfed before, let alone in such a public place, but the rest of them seemed to take it in their stride so she tried to do the same.

She watched, slyly from the corner of her eye, as Ali let the baby take its fill. Sylvie couldn't imagine having a person who was entirely dependent on her. In fact, the idea made her chest tighten uncomfortably, as if she'd become trapped in a small dark space with no way to escape.

'Oh, look at him,' said Vix, one of the other women in the group. 'He's such a dot. And those tiny feet. I just want to eat him up. You're so lucky to have a baby, Ali.'

Ali smiled back at Vix and stroked the baby's hair. 'I know. I'm the luckiest woman alive,' she said.

Contentment radiated from her. Sylvie was baffled.

'Don't you think she's lucky, Sylv?' Vix asked her. 'Isn't he just dreamy? I bet you wish you had one too?'

She threw a grin at Jeremy, and Sylvie watched his response carefully. They hadn't discussed having children yet. It hadn't been relevant to anything about their lives. Sylvie struggled to see how it ever would be.

Jeremy rolled his eyes at the apparent silliness of the question, and then Sylvie realised that she hadn't answered the question and that everyone was waiting for her to speak. She didn't like to be the centre of attention, but that was precisely what she was going to be until she spoke.

'He is very sweet,' she began. 'But I'm not sure motherhood is for me.'

'What? Not now, or not ever?' asked Vix with characteristic directness.

Sylvie knew the answer but felt it might be more politic to be seen to be considering it. She paused for a moment, feigned thought and then said, 'Not ever, I don't think. I'm not cut out to be a mother and I'm certain the human race won't die out just because I don't contribute to its number.'

'That's what I used to think,' said Ali, lifting the baby against her chest and rubbing his back vigorously. 'But now that he's here I wouldn't be without him, would I, my sweet?'

Then the baby gave a resounding belch and they all laughed, and the conversation floated away from her, allowing her to return quietly to the background.

She let her eyes stray over to Jeremy to see how he had taken her comments, but there didn't seem to be anything awry there. Sylvie was relieved. She thought she probably loved Jeremy and she could see them being together forever, but she wouldn't change her mind about babies and he needed to understand that now, before things got any more serious.

Aware of her eyes on him, Jeremy turned in her direction and winked at her.

'Okay?' he mouthed.

She nodded gratefully back.

'No babies?' he mouthed, eyebrows raised questioningly.

'No babies,' she replied, shaking her head.

He gave her a thumbs-up sign and a smile.

◆ ◆ ◆

Sylvie had taken four turns around her morning loop and found herself once again outside their cathedral. She looked at her watch. She had been gone for almost an hour already. Another round would add fifteen minutes to her absence, more if she dawdled.

But she should go back home and get on with her day. She had promised Leonora that they would go swimming later. Sylvie would have preferred an hour or so looking at old favourites in the art gallery or maybe a wander around the cathedral, but this kind of activity was of no interest to Leonora and so Sylvie had long since given up trying. The child was only five, after all. There would be plenty of time for more cultural education when she was a little older, and swimming was fun too – there was nothing wrong with that.

No, she would go home and get Leonora ready, though her heart sank at the thought. No doubt Leonora would be having a debate about something with Jeremy. She was amazingly articulate for so young an age, so that was something to be proud of at least. But what Sylvie wouldn't give for a quiet house some of the time.

At least she had her trip away to look forward to. This time next week she would be at Christine's and they would laugh and chat and drink tea and red wine, and the trials and tribulations of parenthood would just fall away. Christine had never married and was not in the least interested in Leonora, and so Sylvie never felt obliged to discuss her, quite the reverse in fact. She felt a kind of obligation not to talk about her family life. Going to visit Christine reminded her of what her own life should have been – just her and Jeremy and their art.

As she left the cathedral square, Sylvie didn't notice the woman with the dark hair scraped back into a ponytail who was watching her intently.

22

Michelle was glued to the spot. Was it really the woman from the hospital? She was crossing the lawn in front of the cathedral now, about thirty yards from where Michelle was standing. Michelle had only seen her twice, once in the middle of the night and then again standing in the corridor of the maternity ward, but she was certain. She had replayed those meagre memories so many times over the years, making sure that they were firmly embedded in her mind for a moment exactly like this one. The moment when she finally saw her again.

The woman was getting away. Michelle had been waiting for this for five years, scrutinising the face of every stranger, scanning crowds for the kind of wild chestnut hair that the woman Sylvie had had. Always vigilant. And now, when she finally had her in her sights, she was letting her escape. Already she was about to disappear behind the cathedral and down one of the many snickets and alleyways that there were in this part of the old town. If Michelle didn't move quickly she was going to lose her.

Michelle set off, half-walking, half-running in the direction that she had seen Sylvie go. Once she rounded the corner of the cathedral, however, there was no sign of her quarry. Had she disappeared into one of the cathedral buildings? Michelle scanned the doors for signs that one had been recently opened, but there was nothing and there'd been no sound of a door closing either.

Following her gut instincts, Michelle traced the curve of the cathedral yard round and out on to the road behind and there, a little bit further along, was the green leather coat. Sylvie wasn't walking particularly fast. Michelle could easily have caught her up, but she decided against it. What if she was wrong? What if she confronted the woman and it wasn't her at all? This was the closest that Michelle had come to solving the mystery of little Donna, but her instincts were telling her to hold back. She might speak to the woman, discover it was Sylvie, but then she could refuse to listen, or say that she had no doubt that the baby she'd brought home from the hospital was hers. Where would that leave Michelle?

Michelle had worked hard to push all doubts over Donna away during the last few years. Once it had become clear that nobody was going to take her seriously and she had no way of solving the mystery herself, this had seemed like her only option. As she tumbled into bed at the end of each day, exhausted by the basics of caring for four young children, there was no room left in her head for contemplation of something so outlandish.

But now fate had presented her with this chance. There might be a way of deciding the issue once and for all, and even though she had tried to put the question away, she knew that she would never live with herself if she didn't at least try to get to the bottom of what had really happened. The main thing now was to keep Sylvie where she could see her.

She seemed to be walking a circuit of the cathedral because she kept turning left without ever arriving at a destination. It was like a grim parody of their mutual situation. They seemed to be following the route of the huge walls that surrounded the city's ancient castle, turning left until finally, they reached a narrow street with the cathedral once again appearing in view.

Then the woman slowed her pace, pausing briefly in front of a house and then turning into the drive and letting herself in through the front door. The door slammed behind her and then she was gone.

Michelle stood on the opposite pavement, her heart pounding in her chest. Was this where Sylvie lived? Had Michelle finally found her? She had been so close all the time, barely two miles from Michelle's home and yet so far away in this part of the city that Michelle thought she had no business being in.

The house certainly fitted with what Michelle thought she knew about the family. They had seemed far more well-to-do than her and Dean. The way her husband had spoken and dressed, his odd ideas about sketching Sylvie in the bed. And they had named their baby Leonora. That was weird in itself. No one that Michelle knew would choose such a peculiar and old-fashioned name.

It was a huge house. Michelle reckoned that she could fit their tiny place into it at least three times. Double-fronted with two gables and wooden panelling separating four huge bay windows, it was the kind of house that Michelle had rarely even seen, let alone been into. The mere thought of setting foot inside made her feel sick.

Her heart sank. What was she doing here? She didn't belong. She was so far out of where she felt comfortable that it was making her head spin. And what did she think she was going to do now? She could hardly just knock on the door and demand to see their child. She would probably do something really stupid like faint, or not be able to get the words out of her mouth and be left gaping like a floundering fish.

Michelle wasn't sure how long she stood there, staring at the house. Part of her was hoping that Sylvie would re-emerge, perhaps with Leonora, but there was no sign of life. In fact, if Michelle hadn't seen her go in with her own eyes, she would have assumed that the house was empty. Even that was so very different to her own house, where the door hinges would no doubt wear out one day with all the comings and goings.

Then the cathedral bell rang again. Michelle counted ten long chimes. She had to go home, yet she was so reluctant to leave.

But she knew where Sylvie was now. She could go away and collect herself. And then, when she was feeling ready, she could come back and knock on the door, and finally, the mystery would be solved.

Not today though.

With an aching heart, she turned and walked away to start the long descent back to her part of the city.

23

Michelle arrived back at her house with some bananas, a loaf and some mince for their tea, bought as a cover story. She wasn't sure why she felt the need to have had a specific purpose for her trip, but she did. It wasn't like her to just disappear and she had enough spinning round in her head without having to face questions from Dean and the kids.

Back on her street their front door was standing wide open. Donna was on the grass playing quietly on her own. Tina must have been in because her favourite Blondie tape was blasting out of her open bedroom window so that the whole street was being treated to 'The Tide Is High' with Tina's own rendition of the song trilling over the top.

The bonnet of the Cortina was also open and Dean was nose-deep in the engine. Michelle called out as she approached and he looked up.

'Where've you been?' he asked, but his tone was more curious than accusatory.

Michelle held her shopping bag aloft.

'Just went to pick up a few bits,' she said.

He gave her a questioning look.

'I woke up dead early,' she added, grasping at once that more explanation was required. 'And I just fancied a change of scene. I had a wander up the hill. Not been that way for ages.'

'How far did you get?' he asked, disappearing back amongst the spark plugs.

'All the way!' she replied proudly. 'Although I really need to get fitter. Maybe I should take up jogging.'

He withdrew his head from the engine and pulled a face that suggested he thought hell might freeze over first. It was on the tip of her tongue to tell him who she had seen. She'd imagined the conversation as she walked back home, the casual way that she could drop in having seen Sylvie. But now that she was home, she'd lost her nerve. She would tell him, of course she would, but she wanted to get her thoughts straight in her own mind first.

'Cup of tea?' she asked instead.

'That'd be champion,' replied Dean without looking up.

On her way into the house, Michelle paused to speak to Donna. She was much the same kind of child as she had been as a baby: quiet, watchful and entirely self-contained.

'What are you doing, sweetie?' asked Michelle, bending down so that she was at Donna's level. She picked up a book that had appeared from somewhere – school, Michelle assumed – and looked idly at the cover. It was by Enid Blyton. The front had an illustration of some children and a dog. None of her other children had been much interested in books, reading only when forced into it, but Donna could often be found lost in their pages. Michelle wasn't sure that she could recognise any of the words yet, but she saw her daughter's lips moving as if she was reading herself a story.

'Me and Lucy are having a tea party,' Donna said.

She poured very precisely from an invisible teapot into an invisible cup that she then held aloft for Lucy. Lucy might have taken the proffered cup, but as she was also invisible it was hard for Michelle to tell.

Lucy had lived with them for two years or so. Because of the age gap between Donna and Damien and the fact that he was a boy, Michelle had not been concerned to start with, had even encouraged the strange friendship. Now, though, when Donna was at school and old enough to make some flesh and blood friends, Michelle was beginning to worry about it a little. She would have chatted it through with Dean but was reluctant to draw yet more attention to how different Donna was to her siblings, for fear of causing a row.

'That's nice,' she said now. 'Does Lucy like tea?'

Donna pulled a face. 'No, silly,' she said. 'She prefers squash like me. Lemon barley though. Not orange.'

Michelle only ever bought the vibrant orange squash that was cheap in Kwik Save. She had no idea where Donna might have come across the more delicate lemon barley water. It was just another thing about Donna that she didn't know.

'That's nice,' she said again, getting to her feet. 'Can I get you anything?' she asked. 'I'm just going to make Daddy a cup of tea.'

'Why doesn't Daddy make his own tea?' Donna asked, and Michelle was so surprised that for a moment she didn't know what say.

'Well,' she managed after a moment. 'He says I make nice tea, and it's kind to do something for someone else.'

Donna nodded as if this was something she could accept. Then she carried on talking to Lucy, and Michelle knew she was dismissed.

Dean making his own tea, thought Michelle as she made her way to the kitchen. That was a novel concept.

It was later in the day when she could contain what was ready to burst out of her no longer. Dean was in the kitchen cleaning his hands with Swarfega, the smell of it as familiar as the smell of Dean himself.

Michelle took a breath. He would be heading out to the pub shortly so this would be her best chance to tell him what had happened earlier.

'You'll never guess who I saw when I was up Steep Hill,' she began.

She tried to make her voice sound as if this was of no significance whatsoever, but her heart was banging so hard against her ribs that she felt sure Dean must be able to hear it.

Dean shook his head. He started to dry his hands on a tea towel. Normally, Michelle would have ticked him off for that, but she didn't want them to become distracted.

'That woman,' she continued. 'The one from the hospital.'

Dean looked at her blankly.

'In the bed next to mine . . .' she tried.

She really didn't want to spell it out to him, but he still didn't seem to have understood what she was trying to say.

'With the baby . . .' she added weakly.

Dean's expression switched from mild confusion to something closer to irritation.

'Oh,' he said, but his tone didn't invite any further discussion.

He paused, waiting for her to continue, but there really wasn't anything else to say.

'Well, that was all really,' she said. 'Just that I saw her.'

'Did you speak?' asked Dean, eyeing her warily.

'No,' replied Michelle.

Tension fell from his face. 'Right,' he said. 'Good.'

'I know where she lives now, though,' Michelle blurted out. 'I mean, I kind of followed her for a bit and I saw her go into a house.'

Dean hung the tea towel back on the oven door.

'You need to be careful there, Chelle,' he said. He didn't sound angry, but there was a distinct warning in his words. 'Better to let sleeping dogs lie.'

'I know,' said Michelle. 'But I thought maybe I could talk to her, just pretend I recognised her from the hospital, ask how her baby's getting along, that kind of thing.'

'And how would you do that without looking like you'd followed her home?' asked Dean. 'She'd think you were a class one nutcase.'

He did have a point.

'I could maybe go back to that part of town one day . . .' She ran her teeth over her thumb knuckle as she watched his face for clues as to what he was thinking. 'If she was out doing her shopping or something I might run into her again.'

She knew it sounded ridiculous. But then again, she hadn't set eyes on the woman for five years, and yet the moment she'd gone up to the cathedral she had found her straight away.

Dean was shaking his head. 'We're beyond all that now, Chelle. You were ill back then, but you're better now so there's no need to go raking it up again. Donna's our kid. End of.'

Michelle nodded weakly. 'Yeah, you're right,' she said as convincingly as she could manage. 'I'll just leave it.'

'I think that's best,' Dean agreed. 'Have you seen my blue T-shirt? I wanted to wear it tonight.'

'It's in your drawer. The top one.'

Dean left the room to go and find the T-shirt, leaving Michelle on her own. He was probably right that she shouldn't start poking around in it all again, but she wished she could have his certainty about Donna. She had tried, she really had, but there was always that thing in the way, the silent creeping doubt that she couldn't quite believe but couldn't quite dismiss either.

Michelle heard a noise from the room beyond the kitchen. She'd thought they were on their own but now she heard the sound of the door opening and footsteps heading outside. She followed the sound and saw Donna standing on the corner of the lawn looking out at the street beyond.

Had she overheard? Could she have understood even if she had? Michelle tried to replay their conversation in her head, desperately searching for anything that might have made sense to a five-year-old.

24

Donna was quieter than usual at breakfast, pushing her cornflakes round in her bowl but not really eating any. Even if she hadn't understood what she'd overheard the night before, it was obvious that something was wrong. Michelle decided to make more fuss of her than normal, just in case.

'What shall we do today?' she asked brightly. 'Have you got any ideas?'

Normally Donna was brimming over with suggestions of things she wanted to make or play, but today she just shrugged.

'How about Lucy?' Michelle tried again. 'Does she have any ideas?'

'Lucy's not coming today,' replied Donna. 'I don't think she likes me any more.'

Michelle's heart lurched. Lucy was an imaginary friend and so entirely in Donna's control. The idea that even she had rejected Donna was more than Michelle could bear.

'Don't be daft,' said Michelle, putting an arm round Donna's tiny shoulders and dropping down so their faces were level. 'Of course she likes you. We can go down to the rec in a bit if you like. Have a play on the swings and slides. Lucy can come too. Or we can invite Sarah from next door.'

'She doesn't like me either,' replied Donna. A fat tear rolled down her cheek followed by another, and then Donna's little face screwed up as she let herself cry.

Seeing her babies cry always made Michelle want to cry herself. She put her arms round Donna, wrapping her tightly in a hug.

'Well, I'm not sure Sarah likes anyone that much,' she said, and Donna looked up at her through wet eyelashes and gave a tiny smile.

'Lucy doesn't like her,' she said. 'Because she popped my space hopper.'

'That was a mean thing to do,' agreed Michelle.

Sharon had been all apologies when her daughter had taken a potato peeler to the space hopper, but there had been no sign of her replacing it. There was no money for that kind of thing.

'Well, maybe we won't ask Sarah,' she went on. 'Tina might come if we ask her, or the boys.'

As the words left her mouth, Michelle knew this was unlikely. Tina, at twelve, had grown out of the swings and slides and the boys might be there already, but wouldn't be interested in entertaining their baby sister. It was no wonder that Donna had created Lucy to keep her company.

Yet again she replayed Dean's words in her head, analysing them for anything capable of misinterpretation. 'Donna's our kid. End of.' That was a positive statement, but if Donna had heard him then she might be wondering why anyone could have thought that she wasn't.

'I know!' said Michelle, infusing her voice with as much enthusiasm as she could muster. 'Why don't we take a bit of a picnic with us?' As she spoke, her brain scanned through what she had in the fridge to see how practical an idea this was. 'That would be fun, wouldn't it? We can take the blanket to sit on and get some pop from the corner shop.'

'Can we have Tizer?' Donna asked, eyes wide.

'If you like! And maybe some chocolate mini rolls too.'

Donna nodded, her smile returning.

'Lucy would like that,' she said.

'Then that's what we'll do,' replied Michelle decisively. 'Finish your breakfast and then we'll see what we can find to take with us.'

Finally, Donna began to eat her cornflakes and Michelle headed upstairs to find Tina and bribe her to come to the park with them.

The lure of Tizer and mini rolls was too strong for Tina to resist, and she brought a couple of her friends along too, so they were quite a merry band in the end. By the time Michelle tucked Donna in that evening she was back to herself.

'I do love you, you know, Donna,' whispered Michelle as she kissed the top of her head.

'I love you too, Mummy,' replied a sleepy Donna, her eyes already shut.

◆　◆　◆

But nothing had changed. Michelle had seen Sylvie and now knew where she lived. Nothing could reverse that, and faced with the information Michelle knew it was only a matter of time before she made the trip back up the hill. All she had to do was work out what she was going to do when she got there.

That was less easy. Part of her was all for marching up to Sylvie's house with Donna and thrusting the child forward to see what reaction she got. That would never do, though. Even her confused mind knew that. It might have been okay when the girls were still babies. After all, people peered at babies all the time. But now that they were five and aware of what was going on around them, even if they didn't always understand it, it would be unfair to subject the girls to that kind of scrutiny. If nothing else, the events of the last couple of days were enough to show her that.

Without Donna at her side, however, it would be harder to convince Sylvie that she had a point. Unless, of course, Sylvie had been sharing her doubts for all those years. She might be looking at Leonora and seeing things she couldn't explain too. If that was true then Michelle would be pushing at an open door.

But there was no way of knowing which way Sylvie might swing, and so this catapulted Michelle's thoughts back to the same place. She had to talk to Sylvie without the children being there. That way, she could test the water, see if the idea had ever occurred to Sylvie before she got herself in too deep to swim back to safety.

After this conclusion had lodged itself inside her head, Michelle became desperate to act on it. It was like making a decision to have your hair cut. Once it was made, the haircut itself couldn't happen soon enough.

But she wasn't Donna's only parent. There was Dean too. He had told her to let sleeping dogs lie. If she went to speak to Sylvie, then she would be flying in the face of his wishes and whilst she was sure that he was wrong, they were married. They were supposed to work as a team, and she knew exactly what he thought. She couldn't, in all conscience, pretend that she had misunderstood.

She remembered then what Donna had said.

'Why doesn't Daddy make his own tea?'

Why indeed? And why should what he said and thought hold any more water than her own ideas and opinions?

Because it always had?

When it came to something as important as this was that really a good enough reason?

25

Michelle decided that she would go back to Sylvie's house the following Saturday. She had it all planned. She'd leave the kids with Dean, walk up the hill, go to the house and knock on the door. How hard could that be? She wouldn't go so early this time, but she didn't want to leave it too late either. Sylvie's family might be ones for taking day trips at the weekends. The seaside, maybe, or the ice rink in Nottingham. Were they the kind of things that people like Sylvie and Jeremy did, or did they just kick around the house at the weekend like her family? She had no idea. If Leonora really was her daughter, then what kind of life experiences was she having? More than impromptu picnics in the rec, perhaps?

She woke early that Saturday morning. The knowledge of what she was about to do was playing hard in her head, and it was easier to get up than wake Dean with her restlessness.

Only Donna was already up. She was sitting on the sofa in her pyjamas chatting to Lucy, who seemed to be back in favour. Donna's conversations with Lucy were always little more than a murmuring, so Michelle rarely caught what was going on.

'Morning, sweetie,' she said as she came into the room.

'Morning, Mummy,' replied Donna cheerfully. 'Say good morning to Lucy.'

Michelle smiled apologetically. 'Morning, Lucy.'

Donna looked at Michelle, taking in her newish jeans and a top that she only wore when she went out for a drink.

'Where are you going?' she asked.

It was as if the child could look straight into her soul. Michelle shuffled from one foot to the other.

'Nowhere,' she lied, not sounding convincing even to herself. 'Well, somewhere, but I'm only popping out to the shops.'

'Can we come?' asked Donna at once, her face brightening.

Michelle's scalp bristled as she thought fast.

'Erm,' she stalled. 'Well, I'm not doing anything exciting . . .' she tried, hoping that Donna would lose interest but knowing that she wouldn't. To Donna everything was interesting; even taking the bins out could be turned into an expedition.

'Pleeeeeease,' Donna begged. 'Everyone else is still asleep and Lucy and me can't go anywhere until there's someone up to take us. We might be sitting on this sofa for aaaaages.'

'You can always go and play outside,' suggested Michelle, although there was no way this would cut the mustard when set against a trip to town.

Donna gave a huge sigh and Michelle felt herself weaken. Maybe this would go better if she had Donna with her. She would have to be careful how she explained who she was, but she could do that, and if Sylvie were to see the child for herself the problem might become self-evident.

'Okay,' she conceded warily. 'But I'm going right to the top of the hill. It's a long way to walk. You'd better not complain that your legs are tired.'

'We won't,' said Donna, jumping from the sofa and skipping off to find her pumps.

Two minutes later Donna was ready. Michelle found an old receipt and a chewed Bic biro and scribbled a note.

Gone to town. Taken Donna. M x

'And Lucy,' said Donna, taking the pen from Michelle and adding the words in neat round lettering.

Michelle was certain that none of the others had produced anything that was even close to legible until at least their third year at school.

They set off, pointing their noses in the direction of the cathedral. Donna started asking questions almost straight away.

'Who built the cathedral?' she began with, and Michelle was immediately flummoxed.

'I don't know,' she said. 'Workmen, I suppose.'

'Did they get paid?' Donna asked.

'I suppose so,' replied Michelle.

'Not slaves then? Mrs Brook told us that long ago people used slaves to do the things that they didn't want to do. And slaves didn't get paid. That's not very fair, is it, Mummy?'

'No, not very fair at all.'

They continued up the road, Donna's little hand firmly in Michelle's. It made Michelle's heart hurt to think that this beautiful, curious, clever little girl might have nothing to do with her biologically. Part of her wanted to turn round and head straight back home, to put all thoughts of baby swaps out of her mind. Donna was her daughter. Michelle loved her and had provided her with everything she needed for the first five years of her life. And she could continue to do so without anyone questioning anything about it.

And yet here she was, marching the child up the hill to, potentially, destroy her world. The idea made Michelle feel sick and for a moment she slowed her pace. But she couldn't help it. It was as if there were ropes round her wrists physically tugging her towards Sylvie like a primal need that she could do nothing about.

She just had to know.

And she knew she would never rest until she did.

26

Donna didn't complain once about the effort required to get up to the cathedral. Once or twice she passed comment to Lucy about how she was a little bit out of breath, but she kept going with a dogged determination.

When the road narrowed to its steepest section and the surface changed to cobbles, she finally asked, 'Why are we going all the way up here, Mummy?'

'To see the cathedral?' Michelle replied, aware that her sentence had a question mark on the end of it rather than being a definitive statement of intent.

'I've never been to the cathedral, have I?' Donna asked, and Michelle had to admit that whilst the magnificent building could be seen from their house, she had never once taken her children on a visit. That was what school was for, she'd always thought.

'No,' she said to Donna. 'This is your first time. I think you'll like it. And do you know, there's a little stone imp inside, way up high in the roof. If we're lucky, we might see him.'

As she said this, she worried that she might not be able to find the imp. She had been at school herself when it had last been pointed out to her, and she hadn't been concentrating or even all that interested. But if she couldn't find it there would surely be someone who would help her.

Donna nodded approvingly and said something to Lucy that Michelle didn't catch.

'But before we go in the cathedral, there's something else I need to do,' Michelle continued, her guts twisting as she spoke. 'It won't take long.'

'Okay,' replied Donna.

She didn't ask what it would be, blindly taking on trust that whatever Michelle wanted to do would be all right with her, and Michelle felt her guilt rising up like nausea.

'Does the imp move around?' Donna asked a few moments later.

Michelle's mind was on the other reason for her trip and she didn't hear the question.

'What?'

'The imp,' Donna clarified. 'You said we might be lucky to see him. But if he's stone then he must always be in the same place.'

Sometimes Michelle couldn't believe how smart Donna was. It took her breath away.

'He doesn't move,' she replied. 'I just meant that I'm not sure exactly where he is. But I'm sure we'll find him.'

Donna nodded, seemingly satisfied.

Finally, they reached the top of the hill, but instead of turning right towards the cathedral, Michelle steered them left in the direction of the house she'd seen Sylvie enter. Donna seemed interested in the castle, pulling back against Michelle as they walked past so that she could stare up at the stone walls, but Michelle led her on without even mentioning it. She no longer had capacity for anything other than what she was about to do.

Minutes later they were standing in front of the house.

Michelle swallowed. There was still time to change her mind. She hadn't done anything to disrupt the status quo yet. They could just go and find the Lincoln Imp and head back home. But even as she thought this, she knew that was no longer an option. Having come this far, she needed to carry it through to the end if it wasn't going to haunt her forever.

'That's a nice house,' said Donna, bringing Michelle back to the moment. 'I like those big windows.'

'Yes,' replied Michelle, her voice cracking slightly. 'I like them too. Right then, let's go and knock on the door.'

She took hold of Donna's hand and strode to the front door, trying to give herself courage by acting brave even when she wasn't feeling it. When she reached the front door, she pressed the bell hard and then took a step back.

At first there was no sound of movement from inside. The family must be out. Michelle's knees almost buckled with the relief. She was here, she had tried and she had been thwarted by circumstances.

'There's no one in,' she said to Donna. 'Come on, let's go.'

She pulled at Donna's hand, moving her from the doorstep, but Donna resisted, pulling back against her.

'But there's someone coming,' she said. 'I can hear them.'

She was right. Michelle could hear footsteps inside the house and then the door opened and her heart almost stopped beating.

It was Jeremy, Sylvie's husband. He had a huge fisherman's sweater on despite the warmth of the day, and a pair of canvas trousers that were spattered in various shades of orange paint.

'Hello?' he said as the door opened revealing Michelle and Donna on his doorstep. 'Can I help you?'

When she had imagined this moment, Michelle had visualised the bond between parent and child being so strong that Sylvie and Jeremy would immediately be able to recognise Donna as their own flesh and blood. However, Jeremy didn't even look at Donna, focusing his attention entirely on Michelle.

She had a split second to decide what to do next, but something told her that the conversation she wanted to have would be best mother to mother.

'Is Sylvie in?' she asked.

'Afraid not,' replied Jeremy. 'Can I help?'

Michelle's mind was racing. Now what? She could make her speech to Jeremy. He was a parent too, after all. Or she could find out when Sylvie would be back. That felt like the better option.

'Will she be long?' she asked, ignoring his question.

'She's gone away,' he replied. 'To London, to visit her friend.'

'Oh,' replied Michelle. Despite her huge doubts about having the conversation in the first place, she was now burning to offload her concerns about the girls. But she had been stymied.

Jeremy seemed to sense her disappointment.

'I can give her a message if you like,' he said.

Michelle thought. What should she say? *Could you tell her that I think I'm bringing up your daughter and you've got mine?*

'Could you tell her Michelle called round,' she said instead. 'She won't know me, but I was in the bed next to her in the hospital when we had our babies.'

Any hope that the mention of the two babies being together in hospital might trigger some response in Jeremy was immediately quashed. He didn't even draw breath.

'Okay,' he said, putting his big hand on to the door to push it shut.

Behind him the sound of running footsteps on wooden floorboards rang out. Was that her? Was that Leonora? Michelle didn't care about Sylvie's whereabouts. This visit was really about the child. Her child?

She craned her neck, trying to look round Jeremy to catch a glimpse of Leonora, but there was no one there. The footsteps must have been coming from somewhere else in the house. Jeremy, who could see her trying to peer into his home, began to close the door, mild irritation on his face.

'When will she be back?' Michelle blurted before the door closed entirely.

'Not sure,' he said. 'A few days, I think. Bye then.'

And then he shut the door, leaving Michelle and Donna standing like spare parts on his doorstep.

The first thing to race through Michelle's mind was that she was going to have to pluck up the courage to do this all over again. Her heart crashed, but then she reconsidered. That was actually okay. It had been a mistake to bring Donna with her. She understood that now. Next time, she would come on her own.

'Shall we go and see the imp, Mummy?' Donna asked.

All Michelle wanted to do was to slink home and forget about the whole thing, but instead she said, 'Yes. Who's going to spot him first, I wonder. You or Lucy?'

Donna looked at her as if she had a screw loose.

'Well, me of course,' she replied.

27

The trip to Christine's had been everything Sylvie had hoped for. They had fallen on one another like thirsty men on an oasis, each desperate for the other's news, of course, but also to be sated at a deeper level. Christine knew Sylvie better almost than she knew herself, certainly better than Jeremy did in many ways. Time spent with Christine was so effortless. No matter how long had passed between their meetings, it always felt as if it had been but a matter of weeks. They might not know the day-to-day detail of each other's lives, but the really important things could never be lost.

And so, Sylvie had spent the week trying not to complain about Leonora and Christine hadn't once mentioned beds and lying in them.

She had come home refreshed and ready to tackle whatever Leonora had to throw at her. And so far, it was going well. Jeremy had bought Leonora a new transistor radio whilst she had been away. It was a garish yellow with a black plastic wrist strap, and Leonora had taken to carrying it about the house with her, the aerial waving like an insect's antennae. It was tuned to Radio 1 and pumped out pop music from morning to night.

Sylvie had privately thought that, at five, Leonora was too young for such things and that listening to pop music might even do her some harm. All those songs about love and other adult concerns were hardly written with five-year-olds in mind. Sylvie didn't follow the charts herself so only vaguely recognised some of the songs. The one that seemed most popular just then sounded distinctly menacing, opening with an unearthly wailing and then proceeding in a dark minor key which seemed totally unsuitable for a pop song. When she strained to hear the words it seemed to be predicting some kind of urban apocalypse that Sylvie found unsettling. Little Leonora, however, could be heard singing the song at the top of her voice morning and night, untroubled by its predictions.

Despite her doubts, Sylvie had to accept, however, that with her radio at her side Leonora seemed more content, and whilst Sylvie was sure that hours spent in her room listening to music couldn't be good for her, she was glad of the respite it provided. And it had been Jeremy's decision to give her the radio. Any consequences would be his to deal with.

It was Saturday and Sylvie had forgone her morning walk, not feeling quite the same need for the escape since returning from Christine's. Jeremy had popped out on some errand or other, and Leonora was in her room. Sylvie could hear her singing along to the radio. Her little voice was pleasant and quite tuneful, Sylvie thought. Maybe she should introduce her daughter to a musical instrument.

She was just contemplating what might be a suitable choice when somebody knocked on the front door. Putting down her teacup, Sylvie went to open it, her head still full of violins and oboes. There was a woman standing there, younger than Sylvie, with dark shoulder-length hair and a slightly pinched face. She reminded Sylvie of a Modigliani portrait, long and a little pale. Sylvie had no clue who she might be and assumed she was collecting for something.

'Hello,' she said. 'Can I help you?'

The woman didn't speak. She stood staring at Sylvie, her teeth biting down on her lip so hard that it had gone white. For a moment neither of them said anything. Sylvie was used to just looking at people, taking in their features and working out what their story might be. She did it all the time, although rarely as blatantly as this. She was curious as to who the woman might be, but was in no rush to make her state her business. She watched as the expressions skittered across the woman's face, and wondered which one would settle there.

Eventually, the woman spoke.

'You're Sylvie, aren't you?' she asked.

Sylvie nodded. This was even more intriguing. The woman seemed to know her already, although Sylvie had no idea who she might be.

The woman swallowed. 'And you have a daughter who is five?'

Sylvie nodded again.

'You won't remember me,' the woman continued. 'But I was in the bed next to you. In Lincoln County. I was having a baby too.'

Sylvie had very little memory of being in hospital. Giving birth to Leonora felt almost as if it had been an out-of-body experience that she had been looking down on from above. She assumed that was an effect of the drugs they had given her.

'It was very hot,' she said simply.

The woman gave a tight smile and a single nod. 'That's right. It was. Horrible. Anyway, I had a baby too. A girl like you.'

Sylvie had no idea where she might be going with this, but she was intrigued. She stepped to one side, opening the door wider.

'Would you like to come in, erm . . . I'm sorry. I didn't catch your name.'

The woman's eyes opened a little wider and darted from side to side.

'It's Michelle,' she said.

She was as skittish as a colt, Sylvie thought.

'Come in, Michelle,' she said, with what she hoped was an encouraging smile. 'Can I get you a drink? Tea? Coffee?'

The woman, Michelle, didn't move. An invitation to come in didn't seem to be something that she had anticipated. Sylvie watched as she considered the offer. She was an open book, with nothing hidden from view. It was all just written there in her face and body language. And she was nervous, so very nervous, dithering over the decision as if life or death might depend on the outcome.

Eventually, she nodded.

'Thanks,' she said. 'But nothing to drink, thanks.'

Sylvie led them through to the sitting room which was, as usual, in chaos. Jeremy had been looking for an article that he had half-remembered and there were magazines and newspapers open on every surface and across much of the floor. Michelle gave a little shudder when she saw how messy things were. She kept a tidy house then, thought Sylvie, clearing a space on two chairs for them to sit down. Interesting. Sylvie was always fascinated by the lives of other people: they gave her an insight into how hers was supposed to be led.

'And you're sure I can't get you anything?' she repeated.

She really wanted to set this woman at her ease so that she could study her in more detail, but Michelle seemed too anxious to relax. She shook her head again.

Sylvie smiled at her serenely as if to suggest that she should continue with whatever it was she had come to say.

'So,' said Michelle. 'Like I was saying. We both had little girls at the same time. And the thing is . . .' She swallowed, rubbed her thumb into the palm of her other hand. 'The thing is . . . I think they got muddled up. In the hospital, I mean. I think they gave us the wrong babies.'

132

As she spoke her gaze had been on the magazines on the floor, but now she raised her head and looked directly into Sylvie's eyes, searching for a reaction. Sylvie had nothing to give her. For a few seconds she just continued to examine the woman, noticing the amber flecks in her irises, the way her eyelashes curled in slightly before they grew up.

Michelle's eyebrows rose questioningly. 'Did you hear me?' she asked. 'I said I think our babies were swapped. I think we have each other's children.'

Sylvie had heard her. The words were going round in her head.

Hospital.

Swapped.

Each other's children.

The thing was, she was simply too shocked to respond.

28

Michelle wasn't sure that Sylvie had heard her.

'I said I think our babies were swapped,' she repeated. 'I think we might have each other's children.' She couldn't make it any clearer, but Sylvie was looking at her as if she had spoken in Martian.

In the absence of any kind of response, Michelle decided that she should just press on and say her piece.

'My baby, Donna, looked just like my husband when she was born but when we got her home she didn't any more. I noticed pretty much straight away, and I took her back to the hospital but they sent me away again. They thought I was imagining it, like it was some kind of post-natal depression or something. And they wouldn't tell me where you lived. So I couldn't do anything about it. I just kept looking after the baby I had.

'But I've not been sure about her all this time. Sometimes I think she has to be mine. I mean, that makes the most sense, doesn't it?'

She looked to Sylvie for confirmation. Nothing.

'But then I look at her and I can't see my other kids in her at all. And then I'm just not sure any more.'

She was rambling. She knew she was, but she wanted to get it all out before Sylvie could interrupt her with her objections.

Sylvie, however, was showing no sign of interrupting. She was just listening. Michelle kept going.

'And then a couple of weeks back I saw you. It was up near the cathedral. I knew it was you straight away. So I followed you. I'm sorry about that.' Michelle felt heat rising in her cheeks at her admission. 'But I'd been looking out for you for five years. I couldn't let you get away. Not after all that time. And then a few days after that I came round here to talk to you, but you'd gone to see your friend. I spoke to your husband. Did he tell you?'

She paused for a response but there was nothing. Sylvie appeared to have gone into a trance. She literally hadn't moved. She hadn't even blinked. It was spooky and it crossed Michelle's mind that she might be having some sort of episode. Maybe her news had been too much for Sylvie and had triggered something in her head, or a stroke, although didn't strokes look different? The woman was basically catatonic.

Michelle started to worry.

'Are you okay?' she asked. 'Can I get you some water or something?'

Still Sylvie didn't react. Michelle had the impression that she could get up and leave and Sylvie wouldn't even be aware that she was no longer there. She was way out of her comfort zone. When she'd imagined how Sylvie might respond to what she had to say, her having no reaction at all hadn't been on the list.

Michelle stood up. She needed to leave. She didn't know what was going on here but it didn't feel normal. Yes, she had put the cat amongst the pigeons by turning up out of the blue. Of course the idea would take some getting used to, but to not react at all? That was weird.

'Right, well, this has obviously been a bit of a shock,' she said, grabbing for her bag and holding it tight into her chest as if Sylvie might reach out and snatch it from her. 'So I'm going to go. I'll leave you my name and address and then when you've had time to think about it maybe you can write to me and we can meet up and talk about it. You can meet Donna, see if you agree that I might be right. She's lovely, by the way. Smart and funny. You'll like her.'

Michelle cringed as she said this, but she couldn't take it back now. She scanned the paper-strewn room for a pen and spotted a chewed pencil on the window sill. Tearing the corner off a piece of newspaper, she wrote out her name and address in neat capitals.

'Here,' she said, clearing a space on the table and placing the scrap of paper in the centre of it. 'This is where we are. It's easy to find, just straight down the hill. Okay, I'll go now. But please get in touch when you've had a think. We need to talk. We owe it to the girls if nothing else.'

Sylvie was still sitting motionless, like a waxwork, not even her eyes moving.

'Bye then,' said Michelle, and she left the room, crossed the hallway and made her way to the front door. From somewhere in the house she could hear music playing. It was 'Stand and Deliver' by Adam and The Ants and a child was singing along with the words, mimicking the lead singer perfectly.

Was that her daughter? The desire to race up the stairs and find her was so strong that it was all Michelle could do to stop herself. But she mustn't. It would be too much for the child. Seeing the reaction, or lack of it, from Sylvie had shown her that this was a big thing. She'd had five years to get used to the idea that Donna wasn't her baby. She mustn't forget that. Who knew what damage she might do by just crashing into Leonora's life?

Michelle could still hear the child singing upstairs, unaware of what had just happened downstairs. She opened the door and closed it gently behind her.

Then she crossed the drive and stepped out on to the pavement, her heart still pounding in her chest. Turning back, she half-expected to see Sylvie's face at the window but there was no one there. The house looked deserted.

Michelle set off back towards Steep Hill. Well, she thought to herself, at least it's out there. I've told Sylvie what I think and now I'll just wait and see what happens next.

But as she crossed the railway tracks at the bottom of the hill and made her way past the betting shops and the pawnbrokers' towards her house, she couldn't get the image of Sylvie's face out of her head. Something had been very wrong there. A couple of seconds of shock she could have expected, but the woman had sat there for what must have been minutes without moving. She barely even seemed to be breathing.

Guilt started to creep into Michelle's mind. What if Sylvie wasn't well? She'd seemed a bit weird in the hospital that night, but Michelle had put that down to having just given birth. But what if she actually had a condition, wasn't quite right in her head? She thought about a story they'd read at school. There had been a woman in it. Her husband had locked her in the attic and she'd gone completely mad. Or had he locked her up because she was mad? Michelle couldn't remember now. But maybe that was what was wrong with Sylvie too. Maybe she was off her rocker. And maybe, by flouncing in there and telling her that her baby might not be hers, Michelle had made things a whole lot worse.

The hairs on the back of Michelle's neck stood up and she gave a little shiver. 'Someone's just walked across my grave,' her gran used to say when that happened to her.

Thinking of her gran, though, gave Michelle back her resolve. That was why she was doing this. Family was important and the main thing here was that everyone knew exactly who their family was and where they belonged. Until she knew for sure whether Donna was hers or not, Michelle wouldn't rest easy. She was happy to bring Donna up – the child was no trouble at all, a complete sweetheart and Michelle loved her, she truly did – but she had to know whether she really was her flesh and blood.

And that was completely natural, wasn't it?

29

It was only when Sylvie heard the front door bang that she seemed to come back to herself. It was as if she had been in a hypnotic trance and she shook her head to try and get her brain to start ticking once more.

No, no, no, no, no, no, no, no, no, no, no.

This could not be right.

She had not been through the last seven years, sacrificing everything she'd always wanted, changing her life in ways that she had never anticipated when she'd agreed to the arrangement, just to have some total stranger tell her that it had all been for nothing.

No. No. NO.

She stood up, her legs still shaking, and crossed to the table. The scrap of paper on which the woman had written her name and address was sitting there like a little island surrounded by the sea of mess. Without letting her eyes settle on it so there was no danger of reading it and somehow absorbing the details, she picked it up and began to tear it into tiny little pieces. Then, when she could tear it no further, she screwed all the pieces up into a ball, dropped them into the fireplace and put a match to them.

And then it, and the woman with her unwelcome ideas, was gone.

1983

30

'She can't wear that!' objected Tina loudly. 'It's purple.'

'It's not. It's blue,' Michelle snapped back, although she thought the costume she had fashioned from an old dress had a distinctly violet hue to it. 'And anyway, it's all there is so it'll have to do.'

Donna stood on a kitchen chair whilst Michelle pinned up the hem.

'But it has to be blue,' Donna said in a panicked tone. 'Miss Wilson said I have to wear a blue dress and a white headdress.'

Her voice wobbled as she spoke and for a second Michelle felt bad that she hadn't tried a little harder to get something a bit bluer, but she hadn't had time to go further than the nearest charity shop and this had been the only item in there that she had thought might work.

'Don't moan, Donna,' she said. 'It'll be fine.'

But she knew it wasn't, not really. Cross with herself, Michelle stopped paying proper attention to what she was doing and stabbed a pin into the pad of her finger.

'Sugar!' she hissed and pulled her hand out from under the dress to inspect the damage. A bead of bright red blood had formed. She put it in her mouth before it could stain the fabric. It was bad enough that the dress was purple. She didn't need it to be blood-stained as well.

She had at least managed to find a white pillowcase and when she'd finished pinning the hem, she settled it on Donna's dark hair and held it place with a circle of knicker elastic. She stood back to admire her work. Not her finest hour, but it would have to do. It was too late to get anything else now.

'There,' she said, smiling warmly at Donna. 'You look perfect.'

Donna looked back at her doubtfully. 'Are you sure, Mum? I don't want to get in trouble.'

Tina stepped into the breach.

'You look fantastic, Don. The best Virgin Mary that Meadow Street Primary has ever had. I can't believe you're Mary. I only ever got to be a sheep, and not even one of the ones with any lines. Not that sheep can talk, but you know what I mean.'

'You did better than the boys,' Michelle said. 'They were only ever in the chorus.'

'We were lucky that any of us got a part at all after that time Carl was the innkeeper,' replied Tina bitterly. 'He really messed it up for the rest of us.'

'Why?' asked Donna, turning round on the chair to face Tina. 'What did he do?'

Michelle shook her head slowly. It was a funny story but not a parenting moment that she enjoyed reliving.

Tina had no such qualms. 'You know the bit when Joseph knocks on the door and asks if there's any room in the inn?' she asked, barely able to wait for Donna's reply.

'Yes.'

'Well, instead of saying no, our Carl said, "Yes! Come on in!"'

Donna put her hands over her mouth and gasped. 'But that's not right. There was no room at the inn. That's why Mary and Joseph had to go and sleep in the stable.'

'Exactly,' said Tina. 'No one knew what to do. Sean Walsh was Joseph. He asked his question again and when Carl answered the

144

same a second time he just burst into tears. And then that set Mary off. It was Judy Hillier. She's always been wet. Anyway, after that I don't think they trusted any of us White kids in the starring roles.'

Donna stared at her sister, mouth open, and then looked to Michelle for confirmation.

'Is that right, Mum?' she asked, plainly horrified. 'Is that what he did?'

Michelle nodded and tried to keep her face straight. Now, with the distance of ten years between herself and the incident, she could see the funny side, although she hadn't found it funny at the time.

'I'm afraid so,' she said with as much decorum as she could muster. 'But that's all in the past now. And you're going to redeem the White family name by being Mary.'

Donna chewed on the skin around her thumb.

'What if I do something wrong?' she asked shakily.

'You won't,' reassured Michelle. 'You'll be perfect.'

But she looked at Donna in her not-quite-blue dress and her guts twisted.

The front door opened and then closed and Dean breezed into the kitchen in his overalls, his hands still covered in the day's engine oil.

'What's going on here?' he asked, seeing Donna standing on the chair.

'We're just sorting out Donna's costume for the nativity play tomorrow,' Michelle said.

'School nativity plays,' Dean mused. 'Do you remember that time Carl—?'

'Yes,' replied Michelle, sharply closing him down.

Dean seemed to understand that the subject was not up for discussion and dropped it.

'And who are you, Dons?' he asked.

Donna's face crumpled.

'I'm Mary,' she said in a voice so small that it was almost silent.

'Okay,' replied Dean. 'That's great. But doesn't Mary usually wear bl—'

Michelle kicked him on the ankle and Dean recovered the situation promptly.

'You look brilliant, Donna. You're going to be the best Mary that there's ever been.'

Donna didn't look at all sure about that but she managed a weak smile.

◆ ◆ ◆

Later, when Donna was in bed and they were in the kitchen, Michelle making sandwiches for the next day and Dean reading the paper, she said, 'Do you think that Mary dress will be okay? I know it's not the normal blue but it's blue enough?'

'It'll be fine,' he said without looking up. 'It's only a stupid nativity play. I bet most of the kids won't have any costume except a tea towel on their heads. And what does it matter anyway?'

Michelle found it frustrating that Dean was so uninterested in anything to do with school. Granted, the two of them hadn't had the best experience, but Michelle wanted things to be different for their kids. Carl would be leaving later that year so he was probably a lost cause, but Tina and Damien might still get something out of it, and little Donna relished going to school. They had to make sure they didn't do anything that changed that.

'I just want it to be right for her,' she said. 'It's important to her so that should make it important to us.'

'Whatever,' replied Dean. 'I'm sure it'll be fine.'

Michelle should have left it there. She knew she should but she just couldn't help herself. Whenever something big happened to Donna her mind always skipped to the other little girl, the one living up the hill, the one who might be her real daughter. Was Leonora going to be in a nativity play too? She must be. All schools did nativity plays, didn't they? Michelle tried to imagine what Leonora might look like now, at seven and a half, but it was impossible. Whenever she tried this, her imagination wouldn't take her beyond Donna.

Her thoughts escaped from her mouth before she had a chance to stop them.

'I wonder what the other girl is doing,' she said.

'What other . . .' Dean began. Then he stopped and looked up at her. 'Stop that right now. I thought we'd agreed that we weren't going to talk about that again.'

His expression was all warning, but Michelle couldn't hold it in.

'But don't you ever wonder?' she asked. 'She might be our actual daughter.'

Dean stood up, thrusting the chair back with such force that it almost toppled over.

'No,' he said sternly. 'I don't wonder and neither should you. Donna is our daughter and all this harping on about the other kid is stupid and pointless.'

They had been here so many times before and Michelle knew that she was only one comment away from an almighty row. But, like a lemming on a precipice, she was drawn by some unseen force to the edge.

'But what if Donna isn't ours . . .' she began.

'For God's sake, Chelle. Can you not just let it drop? You drive me mental with your endless going on. I'm not sure how much more of it I can take. Just accept where we are. It doesn't matter whether the kids were swapped or not. Donna is here with us. The other one is gone. Nothing to do with us any more.'

He snatched his jacket from the back of the chair and stuffed his arms into the sleeves. 'I'm going out. And I don't want to talk about this ever again.'

Then he picked up his keys and swept out of the room. Michelle heard the front door open and then slam shut.

She dropped to sitting and put her head in her hands. She didn't mean to cause trouble between her and Dean. That was the last thing she wanted. But why couldn't he see how hard it was for her? He seemed to have accepted the status quo and was prepared to go on like that, blocking all other inconvenient possibilities out of his mind.

But she couldn't think like that.

There was always a tiny voice at the back of her mind asking, 'What if?'

31

It was rare that Sylvie saw Jeremy angry. In fact, she mused, he had barely even raised his voice before Leo was born, let alone lost his temper. Now, though, it seemed to happen with a relentless regularity.

First, there were all the low-level triggers that would set him off. Leo refusing to keep her room tidy, her belongings spewing out all over the landing. Leo continuing to eat with her fingers even though she was perfectly adept with cutlery. Leo slinking away, leaving her homework books open on the kitchen table without making any attempt to complete the work.

All these things left Jeremy struggling to find appropriate responses. To begin with he had tried cajoling. This had stepped up a gear to the removal of privileges, and when that failed to get the correct response he mainly just shouted at his daughter.

Leo, by contrast, seemed unmoved by all his attempts to discipline her. She didn't argue back. She just ignored him, watching him sullenly, face expressionless, which made Jeremy angrier still. It became like a contest between them – Jeremy's aim to bend her will to his and Leo's to irritate her father as much as she possibly could.

Today, however, they had reached a new low.

'What I don't understand,' said Sylvie when they were back home and Leo was safely tucked up in bed, 'is why you had to shout at her in front of the whole school. It simply made a bad situation a hundred times worse.'

Jeremy sighed and reached for his whisky, taking a huge gulp before he replied.

'I know,' he said, sounding so plaintive that Sylvie almost felt sorry for him. 'It was stupid, but I couldn't help it. I just saw red.'

'But she does it on purpose,' Sylvie continued, frustrated by what was so very clear to her but which Jeremy seemed unable to grasp. 'She's trying to get a reaction out of you. And you keep obliging.'

Jeremy held his head up with one hand, his elbow resting on the table, and looked at Sylvie. There was so much sorrow in his eyes.

'I know,' he said again. 'But I just can't understand why she has to be so disruptive. Would it have killed her to just be an angel like all the others? She didn't even have any lines. All she had to do was stand there and sing.'

'She said the halo itched. It was the tinsel, I think. She said that before she went on stage.'

'Then she could just have taken it off. She didn't have to frisbee it at the three kings. She's lucky she didn't take that boy's eye out. Coat hangers are sharp, you know. And I bet it leaves a scar. There was enough blood.'

The blood dripping down the king's face and on to his golden robes had been bad enough, but then Jeremy getting to his feet and screaming at Leo to apologise to the child had just made things ten times worse. If there had been anyone in the room who didn't know whose child Leo was at the start of the performance (which seemed unlikely given her reputation) then they must have been in no doubt by the end.

'What are we going to do with her?' asked Jeremy, his voice weary. 'She's seven years old and she behaves like a demon. What will she be like when she's a teenager?'

This thought had crossed Sylvie's mind also. She had no personal experience of teenage girls other than having been one herself, but based on what she could glean from the other mothers, they were not for the faint-hearted.

She reached out and placed a hand on Jeremy's forearm, squeezing it a little in a gesture of solidarity.

'I'm sure it's just a phase,' she said without confidence. 'She'll grow out of it. We just have to be consistent with her boundaries until then.'

Sylvie had read this in a parenting book that she'd borrowed from the library. According to the book, successful parenting seemed to amount to sticking to your guns and saying no a lot, although there had to be more to it than that.

'And don't call her a demon,' she added. 'I'm not sure that helps anyone.'

'No,' agreed Jeremy. 'You're right. It's just that she pushes all my buttons. I can't understand why she is so difficult. Were you like that at school?' He glanced up at her hopefully, and then shook his head. 'No. Of course you weren't. And Jo was a complete angel. If anything it was me that got into bother.'

Sylvie smiled wryly. 'So, it's all your fault then,' she said. 'She's inherited her misbehaving genes from her father.'

Sylvie was trying to lighten the mood, but her comment backfired.

'Of course she hasn't,' he snapped back. 'Do you imagine my mother would have let us get away with the kind of behaviour we witnessed tonight?'

Sylvie inhaled sharply. And there it was, the real root of the problem. She was a terrible mother. No matter how hard she tried to get it right she was just making things worse.

'Jo and I knew exactly what was expected of us,' Jeremy continued. 'Of course, I'm not saying we were perfect, but there were lines in the sand that we knew we shouldn't cross. Leo seems to search out the lines simply so she can march straight through them.'

They sat in silence for a moment. She assumed Jeremy was brooding on why their daughter was such a nightmare, where they had gone wrong and what was to be done about it. But Sylvie's mind was full of the woman with the dark hair who had come calling two years ago and set her world into free fall. As usual, though, when the memory rolled into her mind, she pushed it away.

She would not give it head space.

She simply refused.

1987

32

'So, remind me again?' asked Michelle. 'What time is the film?'

Donna stood, hands on hips, and considered Michelle with the air of a teacher dealing with a particularly unpromising pupil. She shook her head slowly and sighed.

'Don't you ever listen, Mum?' she asked with a grin. 'The film starts at two thirty and it should finish around four thirty, what with the adverts and everything. So then we'll get back here about five, ready for the food and presents and all that. Now, have you got that? I don't want to have to say it all again!'

Michelle saluted.

'Yes, ma'am,' she said. 'Food at five. Got it, ma'am.'

'Good. And can I have the money to buy the tickets, please. Dad said he'd give it to me but he's gone out and he didn't leave me any.'

A current of irritation ran through Michelle. This was so typical of Dean these days, buggering off without doing what he said he was going to do. She fetched her purse from her bag and opened it, but she knew without looking that she didn't have enough. She would have to go to the cashpoint and hope the bank would let her withdraw what she needed to pay for the four cinema tickets.

Donna saw the empty purse.

'I have my pocket money,' she volunteered straight away.

God bless her, thought Michelle. She meant it too. If she'd had to pay for her own birthday treat then she would do it.

'Don't be silly,' she said. 'I'll walk up part of the way with you and get the cash from the cashpoint. I need to get a few bits for the feast afterwards.'

Donna's face relaxed again.

'Don't forget the party rings,' she said. 'And the fig rolls.'

'I swear no one but you eats fig rolls,' Michelle said.

'And it's my birthday,' quipped Donna. 'So that's okay.'

◆ ◆ ◆

They set off in plenty of time. Donna was a stickler for timekeeping and there was no way that Michelle could have been late even if she'd wanted to be.

'I can't believe you're going to be eleven years old,' she said as they crossed the railway lines at the level crossing.

Donna gave a little flick of her head, her ponytail swinging enthusiastically.

'Is that because I'm so very grown-up?' she asked proudly.

'Well, yes. Partly that,' agreed Michelle. And it was true. She could never have trusted the other three with this kind of excursion when they'd been eleven. They either wouldn't have made it on time, or lost the money, or spent it on sweets before they got anywhere near the cinema. 'But it's more that I'm not sure where the time has gone.'

Michelle was almost thirty-seven but she still felt like a teenager herself a lot of the time. Would she ever start feeling like an actual adult, she wondered? She hoped not.

'Well, I can't help you with that one,' replied Donna chirpily. 'You won't forget that Liz doesn't eat hot dogs, will you? She says they make her puke.'

'Nice,' said Michelle. 'But no. I haven't forgotten. I'll get some proper sausages for her.'

They reached the cashpoint and Michelle slipped her card in and tapped the amount into the keyboard, mentally crossing her fingers that her account had enough to cover it. She breathed out again when the machine dispensed the notes without issue, and handed them to Donna.

'Put it in your purse,' she said, but Donna already had the purse open and waiting to receive the money. 'Right, enjoy the film. What is it again?'

'*Police Academy 4*!' replied Donna in frustration.

Michelle flicked her ponytail playfully. 'I know. I'm only teasing.'

'Can I use the change to buy some sweets?' Donna asked, clicking the fastener on her bag.

The others would just have taken the change without a second thought.

'Yes,' replied Michelle. 'But don't eat too many. I don't want you to be too full for your birthday tea.' She thought it unlikely that there would be enough change to buy much so that probably wouldn't be a problem. 'Okay. Off you go. Have a great time.'

'Will do!' sang Donna and then she headed off towards the cinema.

Michelle watched her go and then turned on her heel and made straight for the Mason's Arms.

As she suspected, Dean was propping up the bar lazily watching a game of darts that was in full progress. He didn't see her until she was upon him.

'What the hell are you doing here?' she asked without bothering with any preamble.

'It's Saturday afternoon,' he said as if this explained everything. 'Where else would I be?'

'Er, try at our house giving our daughter the money you promised her for her birthday party.'

Dean's face fell for a second, but then he shrugged.

'I assume you gave it to her,' he said.

'I did, but it was touch and go as to whether there was enough in my account. Imagine if there hadn't been. How would that have made her feel?'

Dean shrugged again as if this couldn't be of less interest to him.

'Look,' hissed Michelle. 'I don't know what's going on with you but we can't carry on like this. You're never at home. You do nothing around the house. And now you're not even stepping up to your responsibilities.'

'If she is my responsibility,' he muttered.

'What was that?' spat Michelle, but she'd heard him clearly enough.

'Well, you're the one that's always saying that she's not mine.'

'Not *ours*, Dean. That's not the same thing.'

'Whatever.'

He turned his gaze to look above her head and signalled to the barman for another pint. It was clear that she was dismissed. Anger rose in Michelle, but she wasn't going to argue with Dean here in front of everybody. She didn't need to be the talk of the street on top of everything else.

'We'll talk about this when you get home,' she hissed instead. 'The girls will be back from the pictures for some birthday cake. It would be nice if you were there too. If you can be bothered, that is.'

Then, without giving him the chance to say that he wouldn't be there, she turned on her heel and stalked out. She could hear laughter at her back and someone saying, 'Who's been a naughty boy, then?'

'Bloody women,' she heard Dean say as the door closed behind her.

33

By the time Donna and her friends arrived back from the cinema, Michelle had the house all ready. She'd bought a pink paper table-cloth that she'd laid on the kitchen table with matching paper plates and cups. Tina had helped her blow balloons up and they'd hung them from the door handles and light fittings. The hot dogs were in a pan on the stove and the sausages for Liz were cooked and waiting.

'It looks great, Mum,' said Tina. 'You've really pushed the boat out.'

Michelle ignored the implications of this, that she always made more fuss of Donna than she ever had done of the others. The thing was, it was probably true. She was always overcompensating for the doubts that confused her mind. It thew everything out of whack so that she couldn't work out what was normal.

'What did I do for my eleventh?' Tina asked.

Michelle tried to remember, but all the parties blurred into one in her head. There had been a lot over the years.

'Swimming at Yarborough?' she suggested, but it was a total stab in the dark.

Tina considered this. 'Maybe,' she said. 'I can't remember.'

The girls' birthdays required more thought than the boys', for whom a football party on the rec with plenty of pop and sweets had generally sufficed.

'But it would have been whatever you wanted,' added Michelle defensively. 'We always tried to make a fuss of you all on your birthday.'

Tina eyed the set table and the balloons and Michelle thought she was going to comment further, but she seemed to change her mind.

And then in came Donna and her friends, giggling with voices raised and clearly on a sugar high. Michelle left Tina standing in the kitchen and went to greet them.

'Hi, girls,' she said, speaking loudly to be heard over the chatter. 'How was the film?'

'So funny,' said Liz. 'There was this one bit when me and Donna laughed so hard I thought I might pee.'

'Well, thank goodness you managed to hold it in,' replied Michelle, throwing a look at Tina, who grinned back. 'So, what do you want to do now? Tea, or do you need a gap to let the sweets go down?'

◆　◆　◆

The party passed without incident and soon enough the guests were making their way home, clutching bits of birthday cake wrapped in kitchen roll. A calm fell upon the house, but it was short-lived. Just as Michelle was tipping half-eaten bread rolls into the bin, Carl and Damien arrived home. At nineteen and sixteen respectively they were both more man than boy, Carl the image of his father and Damien with the gentler features of her own face.

Damien made a beeline for the table and started to hoover up the remaining biscuits.

'What's for tea, Mum?' asked Carl. 'What's the posh tablecloth all about?'

Michelle nodded at Donna meaningfully.

'Oh, the party. How was it?'

Donna beamed at him. 'Great!' she replied enthusiastically. 'The film was ace. You should go.'

'Any hot dogs left?' he asked, stalking round to the stove and lifting the lid on the saucepan. Five flaccid hot dogs floated in the brine. 'Bread?'

Tina threw him an unopened packet of finger rolls.

'Mint,' he said, tearing open the packet. He fished a hot dog out of the pan with his fingers and dropped it into the bread roll. 'Any onions?' he asked.

'Don't push your luck,' said Michelle. 'The ketchup's on the table.'

Damien followed his brother and soon they had demolished all the remaining food. There would be nothing for Dean, Michelle thought. But she didn't care. If he'd wanted feeding then he should have been here when he was expected.

'Can we open my presents now?' asked Donna.

They had a family tradition of not opening gifts until they were all there to watch, but Michelle had no idea when or even if Dean would put in an appearance.

'Why not?' Michelle said, trying not to let her anger show in her voice.

'What about Dad?' asked Donna straight away.

'It's up to you,' she said. 'We can wait for him if you like, but I don't know how long he'll be.'

Or if he even cares enough to come back at all, she thought.

Donna's shoulders drooped, but then she eyed the small pile of presents that her friends had brought and she rallied.

'Let's do it now. Then I can show him what I've got when he gets back,' she said.

'Good idea,' replied Michelle.

I'm going to kill him, she thought.

The gifts were a blue eyeliner and mascara set, a secret diary with a padlock, and three singles – Whitney Houston, Wet Wet Wet and one by George Michael that, going by its title, didn't sound appropriate for an eleven-year-old. Donna was delighted and Michelle had to agree that it was a pretty good haul.

'Can I borrow your record player?' she asked Tina, and Tina nodded at her fondly.

'But no using it when I'm not here, okay?' she added, finger waggling in the air as she spoke.

Donna nodded solemnly and then picked up the records and raced straight upstairs.

As soon as she was out of earshot Carl said, 'Where the hell's Dad?'

'Where d'you think?' Michelle replied.

She had always tried not to speak ill of Dean in front of the kids, but she was almost at tether's end.

'What a dick,' said Carl. 'Fancy missing Donna's big moment. He was always here for our birthdays. Is he bored with being a dad now? Is that it? Or does Donna not matter?'

Michelle was torn between defending her husband and agreeing with her son.

'I don't know what he's thinking,' she said lamely. 'But let's not let him spoil Donna's day.'

Carl paused for a moment, running his hand up and down his taut bicep. 'Is there something going on between you two that we should know about?' he asked.

He looked directly into Michelle's eyes, challenging her to lie to him. Michelle held his gaze even though it felt like he was looking straight into her soul.

'No,' she lied. 'I think he must just have forgotten.'

Carl held her gaze for a moment longer and then broke away. 'Bloody crap effort,' he sniffed.

34

'I'm not going and that's that.'

Leo sat on the sofa, arms folded and face like thunder.

'You will do exactly as you are told, young lady, and you will do it with good grace.'

'Can't make me.'

'I most certainly can. I will drag you there if I need to.'

Sylvie thought that was probably exactly what he would have to do to get Leo to visit her grandparents. That wasn't as easy as it once was, though. Leo was eleven now and quite tall for her age. Jeremy couldn't just pick her up kicking and screaming as he had done when she was a toddler.

Jeremy and Leo glared at one another, neither prepared to give an inch. Sylvie was going to have to stage an intervention.

'Look. Leo. It's not much to ask. Your grandparents would like to see you because it was your birthday yesterday. They are kind and generous and I think they deserve this one little thing.'

Kind might be pushing it a bit, but Margery and Gerald meant well, and they were certainly generous, paying Leo's fees for the smart private school that they spent a lot of time trying to get her to go to.

'And if you come,' she continued, resorting to bribery, 'then your father and I will reconsider the cancelled party.'

Jeremy's eyes widened at this, his face clearly expressing his 'over my dead body' thought, but Sylvie gave him the tiniest shake of the head and somehow he managed to keep his mouth closed.

Leo seemed to be considering this olive branch. Sylvie knew she shouldn't have offered it really. They would never get anywhere disciplining the wayward Leo if they didn't stick to their guns and caved in every time things got tricky, but Sylvie was exhausted by all the fighting. If this was what it took to get Leo to Margery's then she could live with it.

'Okay,' said Leo. 'But we need to agree numbers for the party before we go.'

◆　◆　◆

Leo spent the entire journey plugged into the Sony Walkman they'd given her for her birthday and didn't say a word until they pulled into Margery and Gerald's drive.

'Oh God, give me strength,' she muttered.

Sylvie sighed. 'Leo, please,' she said.

'We'll have less of that, thank you,' snapped Jeremy as he turned the engine off and got out of the car.

The dog – was this one Hogarth? Sylvie had lost track of the line of dogs that led back to old Rembrandt that she'd met on her first visit – bounded out of the house to greet them, wagging its tail with such excitement that it almost made up for the lack of enthusiasm in the car. Maybe it would be infectious, she thought, but with very little hope of it.

Margery followed the dog out and stood expectantly in front of the door, arms folded across her generous chest, matron-style.

'Just behave,' hissed Jeremy and then, 'Mum. How lovely to see you. You're looking well. Dad inside is he?'

Jeremy went into the house to find his father, leaving Sylvie and Leo behind.

'Just try not to wind them up,' Sylvie whispered. 'Then it'll be fine.'

She opened her door and climbed out, Leo following her with a reluctance that wouldn't have been out of place on the gallows platform.

'Ah, Sylvia,' said Margery. 'And there she is, the birthday girl. How are you, Leonora? Did you have a lovely birthday?'

◆ ◆ ◆

They sat in Margery's very formal drawing room, Sylvie and Leo both perching on the edges of their seats as if they might be required to leap up at any moment. On the coffee table sat a loaded tea tray – Sylvie noted the fussy lace-trimmed tray cloth and felt a degree of solidarity with Leo – and some Battenburg cake, which Margery had cut into chunky slices and distributed with steaming cups of tea.

Leo, plate on knee, was dismantling her cake, peeling the marzipan from its edges to release the pink and yellow squares of sponge. Margery eyed her disapprovingly.

'Aren't you a little old to be playing with your food, Leonora?' she said.

Leo gave her most fake smile. 'But it's so delicious, Granny. I want to make it last.'

It might have been charming if Leo had been five years younger and even half-genuine. But Margery either didn't notice or chose to ignore her granddaughter's sarcasm and changed tack.

'So, tell me. How is school? What is your favourite subject?'

Sylvie's spine stiffened. This was unlikely to end well, but Leo was on a roll. She turned up the intensity on her beatific smile and said, 'Oh dear, it's so hard to choose. I love them all so much.'

'Well, there must be a particular favourite,' pressed Margery, seemingly unable to see that she was being played. 'Your father loved art, obviously, but he also had a particular penchant for physics, didn't you, Jeremy dear?'

Jeremy nodded anxiously. He too was worried where this might be going, Sylvie sensed.

'And your Auntie Jo had her music of course, but she was very keen on Shakespeare at school. The comedies, mainly, although personally I always feel that his royal plays are his finest work.'

'I like woodwork,' replied Leo without even a hint of insincerity.

Margery coughed and Jeremy shifted in his seat.

'Very useful subject, woodwork,' muttered Gerald in a rare conversational contribution. 'I always enjoyed it.'

'They package all those practical ones together now, don't they, Leo?' said Sylvie, desperate to mine as much as she could from everything they managed to draw out of Leo. 'Woodwork, metalwork, technical drawing. And of course, you must have studied technical drawing as well, Gerald?' added Sylvie. 'To become an architect.'

Jeremy, seeing the opportunity that Sylvie had opened up, leapt on it.

'Yes. That's very true. Maybe that's where your future lies, Leonora, designing buildings like your grandfather.'

'I like PE too,' Leo continued, pointedly ignoring Jeremy. 'Although I never get picked for the school teams. I can't think why that is. Can you, Granny?'

'Well, I'm sure the standard is very high,' Margery gamely pressed on. 'Your Auntie Jo played lacrosse for school until we became worried that she might damage her hands. But if you keep doing your best then I'm sure you will reap the rewards eventually. Working hard. That's the key to success.'

Leo nodded sagely. If the atmosphere wasn't so very tense then Sylvie would have found her daughter's behaviour funny. She really was manoeuvring Margery quite beautifully, not that that was the point.

'And what did you get for your birthday?' asked Margery. 'Something well chosen, I don't doubt.'

Leo nodded with over-the-top enthusiasm. 'I got a Walkman,' she replied. 'It's blue.'

Margery looked confused.

'A portable tape player, Mum,' explained Jeremy. 'They're very popular.'

'And I got some birthday money too,' continued Leo, 'so I got this.'

She stuck her tongue out at her grandmother to reveal a silver stud right in the middle.

Margery started, pulling away from Leo as if the stud was a dangerous animal that might bite. Jeremy's face went puce.

'I thought we'd agreed that you would take that out,' he said, voice raised.

'No. There was no agreement,' countered Leo. 'You suggested it. I didn't agree.'

'Well, I insist. You will take it out right now.'

Leo just stared at him and made no effort to remove the stud. The words 'make me' floated around the room, mocking them. There was no way that Jeremy could get her to remove the stud without her cooperation, and that was clearly not forthcoming.

'I'm not sure it can be terribly hygienic,' said Margery. 'Having something stuck through your tongue like that. And won't it get caught on your food?'

Sylvie had to admire her daughter's spirit.

'Well, Granny,' said Leo with a cheeky grin, 'we shall just have to wait and see.'

1992

35

Donna was like a cat on a hot tin roof. She paced up and down the kitchen even though the room was only about five steps long, twisting her long dark hair round her finger so tightly that Michelle could see that the tip had gone blue.

'For God's sake, Donna, sit down. You're driving me mental with all this pacing. What on earth is wrong with you?'

Donna gave her a withering look and rolled her eyes.

'I can't believe you've forgotten,' she said with a tut.

Michelle had no idea what it was that she hadn't remembered, but it was clearly important to Donna. She grimaced at her.

'Soz, love,' she said. 'You're going to have to give me a clue.'

Donna's jaw dropped and she stared at her mother and shook her head.

'It's results day?' she said. 'Like, *my* results day. My GCSEs? The most important thing to ever happen to me?'

'Oh! That!' replied Michelle, and immediately felt less guilty.

Exam results were hardly a matter of life and death. They had barely even rippled the water with the others. Carl hadn't turned up for any of his CSEs and so hadn't got anything. Damien and Tina had made a better stab at it, both passing their maths and English at least. And hadn't Tina got one in science?

Michelle couldn't quite remember now. Her other kids weren't stupid – far from it. School just hadn't struck a chord with them. And the day their results came out had left no imprint on her memory. There had definitely been no drama over them, of that she was certain.

But then Donna was a different kettle of fish to the others and Michelle needed to match her reaction to Donna's expectations.

'Sorry, love,' she added. 'I just forgot, what with everything. So, what happens?'

Donna rolled her eyes again. 'I go into school in' – she looked at the clock on the cooker – 'fifteen minutes and get my results.'

'Well, I'm sure you'll have passed some,' Michelle said soothingly. 'You certainly worked hard enough.'

Donna's progression through school had been a revelation to Michelle. She and Dean hadn't been able to get away from the place fast enough, her pregnancy aiding her own escape. The other children had been the same. But a lack of qualifications hadn't held them back. Carl, now twenty-four, was no longer the rogue of his youth and had settled down, working at a garage like his dad. Damien was a brickie and Tina worked in a hairdresser's, learning how to cut, perm and do blue rinses on the job. Michelle was proud of how the three of them had turned out. They all had steady work and only Tina was still living at home.

Donna was staring at her aghast, and Michelle knew for certain that somehow she'd said the wrong thing.

'Some?' Donna snapped. 'Some?! For God's sake, Mum. I'm going to pass them all. In fact, I'm going to smash them.'

Michelle nodded quickly, anxious to undo any harm she'd accidentally done. 'Of course you are, love.'

Donna shook her head affectionately, and Michelle gave her a sheepish grin.

'I sometimes wonder if you're my mother at all!' laughed Donna. 'You can be so clueless at times. Anyway, I'm off. I said I'd meet Lisa on the corner at quarter to.'

She stole the piece of toast that Michelle was holding and slipped out of the room, crunching the toast as she went.

'Wish me luck!' she called through her mouthful.

'Good lu—' shouted Michelle after her, but the slamming door cut her words in half.

What Donna had just said rang in her head, but she dismissed it as the joke it had been. She was Donna's mother, that was in no doubt. After sixteen years of steering her through life, much of it on her own, Michelle couldn't have been prouder of the young woman Donna had become. She rarely thought about the doubts she'd had in the early days. It was hard now to remember what she thought she'd seen, or not seen, in Donna's face but whatever it was, it wasn't there now. Donna was simply Donna, her fourth child. Smart, sassy, thoughtful and kind, she was like a ray of light in all their worlds, and they were blessed to have her.

Michelle stood up and dropped another piece of bread into the toaster. Cupping her mug in her hands she smiled to herself. Yes, Donna would be fine. She was clever. School had said so right from the start. And she was interested in learning too, which was the part that Michelle hadn't managed to get right with the others.

The toast popped and she scraped margarine over it and then a layer of raspberry jam and went to get ready for work. She'd be late herself if she wasn't careful.

Michelle didn't really think about the results again until she was on her way home that evening when it dropped back into her head. She congratulated herself on the fact that she would be able to ask Donna about them without being prompted, but when she opened the front door, calling out a greeting to whoever was there, there seemed to be no one in. She went straight through to the kitchen, noticing that things looked pretty much as they had when she'd gone out. No start had been made on making anything for tea.

There was a piece of paper on the table. Someone had drawn arrows on it pointing towards the centre. Michelle took a closer look. It was Donna's results slip. If Michelle was reading it correctly, it seemed that Donna had got As in everything except French and Biology where she'd got Bs. Michelle stood and stared at the sheet, then picked it up and looked at it more closely in case she had misunderstood. But no, whichever way she read it, Donna had done amazingly well.

And then old doubts, dismissed so readily just that morning, started to creep back into her head. Surely no child of hers was capable of getting results like this, no matter how hard they tried. And brains were hereditary, weren't they? She thought of Sylvie and Jeremy with their smart clothes and their big house. They had done well at school, she guessed. You didn't get that kind of life without having an education behind you.

Leonora must have got her GCSE results today as well, she realised. How would she have done? Maybe if you went to a posh school you stood a better chance of overcoming a basic lack of brain power. She checked herself. That wasn't fair. Neither she nor Dean were stupid. They just hadn't shone at school either through lack of encouragement or lack of motivation, or probably both. And average people did sometimes have bright kids. You heard about it all the time. Plumbers having sons who went on to be vets or doctors. Who was to say that Donna wasn't one of those, or that Leonora wasn't sitting on just as glowing a set of results up at their house?

Michelle had decided that she wasn't going to think about the Donna/Leonora thing any more after Dean left. It had already done enough damage. She couldn't let it spoil anything else. And she had done really well, but at moments like this it was impossible not to wonder. How could she not try to draw comparisons on milestone days? And it was hard. She would celebrate her success with Donna, but in the back of her mind she'd be wondering whether the results were really for Sylvie and Jeremy to celebrate and not her.

36

Donna bounced into the house a couple of hours later, eyes shining.

'Did you see, Mum?' she asked before she was even inside. 'Did you see what I got?'

'I did!' replied Michelle with a grin. 'Come here. Let me give you a hug.'

Hugging wasn't really Donna's thing, but she stood patiently as Michelle wrapped her arms around her daughter and gave her a squeeze. After a moment or two she wriggled free from the embrace.

'Mr Locke said I was a credit to the school,' Donna said, grinning so widely that it was amazing her mouth could form the words. 'Mine are the best results for three years, he said.'

'Look at you, brain box,' Michelle said. 'Seriously though, Donna, I'm dead proud. I really am.'

Donna looked up through the long curtain of hair, her smile bashful. 'Aw thanks, Mum.'

There was a pause, each savouring the moment.

'So, I have to go to Thomas Welbeck on Monday to register.'

Michelle didn't understand immediately.

'Where?' she asked.

Donna gave her the teenage, 'You are really quite stupid, aren't you?' look and said, 'Thomas Welbeck? The school. In town. For sixth form.'

That Donna might stay on at school after sixteen had never crossed Michelle's mind. Her current school didn't even have a sixth form, and as it hadn't ever been an option with the other three children, the idea hadn't registered at all.

'Oh,' she said now. 'Okay. Well, I suppose with results like that it makes sense to do some A levels.'

'And then uni,' Donna added, but she didn't make eye contact with Michelle, as if this were an idea that she was just road-testing.

'Uni? God! Okay.'

It was all coming at Michelle a bit too fast. She wasn't sure how to process it. Not one single person that she knew had been to university. It just wasn't something that people did. She wasn't even sure that she knew what it meant, what was involved in 'going to uni'. Where was it? What did you do when you got there? How much did it cost?

She could feel Donna's eyes on her, trying to gauge her response.

'Well, that would be good. I think. I don't really know much about it to be honest, love. But we can find out, can't we? Just think. A daughter of mine going to university.'

And almost at once, there it was, that nagging doubt that dogged Donna's every step. Exactly whose daughter was it that wanted to go to uni – hers or Sylvie's?

'Have you told your dad what you got?' Michelle asked, more to steer the subject on to a different course than because she cared that Dean had heard the news.

'Yeah,' said Donna with a laugh. 'I called in at the garage earlier. He said I was a chip off the old block.'

The irony of this hit Michelle like a punch in the stomach and tears sprang to her eyes before she had the chance to try to control them, but she was grateful to Dean. There were so many other things that he could have said. She just about managed half a smile, but Donna was too caught up in her own joy to notice her response.

'Right, a gang of us are going out celebrating,' she said, heading for the stairs. 'Not that the rest of them have much to celebrate. Not like me.' She huffed on her nails and polished them on her T-shirt. Her glee was palpable. 'I'm going to get ready.' And then she turned and bounded up the stairs, the thundering of her feet filling the small house.

Michelle made her way through to the kitchen, filled the kettle and flicked the switch. Then she sat at the table as the water came to a boil. She was still sitting there when the water stopped bubbling and she didn't move until it had gone cold again.

The next morning Michelle, Tina and Donna were all up and moving round the tiny kitchen together, none of them getting in the other's way. There was an art to it, developed over many years. The house's only bathroom led off from the kitchen and use of that was also factored into the rhythm of the morning. Often this was done without conversation, details of the day to come being shared on a need-to-know basis only, but today there was something new to talk about.

'So, sixth form, eh, Dons?' began Tina, who was sitting at the table peering into a compact mirror and stroking mascara on to her eyelashes. 'How's that work then?'

Donna was eating a bowl of rice cereal, her spoon banging against the side of the bowl as she struggled to catch the last few puffs.

'You pick your three best subjects and then you only study those.'

'Sounds good. So what are you going to pick? Hard to choose, eh, with all those As.' Tina winked at Donna and Donna gave her a little shove, which almost caused a catastrophe with the mascara wand.

'Not sure. I'm going to talk to them about that when I register. I'm thinking maybe English literature and chemistry. They're my favourites at least. And art, of course.'

'Isn't art just something you do so you don't have to do hard subjects?' asked Tina.

'No, it's an A level just like the others. You can do art at university if you want,' replied Donna.

Michelle couldn't see the point of doing that. Then again, she couldn't see the point of doing any of it. What would Donna do when she'd finished at university? Surely she'd be better using her grades to get a good solid apprenticeship somewhere and working her way up. She knew that this wasn't the time to say that, though.

'Anyway, sixth form is another two years, so we don't need to be worrying about that yet.'

A thought crossed Michelle's mind but it seemed too ludicrous to her that she felt shy suggesting it, even in front of her own kids. She pressed on though. 'So, if you go to uni, does that mean you could get a posh job at the end? Like a solicitor or a teacher or a doctor or something?'

As the words left her mouth she was certain that she had got totally the wrong end of the stick. She had no idea how people got that kind of job; she'd never even considered it before.

'Yeah,' replied Donna, and Michelle immediately felt less stupid. 'You just have to do the right course.'

Michelle was gobsmacked. You just had to do the right course and then you could be whatever you liked. Of course, the teachers had said much the same to her when she'd been at school, but she had never thought to extrapolate that up to any job. Did it apply to anything? Zookeeper? Brain surgeon? Rocket scientist? She assumed it must do. God, the world was so much bigger than she'd even given it credit for. And here was Donna, brave enough to dip her toe in and have a go. It was like a little miracle was happening in her kitchen.

37

Leo hadn't come home.

The last time Sylvie had seen her daughter had been when she'd left the house to collect her exam results the day before. Expectations had been low. Her teachers had made it clear that they weren't hopeful. She would pass, they had said, with a fair wind and a dollop of luck, but no school records were going to be shattered by Leonora Fotherby-Smythe. Not academic ones at least, although she might have been in the running for the most unauthorised absences in a term, her form tutor had quipped.

Sylvie and Jeremy had sat there and listened feeling chastened, as if it were they that had broken the rules and not their daughter. After he had finished delivering the official line of disappointment in Leonora, the tutor had given them a sympathetic smile. They did occasionally get wayward pupils passing through the school apparently, a kind of novelty to be wondered at rather than a problem to be solved. Sylvie was left with the impression that Leo was beyond saving and so the school was simply going through the motions so that no one could say that it hadn't done its duty by her.

Sylvie stood staring at Leo's bed. It was hard to say whether it had been slept in, the duvet all tousled and twisted from previous nights, but something about the quality of the air in the room suggested that it had been undisturbed for some time. And surely, if

Leo had come home the previous night, she would still be sleeping? It was only eight in the morning. She wasn't that well acquainted with the larks.

Sylvie gave a sigh and pushed the door to, so she wouldn't accidentally catch a glimpse inside the room the next time she walked past. She didn't need any reminder of Leonora's absences.

Jeremy was in his studio overhead, his footsteps making the beams creak as he moved about, and she trudged up the steps to pass on the news. When she pushed open his door and peeked in, careful to not disturb him at what might be a vital moment, he was studying a canvas that was resting on an easel in the light from the large gable window. His work had altered over the years that they had been together. These days he worked on landscapes, endless images of the flat fields that surrounded Lincoln, trying to capture how the golden light played on the fields of yellow rape.

Sylvie found the paintings soul-destroyingly dull, but Jeremy had found a gallery on Steep Hill that could sell pretty much all he could deliver to tourists who paused and peered through the windows as an excuse to stop climbing. As long as the price was right, they were happy to take a little piece of the Lincolnshire countryside home with them. Thus far, he had stopped short of painting the cathedral and the castle, complaining that that was too much of a sell-out, but Sylvie suspected it would happen eventually and then his transformation from edgy pop art wannabe to jobbing commercial painter would be complete. Jeremy didn't see it like that, however. He was happy just to be selling, and took a deep pleasure from knowing that his pictures were hanging in living rooms the land over. That seemed to be enough for him. And if he was happy then Sylvie was happy for him.

She took a breath to signal her presence and Jeremy turned round and gave her a welcoming smile.

'She's not come home again,' announced Sylvie.

Jeremy's gaze drifted up to the beams overhead and he sighed. 'Any ideas?' he asked.

Sylvie shook her head. 'Last time it was out on that disused aerodrome towards Grantham but I thought the police had closed that one down.'

'There are legal raves now, with proper organisation. Why does she insist on going to the ones where she's most likely to get arrested?'

Why indeed? There was no answer to this question though.

'That's just Leo, I suppose,' she said.

'Do we know how she did in her exams?' Jeremy asked, turning back to his painting.

'No. But I can ring school and ask,' replied Sylvie. 'Do you think they'll take her back into the sixth form?'

Jeremy tutted. 'I doubt it. Would you?' he asked, but the question didn't require a response. 'How about you ring school,' he continued, his tone a little more positive. 'Let's see what the options are, and then we can sit her down and have a proper chat when she comes home.'

Sylvie nodded. 'I might even pop up there rather than ringing. There's bound to be someone around the day after results. It'll be easier to have an honest conversation face to face. I think, though, that we might have to accept that Leo's school days are over.'

Sylvie went to their bedroom to get herself ready to go to the school. She sat down at her dressing table, stared at her reflection and sighed heavily. Neither she nor Jeremy were living the life they had envisaged when they'd got married, although both for different reasons. Jeremy had wanted to stay in London mixing with the arty crowd and being part of whatever was happening.

And she . . . ? Sometimes, when Leonora was being particularly challenging, Sylvie wanted to hurl the blame at Jeremy's feet.

'This is all your fault,' she might have said. 'If it had been up to me we wouldn't have had any children. Children is not what I signed up for. You knew that. And now we have the child from hell and both our lives are destroyed and it's all because of you and your mother.'

She hadn't ever said that out loud, though. What was there to be gained? They had had Leo. They couldn't run back the clock and unhave her. Looking back was no solution to the problem. There was only forward.

Sometimes, though, Sylvie couldn't help it. Her mind would slip back to 1970 when everything had been perfect. She and Jeremy had been married for a few years. As a wedding present, Margery and Gerald had given them a lump sum, which they had used to buy a three-storeyed townhouse in Belsize Park. Sylvie had loved that house. It had five bedrooms even though there were only the two of them. Two had immediately been commandeered as studios, but the rest of the house they had thrown open to anyone who needed somewhere to crash. So many people passed through over the years that Sylvie would have struggled to remember all their names.

Christine had been in residence for a while and Jeremy's sister Jo, until she had met Mark, got married and moved into a little love nest of their own. Jo was as delightful an adult as she had been a teenager. She filled rooms with her personality and Sylvie couldn't help but adore her. The three women spent hours in the airy kitchen talking and laughing, sharing their dreams over endless cups of peppermint tea.

'When do you think Mark will propose?' Jo had asked them. 'I don't want to push him, but honestly, my best years will be behind me if he doesn't hurry up!'

'You're twenty-four!' objected Sylvie. 'I don't think there's any danger of you shrivelling up just yet.'

Jo sighed loudly. 'I know. But I'm so desperate to get on with things. I want a big house like this and I want to fill it with children and dogs. There's going to be something going on all the time, and lots of music. Definitely lots of music. And laughter. Lots of that too.'

'It sounds exhausting,' replied Christine. She was painting her toenails and, having wound strips of toilet paper in and out of her toes to separate them, she was now applying the silver polish from a little round bottle. 'I'm not interested in getting married. I'll just find a rich sugar daddy who can pay for things without asking any questions.'

Jo leaned over and gave her a friendly but quite hard shove, causing Christine to miss her nail entirely and paint her foot instead.

'Oi!' she objected.

'Well, you can't say that,' laughed Jo. 'You'll put women's lib back by generations.'

'Listen, if he wants to spend his money on me then who am I to object? How about you, Sylvie? Still totally anti the whole children thing?'

Sylvie nodded quietly. She wasn't ashamed of her decision, but it did set her swimming against the tide somewhat.

'I'm not surprised you don't want any,' said Jo, 'given the pressure that Mummy keeps putting you under. She is beastly. I've told her to drop it but I don't think she can. She's just so desperate for grandchildren and as Mark seems to be dragging his heels with my proposal then you're the easiest target.'

'Margery's not the reason,' Christine said. 'You haven't wanted children for as long as I've known you, have you, Sylv? They've never been on the cards.'

Sylvie shook her head in reply. 'I'm just lucky that Jeremy sees things the same way I do.'

'Well, he wouldn't have married you otherwise,' said Jo. 'Nor you him. Don't worry. When Mark and I *finally* get spliced I'll have enough babies for both of us.'

She and Jeremy had never been quite brave enough to confess their child-free intentions to Margery, however. She was still very keen on having grandchildren from both her children and told them so loudly and very often. When babies were mentioned, she and Jeremy made vague noises, as if they were a work in progress, which made Margery and Gerald beam and blush at the same time.

But the best part of living in that house had been the parties. They had been the talk of North London, and creative types of every hue had flocked to spend time under their roof, as if there was some kind of magical quality to the air there. It was hard to imagine now when Sylvie's life was so quiet, but she'd often wondered if Leo's undeniable wild streak could be traced directly back to that time, something inherited from a past she had never known.

Sylvie herself had done her best work in her studio in that house, the window overlooking the patchwork of gardens beneath. She had been completely content. They both were. They were living their perfect life.

Until everything had changed.

But there was no point in dwelling on that. This was her life now, chasing after their recalcitrant daughter and clearing up whatever mess she had made.

That was always assuming Leo was their daughter, of course. Sylvie had never let her mind fully explore those possibilities, and she had never told Jeremy about the day Michelle had come round to the house. How could she put that doubt into his mind, given everything?

However, when life bowled her googlies, as it was doing now, Sylvie had flirted with the idea that Leo, with all her anger and disappointment, was not actually her child and that somewhere out there was another who fitted the bill more closely.

She didn't let herself think about that for long, though, and never seriously. What would be the point? The chances were that Michelle had been mistaken or deluded and quite possibly both. There was nothing in Leonora's appearance that particularly set her apart from Sylvie and Jeremy, although these days, with the hair dye and the make-up it was hard to remember what she really looked like. And Sylvie wasn't sure that she believed in nature proving stronger than nurture. If Leo had turned out to be a wilful and headstrong young woman then who was to say that Sylvie herself hadn't been the cause? She had hardly been a model mother. It was just as likely that Leo had been damaged through her own lack of maternal affection than inherited her discontentment from a different set of parents.

Sylvie stared at her reflection for a moment longer and then went downstairs, leaving all thoughts of the past and what might have been behind.

38

Thomas Welbeck School was a modern comprehensive situated to the east of the city centre. Leonora had been admitted two years earlier after she had been expelled from the fee-paying school that she had been attending. Jeremy had joked that she was simply channelling her namesake, the rebellious artist Leonora Carrington, but Sylvie, and more importantly Margery, hadn't thought it was a joking matter.

Margery and Gerald had been paying Leonora's school fees throughout and Sylvie had been happy to let them. She was their granddaughter after all. But this meant that Margery felt no compunction in telling Leonora exactly what she thought about her behaviour generally and her lack of gratitude in particular. When Leo had been expelled, Margery had come up to the Lincoln house to make her feelings on the subject clear.

'Now, Leonora,' she'd said at dinner, eyeing her granddaughter over the top of her glasses, her tone stern. 'This will not do.'

Leonora stared at her hands, picking at her chewed nails and then trying to scratch what was left of her nail varnish off with her teeth. She didn't speak.

'You are a very privileged young lady,' Margery had continued. 'I hesitate to use the word "spoilt", but you have had every advantage handed to you on a plate. And yet here we are.' Margery sat back in her chair and sucked at her teeth as if contemplating exactly where that might be. 'Your father tells me that this incident is the latest in a long series of misdemeanours.'

Leonora sat back then, slumped in her chair, and eyed her grandmother sullenly, one finger still between her teeth. She raised an eyebrow by way of reply.

'Your grandfather and I are very disappointed,' Margery pressed on, her voice growing louder as she got into her stride. 'I don't know what you think you're going to achieve by this appalling act. Locking a teacher in the stationery cupboard and setting a fire under the door. I never heard the like. It's a terrible thing to do. The poor woman must have been frightened to death.'

Leo had smirked then, unable to keep the delight at her antics off her face.

'And you can stop that sniggering right this second,' snapped Margery. 'It's nothing to be proud of, being thrown out of school. And it will follow you around, you know. Once you've been tarred with something like this it will always be on your record. People will always judge you.'

'Oh, Ma,' jumped in Jeremy. 'There's no need to scare the girl.'

Sylvie thought that she had rarely seen anyone looking less scared than her daughter at that moment.

'Leo has just messed up a few times,' Jeremy continued. 'Youthful high jinks is all. But she's learned her lesson now, haven't you, Leo? And this new school, well, it'll be a fresh start. She'll find some new friends, ones that she feels she has more in common with, and we can put all this unpleasantness behind us.'

Sylvie would have applauded his optimism if she hadn't felt that it was all so very misplaced. It was quite apparent, from her body language if nothing else, that Leonora couldn't have cared less about what she had done. There was no emotion, no arguing back, no screaming that she hadn't asked to be born (and she wouldn't have been alone in that sentiment).

Instead, Leonora was totally uninterested. She seemed to be intending to wait until she had been reprimanded and then leave the room and forget all about it. And that was just the kind of attitude that was likely to get right under Margery's skin. She would be looking for an abject apology, some show of remorse to convince her that all the money that had been spent on education thus far wouldn't have been better spent elsewhere.

But Leonora would never give Margery what she wanted and for that, although Sylvie would never have admitted it out loud, she felt a degree of grudging admiration for her daughter. If she had been able to stand up to Jeremy's family more effectively then they would never have been in this position in the first place, although Sylvie tried to not think like that. It wasn't helpful and didn't take any of them further forward.

'Well, the very least that the girl can do is apologise,' complained Margery to her son.

Jeremy looked at Leonora and nodded his approval of this.

Leonora stared up at the ceiling, folded her arms and muttered something inaudible.

'I beg your pardon,' said Margery.

'I'm sorry that I scared Miss Runton and got expelled from school,' Leo repeated. 'I won't do it again.'

'Well,' said Margery huffily. 'I should think not. Nor do anything that might lead to any more unpleasantness. We can't have it, young lady. It has to stop right now. And let this be a lesson to you, Leonora, that your actions have consequences.'

Leonora threw a glance at Sylvie and Sylvie thought she saw a hint of playful complicity in it. She had always been careful not to let her own feelings show, but perhaps Leo had sensed them anyhow. It was all she could do not to wink back.

And now here she was, going to face yet more consequences of Leo's actions. When she reached the school, the gates were standing open and there were cars in the car park. Someone was inside at least. Sylvie walked up to the main doors and pushed, the doors yielding easily, and went inside. Schools always smelled the same, she thought. Floor polish and chalk and overcooked food. Even though there had been no one there for over a month, the under-lying odours were still lingering.

Now she was here, Sylvie wasn't sure where to go or who she needed to talk to, but she thought maybe the school office would be a good place to start and set off down the corridor in what she hoped was the right direction.

As she approached, a girl with dark shiny shoulder-length hair was just coming out. She turned back to speak to whoever was behind the door.

'I'll bring these back tomorrow,' she said, waving a pile of papers. 'Thanks so much for your help.'

Sylvie stood still and let her pass. The girl smiled her thanks, and then Sylvie pushed open the door and went in.

'Ah. Mrs Fotherby-Smythe,' said the woman behind the desk. 'I was about to ring you.'

39

It was two days before Leonora reappeared. Her hair had gone from a rich aubergine purple to white blonde and was cropped short to her head. It made her eyes look huge, or Sylvie hoped it was the new haircut that was doing that and not anything that was still in her system. Her skin had an unwashed grubbiness about it and there was ground-in dirt under her fingernails and on her feet.

Sylvie was relieved to see her safe and knew that any attempt at a reprimand would be pointless. They had been on this square so many times before and, if nothing else, Sylvie had learned what Margery had never seemed to grasp: that shouting and screaming would make her feel worse whilst not actually getting them anywhere.

'Was it good?' she asked her daughter instead. 'Whatever you've been doing?'

Leo nodded. 'Yeah. It was good.'

'No trouble?'

'Nope. I stayed out of the way.'

'Well, that's something at least. I'm not sure your father would have appreciated coming out to rescue you from another police station. Where was it this time?'

'M25.'

That was a long way from home and Leo was barely sixteen, far too young to be traipsing up and down motorways unaccompanied, but Sylvie knew better than to express any kind of shock. Instead she just nodded as if an event so far away was totally fine with her.

'How did you get there?' she asked.

'Hitched a bit and then got a ride with a mate.'

'Have you had any sleep? Do you need something to eat? You definitely need a bath.' Sylvie gave her half a smile and Leo reciprocated.

'Yeah. I stink a bit,' she said. 'And I'm starving.'

'I went to school,' Sylvie continued, watching Leo's face for clues as to what she was thinking, but there was nothing to see. 'They said you could go back and resit the year if you want. Have another go.'

Leo shrugged. 'I don't think so, do you?' she said.

Sylvie didn't think so either, but Leo was going to have to do something with her life other than hang out in fields and dance the nights away.

'But what will you do, Leo? You can't just go to raves. You need an education or if not that then a job. There has to be some sort of a plan here. And I can't keep protecting you from your dad.'

And then, as if coming in on a prearranged cue, Jeremy threw open the kitchen door and stormed into the room.

'Where the hell have you been?' he roared without any introduction. Sylvie knew that he had been just as worried about Leo in her absence as she had, but nothing about his demeanour would have given this impression to Leo. 'Your mother and I have been worried sick,' he continued. 'It is totally unacceptable to disappear on no notice without saying where you're going or when you'll be back. I was this close' – he held his hand aloft, finger and thumb barely separated – 'to ringing the police and reporting you as missing, although I doubt they'd have believed me.'

Leo just stared at him impassively.

'And your exam results. Let's talk about those, shall we? They're an absolute disgrace. I was ashamed. I am ashamed. You're not stupid, Leo. You have a good head on your shoulders. So why can't you just apply yourself? It wouldn't take much. Just enough to get some qualifications under your belt. Then you can go off and do something else. I understand that you don't like school. I do. I get it. But school matters. The world needs you to at least try. That's how life works. No qualifications. No options. It's as simple as that.'

Jeremy was quite red in the face now, spittle settling in the corners of his mouth. Leo looked as if he was reading her the weather forecast. There was no show of emotion in any part of her body. Sylvie could almost admire her passivity if it weren't for it getting Jeremy so agitated.

'I do have options, as it goes,' replied Leo. 'I'm going to live with some mates.'

'Oh yes,' said Jeremy snarkily. 'And what exactly are you going to do for money? If you think I'm going to support you then you can think again.'

'I'll get by,' replied Leo. 'I don't need much.'

Jeremy's jaw dropped and his eyes darted from Leo to Sylvie and back again.

'Do you hear that, Sylvie? Unbelievable. And what will you do for food, not to mention rent, gas, electricity, the poll tax? Do you have any idea . . .'

Leo shrugged. 'It's all sorted. Don't worry, Dad. I won't be asking you for anything. I'll be out of your hair.'

Sylvie could feel the situation slipping out of control.

'Hang on, Leo. Are you talking about moving out for good? I'm not sure that's such a great idea. I can see that you don't want to go back to school, but how about we give it a few weeks, mull over the options? Then you can decide what you want to do next.'

Leo raised her arms and looked up at the ceiling as if in supplication to the gods.

'Why is nobody listening to me? I know what I want to do next. I'm moving out. Today.'

'Over my dead body,' shouted Jeremy.

'If you like,' replied Leo. 'I'm going for a shower. You mentioned food, Mum. Could you . . . ?'

She gave Sylvie a winning smile and Sylvie rolled her eyes back and nodded. Then Leo left the kitchen and bounded up the stairs, leaving Jeremy struggling to speak.

'Thanks for your support there,' he said after a moment or two. 'You were a great help.'

Sylvie approached him and rested her hands on his shoulders.

'You know what she's like,' she said calmly. 'There's no point getting into an argument with her. Let's let her go. She'll soon work things out for herself.'

'And what if she doesn't?'

Jeremy seemed to be calming down. His shoulders slumped as anger was replaced by a kind of exhaustion and his eyes stared into hers, imploring her to come up with a solution.

'We can't force her to stay here,' Sylvie replied. 'She's almost an adult. We would have to lock her in. Is that what you want? To lock your daughter up like a prisoner?'

Jeremy looked as if his world had ended, his face wretched. 'No, but she's too young. We're still responsible for her. What if something were to happen to her when she was living somewhere else? What then?'

'Then the police will bring her back,' said Sylvie. 'I'm sure it happens all the time.'

'She's not some kid in care. She's loved. She has a home and a family. She's our daughter.'

It was on the tip of Sylvie's tongue.

It would be so simple.

She could give her doubt to Jeremy like a gift. Just a few simple sentences would provide him with the comfort that he so badly needed. She might not be our daughter, darling. She might belong to someone else. Our real daughter might be living a totally blameless life somewhere nearby without us ever knowing.

But what then? Even if they could find Michelle now, after all those years, they could hardly just thrust Leo at her. There was too much water under the bridge. The time for swapping the children was long gone, assuming it had even really been an option in the first place. What would they say? 'Sorry, we didn't believe you when you mentioned it before, but we seem to have totally screwed this baby up so we'll give her back to you to deal with and we'd like our real daughter now, please.'

That wasn't how it worked.

So she swallowed the thought back down.

'We'll get her to tell us where she's living and we'll give her an allowance to help her out until she's ready to make some better decisions,' she said instead.

But Jeremy was still shaking his head and Sylvie wasn't sure that he'd even heard her.

40

It was the week before Christmas but Michelle's tree was still conspicuous by its absence. Donna had been nagging at her to put it up for at least a week but Michelle had been making excuses. She didn't have time to get the box down from the loft. She needed to get some new lights because didn't the old ones give up last year? And wasn't it so much more Christmassy to put the tree up nearer to the big day?

None of it was true. Michelle just couldn't face the forced cheerfulness that the decorations required. You were either feeling it or you weren't. This year she definitely wasn't.

It was at times like this that Michelle really missed Dean. Christmas was difficult enough now that the kids were grown and the day had no real focus, but the prospect of facing it without a companion made her want to close the door against the world and hibernate until it was all over. Although Tina and Donna and probably Damien would be there, it just wasn't the same as having a proper family do with them all crowded round a groaning table.

Christmas had been different when the kids were young. Michelle had loved all that sneaking back from town with bags stuffed with whatever Santa had been begged for. There hadn't been that much money, especially once Donna came along, and she and Dean had had to be creative. It was rare that the actual requested toy could be afforded, but they could generally come up with something that would fit the bill, either from the market or one of Dean's mates who had a knack for acquiring just what was needed.

Then, the presents smuggled into the house and hidden as well as was possible in such a tiny space, Michelle and Dean would crack open some tins and, when they'd drunk enough, they'd dance in the front room to Christmas songs. They made proper Christmas songs back then, Michelle thought wistfully, ones you could really let your hair down to.

Dean had his new life now. Michelle had worried that when he left her, he would fall straight into the arms of Linda from next door but one. In some moments, the thought of Linda's smugness at finally having got her man was almost worse than the pain of Dean's departure. Michelle suspected that the pair of them had had their moment, but it hadn't worked out, which was the main thing – or at least, not long enough for Linda to take any pleasure at her expense.

In fact, Dean now lived in a different part of the city, shacked up with his new girlfriend. There was talk of them trying for a baby according to Tina, and this had wounded Michelle almost as deeply as the fact that he had gone. He already had four children. His real children. What was he doing thinking about having more? Michelle knew that she was still young enough to have another baby if she wanted, but she really didn't. That part of her had been spent by the ones she had. But it was different for men, wasn't it?

She rarely saw Dean these days, although he was still working at the garage as far as she knew, and he'd stopped sending her money once Damien turned eighteen. He had refused point-blank to send anything for Donna.

In her heart, Michelle knew that she was the one who had broken their marriage. Everything would have been fine, she knew, if she'd just been able to get over the Donna thing. If she could have accepted that the child was theirs, or wasn't but she hadn't minded, then it would all have been forgotten about.

But she couldn't let it go. Whenever she was tired or upset or drunk, snippets would leak out of her. A comment here, a shake of the head there – never when Donna was there to see or hear but often enough that Dean knew she was still dwelling on what might have been.

'For God's sake, Chelle,' he'd say. 'Just drop it. You've got to let it go. You're driving me mad. You're driving yourself mad. And there's absolutely nothing that we can do about any of it anyway.'

'But don't you ever wonder,' she'd add, pushing on when she should have retreated. 'Aren't you at all curious?'

Dean folded his arms across his chest and looked her straight in the eye.

'No,' he said firmly. 'I don't wonder and I'm not curious. As far as I'm concerned she's our kid. And that's the end of it. And you need to stop talking about it. One of these days she'll hear you, and then what?'

Michelle sometimes wondered if Donna could remember their trip to the posh house by the cathedral. She'd only been five and it hadn't been much of an event to stick in her memory – a short conversation with a strange man. Nothing particularly noteworthy, unless, of course, you knew that the man in question might be your father. But Donna had never mentioned the trip again and so Michelle had to assume that it had gone the way of many child-hood memories. And she should have let her memories leave her in the same way, just drifted away on the breeze.

But she hadn't. She had needled away at it whenever she got a chance. She had cast around all that doubt like so much confetti without realising the damage she was doing.

One night, not long after Donna turned eleven, Dean had come home from the pub more riled up than usual. He slammed the front door without caring which of his children he woke. Michelle was sitting up watching the dregs of the evening's television, not really interested but without the energy to take herself to bed. With a house full of teenagers, there were rarely moments when she could hear herself think and late at night when they were asleep was sometimes the only time she could find peace.

Michelle flinched as Dean stormed in.

'Shhh,' she said. 'You'll wake the kids.'

She turned to look at him and that was when she saw it. There was a fire about him that wasn't usually there. His eyes were bright despite the alcohol, and his movements were precise and focused.

'I'm on to you,' he said with an air of triumph in his voice. 'I think I've always known, but I was kidding myself before.'

'What are you on about?' Michelle asked without much enthusiasm. 'Kidding yourself about what?'

He took his jacket off and threw it on to the sofa next to her but he didn't sit down. Instead he bounced on his toes, a ball of unspent energy.

'The reason why you keep going on about that baby not being ours. Linda was right all along, wasn't she?'

'Linda? Right about something? I very much doubt it,' replied Michelle scornfully, but inside her fear was beginning to grow. She didn't like how this was going at all. 'Right about what?' she added, doubt creeping into her voice.

'She said that baby looked nothing like me right from the start. And you said it wasn't ours. I think Linda's right. You only said that because you *knew* she wasn't mine. You made up the whole swapped baby crap just to cover your tracks.'

Michelle wanted to laugh. This was not new ground. They'd stood on this spot before.

'But she doesn't look like me either,' she said, raising her hands questioningly and shaking her head. 'Nor like the other kids.'

He was being ridiculous. It was the drink talking, she knew, but there was something about the fire in his eyes. This time it wasn't just smouldering; it was burning bright. Michelle didn't like it one little bit.

'I know,' he replied. 'That's pretty convenient, isn't it? Makes your story work even better, if she doesn't look like any of us.'

Michelle was lost.

'Well, no. Not really,' she said. 'It's just how it is.'

Dean stood in front of the television, swaying slightly.

'Well, I'm not buying it any more. It's been niggling away at the back of my head all these years, why you were so obsessed with her not being ours. And now I get it. It's all been a cover story to hide the fact that you knew it wasn't my baby right from the start.'

Michelle laughed out loud. She couldn't help it.

'So, what? You think I was having an affair,' she scoffed. 'I was twenty-five years old with a full-time job, three children under eight and a husband that I loved, and you think that I had the energy to think about having an affair, let alone to actually want to do it?'

Dean tightened his jaw a little, wavering slightly, Michelle thought, but then he said, 'Yes. That's precisely what I think.'

'But who with?!' Michelle asked in astonishment. 'And what happened to them? Did they get me up the duff and then mysteriously disappear?'

Dean shrugged. 'Yeah,' he said, less sure of himself now. 'It makes sense to me. I've never believed that baby swap bollocks. It's stupid. Who comes away from hospital with the wrong baby?'

'Well, I think we did,' Michelle said, her voice louder now too.

'That's crap and you know it. You cooked it up to hide the fact that you'd been playing away.'

'No! That's just not true. I wouldn't. I didn't!'

But she could feel that this was getting out of hand. If she didn't close the row down now then things would be said that they couldn't unsay. And Donna might hear them.

'Look,' she said more quietly. 'Let's just go to bed. We can talk about this in the morning.' She wanted to tell him again that he was wrong, but didn't want to set him off on yet more ranting.

'You go,' he mumbled, dropping down into the sofa. 'I'll sleep here.'

This was a first. Dean had slept on the sofa when he was too drunk to get up the stairs but never had he chosen to be there of his own accord.

'Don't be silly,' she tried. 'Come to bed.'

But he lay down, rearranging the cushions into something more comfortable.

'I'm fine here,' he said gruffly.

So, she'd gone upstairs to find him some blankets and then left him to it.

Michelle had never worked out what had started him off down this path, but once he'd got the idea in his head there was nothing she could do to shift it, and gradually, over the next few months things between them had deteriorated until there was nothing left and he had packed a bag and gone, leaving her first shattered and then angry.

It had been the coward's way out, she could see that now. Someone, Linda, must have planted the seed in his head and he had let it grow into a full-sized triffid without really thinking about how likely any of it might be. That she would have had an affair was as unlikely as their baby getting swapped in the hospital. But Dean had chosen not to see that.

Yet despite it all Michelle still loved him. She had tried really hard not to, but somehow she just couldn't help it. He was ingrained into her. She supposed that he had been in her skin so long that it was hard to scrub him away.

41

Unsurprisingly, Donna seemed to be going great guns at Thomas Welbeck School. She had thrown herself into her studies and now, judging by the new names that Michelle kept hearing over the tea table, she seemed to have found herself a group of friends too. She hadn't brought any of them back to the house as yet, but when Michelle asked her about that she had just laughed and made some comment about it not being primary school. Still, Michelle was curious. She'd like to have seen what kind of girls her daughter was hanging round with.

'You're not ashamed of us, are you?' she'd asked gently, conscious that her new friends might be very different to them, but Donna's smile had been so open and genuine that she knew at once that she was wide of the mark.

'God, no!' replied Donna. 'But it's not really what we do. Some people live miles away and it's hard to get back home if you miss the bus. It's easier if we just see each other at school. But maybe one weekend . . . ?'

Michelle had got her head round the fact that Donna had gone into the sixth form now. She'd even started bragging about it to anyone who showed any interest.

'Ah yes, our Donna. She's the brains of the family. Doing A levels now, you know. Talking about going to university next.'

Every time Michelle said the word 'university' she could feel herself almost stumble over the syllables in her attempt to make it sound natural. Sharon next door, Donna's biggest fan, always gave the most gratifying response to news.

'God, she's brilliant, that one,' she'd say. 'Brains the size of a planet and dead lovely with it. You never see her without that smile either. It's like she can't pull any other face.'

Michelle always felt the need to defend her other children.

'Well, the others aren't thick,' she'd say. 'The thing that's different about Donna is that she's interested in what they teach at school. But she has her moments too, you know. It's not all sweetness and light.'

Just the week before there had been an incident.

'I'm going to London on Saturday,' Donna had said when she bounced in from school.

Michelle, who was working her way through the crossword in her magazine, didn't look up.

'Oh yes?' she said. 'What for?'

'There's a rally. A group of us are going to go.'

'What do you mean, a rally? Like a protest march?'

Donna's eyes were shining, lighting up her whole face. 'Yes. Vicky heard about it. It's about the riots in the summer and getting the government to see that there's real poverty in this country. Someone needs to do something, so we are.'

Michelle wasn't particularly well informed politically but this all sounded a little vague, even to her. She wasn't sure it was really Donna speaking either. It sounded more as if she was just parroting what she had heard others say.

'I'm not sure that's a great idea,' Michelle said, focusing hard on her tone so she didn't accidentally trigger a row. 'And it's nearly Christmas. London will be heaving.'

'Well, that's the point, Mum,' said Donna, flopping down at the table and slouching in a chair, legs splayed. 'Maximum publicity. We go down there. We march on Parliament. We show the Tories that we've had enough. Labour is miles ahead in the polls. The government just needs a little push and then it'll topple over and take all its cronies with it. You just have to look at Black Wednesday to see that they don't know what they're doing.'

Michelle didn't know what Black Wednesday was, and she wasn't convinced that Donna did either, but she did have that fire of youth that was powerful enough to overcome a lack of actual knowledge. Michelle, more jaded with each passing year, had to admire her passion, but she couldn't help but think that Donna had the wrong end of the stick here, not least about how democracy worked.

'It's not like Jenga, you know,' she said. 'You can't just wobble one bit of the government and it all comes crashing down. You have to have elections and stuff.'

'God, I know that, Mum,' snapped Donna. 'I'm not completely stupid.'

'Well, then you'll know that protests need a focus. You can't just go and protest about everything.'

'Why not?' Donna stared at Michelle, eyes narrowed.

'Well, because no one will take any notice for a start.'

'They have to take notice. There'll be so many of us that we'll be impossible to ignore.'

Michelle pulled a sceptical face. 'If there are that many of you then the police will only let you march down out-of-the-way streets. You won't get within a million miles of the Houses of Parliament.'

'Like we're going to march the route the police give us,' Donna scoffed.

'I'm not sure you get much choice. A policeman on a horse with a truncheon can be very persuasive. Who else is going on this jaunt?'

'It's not a jaunt,' Donna spat. 'Me, Vicky, Jess and Chloe. Vicky says there's a coach going down but we don't know about that yet. Anyway, she says she'll get me a seat on it.'

Michelle put her hand up.

'Hold your horses,' she said. 'We don't really know what's involved. And there were those bombs in Oxford Street last week,' she added, suddenly remembering. 'It's not safe down there at the moment.'

'Don't be so stupid, of course it's safe,' replied Donna, and Michelle flinched.

'I'm not stupid, and how do you know?' Michelle shot back. 'This is not the time to be going to London and definitely not on such a flimsy arrangement. You're only sixteen, Donna. I know you think you're grown-up but you're really not.'

From dealings with her other kids, Michelle knew that this was like a red rag to a bull, but it didn't make it any less true. Donna sat up in her chair, as if this would add strength to her argument.

'Vicky says this is exactly the safest time because the police and that will be all over everywhere. No one will be able to bomb anything.'

Michelle wasn't sure she liked the sound of this Vicky, and the more she heard about the 'plan' the more determined she was that Donna wouldn't be involved.

'Be that as it may, you're not going.'

'I bloody am and you can't stop me!'

She was right on that score. Donna earned her own money and Michelle could hardly lock her in the house.

'Well, put it this way then. I don't think it would be very clever to go. And I assume that when you think about it properly you will agree with me.'

This was a low blow. Michelle knew that Donna prided herself on thinking things through. Now, though, she was clearly too angry to discuss it any further. She stood up.

'Oh, for God's sake. You're so controlling. It's pathetic. I'm not a child, you know. And I'll go if I want.'

Then she stormed out of the kitchen, thundered up the stairs and banged her bedroom door shut behind her.

But she hadn't gone on the rally. Sense had prevailed, as it usually did with her.

Generally, though, Michelle had to agree with Sharon's assessment of her. Donna did always seem to see the cheery side of the world. Life came more easily to her than it did to others, as if the dice were permanently loaded in her favour. Even when she faced challenges – the fact that there was no money to buy the latest clothes or music being the most common – she rarely did it with bad grace. Rather than complaining, she'd just gone and quietly got herself a job waitressing in a restaurant and so made money for herself. She even offered to pay some rent to Michelle, which had brought tears to Michelle's eyes.

'Well, Tina pays rent,' Donna had argued. 'So I should too.'

'But Tina works full-time and is old enough to have moved out years ago. It's different for you,' Michelle had argued.

Donna had shaken her head, and Michelle had found two twenty-pound notes neatly folded in her purse later.

◆ ◆ ◆

'Are we going to put the tree up today?' Donna had asked the day before. 'There's only a week to go and I've got things I need to put under it.' She gave Michelle a knowing wink.

Michelle was always nervous about putting presents under the tree too early. Anyone could look through the window, see them just sitting there and decide to break in and nick them.

'Let's do it tomorrow,' she said. 'I'll get us a bottle of wine and we'll do a proper job with carols and everything. I might ring Carl and Damien, see if they want to pop over. We could make a thing of it. All of us together.'

All of them except Dean, Michelle thought but didn't say.

The next day, Saturday, Michelle woke feeling more optimistic than she had done in a while. She had been in touch with Damien and Carl and they'd both said they'd come, drawn by the promise of a meal that she hadn't really offered but was happy to provide if it meant that they would all be together.

'The boys are landing around three,' she told Donna and Tina, even though her sons had been men for years, and when they arrived, tumbling into the tiny house in pre-Christmas high spirits, she was almost overwhelmed by her feelings for them all. She watched as the four of them worked together to dress the tree whilst she sat on the sofa. There really wasn't room for everyone to be on their feet at once.

They told tales of Christmases past, argued over where some of the decorations had come from.

'I nicked that fairy from the tree in school,' claimed Damien, only for Carl to set him straight.

'Nah, that was me, that was. It was right at the top and I had to sit on Frank's shoulders to reach it. Nearly brought the whole bloody tree down. It was definitely me.'

'The times I went down to that school to dig you out of the holes you'd got yourself into, Carl White. You were a bloody disgrace!' laughed Michelle.

Carl gave a little bow. 'At your service. Hey, Dons, you've got way too many of those ball things on your side. Chuck a couple my way.'

Donna tossed him a silver bauble and he reached out and caught it with one hand and then attached it to a branch on his side of the tree.

Michelle could feel a warmth building inside her. These were her children. Her almost all adult children. They'd done a good job, her and Dean. They'd created four independent people each making their own way in the world.

And, despite whatever Michelle may have thought over the years, Donna fitted in just as much as any of the others. Tina, Carl and Damien were her siblings. No, she still didn't look like them, it was true, but then Tina looked nothing like the boys either. Donna had once explained the biology to her. Siblings weren't guaranteed to look alike, apparently. It was all a matter of luck as to what features you were born with. Could it be that the magic combination of DNA that had created Donna was simply drawn from a different corner of the melting pot to the others? Another egg or different sperm and she might have turned out to be the absolute double of any one of them.

It made Michelle's insides clench when she thought of the doubts that she had been harbouring for the last sixteen years. She wanted to believe that she had treated Donna no differently to the other three. She had certainly tried to treat them all the same. Of course, Donna had been different, but that was just Donna and nothing to do with the way Michelle had responded to her.

Or maybe Michelle was wrong about that. Was the quiet watchful child with the invisible friend a by-product of always feeling that she didn't quite fit in, even if she couldn't understand why that might be? Michelle had to admit to herself that part of that might be true.

But there was nothing quiet and watchful about Donna now. At sixteen she was confident and self-assured. She knew who she was and what she wanted to achieve. She was focused and determined, both qualities, Michelle thought with a fizz of pride, that she herself had displayed throughout her own life.

And who was to say that Donna hadn't been born with those things already hardwired into her? Where did it say that Michelle White couldn't give birth to a child who was going to make more of herself than her circumstances might suggest?

Where indeed?

42

When they'd run out of decorations to hang and finished bickering about whose side of the tree was better, they all decided that it looked very festive but that now they needed to go to the pub to ramp up the Christmas spirit.

'But what about tea?' objected Michelle. 'I got some food in specially.'

'We'll pick up some chips later, Mum,' said Carl. 'Let's go out. All of us. It'll be a laugh.'

He was right. It would be, and Michelle couldn't remember ever having done it before. Donna had been too young for one thing. Technically she still was. She looked at her daughter, trying to gauge whether she could pass for eighteen, even though she knew the pub was full of underage kids.

Damien seemed to read her mind. 'Don't worry about Dons. No one will care. Just stay with us and keep quiet,' he said to Donna with a grin. 'Like you do the rest of the time!'

Donna gave Damien a shove that almost sent him crashing into the newly dressed tree.

Michelle sighed. They could eat the lasagne she'd bought any time and, if she was honest, after the wine she wasn't sure she could be bothered heating it up any more anyway.

'Okay,' she said. 'Let's go.'

They didn't tend to drink at their local pub. There had been some nastiness between Dean and the landlord back in the seventies and even though that landlord had long since moved on and Dean no longer lived with them, old habits died hard. So they walked past that one and to the next one along, the Ring O' Bells.

It was an overcast December night with the kind of dull damp cold that creeps into your bones, but, with the windows of many of the houses cheery with light-up Santas and fake candelabras, everything looked so bright and welcoming that Michelle didn't really notice.

The pub was festooned with lights too and, despite it being barely past six o'clock, it was clearly already bursting at the seams inside. Punters spilled out of the door and on to the pavement, each clutching a pint glass, and the family had to shoulder their way inside, apologising to those they nudged as they went.

Inside, the stuffy heat created by so many bodies all crammed together was almost overwhelming after the chill of the night outside. The air was thick and Michelle felt as if she were struggling to fill her lungs. She wanted to tear off her coat for fear that the sudden change in temperature might make her faint, but there wasn't enough wriggle room, so she concentrated on finding somewhere for them to stand whilst Carl went to the bar.

As she surveyed the throngs of people, a woman she knew a little waved at her.

'Hey, Chelle. We're just leaving. Do you want this table?'

Grabbing Tina and Donna, Michelle shoved her way through, and the three of them dropped into the seats as soon as the previous group stood so there would be no danger of someone else stepping in and stealing them from under their noses.

The room suddenly felt less full now that they had somewhere to sit and Michelle, relaxing, shrugged off her coat and laid it across the window ledge behind her.

'I can't believe how busy it is,' she said, her mouth falling open.

'It's Christmas, Mum,' replied Tina with a broad grin.

It was, and coming out was starting to feel like it was just what Michelle needed. Maybe she just needed a decent night out to remind her how much fun Christmas could be.

Carl was making his way across the room carrying a round metal tray stacked with five pint glasses, Damien following in his wake. People parted for him to get through, seemingly each understanding the problem of carrying full drinks in a crowded pub, and soon they were all sitting together, the drinks distributed.

Relaxed and happy, they chatted about their plans for Christmas Day.

'Me and Casey are going to her mum's,' said Carl. 'They eat Christmas dinner at teatime there. How weird's that?'

'What about the turkey sandwiches?' asked Damien between swallows of his pint. 'When do they have those?'

Carl shook his head. 'No idea, mate. I'm just doing as I'm told. No jeans' – he pulled a face that said this was also unbelievable – 'and Christmas dinner at teatime. Bizarre.'

'You'll have to come to us next year,' suggested Michelle.

She had barely got her head around this Christmas, let alone next, but if Casey's family got to see her son on the big day and she didn't then she needed to redress the balance.

'He won't be with her next Christmas,' teased Tina. 'When have you ever known our Carl to hang on to a girl for more than a few months? And she's nice, is Casey. She'll soon kick him into touch when she realises what a scumbag he really is.'

'Oi!' responded Carl indignantly. 'We'll have less of that. It's actually going pretty well, as it happens. I might even pop the question one of these days.'

'Never!' said Tina with a laugh. 'Super-stud Carl White settling down. I'll believe it when I see it.'

Michelle's heart gave a little flutter. 'Really, Carl. You think she's the one?'

Carl shifted in his seat, looked down at his pint and shrugged. 'Well, I'm not making any promises. But yeah. I like her.'

'See!' said Tina, a note of triumph in her voice. 'He's backing out of it already. Hell will freeze over before my brother makes an honest woman of anyone.'

The banter continued but after a while Michelle noticed that Donna wasn't joining in. This wasn't unusual. Donna was often happiest watching things unfold around her. This time, however, she had her eyes trained on a group at the far end of the bar. Michelle followed her gaze but Donna spoke before she had found the target.

'Isn't that Dad over there?' she asked.

Michelle's stomach gave an involuntary flip and she followed Donna's gaze. She picked Dean out immediately. Even though he was standing with his back to them, she would have known that shape anywhere. He was with some of the other mechanics from the garage. It must be their Christmas night out, she thought. The pub was still the nearest to where he worked, even if he did live on the other side of town now.

'Looks like it,' she said.

Her heart, risen sky-high just two seconds ago, crashed. Why did he have to be in here when she had been having such a lovely time? Seeing him, especially when the rest of them were all together, just reminded her of everything they had lost and it started an ache deep inside her core. She wanted it to go away. She wanted him to go away.

She tried to reposition herself so that she didn't have him in her line of sight, but now that she knew he was there she found her eyes kept sliding across to him. She stopped listening, missing parts of what her children were saying because her head was occupied with her own thoughts.

'Don't you think, Mum?' asked Tina.

Michelle wrenched her attention away from Dean and back to her daughter.

'I'm sorry, love. What did you say?'

'I was just saying that I don't give Charles and Di long. They'll be divorced before you know it.'

'They can't get divorced,' said Damien. 'He's going to be king. You can't have a divorced king.'

'Well, they're obviously no good for each other. Much better to call it a day,' Tina replied. 'Mum agrees, don't you?'

Divorce, even if it was the most talked-about one in the country, was not what Michelle wanted to be discussing just then. Seeing Dean had already spoiled her night. Talk of divorce would no doubt tip her into a malaise.

'I think it's none of our business,' she said shortly and Tina, who had been expecting wholehearted support, looked a little nonplussed. 'Now, whose round is it?' Michelle continued. 'Or is it mine? Shuffle over, Damien, and let me out so I can go to the bar. Same again?'

She stood up, straightened her top and ran a finger under her eyes to wipe away any wandering mascara, and then headed to the bar, conscious of how her body might look with every step. He might be her ex but that didn't mean that she didn't want to look at her best, remind him what he'd let slip through his fingers.

43

Michelle didn't know what she would say to Dean if the opportunity presented itself. He wasn't even facing her way and for all she knew he had no idea she was even there. But something was compelling her to move towards him. She knew it was probably the booze, but she couldn't help herself. A part of her would always love him.

To stand anywhere near where he was, she would have to go quite out of her way and she was just considering whether she ought to when a huge gap opened up at the bar right behind him. Michelle made a beeline for it. Surely this was fate on her side.

She stood, waiting for the bar staff to get to her. She was two people away from Dean. She could reach out and touch his shoulder if she wanted to. And she did want to, she really, really wanted to create a connection between them, but she kept her hand in her pocket. He was no longer her Dean. He had a new life now, had chosen someone else, and she would only set herself back if she tried to disrupt that. But if he saw her and maybe remembered for a few minutes just what they'd once had, how bad would that be?

Her eyes darted between the barman and the back of Dean's head. She willed him to see her, but he didn't seem to be responding to her thoughts. Then her turn arrived and she was forced to shift her attention back to ordering her round.

As she did this, she saw out of the corner of her eye one of Dean's colleagues nodding in her direction, in a silent signal to Dean. Seeming to understand the message, Dean turned round, and Michelle could feel his eyes on her. She turned to face him, feigned surprise and smiled.

'Oh, hi. Fancy seeing you here,' she said as naturally as she could.

'Yeah. Just in for a few drinks after work,' he said. 'Christmas and all that.'

She could tell from the way he formed his words that they must have been in the pub for a while.

She nodded. 'We're all over there,' she said, cocking her head in the direction of their table.

'Oh, right,' he said. 'Well, maybe I'll come over and say hello in a bit.'

Michelle's heart stopped beating for a second and then lurched back into action at a far faster speed. She hated that her body was being so disloyal to her mind, but she had no control over it. The main thing was to make sure that Dean had no idea of the effect he was having on her. She tried to play it cool.

'Do that,' she said. 'Be nice to see you.'

'That's seven fifty,' said the barman, putting the last of the pints on the tray.

Flustered by having to shift her focus away from Dean, Michelle scrabbled in her bag for her purse and counted out the coins in the palm of her hand. She handed them over and turned to Dean, but he had spun back to face the other mechanics. She had been dismissed.

Trying not to give anything away of the turmoil that was boiling inside her, she carried the drinks back to the table. It wasn't easy as her hands were shaking, and a fair quantity of the beer ended up on the tray.

'Did you speak to Dad?' asked Tina as soon as she sat down. 'Is he coming over?'

'He says he will in a bit,' Michelle replied as she tried to regather herself. The tray was swimming in spilt beer and the glasses dripped as she handed them out.

'He looks good,' continued Tina.

'He looks pissed,' contradicted Carl. 'I can see him swaying from here!'

'It's the garage Christmas night out,' said Michelle, but her voice was barely audible.

It took Dean another hour before he came over and by then Michelle had decided that he wasn't coming and had relaxed again. The pub was still busy but less rammed than it had been. She saw him saying goodbye to one of his workmates near the door with much hugging and slapping of backs. Then he began to meander across to their table.

'Hey up,' said Damien, cocking his head in Dean's direction.

'Hiya, Dad,' said Tina when he got within earshot. 'Merry Christmas.'

Dean was quite a lot drunker than he had been before. His eyes were glazed and he held his mouth in a dopey smile.

'Well, well,' he said. 'And what have we here?'

He reached the table.

'Budge up,' he said, shoving Carl across the bench seat with his hips to make enough room to sit down. The bench wasn't really long enough to accommodate another person and Donna almost fell off the other end.

'Oi! Careful, Dad,' said Carl. 'You'll have our Donna on the floor.'

'Less of the "our",' said Dean, his head wobbling from side to side as he spoke.

Michelle threw him a warning look, but subtlety was going to be lost on him in this state.

'Dean. Shush,' she said under her breath.

'What?' he replied indignantly and at exactly the same volume as before. 'I'm only telling it like it is.'

'Dean!' Michelle repeated more urgently. 'Don't.'

But Dean was having none of it.

'Don't what?' he asked, his tone now more aggressive. 'She's not "our" Donna. No point pretending otherwise.'

Michelle's heart began to pound in her chest. She wanted to look at Donna, to make sure that she hadn't heard him, but she didn't want to make things worse by drawing any attention to her either.

But Tina had heard all too clearly, it seemed.

'What are you on about, Dad?' she asked.

'Ask your mother,' Dean said. 'Get her to tell you her cock-and-bull story. Because it's all bollocks, Chelle. We both know that.'

Michelle glanced at Donna. Colour was draining from her face as she looked from Michelle to Dean and back again.

'What's he talking about, Mum?' Donna asked in a voice barely audible over the noises of the pub.

'Nothing, love. He's just drunk, that's all. You take no notice.'

'I may be drunk,' said Dean, carefully enunciating each word in turn, 'but I'm not wrong. I'm not your dad, Donna. Never have been. Never will be.'

Donna's mouth fell open and the others glanced quickly from one to another to see if anyone else knew what was going on.

'It's not true, Donna,' said Michelle, reaching her hand across the table to take Donna's, but Donna was completely unresponsive. She was just staring at Dean.

But Dean wasn't finished. 'Your mother gave me this crap that you weren't ours. She reckons we brought the wrong baby home from the hospital, but I know that was just to cover up the fact that she was playing away.'

'Right!' said Michelle, suddenly springing to her feet. 'That is enough. We're leaving. Come on, kids.'

But no one moved, either too shocked or too curious to respond.

'What are you saying, Dad?' asked Carl, his face creased in confusion.

'Just that. Your mother has always said that Donna isn't ours. Reckons that the woman in the bed next to her got our kid and we got hers. Like that could ever be true. More likely she had a fling with some low life and tried to pass the result off on me.'

Michelle's cheeks were burning. Dean was now speaking loudly enough that those around them could hear him and several people stopped their own conversations to listen in.

'Come on, Donna,' urged Michelle. 'Let's go home. We can talk about this properly there.' She tried reaching for Donna's hand again but Donna still ignored her, transfixed by Dean. Michelle wished she could tell what was going on in her head so that she could say the right thing to her, but as ever, Donna was giving nothing away.

Michelle stood up, walked round the table and put her arm around Donna.

'We're going home right now,' she said.

Donna was biddable in her shock and Michelle grabbed their coats and steered her in the direction of the door, scowling at the onlookers as if to tell them to mind their own business. Tina followed her but Carl and Damien stayed where they were.

'We'll see you later, yeah, Mum?' Damien called after her, but she didn't reply. All her attention was focused on getting them out of the spotlight.

Finally, they reached the door and virtually fell out into the cold street beyond. There were a few other revellers around but Michelle ignored them. She wrapped Donna's coat over her shoulders as if she had been in an accident.

Then she led her away.

44

Sylvie stood on the street and looked at the boarded-up house. She had never been to this part of town, had had no need to. When she had become pregnant and Jeremy had suggested that they move out of London to somewhere more rural, she had been so numbed by the whole business of having a baby that she had just gone along with it. Jeremy had been on childhood holidays to Lincoln to visit a favourite aunt and had fond memories of the place. He had found their house without her help and she had just moved in and begun to live in its environs. And with a stab of shame, she realised that she had taken no notice of the rest of the town at all.

She checked the address that Leo had given her. This was the right road, and the house was identified by a number daubed on to the bricks in dripping white emulsion. This was definitely the place.

Sylvie shivered at the thought of what she might find behind the chip-boarded windows. She had never been in a squat before Leo had moved into one. Even when she and Jeremy had been living in London and spent their days with impoverished artists, they had all paid their own way. No one had simply acquired an empty property and adopted it as if it were their own. But things had changed. Squatting appeared to be a way of life now.

This was the third squat that Leo had lived in since August and it looked even more rundown and decrepit than the first two. Sylvie wouldn't have thought that was possible, but she was learning not to have any expectations.

The main thing was that Leo was well and happy and she considered this to be her home. Home. Sylvie shuddered again. This was no home, not to Sylvie's mind. But it was where Leo was choosing to live so she needed to accept it. She continued to tell herself that it was only a temporary state of affairs, but the longer the situation continued the harder that was to believe.

Taking a deep breath, she knocked on the door. There was a doorbell, but judging by the wires that were poking out of it she assumed that it wouldn't be working. Did the house even have an electricity supply? Or water? What did they do for sanitation?

She was just running through these horrifying thoughts when the door swung open. A young man stood there dressed in an over-sized mohair sweater, jeans and a Santa hat.

'Alright,' he said.

'Is Leo in?' Sylvie asked. 'She knows I'm coming.'

He nodded. 'I'm just on my way out but she's upstairs,' he said. 'Merry Christmas!'

He stepped past Sylvie and set off down the road, the pompom on his hat bouncing with each step he took.

Sylvie stepped into the dark hall. Her natural instincts were to leave the door open behind her for an easy egress should the need arise, but she pushed it closed anyway. Even if the people who lived here had adopted an unconventional lifestyle, they were still entitled to a little privacy.

With the windows boarded up, there was very little natural light and it took Sylvie's eyes a moment to adjust to the gloom. The walls had once been papered with Anaglypta and painted magnolia, but there was so much graffiti that you could barely see the original colour and much of the wallpaper hung away from the walls in long damp strips. There was a door to her left and right and the stairs were straight ahead of her. The young man had said that Leo was upstairs and so, calling her daughter's name out tentatively, Sylvie stepped on to the staircase. Any carpet that there might once have been had long gone and the treads were edged with vicious-looking tacks and creaked as she put her weight on them. One step had rotted through entirely.

'Leo,' called Sylvie again as she reached the top. 'It's me. Are you here?'

The house felt very still and for a moment Sylvie was sure that she was the only person there. Then she heard some movement and Leo's smiling face appeared from one of the rooms.

'Hi, Mum,' she said. 'Come in.'

Her daughter looked well. Her pixie haircut was now a vivid pink, which suited her. Sylvie scanned her face, searching for signs of anything untoward, but her skin was clear and her eyes were bright and Sylvie let herself relax.

She stepped into the room and smiled. Even though the room had been stripped back to nothing more than its skeleton, there was something about it that shouted Leo. She had put the mattress slap-bang in the middle of the room rather than pushing it against a wall. Her clothes were hanging on an old-fashioned hat stand. Leo saw her looking at it.

'Do you like it?' she asked proudly. 'I found it in a skip.'

'It's very inventive,' replied Sylvie. 'And I love the artwork.'

The walls had been decorated in an intricate doodle that ran from the top of one corner to the bottom of the opposite one. The pattern was built up of swirls and feathers with delicate flowers and tropical-looking leaves in and amongst them. Sylvie went to examine it more closely.

'It's beautiful,' she said, tracing the line of a monkey's curling tail with her finger. 'Did you do it?'

'Well, don't look so shocked,' snapped Leo, her voice a little defensive. 'I am the product of two artists, you know. It'd be a bit shit if none of your talent had rubbed off on me.'

'I'm sorry,' said Sylvie quickly. 'It's just I've never seen you doing anything like this.'

Leo just shrugged.

'So,' said Sylvie, leaving the doodled wall and dropping to sit on the mattress. 'How have you been?'

Leo sat down next to her, making Sylvie bounce as the mattress springs repositioned themselves.

'Pretty good. It's nice here. The neighbours leave us alone and the police haven't been yet.'

'How many are there of you?'

Leo counted them off on her fingers. 'Dessie, Spider – I think you met him at the door, he's nice. Chrissie. She's a bit of a warrior. She picks holes in everything, you know. It's all capitalist conspiracy this and slam the patriarchy that. It gets a bit tired after a while.'

Sylvie marvelled at how mature her sixteen-year-old daughter sounded.

'And then there's Tosh but he's not here at the moment.'

Sylvie resisted asking where he might be. She hoped it wasn't anything unsavoury or illegal keeping him away.

'Are you the youngest?' she asked instead.

'I don't know. Everyone lies about their age so it's hard to tell. They think I'm eighteen.'

I very much doubt that, thought Sylvie.

'Did you see that I topped your bank account up again?' she asked.

'Yeah. Thanks for that, Mum. You're a lifesaver.'

Sylvie smiled, partly to acknowledge Leo's thanks and partly in relief that she looked so well.

'Dad sends his love,' she said, but the words came out too brightly and it was obvious that they weren't true.

'You don't have to do that,' Leo said. 'I know where I stand with Dad.'

'He's just finding it hard to process,' Sylvie replied. 'He hates that you're living away from home like this. He wants you to come back. And you can't blame him for that.'

'He wants to be able to control me, you mean. He wants me to do exactly what he wants so that he can report back to Grandma about how wonderful I am and what a great return on her investment I'm turning out to be.'

'Oh, that's not true,' objected Sylvie. 'He loves you very much. And don't worry what Grandma thinks. It really isn't any of her business.'

But it was her business, Sylvie thought. The baby that she and Jeremy had had was very much Margery's business, and Sylvie couldn't help the sneaking admiration that she felt for Leo for kicking back against them. If Sylvie had been strong enough to do that in the first place . . . but then she wouldn't have had Leo.

'Will you come to us for Christmas Day?' she asked.

Leo pulled a face. 'I'm not sure. We're having a bit of a do here. Spider's doing his world-famous nut roast. And it's not like Christmas at home is any fun.'

Sylvie shrugged. Leo was right. It wasn't.

'Okay,' she said simply. 'But we'd still love to see you. Both of us,' she added.

Leo raised her eyebrows sceptically.

'Honestly! Perhaps you could come after Boxing Day is over. Things are generally a little better by the twenty-seventh.'

'We'll see,' replied Leo, but Sylvie could tell that she was actually saying no but trying not to hurt her feelings.

Sylvie changed tack. 'Are you hungry? I saw a nice-looking café just down the road. Shall I take you for some lunch?'

Leo grinned at her.

'That'd be ace,' she said.

45

Christmas was always excruciating. It didn't matter how Sylvie tried to arrange the day. Whatever they did would inevitably end up being shrouded in misery. Even in the odd moments when Jeremy managed to forget what had happened on Christmas Day, 1974, the release would only be for a minute or two before the memory slipped back into his mind. Then there would follow a period when he felt so guilty for having enjoyed himself even for a moment that his misery was increased.

Over the years, Sylvie had suggested various alternatives to the kind of traditional day that they had enjoyed before – that they go abroad to somewhere where Christmas wasn't celebrated, or treated the day just like any other without any of the usual festivities, but Jeremy had refused. Sometimes Sylvie thought that he actually enjoyed wallowing in his self-pity, but given what had happened she really couldn't blame him.

And this year there would be no Leo either. The mere thought of a day with just the two of them was exhausting. Sylvie had never thought she might miss the argument-filled Christmas Days when Jeremy and Leo were at each other's throats from morning until night, but this year even that looked preferable to what lay ahead.

Not for the first time, Sylvie contemplated inviting Christine to come and stay without telling Jeremy. Christine could just turn up on the doorstep – surprise! But as usual she rejected the idea. How could it be fair to inflict their horrible Christmas on anyone else, least of all lovely Christine? No, she would just have to deal with it as she had done all the other ones over the last eighteen years.

Sometimes Sylvie tried to remember how their Christmases had been before the accident. She would see Christmas tree lights twinkling in the windows of the houses and wonder. For a moment she'd feel like the little match girl from the story, until she got hold of herself and remembered how fortunate she really was. She had Jeremy and their lovely home and their work. And there was Leo, of course. Nothing about Sylvie's life merited complaint. But each year, the memories of those early, untroubled Christmases became fainter. Soon they would leach away entirely so that only the silty dregs remained like the end of a bottle of red wine.

Having tried everything she could think of to improve their festive period at home with no success, she now did the bare minimum. They always had a tree – Sylvie loved its twinkling glow and the way the glass baubles reflected the light as they span slowly from their strings – but she didn't bother with any other decorations. She served duck instead of turkey and didn't buy Christmas crackers.

They did exchange gifts, however. With a child in the house, that part of the festive season could never be ignored, and Sylvie always took great care with the wrapping, using bows and ribbons and beautifully decorated labels that she drew herself as if trying to decant the whole of Christmas into that one little part of it. Now that Leo was neither a child nor in the house, even the idea of gifts seemed suddenly unappealing. Sylvie had steeled herself in readiness for what was to come.

That day she and Jeremy were having breakfast. Jeremy had finished all the commissions that he'd had in the run-up, having had to work hard to get them all out in time. Now he looked tired but emitted a kind of happy contentment from a job well done. If it weren't for the proximity of Christmas everything might have been very satisfactory.

Sylvie poured a fresh cup of coffee for them both.

'Thanks,' said Jeremy without looking up from the newspaper.

'I thought I might go to the carol service at the cathedral this evening,' said Sylvie.

'Uh-huh,' said Jeremy.

'You don't want to come?' She asked the question lightly, knowing the answer already but still hoping that this might be the year that something changed.

'I don't think so,' he replied. 'But you go. It'll be wonderful. Busy though.'

'Yes. Packed with all us heathens coming out of the woodwork for their once-a-year visit,' replied Sylvie with a smile. She paused, ran her knife over her already buttered toast.

'I saw Leo yesterday,' she began.

Jeremy didn't respond, but a slight stiffening of the way he held himself told her that he was listening.

'She seems well. The new place is . . . well, it's okay. She's drawn this amazing frieze across her wall. You should go and see it. It really is very intricate; beautiful, in fact.'

Jeremy gave a single nod but didn't speak.

'She says she won't come home for Christmas. They've arranged something for all her housemates. They're having a nut roast, she said.'

'Housemates? Nice way to describe them,' said Jeremy.

'Oh, you know what I mean. I think it's good that she's settled there with them. She seems happy, Jeremy. That has to mean something. I'm pleased for her.'

Jeremy made a noise between a word and a grunt that Sylvie took to be an agreement.

'So it'll just be the two of us,' she continued brightly. 'I thought we could perhaps do something a bit different. Go away maybe. I know it's short notice but I could call into that travel agents' on the High Street. I'm sure they would be able to find us something.'

Her heart was pounding in her chest now. She hadn't realised how much she wanted to go somewhere else until she voiced it out loud.

Jeremy didn't say anything straight away, which meant that he hadn't rejected the idea either. She hardly dared breathe.

'It might be good for us. To be somewhere different.'

She reached across the table and rested her hand on his. She could feel his warmth through her palm.

He was silent for a second longer and she was beginning to hope that he might agree – Great idea, darling. Go and see what they still have available. In fact, why don't I come with you? In her head, he had already started down this path, so when his actual reply came, stark and cold, it took her by surprise.

'I don't think so. And what would Mum think?'

And so that was that. Another cold, dark Christmas entombed with his misery.

'Okay,' she said quietly. 'It was just an idea.'

◆ ◆ ◆

The last big brash Christmas that they had enjoyed was in 1973 and Sylvie remembered it with crystal clarity. They had still been in the house in London together with all their lost souls and hangers-on. Jeremy always let it be known that their house was open at Christmas to anyone who was in need of company, and there was usually at least one person who turned up that no one they knew laid claim to. A friend of a friend of a friend, maybe.

It was no bother. As long as the guest didn't try to steal anything they were welcome.

Sylvie and Jeremy would spend what felt like days peeling vegetables and Christine would buzz about looking busy but actually achieving little more than ensuring that bottles were always open. They made decorations out of the bizarrest raw materials. Baubles fashioned from washing-up gloves filled with water, stars carved from root vegetables that always started to rot before Twelfth Night. There were endless paper chains because Sylvie found the process of making them therapeutic and began cutting and sticking loops of paper together long before they needed to be hung up, resulting in miles and miles of the things. There was a special energy to the place. It was always a vibrant house with all the comings and goings, but at Christmas it seemed to light up as if someone had plugged it into the mains.

That year they had been invited for Christmas with Margery and Gerald. Jeremy's sister Jo would be there with her husband Mark and their baby boy John-Paul, who had recently turned two.

'Jo says that John-Paul really understands about Santa now that he's a bit older,' Jeremy said when he came off the phone to her the week before Christmas. 'She says they've decided to go to Mum and Dad's this year, let them make a bit of a fuss of him. Bit of a last-minute thing. I was wondering, how do you fancy going too?'

Sylvie fancied it about as much as hanging out under Blackfriars Bridge on Christmas Day. A couple of days of Margery cooing over John-Paul and making snide comments about how it would be lovely if she had a grandchild from each of her children was more than Sylvie could stomach.

'But we can't,' she said, trying to disguise the panicked squeak to her voice. 'We've invited all those people to come here. We can hardly just say we've changed our mind and let them all down.'

'I'm sure they wouldn't mind,' Jeremy replied.

'Of course they would!' Sylvie objected. 'They're all looking forward to it. I'm looking forward to it. I've ordered two turkeys from the butchers' and everything. What would we do with those? And what about Christine? She'll have nowhere to go if she can't come here.'

Jeremy twisted his lip as he thought about it. Then he gave a heavy sigh.

'Yes, I suppose you're right.'

Sylvie almost let out a whoop of relief, but managed to hold it in.

'We'll go next year,' she said. 'We can let everyone know that we won't be here in plenty of time so they can all make other arrangements.'

Jeremy was coming back round to the idea of a big riotous Christmas at home. Sylvie could see the light returning to his face.

'Yes,' he agreed.

Best Christmas ever!

46

Donna was still trembling under Michelle's arm when they finally reached the house. She hadn't said a word all the way back. Tina had rattled off a string of questions but when Michelle failed to answer any of them, she'd finally given up and trudged alongside them in silence.

Michelle slipped the key into the lock and opened the door. They had left the Christmas tree lights on when they'd gone out and now the garish, cheerful brightness felt horribly out of place. Michelle's first instinct was to switch them off, as if someone had died, but immediately decided against it. This conversation had to be as natural as it could be and extra drama of any kind wouldn't help. To that end, she needed to get rid of Tina. She and Donna needed to be on their own.

She gave Tina a meaningful stare and nodded at the door. Tina stared back as if to say, If you think I'm missing this then you're barmy.

'Tina. Would you mind going upstairs,' Michelle said softly but quite clearly. 'I want to talk to Donna on her own.'

'But I should be here,' objected Tina stroppily. 'This affects me too, you know.'

'Please, Tina,' said Michelle, and Tina let out a huff and headed towards the door, muttering under her breath.

When she had gone, Michelle put her arm around Donna and led her to the sofa.

'Sit down,' she said. 'We need to talk about what just happened with your dad.'

Donna did as she was asked, unnervingly compliant.

'What did he mean, Mum?' she asked as soon as her bottom hit the sofa. 'When he said I wasn't his baby? What did he mean by that?'

'He was just drunk,' replied Michelle, hating herself that she was deflecting, but not quite ready to voice to Donna what she had been hiding for so many years.

'He was, but he knew what he was saying,' Donna replied. 'He meant it.' She looked up at Michelle, her dark eyes brimming with tears.

There was no way out of this, Michelle could see that. Inwardly she cursed Dean for putting her in this horrible position, but she gave Donna what she hoped was a reassuring smile.

'I didn't have an affair,' she began. 'He's wrong about that. I wouldn't. I love your dad.'

Something that might have been relief washed across Donna's face.

Michelle swallowed. 'But the thing about the swap,' she continued.

Donna was instantly on edge again, her face taut with the strain of waiting to hear her fate.

'I have to confess that I did wonder about that.'

'Why?' she asked. 'Why did you wonder?'

She looked so desperate, every part of her face begging Michelle to say that it was a misunderstanding, that Dean had been messing about in some ill-judged Christmas joke.

But Michelle couldn't. She had to be straight with Donna. She wished with everything she had that it wasn't true, but she had no choice. Dean had boxed her into a corner.

It was so hard, though. It was difficult enough saying out loud that you thought the baby you were bringing up wasn't yours. It was immeasurably harder to explain it to the baby herself.

'Well,' Michelle began. She took a deep breath, bit her lip, searching for strength from somewhere inside herself. 'When I went into hospital, I had a baby girl.'

She paused. Normally when someone was telling a story like this they would say, 'When you were born' or 'When I had you'. Yet these words were not available to Michelle. It felt wrong not to be able to offer Donna this simple comfort, but she had started this now and she needed to be completely honest.

'The night she was born,' Michelle continued, ignoring the awkwardness of the pronouns, 'another baby girl with dark hair and a similar birth weight was born as well, and the mother was put in the same room as me. My baby was good as gold and was sleeping but the other baby was fussing and wouldn't settle, so the midwife came and took them both away to look after them in the nursery.'

Michelle was looking straight into Donna's eyes as she spoke and she could read the fear in them, see the colour slowly draining from her face.

'The next day the midwife brought our babies back and then pretty much straight away your dad arrived with the other three to take us home.'

The baby in this part of the story had definitely been Donna and Michelle relaxed a little as she continued.

'But when I got home, the baby, you, didn't look as much like your dad as the one I'd held straight after giving birth. And they had lost the little outfit, the one I'd dressed my baby in. And you were so quiet. You barely cried. The other three had all screamed their heads off from the get-go but you were a dream child. It all felt a bit strange, to be honest, and so after a day or two I started to wonder if maybe I had got the other lady's baby and she had mine.'

Donna put a hand up to stop her. 'But you said that your baby, the one you had in the hospital, was quiet and good as gold,' she said. There was an urgency to her voice and her eyes were wide. 'Well, that sounds just like me, doesn't it? So that must mean that I was the one that they took to the nursery.'

Michelle nodded but her brow wrinkled. 'Yes,' she said. 'I thought that to start with. But then as you grew you didn't look anything like your brothers and sisters. And you're so smart. No one in our family has ever been as clever as you are. And the other couple, the parents of the other baby, well, they looked like they had a bob or two and they talked posh, not like me and your dad. It stands to reason that they would have had a smart baby.'

Donna's face fell into a frown.

'No, it doesn't,' she said, desperate to contradict at least one part of what she was hearing. 'We did it in biology. You can have smart kids born to stupid parents. It happens all the time. Not that you and Dad are stupid, but you know what I mean.'

Michelle shrugged. 'Well, something didn't feel quite right to me,' she said.

Donna shuddered and squeezed her lips together, trying to stop her emotions escaping. Her reaction was so like her. She was trying desperately hard to be brave, Michelle thought, but she was too young to have to deal with what she was hearing. Then again, were you ever grown-up enough to have your world blown apart?

'So, what did you do?' asked Donna. 'When you thought I wasn't yours.'

'I went back to the hospital and I told them, but they thought it was the baby blues or something. I don't know. They didn't believe me anyway. And they wouldn't give me the address of the woman in the next bed, so there was nothing I could do other than just bring you back home and get on with bringing you up the best I could.'

Tears were streaming down Donna's cheeks now. She tried to wipe them away with the back of her hand but as fast as she moved them they reappeared, her cheeks glistening in the lights. Michelle reached for a loo roll that was sitting on the carpet by the sofa and tore off a handful of sheets, passing them to Donna. Donna blew her nose and sniffed.

'But I loved you, Dons,' she added. 'I've always loved you.'

The words sounded so hollow in light of what she had just told her.

Donna didn't respond to that. She didn't shrug, but she might as well have done.

'And what about Dad?' she asked after a moment or two. 'What did he think had happened?'

Michelle moved across and put her arm around Donna, squeezing her into her own body, but Donna pulled away. That stung. Donna had never rejected her before. Michelle dropped her arm.

'Your dad never believed you'd been swapped,' she said, and a tiny smile crept on to Donna's lips. 'But then he got it into his head that you were mine but not his.'

The smile was gone.

'What? Like you had an affair or something?'

Michelle nodded. She could feel tears building up behind her own eyes and blinked hard so they wouldn't trickle out.

'Is that why he left us?' Donna asked.

Michelle nodded again. 'Well, not the only reason. But once he started thinking like that, something between us just broke and we couldn't fix it. We tried, well, I did. But it was no good.'

Michelle's heart was hurting, actually physically hurting. Was this what it felt like to have a heart attack, she wondered? She put her hand to her chest, pressed hard to try and make the pain go away, but it stayed right where it was.

Donna sat still for a moment, her eyes fixed on the floor, and didn't speak. She was taking it all in, Michelle knew, processing. She had always responded to new information like this, ever since she'd been a very small child. Quietly, thoughtfully.

She was quiet for so long that Michelle was on the verge of trying to make her speak. Then she said, 'And what do you think now? Do you still think I belong to someone else?'

This was it. The million-dollar question; the one that Michelle had asked herself over and over. She reached and took Donna's hand in hers, squeezing it tightly. It was cold and felt clammy against her own.

Michelle found Donna's eyes and held her gaze. She took a deep breath.

'No,' she lied. 'Of course not. You're our child.'

47

Donna stood up slowly, shrugging off Michelle's attempts to grasp hold of her.

'I don't believe you,' she said. 'You always were a shit liar. You know that I'm not yours. You've known since the start. Why else did you go to the hospital and try and swap me back? At least Dad's being honest with me. It might have taken him sixteen years but he got there in the end. But you . . .'

The look that Donna threw Michelle was like nothing she had ever seen on her child's face before. There was hurt there and disbelief, but mostly there was contempt. It pierced right into Michelle's heart, as sharp as a spear.

'But Donna, you don't understand . . .' Michelle tried, desperate for something other than this disdain, but Donna wasn't listening.

'Shut up!' she screamed. 'I don't want to hear any more.'

She was making for the door. Michelle stood up and grabbed for Donna's hand to try and pull her back, but Donna wrenched herself free.

'Leave me alone! Don't touch me! I hate you!'

'Donna, wait. Please don't go,' Michelle pleaded. 'It's horrible that you've had to find out like this but—'

'You'd have preferred that I never found out at all,' Donna spat, her face contorted by her anger. 'You would have let me carry on, never knowing why I'm a misfit. I've always felt like I didn't belong. Do you know that? There's always been something that just didn't feel quite right. But now I know, don't I? I don't belong. And I never have. And you knew and didn't tell me. What kind of person does that? What kind of mother?'

'It wasn't like that,' Michelle began.

'No? Well, that's how it feels at this end. But, I suppose, if you knew I wasn't really your concern then it starts to make more sense.'

Michelle was wounded by Donna's words but fought on desperately. 'I didn't tell you because I wanted you to grow up safe and happy. And I had no proof. It might all be in my head like your dad thought. Why would I tell you and risk hurting you when none of it might be true?'

'Because that's what any decent human being would have done, any decent mother.'

Then Donna threw open the door and charged up the stairs.

Michelle shouted after her, 'But I love you, Donna. I always have, right from the start.'

But it was futile. She couldn't make her listen, let alone understand.

Michelle fell back on to the sofa, her head in her hands. She heard Donna's bedroom door open and then slam shut with such violence that the walls of the house shook.

Almost at once, Tina was there.

'Shit. What's happened?' she asked.

Michelle shook her head but didn't look up.

'Go to bed,' she said.

'But what's going on? What's up with Donna? Mum, you have to tell me.'

But Michelle had had enough.

'JUST GO TO BED!' she screamed.

But Tina didn't leave. She sat down next to Michelle and slipped an arm around her, squeezing gently.

'It'll be okay, Mum,' she said gently. 'We'll sort it.'

Michelle leaned into her and let go. She sobbed until she had nothing left. She sobbed all the tears that she had been holding in for sixteen years. She sobbed out all her doubts and fears, all the worries about Donna, all the moments she'd spent wondering about where Leonora was, what she was doing. She let it all flow out of her until she was empty.

◆　◆　◆

'We should go to bed,' Tina said when Michelle had finally stopped trembling.

'You go. I'll be up in a minute.'

Tina eyed her doubtfully for a moment. 'Okay, but don't stay up too long. You need to get some sleep.'

She let Michelle go and then stood up and headed for the stairs.

'Night then, Mum,' she said, and then was gone.

Mum. Such a simple word, so easily used.

And yet so very, very complicated.

'Night, love,' replied Michelle, her voice cracked and broken.

Michelle knew Tina was right. She should go to bed, but she wouldn't sleep so what would be the point? Instead, she wandered into the kitchen, picked things up and then put them down again. There were the dregs of a bottle of wine left and for a moment she contemplated drinking them, but then thought better of it. What would that achieve? Instead, she filled the kettle and flicked the switch. She didn't want tea either, but she had to do something, anything to stop her from thinking.

It was no good, though. Everything was whirling round in her head. How Donna had looked at her, the things she had said. Would she really hate her? Michelle wouldn't blame her if she did. She probably deserved that.

But it felt so unfair. None of this was Michelle's fault. She had tried so hard to do the right thing. She had asked questions and then, when no one seemed to believe her, she had worked to bring Donna up just as she had the others. She'd swear that she hadn't done anything differently for any of her children. Any differences there were between them came from Donna herself.

Yet, despite all that, Donna had said that she'd always known she didn't belong.

Was that Michelle's fault?

Had she really been treating Donna differently for all those years without realising?

Had her own doubts coloured everything?

How would she ever know?

God, she could kill Dean, she really could. What had he done?

The kettle boiled and she made the tea blindly without really being conscious of what she was doing. Then she sat down at the kitchen table, cupping the mug in her hands and breathing in the steam.

It was no wonder that Donna was angry and upset, Michelle told herself, trying to square it all in her head. It was so much to take on board, but maybe once she'd had a chance to think about it, to process it a bit, she would come round. She would see that Michelle had been in an impossible situation and had done her best. Surely she would? And now that everything was all out in the open there would be no need for it to be hidden. Perhaps they could move beyond it, forget that it had ever been a part of Donna's story. After all, to all intents and purposes Donna was her daughter now, whether she was biologically or not.

Except, Donna didn't know all of it. There was still one crucial part of the tale that Michelle had held back. Her mind tripped to that day eleven years earlier, to the large, messy house at the top of the hill, to the woman who had sat, catatonic, in the face of Michelle's claims. She hadn't told Donna that, had she? She had failed to mention that she knew the other mother's name, or her first name at least, and where she lived.

Although, the part that even Michelle didn't know, the part that had haunted her ever since she'd left the woman staring into space, was what had happened to Sylvie next. Michelle had strolled into her life and dropped her little bombshell, but what had the consequences of that act been?

Michelle had no idea. She'd never let herself think about Sylvie again in case her visit had caused some irreparable harm. Michelle hadn't been sure that she could deal with the guilt on top of everything else, so she had just buried the experience at the back of her mind and left it there to rot.

But what should she do now? Ought she to tell Donna where the woman who might be her mother was, assuming that she was still alive and well and living in the same house?

Or should she keep that to herself?

Yet again Michelle found that she had no idea what to do for the best.

48

When Michelle woke up the next morning she found herself on her sofa and not in her bed. She was chilled to the bone and had a crick in her neck to go with her deepening sense of dread. Turning over and groaning as her spine complained, she listened for signs of life in the house, but there were none. She had no idea what time it was, but it was no longer dark outside. The Christmas tree lights were still burning, their bulbs a pale imitation of their night-time selves in the stark December morning.

She sat up gingerly but decided that her body had survived the experience without too much damage. She hoped her relationship with Donna could say the same. Would she have calmed down a little by now? Certainly, it wasn't in Donna's nature to stay angry about anything for too long, but then she had never had to face anything like this before. Who knew how she might react over the coming days?

Well, there was only one way to find out. Michelle stood up. Her mouth felt furry and she could tell her eyelashes were sticky with yesterday's mascara. She must look a sight, but that was the least of her concerns. She needed to go and check on Donna before she did anything for herself.

She made her way up the stairs and knocked lightly on Donna's door. Nothing.

'Donna,' she whispered, not wanting to alert Tina to the fact that she was awake.

There was no sound from Donna's room.

'Donna? Are you up?' she said, a little bit louder this time, but there was still no reply.

Gently she pushed the door handle down, flinching slightly as it creaked, and inched the door wide. She had no idea what mood Donna would be in and her heart thumped hard against her ribs as her anxiety grew. It would be all right as long as Donna didn't look at her like she had done the night before. She could deal with another row, even a humdinger of one. It might clear the air between them. What she couldn't bear, though, was the rejection that she'd seen in Donna's face. That had hurt more than anything Donna had said.

It was still dark in the room, the curtains drawn so that only a dull filtered light made it through. The duvet was ruffled so at first Michelle assumed that Donna was still in bed, but when she looked more closely it was too flat to have anyone asleep underneath it.

In two strides Michelle was at the bedside, from where it was immediately obvious that Donna wasn't there. Her head spun one way and then the other as she searched, but the room was tiny. It was clear she was there on her own.

Where was Donna? Michelle had been asleep downstairs, so surely she would have heard someone opening and closing the front door. Then again, maybe not. Might Donna be in the kitchen? It was difficult to see how she would've got there without Michelle coming across her, but it was possible.

Michelle turned on her heel and raced down the stairs, taking them two at a time, but there was no sign of Donna there either. She was definitely not in the house.

Her running about must have woken Tina, who appeared in the kitchen moments later.

'Did you get much sleep?' she asked, making her way across the room to flick the kettle on.

Michelle shook her head, distracted. 'Donna's not here. She must have gone out. Where will she be? Do you think she's all right?'

'Donna?' replied Tina. 'God, yes! She's always all right. We could get the four-minute warning for the end of the world and our Donna would take it in her stride. She was pissed off last night, but it'll all be water under the bridge today. You'll see. She's probably just gone to buy milk or something.'

Seizing on this idea, Michelle swung the fridge door open and then was disappointed to see two full cartons nestling in the door.

'So, what's it all about, then?' asked Tina, fishing two mugs from the cupboard and standing them on the counter. 'Is it right what Dad said?'

Bloody Dean, Michelle thought. What had he started with his stupid drunken one-upmanship? It was bad enough that she'd had to explain things to Donna, but was she now going to have to have the full post-mortem with Tina as well? At least Tina would pass the story on to her brothers, she assumed, saving her from having to tell it for a third and fourth time.

'No,' Michelle said decisively. 'It wasn't right. I did not have an affair and I most definitely didn't get pregnant by someone else.'

A fleeting look skittered across Tina's face. Michelle knew it was disappointment. Tina always had loved a drama, and it appeared that a drama at the expense of her own family's stability would fit the bill just as well as any other.

'So why did he say you did?' she asked, bold as brass.

It really was none of Tina's business, Michelle thought, but she knew that if she took that line Tina would only assume that she was lying and that Dean was right.

'There was a time,' Michelle began, 'a while ago, back when Donna was a baby, when I thought that she might not have been ours. Your dad didn't believe me and over the years he managed to switch that into meaning that I was covering up an affair, which I wasn't.'

'Not yours how, exactly?' Tina asked.

Michelle closed her eyes.

'It doesn't matter,' she said, and tried to shut the conversation down by making the tea.

'Like hell it doesn't,' replied Tina. 'Come on. Tell me.'

So Michelle began the whole sorry tale again with Tina nodding and clarifying things as she went. When she got to the end, she blew out a long breath and looked Tina in the eye.

'So,' she said. 'That's it.'

Tina leaned back in her chair, lacing her fingers in front of her stomach.

'What a load of bollocks,' she said. 'Of course she's your kid, yours and dad's, I mean. I agree she doesn't look much like you but she's the double of Damien. And she's calm under pressure which is just like you. And she can sing like me.'

Was she right? Michelle had spent so long looking for the differences between her children that she hadn't noticed that in many ways they were the same.

Tina was on a roll now. 'I'll give you that she's brainier than the rest of us,' she continued. 'But I can do stuff that the boys can't do, and the other way around. We're all different. So this swapped in the hospital crap, that's completely mad, Mum. Stark raving bonkers. That's just post-natal depression talking which isn't surprising given that you were trying to bring us all up and when you were so young yourself.'

Tina paused for breath, her forehead creased in thought before she asked, 'Is that really why Dad left? All that rubbish he said last night about you having a bit on the side? Was that it?'

Michelle nodded, her eyes filming over with unshed tears.

Tina's jaw tightened and her eyes narrowed. 'Then he's more spineless than I thought he was,' she spat. 'Anyone can see you'd never have done that. It's just not in you, Mum. What a moron! I've got a good mind to go round there . . .'

Michelle put a hand up. 'Stop! Don't do that. You'll only make things worse. That ship has sailed, and I'm okay with things the way they are. What's important now is that we find Donna and make sure that she knows that she's loved and wanted. She needs to know that she's my daughter.'

49

Donna sat on the iron railings of the footbridge and dangled her legs over the water. Ever since she'd been small she'd loved this place. She must have sat there for hours over the years, at first with her friend Lucy and then later, when she'd grown out of having an invisible friend, on her own. This was where she came to think, to mull things over, plotting and planning her life out as it spread ahead of her. So, when she'd fled from the house this was the obvious place to come.

She had lost track of the time but had she been here for an hour now? Two maybe? She didn't know. Her eyes felt swollen from crying and the skin on her face was tight where the salt still sat on it, but there were no tears left.

She was empty.

Hollow.

Numb.

She couldn't find a way of responding to what she'd learned that felt big enough. Carl might have put a brick through a window or two if it had been happening to him, but that wasn't her way. She thought about screaming, long and loud. Wasn't that what you did when emotions were too big to handle? But when she opened her mouth to try, nothing had come out. It felt fake and contrived, and she caught herself worrying that people might think she was being attacked and come running to help. Tina would have just let rip, she knew. She would have screamed the houses down. Tina was all about the drama, but she wasn't Tina either.

Who was she? That was what she really needed to know.

Donna let her eyes drift in and out of focus. It made the world go blurry and that suited her just fine. She didn't want to be in the world right now. It wasn't what she thought it was. It didn't feel safe.

Then again, she couldn't live her life in soft focus. That was no solution. She pulled her vision back.

She'd always loved this bridge partly because of how far away you could see. Facing one way there were views up towards the cathedral in the distance, and in the other you could see the floodlights of the football stadium, standing sentinel over the rows and rows of terraced streets. Not that she could see much now. One or two houses had lights still shining inside, but mainly the streets were dark, lit only by the soft yellow glow of the streetlamps.

Beneath her feet the water in the dyke was black, calm and still. It rarely moved much unless they'd had rain. The dyke had been dug in Saxon times. She knew that because she'd looked it up in the school library. It was there to stop the river flooding. The dyke was full now, in the dead of winter, but in the summer she'd been born, in the great heatwave of 1976, the dyke had been as dry as a bone. Her dad had told her that. You could walk right along the bottom of it, he'd said, and never get your feet even damp.

Her dad. Donna felt the tears start to gather in her eyes yet again and her throat thickened. Was he actually her dad or just some random man that fate had placed in her path? What about her mum and her brothers and Tina? Were any of them who she thought they were? What was she supposed to do with the idea that her presence in the family she had always known might have been a mistake? How could you have a family for sixteen years and then suddenly lose them all in the space of a couple of hours? Donna couldn't get her head around it.

The metal bars of the barrier were seeping the warmth out of her. Her hands were so cold that she couldn't bear to hold on any longer. She pulled her coat sleeves down to cover them but it was probably too late to warm them up, and the cold was permeating her jeans too, her thighs numb. If she didn't move soon they'd find her in the morning frozen to the spot.

Shivering, she got down and set off walking, huffing her breath out on to her frozen hands in a feeble attempt to get some heat into them. She didn't know where she was going. It didn't matter anyway. Nothing mattered any more.

The streets were quiet. Christmas lights burned in a few of the windows and there was the odd cat prowling, but no people. This was how Donna liked it. These were her streets and she knew them like the back of her hand, each shortcut and alleyway. She could navigate them all. That's what happened when you belonged somewhere. You could be there at any time of day and night and always feel safe.

But now they were telling her that she didn't belong, that these weren't her streets at all. She had landed in them by accident rather than by design. If what her mum had said was true, she should have been living somewhere else, have a totally different life with totally different people. Was she even called Donna? She couldn't be. The chances of two babies in next-door cots being given the same name was infinitesimally small.

All of a sudden, there was nothing to grasp hold of. No part of her life was secure. She felt completely untethered from reality, like Major Tom in the David Bowie song, just floating further and further away without any hope of getting back to the life she knew.

And it was terrifying.

A fox crossed the road in front of her, its eyes glowing red in the light from the streetlamps. It stopped and stood stock-still and stared warily: friend or foe? Donna took in its brindled coat, its white bib and unfeasibly fluffy tail. Everyone knew there were foxes around but you rarely saw them unless you were out late at night, or early as it was now. Donna had seen a couple over the years but never as close up as this one. She could even make out its black whiskers.

They stood there, eyeing one another, and then the fox, as if it had lost interest in her, sauntered off across the road and down an alleyway. Donna swallowed back yet more tears. Even the fox didn't want her.

She was of no consequence to anyone.

Maybe it would be best if she just left home so that no one would need to deal with her ever again. There was a squat on the road behind theirs. Donna walked past it on the way to the corner shop. The windows were boarded up but there were people living inside. She'd heard someone playing a guitar once, an upbeat country number with a catchy rhythm. She had always felt sorry for the occupants. Where were their families? Why had they ended up living in a derelict hovel? But when she'd heard that music it had made her think about things differently. They didn't sound miserable. In fact, they seemed to be having a better time than her as she trudged to pick up some milk for her mum.

She could find a squat of her own. She had some money saved, and she could finish her A levels from anywhere. No one at school would care where she was living as long as she handed her essays in on time. Perhaps she could knock on the door of the squat round the corner. Was that how it worked? Would they let her in out of some kind of displaced person's solidarity?

But running wasn't the solution. Donna knew that. No matter how lost she was feeling right now, she was loved. Despite the row with her mum last night, despite all of it, of that she had no doubt. Even though it appeared that they had all been living a lie, she had been cherished and cared for always.

Surely that spoke volumes, the fact she'd had no inkling whatsoever of any of it? Either that or she had been particularly unobservant, and she didn't think that was true.

So that had to be a good thing, didn't it? She had grown up in a house surrounded by love and affection with brothers and a sister who looked out for her. Yes, she might always have felt a little bit set apart from them, but it hadn't been a bad feeling. That was simply part of who she was and it didn't change the basic fact.

She was loved.

Donna stood still and let this thought cement itself in her mind. She didn't know what the solution was, but she knew what it wasn't. Running away would solve nothing.

The sky was lightening now as the new day approached. Traffic rumbled in the distance and she could hear voices as people began their Sundays.

She turned on the spot and set back off the way she had come.

50

By the time Donna got back to the house she was so cold that she could no longer control her jaw. It vibrated violently along with the rest of her, hands shivering so much that she struggled to get her key into the lock. She was about to give up and just knock when the door flew open and Michelle rushed over, hurling arms around her and squeezing the breath from her.

'God, Donna, where've you been? I was so worried. I didn't know what to think when you weren't in your bed.'

Michelle pulled away and reached out to touch her cheek with the back of her hand.

'You're frozen solid. You'll catch your death. Come in and we'll get you warm. Tina! Donna's back. Grab the duvet off her bed and bring it down here, will you?'

Michelle steered her into the front room without releasing her which made walking awkward. Donna could feel her mum's body heat seeping into her through her clothes, and she shivered even harder.

'Look at you! Your lips are blue! How long have you been out there? Quick. Sit down. I'll get you a cup of tea. Tina! Stick the kettle on.'

'Give us a minute,' shouted Tina, emerging seconds later from upstairs almost entirely engulfed by Donna's duvet. 'I've only got one pair of hands.'

She dropped the duvet on top of Donna.

'Where've you been?' she said, not unkindly. 'Mum was worried sick. And I was a bit too.' She grinned at her. 'Bloody idiot,' she added, thumping Donna affectionately on her arm. 'Running off in the early hours. What kind of nutter does that?'

'Just make her some tea, Tina,' interrupted her mum. Or Michelle? Donna had no idea what she was supposed to call her, but settled on Mum purely because that was easiest.

Her mum sat down next to her, fussing with the duvet so that only Donna's head remained uncovered.

'Where did you go? What have you been doing?'

Donna's jaw had finally stopped shivering so she was able to speak. 'I've just been wandering about,' she said flatly. 'I saw a fox. A big one. Just standing there in the middle of the road like he owned the place.' Why was she talking about foxes when there were much more important things to be said?

'They're a bloody nuisance, those foxes. Always in the bins. But are you okay?'

The concern on her mum's face was so deep that Donna immediately felt guilty about causing it, but then she pushed the thought aside. She had nothing to feel bad about. None of this was her fault.

'I'm so sorry about last night,' her mum went on. 'I didn't mean to upset you like that. I just . . .'

She needed Donna to say she was forgiven. Donna knew it. And she looked as if she had barely slept either, her eyes dark and her skin sallow, anxiety coming off her in waves. Donna noticed her jagged little movements, each one skittish and unsure, and her voice trying oh so hard to sound normal, yet being so wide of the mark.

But Donna wasn't there yet. Yes, she'd come back, but that was mainly because she didn't have any other options. But forgiveness . . .

She kept her eyes low and focused on the carpet. She couldn't look at her mum. Partly that was because she knew her resolve would weaken if she did and she wasn't ready for that, but mainly she was scared of what she might find in her face. That face had been more familiar to her than any other, a place of safety throughout her life. Would she ever be able to look into it again without searching it for some shadow of her own features?

'I'm so sorry, Donna,' her mum tried again. 'I never wanted you to find out like that.'

'To find out like that, or to find out at all?' Donna asked bitterly, unable to resist looking up. She needed to see her mum's face, to judge what was going on inside from what she displayed on the outside.

Her mum blew out her lips. 'Honestly? I don't know. I mean, I definitely didn't want you to find out like that. I'll kill your dad. I really will. But finding out at all . . . ? I don't know.'

Her mum's eyes were swimming with tears. She squeezed them tightly closed, trying to blink them clear.

'I just never knew what to do for the best,' she continued. 'It's only ever been me, you see, that thought there might be something not right. No one else noticed. Your dad said I was mad. That's how he came up with that stupid affair story. It was the only way he could deal with what I was saying. But why would I tell you something so devastating unless I was absolutely certain that I was right?'

Donna could see that, and looking at how she had reacted to the news last night, her mum had probably been wise to keep it to herself for all those years. But it was out now. There was no putting the genie back in the bottle.

Donna felt a slight lightening inside her. They hadn't all known and kept her out of the loop. No one had been talking about her behind her back, making jokes at her expense. It had been a secret.

'I'm sorry I stormed off,' she said quietly. 'It was the shock. I didn't know what to do. But then, when I was out there, I didn't know what to do either. It's like I'm lost. I don't know where I am any more. Or who I am either?'

Tears stung her eyes again and, driven purely by instinct, she reached her arms out from under the duvet to let her mum hold her. Her mum pulled her in close, wrapping her and the duvet into a hug, and rocked her slowly backwards and forwards, one hand stroking her hair. Donna felt very small, and very safe.

'There's no need to be sorry, Donna. None at all. I'm the one who should be sorry for causing all this mess with my stupid insecurities.'

'Was it my fault Dad left?' she asked, the thought just occurring to her. That was all she needed, the break-up of their marriage on top of everything else.

'No, no, of course it wasn't,' her mum replied quickly. 'Don't be thinking that. It was just one of those sad things that happens sometimes. Nobody was to blame, and most definitely not you.'

Donna leaned harder into her mum, as if she was trying to meld their bodies into one. They continued to rock gently.

Tina appeared then with three steaming mugs of tea that she set down on the coffee table. Donna pulled away from her mum and wiped a hand across her eyes. Tina looked as if she was going to settle herself down in one of the armchairs but her mum gave her a look.

'What?!' said Tina indignantly. 'Am I not allowed to be part of this? I do live here too, you know.'

'It's not that,' began her mum. 'It's just that Donna and me still have a lot to discuss, and I think it would be better if we did that on our own.'

A lot to discuss? Donna's ears pricked up. What else was there? Surely they had covered it all? Her mum had said that she didn't know whether she was right or not about the swap thing so that was that boxed off too.

Tina let out a harrumph, stood up and picked up her tea.

'Okay,' she said grudgingly. 'I'll go and have a bath, but then I want stuff to get back to normal around here. It's nearly Christmas, for God's sake. We can't be doing with all this doom and gloom hanging over us. Get it thrashed out between you, and then we can forget all about it.'

She left the room, closing the door firmly behind her.

As soon as she was gone, Donna turned to her mum, her heart beating hard behind her ribs.

'What is it you're not telling me?' she asked. 'What else do you know?'

51

Donna watched as her mum picked up her mug and blew lightly on the steaming tea. It was obvious that she was playing for time, but Donna had nowhere to go. She could wait here for as long as it took.

Michelle let her gaze drift up to the ceiling and then back down to Donna. She pulled at the skin of her knuckles with her teeth. Donna wasn't sure she had ever seen her look so uncomfortable and she didn't like it. It didn't bode well for whatever was coming next.

'Whatever it is, Mum, I can handle it,' she said, trying to sound reassuring. She wasn't sure that she could, though. As her mum built herself up to speaking, Donna tried to imagine what else there could possibly be to come out, but the thought made her feel sick.

'The thing is . . .' Michelle began. 'And I don't want you to think badly of me. I was just doing what I thought was right. You have to understand that, Donna.'

Donna nodded furiously. She would understand anything if only her mum would hurry up and tell her what it was.

'So, one day . . . It was when you were five . . . I was up at the top end of town. Up by the cathedral, you know.'

Donna nodded again.

'And I saw this woman. I wasn't sure to start with. I thought it was, but I couldn't be certain.'

'Be certain about what, Mum?' asked Donna. Her pulse was throbbing in her temples, forcing her blood through her veins, but it felt as if she was barely sucking in enough air to keep her heart beating.

'That it was her.'

Donna wanted to scream. It was so frustrating. She had no idea what her mum was trying to tell her and the facts were dripping out as slowly as treacle from a tin, but there was no point trying to hurry her along. She just needed to be patient, follow the story at the pace that Michelle felt comfortable telling it. She swallowed down her exasperation.

'So, I followed her,' Michelle continued. 'She was just walking in a big circle through the streets, but eventually she ended up back at this beautiful house. Huge, it was. Dead posh. Right next to the castle. I decided that that must be where she lived so I waited outside. And I was going to go and knock on the door, but I lost my nerve. I needed to think about what I was doing before I went barging in there, make sure I knew what I wanted to say, you know?'

Donna didn't know at all and she was all out of patience. 'What are you trying to tell me, Mum? Because I'm not getting it. Who was she, this woman? Why were you following her? You're not making any sense.'

Michelle put her hands over her face and bent her head.

'It was *the* woman,' she said through her fingers. 'The woman from the bed next to mine in hospital.'

Adrenaline made Donna's scalp tingle. She held her breath as she processed what her mum was telling her.

'So she was . . . ?' she began.

Michelle lowered her hands and looked straight into Donna's eyes. 'Yeah. If I'm right about the baby swap thing, then she was your real mother.'

Donna leapt up out of her seat. The duvet fell to the floor and she nearly sent her mum's cup of tea flying. It was an involuntary reaction. She didn't know what to do with this new information. Part of her wanted her mum to stop talking right then so they could forget there was any possibility that she was somebody else's daughter.

But the other part was thirsty for knowledge and so very, very curious.

'What did you do?' she asked, her voice coming out as barely a whisper.

Michelle shook her head. 'Nothing that day. I was too shaken up. I just watched her go in and then I came home to think about everything.'

'And then . . . ?' Donna breathed, hardly daring to ask the question.

'And then we went back,' Michelle said.

'We?'

'Yes. I took you with me. I don't know why. I wasn't going to, but then you wanted to come up to town and for a mad moment I thought it might help if you were there. Actually, I don't know what I thought really. I was hoping that if I had a little girl with me she might not just slam the door in my face.'

'And?' Donna was hardly breathing at all now, snatches of air making it into her lungs without any help from her.

Michelle swallowed. 'Well, we knocked at the door and the man answered, the husband. I recognised him from the hospital too. He was called Jeremy. I remembered that. She's called Sylvie, the woman. But she wasn't there. She'd gone away. So I said to say that I'd called and then we left.'

Donna felt the disappointment rush through her, although she wasn't sure what she was disappointed about. If the woman, Sylvie, had been there and had spoken to them and her mum had never said anything about it then wouldn't that mean that she'd been covering up an even worse secret? That would make everything ten times more awful. But luckily the two women had never met, so that was okay.

Michelle turned to face her, looked carefully into her eyes. Donna tried to read what was going on behind them but she couldn't find enough to grasp on to. There seemed to be new lines in her mum's face since yesterday. Was that even possible?

'Do you remember that day?' Michelle asked, cutting through Donna's thoughts. 'Do you remember us going?'

Donna trawled through her memory banks for something that might match what she was being told but found nothing. She shook her head. Michelle let out her breath, her shoulders sagging in relief.

'That's good at least,' she said. 'I always worried that I might have made a massive mistake, dragging you up there with me.'

This wasn't everything. Donna could tell from the inflection in her mum's voice that she hadn't finished yet, and she braced herself for what was coming next. It was obvious from the way Michelle was pulling at the skin on her throat that she still had more to tell and was worried about doing it.

They must have met, then, Donna thought, not when she was there but at some other time. The two women who might be her mother had met to talk about her and no one had ever said a word. Donna couldn't process how this made her feel, but this wasn't the time to focus on that. She needed to be told all the facts before they slipped back into the dark recesses of her mum's head.

'So, did you go back?' she asked. 'Did you try again?'

Michelle gave a tight little nod.

Donna's stomach flipped and for a second she tasted bile. She willed herself to hold on to control. Could she hear whatever it was that Michelle was so reluctant to tell her? She wasn't sure, but she knew she had no choice if she ever wanted to live in peace again.

'And she was there the next time,' Michelle continued. 'She invited me in. She was so kind and friendly. And I went into her house and I told her what I thought had happened.'

Donna didn't think she could bear it any more.

'And??' she asked, unable to keep the frustration out of her voice now.

'And, well, nothing,' replied Michelle, her eyes meeting Donna's squarely once again. 'I told her and she . . . Well, she kind of went into a trance or something. She just sat there. She didn't say a word. Nothing. It was like I wasn't even there. I didn't know what to do so in the end I just left.'

'You mean she didn't say anything about me?' asked Donna. 'Not a word?'

Michelle nodded. 'It was really weird. I assumed she'd gone into some kind of shock. I couldn't get her to respond to me at all, so I just left. I felt awful afterwards, in case I'd done some real damage just barging in there like that, but I didn't know what else to do.'

Donna didn't know what to make of any of it.

'And you never went back?' she asked.

Michelle shook her head. 'I left her my address, I wrote it down on a piece of paper for her, but I never heard anything so I assumed that she thought I was mad, just like your dad did. I decided to put the whole thing out of my mind and forget about it.'

She hadn't forgotten about it though. Donna could tell. It had been eating away at her all this time. Donna wondered how she had been able to bear it.

Then something else occurred to her and her heart began to bang in her chest all over again.

'But you know where the house is? You could show me?'

The colour drained from Michelle's face and Donna immediately felt horrible for asking, but then Michelle nodded.

'Yes. I know exactly where it is.'

52

There were Christmas cards lying on the doormat when Sylvie went downstairs to make Jeremy a cup of tea. Six in total; two in cheerful red envelopes and all of them with a serene image of the Angel Gabriel, that year's Christmas stamp, stuck in the corner.

Usually Sylvie enjoyed the Christmas cards. She wrote them with gusto, generally when Jeremy was out, filling every available corner of space with their news and hoping that the ones she got in return would be similarly informative. Who wanted a Christmas card that was simply signed by the sender?

But somehow this year her secret and quite disloyal enthusiasm for the festive period had waned. She wasn't sure whether it was because Leo wouldn't be there with them or simply because after so many years of having to suppress her excitement it had finally given up and gone to spend Christmas with someone more deserving of its attention.

She was tempted to just ignore the cards, leaving them there on the mat, but then Jeremy would probably just drop them into the bin unopened and she couldn't have that. So she bent down and scooped them up, taking them with her to the kitchen.

It was the work of a moment to identify the senders once she could see the handwriting. They were people whose paths had crossed with theirs over the years, mainly from their days in

London, others from Leo's former school in Lincoln but who lived far enough from them to merit a stamp. When she saw the final one a smile came to her lips – Christine. Her lack of enthusiasm dismissed at least for the moment, Sylvie slipped her finger under the flap and tore the envelope open.

The front showed a picture of a reindeer that appeared to be answering a call of nature and the words Special Delivery in glittery letters across the top. Sylvie laughed to herself and opened the card.

Saw this. Thought of you. Everyone needs a bit of reindeer shit for Xmas. Hope all's well. I know you'll say no but I'll ask anyway. Do you want to come to mine for the festivities? Leave misery guts behind to wallow. You come here and we'll drink gin and laugh at Only Fools and Horses like it's actually funny.

Merry Xmas and all that crap,

C x

Christine invited her for Christmas every year and Sylvie had always declined, citing a need to stay by Jeremy in case he needed her, but this time she was sorely tempted to go. What was keeping her here? Jeremy would barely show his face until it was all over and Leo wasn't coming home. Why shouldn't she spend a couple of days with Christine? Jeremy might even welcome the time to himself. She knew she most definitely would.

Feeling her resolve strengthening, she slipped Christine's card back into the envelope and went to talk to Jeremy.

He was, as ever, in his studio. Sylvie knocked lightly on the door and then went in without waiting for a response. The Christmas commissions all duly dispatched, he seemed to be working on something different, and was standing staring at his easel, three paintbrushes in his hands and a pencil behind his ear.

Sylvie went and stood behind him to take in the work. It was a jumble of bodies, all rendered in simple lines and with the rounded edges of cartoon figures but painted in dark greens and blues, the colours at odds with the subject matter. It reminded her of Keith Haring's work and she pushed down the thought that her husband only ever managed to create in the style of another.

'That's interesting,' she said. 'New?'

Jeremy nodded his head. 'Been wanting to try it out for a while but I just had to get that other stuff out of the way first. I'm not sure about the palette. Wondering whether it might not work better in reds and oranges. What do you think?'

Sylvie looked hard, cocking her head one way and then the other.

'The dark colours make a better foil for the images,' she said. 'It's more striking like that. I'd keep going and see where it takes you.'

Jeremy stared at his work a little longer and then made a little sound of approval. 'I think you're right,' he said.

Sylvie waited for a beat or two and then began.

'We've had a card from Christine,' she said.

'How is she?' asked Jeremy. 'Still as mad as a box of frogs?'

'The card's got a crapping reindeer on the front,' replied Sylvie, 'so yes, I suspect she is. She's invited me to go for Christmas.'

'As usual,' replied Jeremy, dipping his paintbrush into a forest green colour and then mixing it into some black. 'I wonder if one year she'll just give up asking.'

'Actually, I thought I might go this year. I haven't seen her for a while and now that Leo is going to be away and you . . . well . . . I just thought I might. Would that be okay?'

Jeremy didn't stop what he was doing but Sylvie could sense first a tension and then a relaxing as he considered his answer.

'That's fine by me. I can keep myself busy and it would be nice for you to see Christine.'

Guilt washed over Sylvie but it was tempered by her longing to leave.

'Are you sure?' she asked. 'If you'd rather I stayed here then I will do.'

'No, it's fine,' replied Jeremy, speaking with more conviction now as if his decision had settled. 'You go. Say hello from me. Tell her she needs to get herself up here for a change. It's years since I've seen her. Feels like it anyway.'

It had been years and Sylvie knew that Christine kept away because she found Leo, and everything she represented, challenging.

'I'll tell her,' she said with a smile. 'I thought I might go tomorrow if that's okay. I'll see if I can get a train ticket, but I imagine most people are coming away from London at Christmas, not going into it.'

'Probably,' replied Jeremy. 'You go. Stay as long as you like. I'll be fine here.'

Sylvie could see that she was losing his attention as he slid back into his work.

'And I was making you a cup of tea! I'm sorry. I got distracted. I'll go and do it now.'

But Jeremy was lost in his painting and didn't seem to notice as she slipped out.

53

Christine lived in a tiny studio flat at the top of a Victorian town house in Stoke Newington. It had a bedroom, a bathroom and everything else was crammed into one large living area. The flat was jammed with the things that Christine had acquired over the years. There was an eclectic mix of furniture, including a sagging sofa bed that was lumpy as a seat but quite remarkably comfortable to sleep on. Every inch of wall was covered with artwork, all hung with no thought for its neighbours, the only deciding factor being whether the allocated space could accommodate the frame. Many of the artists, who had been struggling when they'd given Christine the pieces, were now famous and the collection was probably quite valuable. Not that Christine would have sold it. The art was a tangible connection to a long-lost life.

As well as her paintings, Christine also loved plants and they balanced on every surface, growing lush and green, apparently delighted to be living in such cramped quarters. There was, at least, plenty of natural light from the large windows. It was chilly though. They clearly couldn't be tropical houseplants.

When she opened the door, Christine immediately took Sylvie in her arms and squeezed her tightly.

'I can't believe you're here,' she said.

'Well, it's really me,' replied Sylvie into Christine's hair. It fell in silvery curls over her shoulders, soft and lovely. Sylvie's own hair was not showing any signs of going grey as yet, but she almost envied Christine hers.

'Let's have a drink to celebrate!' said Christine, pulling away and heading towards the kitchen area. 'You sit down, make yourself at home.'

Sylvie avoided the lumpy sofa and chose an armchair instead. It was newly upholstered in a heavy tweed.

'This is nice,' she said admiringly as she sat down.

'Evening classes,' Christine replied without turning round. 'Gin suit you? Or I've got some vodka and there's a bottle of red wine somewhere.'

Sylvie couldn't remember the last time she'd had a drink in the day, but in for a penny and all that. 'Gin's fine as long as you've got tonic. I'm not drinking it neat!'

Christine found two glasses of differing sizes, poured a generous measure into each and topped up with fizzing tonic water.

'Can we live without ice and a slice?' she asked as she offered one of them to Sylvie.

'We can,' confirmed Sylvie.

She lifted the glass to her lips and took a large gulp. The alcohol seemed to hit her bloodstream instantaneously and she kicked off her shoes, tucked her feet underneath herself and felt her body relax into the chair.

'Oh, that's nice,' she said, more to herself than to Christine. 'Now, tell me everything.'

They spent the afternoon swapping news. As Christine was childfree, Sylvie was relieved of the obligation to talk about Leo and she found it refreshing. When she was here it was as if she could be her real self, the Sylvie she would have been if her life had followed the path she'd been expecting it to.

The subject of Leo did come up from time to time, however, as Sylvie shared the news from her life.

'Leo has moved out,' she told Christine. 'She's living in a squat in town. It seems all right. Her housemates look out for her because she's so young.'

Christine raised an eyebrow. 'Did she go out in a blaze of glory?' she asked.

'A row, you mean. No. We seem to have moved through the arguments stage. This time she just disappeared for a few days after her exam results, and when she came back she'd sorted everything out. Where to go, who with, all of it. She doesn't ask us for anything. Scarily independent in fact.'

'Just like her mother, then,' replied Christine, and Sylvie felt the uncomfortable tug that pulled at her every time this kind of comparison came up. Sylvie had never told Christine about the visit from Michelle all those years before.

She had never told a living soul.

'She needs to be careful, though,' Christine continued. 'The police are cracking down on squats. There's talk of a new bill going through Parliament and a lot of councils want their patches clearing. God knows why, because all it does is push people on to the streets which gives rise to a whole load of other issues.'

Christine worked in the housing department of the neighbouring London borough and could tell heart-wrenching stories about some of the things she saw.

Sylvie nodded. 'I'll tell her,' she said.

The afternoon slipped into a comfortable level of nostalgia. They took a tour of Christine's art, reminding each other of the artists and the things they knew about them.

'That little Hockney probably needs some insurance, you know, Chris,' Sylvie told her. 'Do you remember when he painted it, in that godawful flat in Shepherd's Bush?'

'I wonder if he'd remember us now?' Christine mused. 'And dear Peter. He was always around. Wasn't he there that Christmas?' Christine's hand shot up to her mouth. 'God, I'm so sorry, Sylv. I shouldn't have mentioned it. You're here to forget about all that.'

Sylvie flapped her hand in the air. It looked like a regal wave – she must be drunker than she'd thought.

'It's fine,' she said. 'Really, don't worry. It's Jeremy that goes into a tailspin over it, not me. I mean, it was sad and everything, but I don't fall apart at the mere mention.'

For a moment, the two women sat quietly with their own thoughts. Christine had lit a fire in the grate and the flames crackled. Somewhere the other side of a wall someone was playing 'Do They Know It's Christmas?'

They had been debating what was the best Christmas tune ever on the Boxing Day when Jeremy's father had telephoned with the news. It was strange that Sylvie could remember that tiny detail. Jeremy had always said that the entire day was a blank in his head, all its memories entirely subsumed by just one, the last one. Sylvie remembered the discussion because her favourite had always been 'The Power of Love', which Jeremy insisted wasn't a Christmas song at all and that putting the nativity story on the video wasn't enough to turn it into one.

And then the phone had been ringing. It was a Christmas miracle of a sort that anyone had heard it over the racket they were making debating the songs.

'Jezzer, your dad's on the phone. Needs to speak to you,' someone had called out over the laughter. Sylvie had never known the man's name, just one of the waifs and strays that their house seemed to attract.

Jeremy had put his hand up to draw a halt to the argument.

'Hold those thoughts,' he had said portentously, and wandered out into the hallway to take the call.

A few minutes later he came back in. His face was as pale as alabaster and Sylvie knew instantly that something dreadful had happened. The room slowly fell silent as each person realised that the atmosphere had changed and turned to look at Jeremy. Sylvie stood up, immediately sober.

'What is it?' she asked urgently. 'What's happened?'

Jeremy's jaw hung slack and his eyes seemed to be focused somewhere in the middle distance rather than on any of them.

'They're dead,' he said.

Sylvie frowned. 'Who's dead? Who are you talking about?'

'Jo and Mark and baby John-Paul. They're all dead.'

Sylvie had felt as if all the oxygen had been sucked out of her. That couldn't be right. They had only seen Jo the week before to exchange presents, and there were plans to go round to their place the following week as they'd miss each other on Christmas Day. They couldn't be dead. It made no sense.

A second later a whispering started up around the room as those who understood filled in those who didn't.

'That's his sister and her family,' Sylvie heard. 'All of them together. Shit.'

'Must have been an accident, car crash I assume. God, poor Jeremy. And at Christmas too.'

Sylvie pulled herself together and rushed over to Jeremy just in time to catch him as he swayed and then collapsed to his knees. She couldn't hold his weight but she broke his fall a little and then she too dropped and threw her arms around him. He didn't respond to her touch. He just shook his head slowly.

'They can't be dead. They can't be. How can that be true, Sylvie? Not Jo. Not darling Jo. Not my baby, baby Jo.'

And then he started to cry. Sylvie had never seen him cry before. His bottom lip trembled and then his face seemed to collapse, hideously disfigured by the shock. And he howled. Sylvie tried to hold on to him, to offer him some comfort, but he seemed oblivious to her. He had been entirely locked into his own anguish.

Christine reached for the gin bottle and refreshed their drinks and Sylvie let the memory recede.

'I suppose you can't really blame Jeremy for hating Christmas,' Christine said. 'Not after everything he went through that year. It just tainted all of the rest of them.'

Sylvie sighed. 'No, I suppose not,' she said. 'But if I'd known then that that one day was going to change the entire direction of the rest of my life . . .'

Christine sat back on the sofa and shook her head.

'How could you have known? Which of us gets to see what's just around the corner? We simply have to deal with what gets thrown at us. Me, I get life as a spinster in a pokey rented flat surrounded by art I can't afford . . .' She gestured at their surroundings expansively. 'And you get a child you didn't want and shit Christmases!'

And when she put it like that, and after all the gin, the situation seemed hilarious. Sylvie laughed until tears poured out of her and she was no longer sure if she was laughing or crying at her fate.

54

'You can't just go storming up there, Donna,' said Michelle. 'Not at Christmas.'

Donna thought that as Christmas was a time for families and getting together it was exactly the right time to go and meet the people who might (or might not) be her biological parents.

'I'm not going to storm anywhere,' she replied in her best no-nonsense voice. 'I'll just go and knock on the door like a perfectly normal and polite person.'

'And say what, exactly?' Michelle folded her arms across her chest and stared at her, lips squeezed into a tight line across her face.

This was a good question. Donna really didn't have any idea how you started a conversation like the one she needed to have. She just knew that she needed to do it.

'Well, not what you said when you tried to talk to them,' she said with a grin in an attempt at humour.

It worked, just as she'd hoped it would. Michelle unfolded her arms and cocked her head to one side, her mouth twisted into half a smile.

'Yeah,' she said. 'Well, I wouldn't recommend that approach, unless catatonic is what you're aiming for.'

'Not particularly,' replied Donna. 'But I have to try. You can see that, Mum, can't you?'

Michelle nodded. 'I can,' she said. 'But not before Christmas, that's all I'm saying. Give yourself time for the dust to settle. Don't go in like a bull in a china shop. You might only get this one go at it and you don't want to mess it up.'

That was true enough.

'Okay,' Donna replied. 'I promise. But will you at least take me and show me the house?'

She could see Michelle thinking about this, weighing up the harm in revealing the key to the whole situation against the benefit of keeping it to herself. She seemed to reach a decision and she let out a loud sigh.

'All right. We can go this evening after work. It'll be nice to see the lights and what have you anyway. But I mean it, Donna. There'll be no knocking on the door, not until Christmas is over. Okay?'

Donna nodded reluctantly.

◆　◆　◆

After they'd eaten their tea, Donna and Michelle wrapped themselves up in coats and scarves ready to walk up to the house. Tina was out with a friend so there were no difficult questions to field about where they were sneaking off to. They just locked the door and set off.

'You know they might not live there any more,' Michelle said as they waited at the level crossing to get over the railway line. 'They could have moved. It's been more than ten years since I went before. A lot can happen in that time.'

She was right, of course, but something inside Donna told her that nothing would have changed. She needed to straighten this out and the universe was going to help her do it. And her family hadn't moved house in all that time so hopefully this couple, Sylvie and Jeremy, would be the same.

Donna's mind tripped over the names as she thought them. They didn't come naturally to her. They were rich people names. She'd never met a single Sylvie or Jeremy anywhere. How could that be where she really belonged? With this couple in their big house and their posh-sounding names? Not for the first time the thought made Donna feel queasy. She was so desperate for the answer and yet at the same time she didn't want to know. It was a bit like waiting for her exam results – only a million times worse.

There were Christmas lights strung across the High Street – stars and Christmas trees each made up of hundreds of individual little twinkles. The shops were closing up for the night, but they all had festive displays shining in their windows. The last few shoppers beetled about purposefully, laden with plastic bags of booty.

The closer they got to the cathedral the less brash the decorations became. Donna peered into the windows of any houses that still had their curtains open and saw trees sparsely decorated in just one colour, so different to the chaos of their tree at home. It felt like they were Cathy and Heathcliff, peering in to watch the rich kids at play.

Michelle was very quiet, partly because of the physical effort required to scale the hill but also, Donna decided, because she was lost in her own thoughts. Donna was happy with that. The space in her own head was somewhere that she could happily occupy at any time.

When they reached the top of the hill with the cathedral to the right and the castle to their left, Michelle took her arm and gave it a little squeeze.

'It's this way,' she said, and led Donna down a road that ran in front of the castle gates.

Donna's heart was going like the clappers now. She didn't know whether she was excited or scared. Probably a mixture of both. They carried on down the narrow road until Michelle stopped and cocked her head at the house on the opposite side.

'That's the one,' she said.

It was pretty much exactly as her mum had described. Big and grand. But, unlike the other houses in the street, it had no Christmas lights at its windows and nothing twinkling in the garden.

Disappointment washed over Donna. 'It doesn't look like they're at home,' she said. 'And there are no decorations. Do you think they've gone away?'

Donna tried to ignore the expression of relief that had settled across her mum's face. But then, as they stood there staring up at the house, a light went on. It made Donna jump. It was on the first floor and was followed by another that must be for the stairs and then another in what looked like the hall. Whoever was there was making their way down through the house.

As the figure crossed the hall, they got a glimpse of him. He was wearing a huge woollen jumper in a navy blue cable-knit design. He had dark hair but more than that Donna couldn't make out.

'Is that him?' she asked Michelle. 'Is that Jeremy?'

Michelle sucked a breath in through her teeth and nodded.

'I think so,' she said.

'So, that's good,' replied Donna. 'At least they haven't moved.'

Michelle agreed, but she didn't look as if she thought the news was really that good. Shivering, she pulled her scarf more tightly around her neck.

'It's freezing out here, Dons. Can we go home now?' she said.

'Okay.'

Donna had done what she needed to. She'd seen the house. Now it was up to her. No matter what she'd told her mum, *she* could decide when she wanted to knock on the door and there would be no one to stop her.

'Yeah,' she said, turning to her mum with a smile and a fake shiver. 'Let's go home before our bits drop off.'

55

The prospect of the forthcoming visit didn't leave Donna's mind for more than a minute or two from that point on, but her mum was right about one thing. She couldn't just turn up and drop her bombshell on Christmas Day. She decided that Christmas Eve and Boxing Day were out as well, which left the twenty-seventh as her first possible opportunity. She would take herself off in a quiet moment when she was unlikely to be missed and get it over and done with.

With that decision made, Donna was able to enjoy her Christmas. The family gathered and the celebrations were as raucous as usual. Nobody mentioned anything about baby swaps, which must have taken a gargantuan effort, particularly on Tina's part, and Donna was grateful that they had all tried so hard to party around the elephant in the room.

Her dad didn't show his face, but she hadn't expected him to. He still owed her an apology, she felt, for his outburst in the pub, but she knew that hell would likely freeze over before he said sorry for something without being bounced into it by someone else, and she wasn't about to be the one to prompt him. No doubt Tina would shame him into it before too long.

In any event, Donna thought it would be better to deal with her dad after she'd had her conversation with Sylvie and Jeremy.

Then she should have an idea of how likely her mother's theory was to be true and so what to do about her dad's attitude. But that could all wait for now, and she got on with the task of having fun.

When the twenty-seventh dawned, she got dressed carefully, mindful of what each item of clothing might say about who she was. She hadn't breathed a word of her intentions to her mum or Tina and had her excuses as to where she was going ready, but in the end she didn't have to use them as the house was empty when she set off to walk up the hill. Donna was relieved. It felt as if her stars were all aligning. Was this a good sign for what was to come? She really hoped so.

She made her way up past the shops. Even though the same decorations hung in the windows, they had all lost their lustre somehow, like a tatty poster for an event that had been and gone. The Boxing Day sales had begun and the atmosphere had switched from an excited sense of anticipation to something altogether more tawdry.

Cutting her way through the bargain-hunters, Donna made her way up the near-vertical slope for the second time that week, wondering as she passed the quirky old buildings with their funny stone windows why she didn't come up here more often. It was so very different to her part of the town. It barely felt as if it could be the same place. But, she wondered, what if this was where she should have been all along? What if these ancient cobbled streets with their elegant buildings were her real destiny rather than the rows and rows of terraced houses she knew so well?

Donna didn't like to think like that and she dismissed the thought as quickly as it had come. She belonged where she had always been, with Michelle and Tina and her brothers. Whatever she was about to discover up here was a completely different matter. She wasn't going to let it alter what already was.

She reached the house and stood on the opposite pavement, shrinking back into the ivy that tumbled over a garden wall so that she didn't stand out. The houses up here seemed so quiet: such a contrast to their street, where there was always music blaring and people shouting out to one another from top-floor windows.

For a moment, she allowed herself to reconsider her decision to knock. She didn't have to do it. There was no compulsion, nothing that said it was her duty. Her life could continue perfectly well as it was without ever meeting these people.

But she knew none of that was true. She would always have to know. This was something that she would never get out of her system unless she had at least tried to get to the bottom of the mystery.

She wouldn't let it make any difference though. Michelle was her mum, Dean was her dad (despite him choosing to be a dick about it just then) and whatever or whoever was waiting behind the door opposite was never going to change that. At best, she would discover something that enhanced her world. At worse she could just walk away and leave it all behind.

She checked for cars and then crossed the road, striding confidently until she reached the heavy black door.

And then she pressed the bell.

56

Sylvie had been away for almost a week and she really needed to think about getting back to Jeremy and her real life, but it was just so very relaxing in Christine's cosy little flat. When she was there she could forget about the struggles at home and just be herself for a while. Christine had been on call over Christmas and had gone out a couple of times to deal with emergency housing issues, leaving Sylvie to luxuriate in the solitude, plucking books from shelves at random and losing hours between their covers. She had even got out her sketch pad and made some preliminary drawings for a couple of ideas that were starting to bubble up in her head.

But now there was nothing stopping her from heading back home. It wasn't that Jeremy was difficult to live with – he really wasn't – but he was always there in the house, so Sylvie rarely found the peace she craved. And even though Leo, by contrast, was rarely at home, her spirit and the unspoken arguments that she provoked were scattered about the place like unexploded bombs just waiting to be detonated.

Sylvie didn't want to outstay her welcome, however, and she couldn't prolong the inevitable indefinitely.

'I think I'd better be heading home tomorrow,' she said as she and Christine sat around in dressing gowns and pyjamas enjoying a wholesome breakfast of crunchy toast and thick-cut orange marmalade.

'No need to on my account,' said Christine through a mouthful of crust. 'You can stay as long as you like.'

'I know,' replied Sylvie, 'and I'm really grateful, but . . . well, you know how it is.'

'Sadly, I have no idea,' replied Christine. 'Who is there to care what I get up to? But I do understand. Tomorrow it is then. Shall we cook something delicious tonight and have a proper blow-out to mourn your departure?'

'Yes! Let's.'

They spent their day choosing a menu and sourcing the ingredients, and then as the sun dropped behind the rooftops late in the afternoon, they began to cook. Christine opened a bottle of wine and then another and by the time the food was ready Sylvie was quite drunk and had no appetite at all. She did her best, though, picking her way through the dishes until the meal was complete and they had retired to the more comfortable chairs to see out what was left of the evening. Christine lit the fire and they huddled round it, pulling the chairs closer to get the full benefit of its heat.

Their conversation meandered its way round to Leonora. Having roundly avoided her daughter as a subject until then, Sylvie found that she had a lot to say.

'The thing is,' she confessed, staring into the flickering flames of the fire, 'I've never been any good as a mother. I just don't have it in me. So it's no wonder that Leo's turned out the way she has, so wayward and difficult.'

Other people might have leapt in to contradict her, but Christine knew her and the truth of the situation and so didn't. Sylvie was grateful. It was exhausting having to restate that which was patently true. She didn't have a maternal bone in her body.

'You might not be a natural mother, Sylv,' Christine said, 'but how Leo behaves now is not your fault. She's her own person and responsible for her own actions. And it's not fair to judge you when you never wanted kids in the first place. You always said that. Right from the start.'

Sylvie nodded, aware as she moved her head of how drunk she was.

'I did, didn't I?' she replied thickly. 'I always said that. You can marry me, Jezzer old man, but you won't be getting any sprogs out of me so you'd better understand that right now.'

Christine smiled fondly at the memory.

'So it's not surprising that I'm so crap at it. At being a mother.'

'You're not crap at it,' objected Christine. 'Leo has been a challenge to deal with, due, in no small part, I imagine, to how Jeremy has dealt with her over the years. If anyone is going for Crap Parent of the Year then I'd say it should be him.'

'I'm not sure that's fair,' Sylvie replied, thoughtfully. 'He does his best. It's just that Leo could never quite match up to his expectations.'

'You mean she isn't Jo,' said Christine, pulling a face that suggested this was incontrovertible.

Sylvie sighed deeply. 'Dear, sweet Jo,' she said. 'She'd have been forty-six now. Hard to imagine, isn't it? And the silly thing is, I really think Leo would have loved her. If Jo had been around maybe things might have been easier . . .'

But, she thought, if Jo had still been alive there would have been no Leo.

'I wonder if I'd been more natural with her when she was a baby,' she mused, harking back to her own failings rather than Jeremy's, 'if I could have managed all that mother-baby bonding business then maybe she would have turned out differently.'

Christine shrugged, flicking the ash of her cigarette on to the coals. 'Who's to say? Nature or nurture? It's the age-old conundrum.'

They sat in silence for a moment.

'Actually,' said Christine, draining the last of the wine into Sylvie's glass. 'If we're casting blame then surely some needs to be cast in Margery's direction. If she hadn't bullied you into it in the first place . . .'

'She didn't bully me into it,' protested Sylvie.

'Oh no? Well, what would you call it?'

Sylvie thought for a moment, replaying the scene in her head. Jo had been dead for over a year then, but Jeremy's grief was showing no sign of abating. He had no interest in anything. She had to remind him to eat and even then he picked at his food so that he became scrawny and gaunt. Sometimes it was all she could do to make him speak. He seemed to have withdrawn so deeply into himself that she began to worry that he would never come back to her.

Margery rang to speak to him every Saturday and Sylvie generally handed the phone straight over to him without exchanging more than pleasantries, but one day it was her that Margery wanted to speak to.

'Sylvia,' she said. 'Wait. Don't go just yet.'

Sylvia had already drawn breath to call Jeremy to the phone and this change of routine threw her.

'Yes?' she said suspiciously.

'Now listen,' continued Margery in her customary clipped tones. 'I'm terribly worried about Jeremy . . .'

'Well, yes,' agreed Sylvie, 'so am—'

'He doesn't seem to be able to put this behind him. He and Jo were so very close, you understand. I am worried that he might' – she dropped her voice to a stage whisper – 'do something stupid.'

The thought that Jeremy might end his own life had occurred to Sylvie too, although she hadn't taken the idea too seriously. Jeremy wasn't the sort.

'Oh, I don't think . . .' she began.

'So Gerald and I think it would be best all round if we paid for you to go and see someone.'

Sylvie was completely lost.

'Go and see who?' she asked.

'A man,' said Margery gruffly. 'You know, a doctor. Someone who specialises in fertility issues.'

'But . . .'

'We think that the sooner you two have a baby the quicker Jeremy will recover. If he has a child of his own it would help him look more positively on life. And obviously we have been very patient waiting for you to produce a grandchild under your own steam but enough is enough. As I say, we will pay. You can see the best man on Harley Street. I have the name here. Do you have a pen?'

The words were coming at her too quickly to process. She needed to stop Margery, to explain, but Margery was like a devastating landslide, flattening everything in her way.

'Yes,' replied Sylvie, reaching for the pad by the phone. She took down the name and number. 'Thank you,' she said automatically.

'Now, you make sure you ring him,' Margery was saying. 'Don't tell Jeremy. He has enough to worry about. The problem won't be with him in any event. We Fotherby-Smythes never have any difficulty in that department. So, you pop along, get the issue resolved and then we could have a new baby in the family by this time next year. And now, I'll speak to Jeremy if you could put him on the line.'

Sylvie had put the phone down in a daze and wandered away to locate Jeremy, her head spinning from the very many things that were wrong with what Margery had just said.

'She didn't bully me,' she said to Christine now. 'She made me think, that's all. And I decided that the greater good would be done for the largest number by my having a baby.'

'Hmmph,' said Christine, sliding even deeper into her chair and eyeing Sylvie sceptically.

'It was his pain I couldn't stand,' Sylvie continued. 'Jeremy's, and his mother's too I suppose. Their terrible, awful grief. Margery and Gerald had not only lost Jo and their grandchild, but also the hope of any more, unless I changed my mind.'

'She blackmailed you,' said Christine. 'She put you in a position where you couldn't possibly say no. What if she'd been right and Jeremy had ended it all? Where would that have left you when she'd basically said that having a baby would fix him? How would you have felt then? The whole thing was appalling.'

Sylvie shrugged. They were where they were. There was nothing to be gained by raking it all up now.

'Nobody held a gun to my head,' she said.

'As good as,' muttered Christine.

Sylvie smiled at her fondly. 'You are the best friend a girl could have,' she said.

'And you are the kindest, most selfless person I know,' Christine replied. 'A toast!' She reached for her glass, found it to be empty and put it down again. 'Bugger! Out of booze.'

Sylvie shook her head, the movement extravagant and exaggerated. 'No, no, no, no,' she said. 'That's not true.' There was a slur in her voice now.

'It bloody is! You offered to have a baby you didn't want out of pure love for your husband, so that he could please his grieving mother. I wouldn't have done it. I doubt anyone would. But you did.'

Sylvie's bottom lip stuck out. 'I'm not sure I should have done,' she said. 'Look how it turned out. I made such a hash of it and now Leo barely speaks to Margery which just makes not having Jo even harder to bear. They lost their beautiful, talented daughter and her gorgeous baby and got Leo instead. Not that great a bargain whichever way you look at it.'

She closed her eyes and her head swam a little. She opened them again and waited until the room steadied itself.

'God, listen to me,' she said. 'What do I sound like? How can I say these terrible things about my own child?'

'It's the wine talking,' replied Christine. 'And it's only me listening, which is basically like talking to yourself. But you're wrong, Sylv. Leo is troubled, I agree. But fundamentally she's a good kid. She's smart and sassy and she knows how many beans make five. She's going to grow into herself, you mark my words. And then she'll realise what a pain in the arse she's been. Wait until she has kids of her own! Then she'll get it.'

Sylvie stared deep into the fire. There were no flames now, just the deep tiger-orange of the glowing coals.

'Do you think Jeremy blames me?' she asked, her voice barely above a whisper.

'No!' The reply came firm and clear. 'Of course not. Why would he? Like I said, he's just as much Leo's parent as you are. If there was any blame to be apportioned – which there absolutely isn't – then he would need to take his fair share.'

Sylvie nodded. She could see that, she supposed.

Her mind trailed back to that day eleven years before when a stranger had appeared at her door and given her a way out. The child might not be hers after all, she had said. All of Leo's faults, her tantrums, her refusal to engage, her lack of interest in anything around her, that might all have been nothing to do with Sylvie. They could have started again, a clean sheet, a fresh start with a different child.

But the thought that she might have gone through with having a baby, struggling to create a relationship with her against all her natural instincts, doing it for Jeremy on the say-so of his mother, only to be told that it was all to no end because the child wasn't theirs anyway – that was more than Sylvie could handle.

Not even Christine knew about that conversation. Every so often, she would get the thought out and examine it, run through the possibilities that it offered in her head. But then she always put it back in the box and locked the lid tightly shut.

There was one thing that Sylvie knew for sure.

Nothing good would come of revisiting it.

57

Donna stood and waited for someone to answer the door, her palms clammy and her heart in her mouth. Who would it be? Sylvie? Jeremy? Or even their daughter? Donna hadn't really considered the other child, the baby who might be her mum's true daughter. She would be here as well, Donna assumed, so it could be any of them who opened the door. She swallowed down a wave of nausea as her stomach roiled, and stood her ground.

After a moment or two she could hear someone moving around inside and then the door opened wide and there stood the man they'd seen before, Jeremy. He had dark hair, greying at the temples, and the start of a scruffy grey beard, as if he hadn't shaved over Christmas. Paint speckled his clothing and there was a little on his face, a spattering of dark green freckles. There was nothing familiar about him, no shared features that she could see.

She felt a tremor of disappointment. What had she been hoping for? Had she assumed that she would see these people for the first time and something about them would speak to some inner, hitherto undiscovered part of her consciousness? Well, yes. That was exactly what she had been expecting. But maybe it wasn't as simple as that.

When Jeremy saw her, his expression was momentarily confused and then he offered her a bemused smile.

'Hello,' he said. 'Can I help you?'

Donna had rehearsed her lines beforehand, running over them in her head with various alternatives to cover the responses that she might get.

'Are you Jeremy?' she began, mentioning his name to show that she wasn't just a time-waster.

'I am,' he said.

'Good. Could I come in for a minute?' she continued. 'I have something I need to talk to you about.'

Jeremy's eyebrows pulled together, changing the shape of his face, and Donna wondered if the expression might be a familiar one. Something about the shape of his eyes, maybe?

'How very intriguing,' he said. And then his face darkened a little. 'You're not something to do with Leonora, are you? Has she sent you here for cash? Because if she has you can tell her to come herself and do her own dirty work.'

This wasn't in the script, and Donna was thrown for a second. As she was working out how to respond, he scrutinised her face and then his own softened as if he had answered his own question.

'No,' he said. 'You're not here for Leonora, are you?'

Donna shook her head.

'Okay then. You'd better come in.'

He gestured for her to enter and then led her into the kitchen.

The room wasn't that tidy. It was clear that he hadn't washed up for a day or two and there were plates and cups piled high in the sink. Beneath that, though, the room was clean and cared for.

'Excuse the mess,' he said. 'My wife has gone away for a few days and I've let standards slip just a little. Our secret.' He put his finger to his lips and winked at her.

Donna immediately warmed to him. He seemed relaxed and very open. But his wife, Sylvie, was away so did that mean there were only the two of them in the house? Should she be cautious? Was she safe?

Her gut told her that she was, perfectly.

'Coffee?' he asked. 'Or tea maybe? You'll have to forgive me. Having been on my own for a while, I have an urge to chat with another human. Tell me if I'm behaving oddly and I'll stop.'

He grinned at her again and Donna offered a tentative smile back.

'Oh, look,' he continued. 'You do think I'm odd. I'm sorry. I'm not really. I'm perfectly normal, honestly. Now did you say tea or coffee?'

'Tea, please,' replied Donna.

This was fun. Maybe she would never have to tell him why she had come and could just watch his one-man show instead.

'Did you have a nice Christmas?' he asked as he scooted around the kitchen making the tea.

'Yes, thanks,' she said. 'It was lovely. Did you?'

He had his back to her at this point and he shrugged.

'I don't really buy into the whole festive season,' he said, 'but I enjoyed myself in my own way.'

'That's good,' replied Donna. 'How come you don't do Christmas?' she heard herself say, bolder than she'd intended.

'Oh, it's just not my kind of thing,' he said vaguely. 'Tea.' He handed her a mug of tea and gestured at a chair. 'Please. Sit down and then you can tell me why you're here.'

Donna had relaxed without realising it, but now the knots in her stomach retied themselves. She pulled back a chair and sat down.

'Well,' she began. 'You're going to think this is a bit weird.'

'I can handle weird.'

'I was born in Lincoln Hospital on the twenty-sixth of June 1976. It was a Saturday,' she added unnecessarily.

'That's a strange coincidence. My daughter Leonora was born on that self-same day,' Jeremy replied with a bemused air. Nothing about him suggested that he thought this in any way peculiar.

So, Leonora was the other baby, Donna thought. And she had already been mentioned by Jeremy. Donna struggled to remember what he had said. Something about her being a messenger for Leonora, and cash. Did that mean Leonora didn't live here with them? That was strange. They were only sixteen, after all, which was quite young to be living away from home. Wildly Donna's brain fired with alternative reasons. Did Leonora know that she was with the wrong parents? Had someone else turned up to claim her and caused a rift? Who could that have been? Michelle, Dean, someone else entirely?

But she had to bring herself back under control. She needed to focus all her attention on what was going on right now, not speculating as to what might have happened before.

'Yes,' she said, trying to keep her voice steady. 'My mum told me that your little girl was born the same day as me. My mum and your wife were in beds next to each other.'

Would he see where she was going with this? Might he reach the obvious conclusion before she had to spell it out to him?

But it appeared not.

'Well, isn't that a turn-up for the books,' he said. 'So your mum and Sylvie have kept in touch all this time. That's nice. Sylvie never mentioned it but that's Sylvie all over. She can be very puzzling sometimes; a woman of mystery.' His eyebrows shot up and his expression softened, as if this was something he was particularly fond of about his wife.

Donna's mind flew over the various scripts she had written for herself, trying to work out which one would best fit.

'My mum thinks that you took the wrong babies home.'

Jeremy's face broke into a wide smile as if this was funny, but then he seemed to consider what she had said and the smile was replaced by confusion as he tried to process the implications. Donna paused, giving him time.

'Hang on, let me get this straight . . .' he began, his fingers on his lips in thought. 'If your mum is right, that would mean that Leonora isn't actually our daughter . . . and . . . you are?'

He spoke ponderously, chewing each word over as he went, and Donna had no idea what he was actually thinking. Was he about to burst into laughter at the preposterous idea or was he giving it genuine consideration? She couldn't tell.

She met his eyes with hers and nodded.

'Well, I'll be damned,' he said throwing his head back and looking up at the ceiling.

Donna sat perfectly still and waited. Her eyes drank his in, searching for any sign that her mother might be right, but how was she supposed to find traces of herself in this middle-aged man? It was impossible.

After a moment or two, he straightened back up and turned his focus on to her. His eyes scanned every inch of her face and Donna could feel herself blush under his scrutiny.

'How long have you known that your mum has this theory?' he asked.

'Since a couple of days before Christmas,' she said.

'And how did you know where to find us?'

'My mum saw Sylvie, your wife, once. It was a long time ago. I was only five. She followed her here.'

'But she decided not to do anything about it?' Jeremy asked.

Donna's insides clenched. Had she just inadvertently walked into something that was going to throw the conversation off track? She thought about lying, telling him that Michelle had done nothing with the information, but she didn't know enough about how the land lay. Better to just be honest, she decided.

'She came and knocked at the door. You answered the first time, but Sylvie was away.' Like now, she thought but didn't say. She wondered what kind of a marriage this really was. 'And then Mum came back and she told Sylvie what she thought had happened. But Sylvie . . .' How to describe Sylvie's strange reaction to the news? She could hardly say that she fell into a catatonic trance. It seemed impertinent. '. . . Sylvie seemed a bit shocked and she didn't say anything. Mum just left in the end. She gave Sylvie her address but she never heard anything from her.'

Jeremy nodded slowly.

'And then a couple of nights before Christmas, my dad got a bit drunk and he said something and I asked some questions and that's when Mum told me.'

Jeremy rubbed at his chin and eyed her. She still had no idea what was going on in his head.

'So your mum, what's she called?'

'Michelle.'

'So Michelle thinks you and Leonora were swapped in the hospital somehow. Yes?'

Donna nodded.

'And, just so I'm completely straight here, you're saying that that would mean that *you*' – he emphasised the word – 'are actually *our* daughter, and Leonora is hers.'

Donna nodded again, catching her lip between her teeth and not letting her gaze drop from his eyes.

Jeremy continued to stare at her so hard that it was like a laser boring into her.

And then he began to laugh.

58

Jeremy's laugh was deep and full. And it didn't stop. He laughed until his eyes watered and he had to gasp in large mouthfuls of air. When he looked as if he was going to recover himself, his lips would start to tremble and he would start again.

Donna had no idea how to react. Did he think she was joking? She had just said that she might be his daughter and now he was laughing as if she'd told him a side-splittingly funny joke. It was disconcerting, and then it became irritating and finally annoying.

'Look, maybe I'd better go,' she said, getting to her feet. She wasn't about to sit here and have this total stranger laugh at her for no obvious reason.

Jeremy put his hand out to stop her and made a concerted effort to get some words out.

'No, no. Please stay. I'm sorry. I'm okay . . . I'm okay now.'

He took two deep breaths and closed his eyes, recentring himself. When he opened his eyes again, now red-rimmed and watery, she could see that he was working hard to keep control.

'Forgive me,' he said stiffly. 'That was an appalling reaction to such serious news. I'm not sure where it came from but please accept my deepest apologies. It is obviously not a laughing matter.' But then his shoulders hunched again and he pressed his lips tightly together to prevent another hoot escaping. It wasn't entirely successful.

Donna tutted and pushed her chair away from the table.

'I think I've made a mistake coming here,' she said. 'I'll just . . .'

Jeremy leapt to his feet. 'No. I'm sorry,' he said again. 'Don't go. Just let me explain.'

Donna considered her options. She could leave, but then she would never get to the bottom of this or find out what was so very funny, either.

'Okay,' she said sceptically, sitting back down. 'But please could you stop laughing.'

Jeremy nodded. 'Yes, yes. Of course. Forgive me,' he said, wiping the moisture from his eyes with the tips of his fingers.

'So, here's the thing,' he began. 'We do have a daughter born on the same day as you, as I mentioned. Leonora. She's not here. She moved out in August, lives in a squat somewhere. She's been' – he tapped a paint-speckled finger against his lips – 'shall we say, a difficult child. The thought that we might have had the wrong baby all along . . . well, you can maybe imagine . . .' He looked at her expectantly, clearly hoping that she would understand at once.

Donna wasn't sure what he was getting at. He seemed to be saying that he was looking for an excuse to absolve all responsibility for this Leonora, so that he could wash his hands of her. She wasn't at all convinced that that was as hilarious as he seemed to have found it. She gave a non-committal shrug.

He was staring at her now, scrutinising her features one by one. Donna felt her cheeks start to burn again and she lowered her head. She could sense him shifting his position, altering his gaze in response.

'I'm going about this all wrong, aren't I?' he said. 'Forget about my troubles. Tell me something about you. Let's start with your name. Is that okay?'

Donna thought that it probably was, but she was feeling far more cautious than she had been.

'Donna,' she replied. 'My name's Donna.'

He nodded. 'And you live in Lincoln?'

Donna nodded.

'And your mother, well, the woman who brought you up, she came here once, you say, and spoke to me?'

Donna nodded again.

'I'm afraid to say that I have no memory of that at all.' His brow creased as he attempted to dig deep into his past. 'And then she came again and spoke to Sylvie, my wife? Funny that Sylvie never mentioned that.'

He seemed to be considering that point, mulling over it for a moment, but Donna had the impression that he wasn't questioning her version of events.

'That's what my mum told me,' she replied cautiously.

There was something a bit off about the atmosphere. It wasn't that she felt threatened. Jeremy seemed like a nice enough bloke. But there was an undercurrent here that she didn't quite understand. It was as if she had walked into the middle of a conversation and was struggling to catch up.

'And now that you're here,' he said, 'what do you think?'

His expression was loaded with significance but Donna wasn't sure what he was getting at. She shifted in her seat.

'How do you mean?' she asked.

'Well, does anything feel familiar? Are you looking at me and thinking that there might be some connection between us?'

Donna had been asking herself the same question ever since he'd opened the door. There had certainly been no immediate sense of shared genes. He was an older man with a grey beard. It would be hard to find traces of herself in him at the best of times, let alone when just staring at his face felt so awkward and quite rude.

She shook her head.

Jeremy took a deep breath and let it out slowly. 'Okay. Here's what I think we should do,' he said. 'You go home now. We both have a think about what we want to do next. I can talk to my wife etcetera. And then we meet again in, say, a week. Somewhere neutral. At which point we can have a chat about where we should go from here. How does that sound?'

Before she had arrived here she had wanted immediate answers. She had hoped to look into Jeremy's face and see that they were clearly related. Or not. She hadn't minded which.

But now, she understood that this was a whole lot more complicated than she'd originally thought. A week's breathing space was probably exactly what they both needed. She could talk to her mum too, see how she wanted to play it.

'Okay,' she heard herself say. 'That sounds good.'

'How about we meet a week today? What would that be?' He stood up and walked over to a calendar hanging on the wall. 'Sunday the third,' he said. 'New year – new beginnings and all that. Or not,' he added, and raised an eyebrow.

'Where should we go?' she asked.

Jeremy considered his answer. 'It needs to be somewhere inside,' he said. 'In case of bad weather. And quiet so that we aren't in anyone's way. Bit tricky at this time of year when everywhere is so busy.' He paused, and then seemed to hit on an idea. 'How about the art gallery?'

Donna had never been to the city's art gallery, wasn't even sure quite where it was. It seemed a strange choice, but then, she supposed, they wouldn't be able to have a full-blown row in there so maybe that would be good.

'Okay,' she said. 'How about two o'clock?'

'Yes. That's fine,' Jeremy agreed. 'And we won't exchange telephone numbers so if the other party doesn't turn up we'll know that they've decided against going any further. Although,' he said, scratching his beard, 'I suppose you know where we live so that doesn't quite work.'

Donna thought about it for a moment. 'Well, how about we say that if you don't turn up next Sunday then I won't ever come here again? I know that means that you're having to trust me, but I'm quite trustworthy.'

She gave him her most winning smile and he smiled back. Was there something there, she wondered? Something about the way his eyes crinkled, the turn of his mouth?

'I bet you are,' he said. 'Okay. That sounds like a plan to me.'

Donna got to her feet. Now that the arrangement had been made she found that she was quite keen to get out of the house and remove the pressure from herself. She left the kitchen and headed for the front door. When she got there she turned and paused.

'Well, I'll see you next Sunday at two then,' she said.

'Or not,' replied Jeremy.

'Or not,' she confirmed.

59

Donna left the house and strode up the way she had come without once turning round, but when she got back to the open cobbled square she felt her knees start to buckle and she let herself drop on to an empty bench. The day was dank with drizzle floating in the chilly air and she realised she was trembling, but she wasn't sure whether it was the cold or her adrenaline that was the cause.

What had just happened? She tried to piece the encounter together from the moment Jeremy had opened the door. She had learned that he and Sylvie were still married, although she was away on her own, and that their daughter, Leonora, had moved out. That seemed to be a rundown of all the actual facts.

Yet the facts were such a small part of what she'd gleaned. The trouble was, she wasn't sure she totally understood the rest. His laughter, now that had been really weird. She knew that people sometimes reacted to shock or stress with a totally inappropriate response, like giggling at a funeral, but to laugh so hard and for so long, and when there wasn't someone else there to egg you on – that was strange.

And what about Jeremy's suggestion to walk away if they chose to? That had sounded quite reasonable when he had proposed it, but already she was changing her mind. Surely they needed at least one meeting, all of them together. After that they could decide what to do next. The idea that he and Sylvie might not turn up at the art gallery, bringing an end to the whole mystery, made her heart beat a little faster. If that happened, she would be left with so many unanswered questions that would never be resolved. She wasn't sure she would be able to live with not knowing the truth, not ever meeting the woman who might be her mother. Would she even be able to keep her promise and stay away from them?

But as she sat on the bench, the damp seeping into her coat, she realised that Jeremy was right. If they did meet up, there would be no going back from it. Right now, the whole baby swap theory was nothing more than a notion that her mother had once had. There were things about her and her family that pointed to her mum being right, but there was also plenty of evidence against it.

If they formalised the situation by all being in a room at the same time to discuss what they thought, what the next steps might be, where they went from there – well, that was something different entirely. It went from being a whimsical idea to something that might change lives, and she supposed they all had to be certain that they wanted that particular can of worms opening.

When she got back to the house she had barely taken her coat off before her mum appeared. Although Donna had been careful to sneak away to carry out her errand, there must have been some clue written on her face because her mum knew as soon as she saw her.

'You've been, haven't you?' Michelle said. 'You've been up to see them.' Her eyes were wide and she looked more frightened than curious.

Donna nodded.

'And?' asked her mum urgently.

'Not much. He was there. She was away. He invited me in. I told him what I had to say. He suggested that we meet again in a week when we've all had a chance to think about what we want to do. If someone doesn't show up then the others will know that they're not interested in taking it any further.'

Something was telling Donna that she should only give her mum the bare facts, and delivering them like this, simply and without elaboration, made the task easier. As she spoke, she felt instinctively that it would be wrong to mention Leonora, although she wasn't quite sure why. It might distress Michelle to hear that she was living in a squat, even if she was perfectly happy there. No one liked stories of family disharmony, except in soap operas.

But something altogether less altruistic was also holding Donna's tongue. There was a chance that this Leonora was Michelle's actual daughter. That triggered an emotion in Donna that she wasn't familiar with and didn't like.

Jealousy.

If Michelle started to worry about Leonora's well-being, then that would lead to something complicated in Donna's head that she didn't want to examine too closely. *She* was Michelle's daughter, not this imposter she'd never even laid eyes on. Why tell Michelle things that might push her towards Leonora?

But being jealous was totally the wrong response here. She knew it was, and yet she couldn't help it. How was she expected to go from being Michelle's daughter and the apple of her eye one week to being usurped by a total stranger the next? If that was what was going to happen then she needed to build herself up to it and she definitely wasn't about to help the process along.

On top of that, the chances were that Leonora was living somewhere nearby, maybe even in that squat she'd seen. The thought that Michelle and Dean's real fourth child might be just around the corner made Donna's insides clench.

Realising that her mum was speaking to her, she pulled herself back to the conversation.

'And what did you think?' her mum asked. 'Was he a nice bloke?'

Donna shrugged. 'Well, he listened to me and he didn't slam the door in my face,' she said. 'But it was hard to tell more than that. He seemed okay.'

Michelle turned away, busying herself with tidying the already tidy table as if she were placing no importance whatsoever on the next part of the discussion.

'And did you think . . .' she began. 'Did you . . . ?' She seemed to be struggling to formulate her question in a sensitive way.

Rather than letting her stumble on, Donna interrupted her. 'Did I think he might be my dad, you mean?' she asked.

Michelle nodded gratefully.

'Honestly? I haven't a clue. I couldn't say he definitely isn't but I couldn't say he definitely is either. I'm not even sure how I'd know, unless I looked exactly like him, which I don't.'

Michelle blew out her lips.

'What if I've started all this for nothing?' she said quietly.

'Well, for that reason alone we need to find out the truth,' said Donna. 'Otherwise it's going to nag away at us forever.'

She smiled at her mum, tried to make it look convincing. But actually, Donna wasn't at all sure that any of this was the right thing to do.

Not now. Not ever.

60

Sylvie caught a taxi from the station up to the house feeling restored by her trip to Christine's. She was ready to step back into her own life with her battery recharged. And she'd really missed Jeremy. She was looking forward to sharing her ideas for the new projects, and to see what he had been working on whilst the rest of the country had been celebrating Christmas.

She thought about taking a detour to Leo's house on the way but decided against it. She would get home first and unpack and then she could make a plan to visit Leo the following day, hear how the nut roast had gone down. It was amazing how a few days away made everything seem exciting and full of possibility where previously it had been humdrum or burdensome.

There were lights shining out from the windows as she stepped from the taxi and paid the driver. She found her keys and went inside. The house felt warm and welcoming and she could smell onions and garlic frying. Dinner was clearly in progress.

'Jeremy! It's me. I'm back,' she called before the front door was even closed behind her.

Jeremy was in the kitchen as she had assumed and he came bounding out to meet her, engulfing her in a huge hug. He hadn't shaved whilst she'd been away and his new bristles scratched her cheek. His clothes smelled of turpentine and cigarettes.

'Hello there, Sylph,' he said into her neck. 'It's so good to have you home.' He squeezed her tightly and for longer than she might have expected.

Eventually she wriggled free. 'It's good to be back. Did you miss me?'

'Every second,' he said.

She eyed him suspiciously. 'What's going on?' she asked, a laugh in her voice. 'Normally when I'm away you lock yourself in your studio and barely come out except for food. And now you're saying that you actually noticed that I was gone.'

'I did,' he replied, his voice urgent. 'I always do. It's very quiet when you're not here.'

And when Leo isn't here either, she thought. Jeremy would never concede the fact, but she suspected that he missed having her around too, even if it was only to argue with.

'Well, I'm back now,' she said, 'so you can stop pining. I'm parched though. British Rail tea does not improve.'

She left her case at the door of the stairs and moved towards the kitchen.

'How's Christine?' Jeremy asked, following her through.

'She's fine. She never changes. She sends her love.'

'That's nice.'

'And did anything happen here?'

There was a pause, the briefest hiatus, but it was enough to make Sylvie turn round and look at him curiously.

'Something did, as a matter of fact. We had a visitor.'

'Not the police?' asked Sylvie at once, her mind suddenly swamped with all the things that Leo might have been involved in.

Jeremy shook his head. 'No, no. Nothing like that. No, this was a young girl. Same kind of age as Leonora. In fact, exactly the same age as Leonora.'

Sylvie went cold. She could actually feel her blood freezing in her veins just like they said it did in bad novels. She had known that this would happen one day. She had tried to push it from her mind, hoping that Michelle would have forgotten all about it over the years, but in her heart she'd always known it would raise its head again. And now it had.

'Oh?' she said, turning round so that Jeremy couldn't see her face. 'Who was that then?'

'Shall we sit down?' asked Jeremy. His tone was different now, not angry but firm, as if he would brook no nonsense.

Sylvie concentrated on making the tea. She wasn't ready for what she suspected was coming. It wasn't fair that it was being dropped on her like this with no warning, no time to prepare herself.

Jeremy waited until the tea was ready. She could feel his eyes on her as she moved, but he didn't speak until she finally placed two mugs on the table. He nodded at the chair opposite him and she pulled it out and sat down.

'This is all very formal,' she said, trying to make her voice sound light. 'I feel like I'm being interviewed.'

'So, this visitor,' Jeremy continued, completely ignoring her attempt at levity. 'She had an interesting tale to tell.'

Sylvie wished he would just get on with it. Did he know that she had heard it before or not?

'Oh yes?' she said, her voice coming out a little higher than it ought to.

'She told me that she was born on the same day as Leonora and that her mother had told her that there might have been some mix-up or other at the hospital and somehow we and her family had ended up with each other's babies.'

What was she supposed to do? Should she look surprised, or even shocked, by this news?

'That seems unlikely,' she said, fearful that her voice would let her down. 'I'm sure that sort of thing doesn't happen.'

Jeremy pressed on. 'She also said that her mum had been here about ten years ago and told you this but that you hadn't said very much to her.'

Could she pretend that she had no memory of the event? She decided that she couldn't. It wasn't the kind of thing that was easy to forget.

'Someone did come to the house once,' she began, trying to sound as if it was all a little vague. 'And she did make some ridiculous claim along those lines, but it was so madly unlikely that I thought she must be a little bit unhinged and just ignored her. In fact, I'd forgotten all about it.'

Why had she said that? It was such an obvious lie and Jeremy would never believe her.

'Well, now the girl knows and she wants to talk about it too,' he said.

Sylvie stared deep into her tea, not daring to meet Jeremy's eye in case he read the shame in her face.

'What did you tell her?' she asked, her voice quiet and flat.

'Nothing. I listened to what she had to say and then I sent her away. We've arranged to meet on Sunday with you and her parents, and Leonora. But I left us some wriggle room. I said that if anyone doesn't show up then we'll know that they don't want to take it any further.'

Sylvie nodded, absorbing what had just been said. Well, that was good. They just wouldn't go and then that would be the end of it.

Jeremy was entirely focused on her now. She could feel his stare drilling into the crown of her head. Slowly she raised her eyes and met his.

'But what I want to talk about,' he said, 'is how come you knew and never said.'

61

How did you go about finding out who your biological parents were? Donna wondered. It was all very well having this plan to meet and talk about things, but if they did decide that both families wanted to know more, what would they do next?

Donna thought about asking at school, but as she was new there she didn't even know who the biology teachers were. She considered going back to her old school and asking, but she wasn't sure her old teachers would know the answer. She hadn't realised the meaning of the expression 'quality education' until she'd moved to Thomas Welbeck High.

There would definitely be a way of discovering where a child belonged, though. You could do paternity tests, she knew. So surely checking the baby against both parents couldn't be that hard. Would it cost money? Probably. She only had what she earned at her waitressing job, but maybe Sylvie and Jeremy would pay. They didn't look short of a bob or two.

If she and this Leonora had been swapped then perhaps her mum could sue the hospital for its mistake, although she really couldn't see what the point of that would be. If they had been swapped then it wasn't as if anyone would have done it on purpose. It seemed a bit harsh to her to try and screw some cash out of the hospital, although she was pretty sure her dad might think differently.

But this idea of what she might have lost because of the alleged swap took her straight back to where her mind had been wandering ever since her dad had let the cat out of the bag. What had she actually missed out on, if she had been brought up by the wrong family? How might her life have been different? Lots of kids dreamt that they had been adopted at some stage, conjured far more interesting histories for themselves than their real lives offered. Donna had done it herself, whispering her secret dreams to Lucy when no one was listening, but unlike all those other children, she would find out what her other life might have been.

Some differences were obvious. First, there was the money issue, growing up in a house where there was enough to go round. Sylvie and Jeremy were quite obviously wealthier than Michelle and Dean, but she had hardly been living hand to mouth for all these years. Yes, money was tight at home sometimes, but they got by well enough. She had never not had what she needed (as long as you didn't count the latest fashions and holidays in the Caribbean).

There was school too. Sylvie and Jeremy would probably have sent her somewhere better than the local school she'd been to, but she'd got great results in spite of that and she was doing well with her A levels. If this Leonora girl was living in a squat then it sounded like she'd dropped out, so wherever she'd gone it couldn't have been that amazing. Donna appeared to have had the better deal there too. Plus she had Tina and Carl and Damien. Leonora was an only child. Jeremy looked too old to have any more kids and he must have been already pretty ancient when Leonora was born. How much fun could it have been to be brought up in that massive house on your own with old parents and no one else around? Not much, she guessed. Maybe Leonora had exactly the right idea leaving home. Maybe if Donna had been living there she would have done the same thing. Then again, Jeremy had seemed nice. It wasn't as if he was a tyrant who would have driven his child away. And she wasn't Leonora.

Donna concluded that she didn't know what to conclude. The whole situation was very confusing, but there was one aspect that was more straightforward.

Sunday.

She had two simple options. Either she turned up or she didn't. If she didn't turn up then that would be an end of it. She could push the whole thing to the back of her mind and never think about it again – like that was ever going to happen!

Donna knew she had to go. It was a compulsion. She had no choice even though it wouldn't guarantee an answer to the question, was only the next step on the journey, an indication that she was willing to talk about it some more. She might never uncover the truth of what had really happened in that hospital but she had to try.

That was the key for her here, she decided. What had happened. It wasn't that she wanted to abandon Michelle and Dean in favour of the other two. She didn't suddenly feel as if they weren't her parents. She loved them. She would always love them. They had brought her up. They were her mum and dad and always would be.

But balanced against that, she knew she had never quite fitted in at home. There was something about her that stood her apart from the rest of her siblings. For her, the sense of belonging that they all seemed to share had been missing.

If going to the art gallery on Sunday held any purpose for her it was that. She wanted to know where she fitted, not so she could uproot herself, change her life and try to recapture what might have been. She simply needed to know who she was so that she could make sense of what she already had.

62

Michelle had no idea what to think. The inside of her head felt like one of those typhoons you saw on the news. Everything was being picked up from where it had always been and thrown about willy-nilly by a force that she couldn't control. As soon as she settled on one way of looking at the situation, the wind would blow everything around and she wouldn't know where she was again.

She had known that Donna would go back to the house and knock on the door. Hadn't she done the self-same thing as soon as she had first spotted Sylvie all those years before? The temptation was irresistible. To have the chance to lay eyes on the people who might be your biological parents so you could see them for yourself and draw your own conclusions? Who wouldn't do that? Well, no one that she could imagine, at least.

But no conclusions had been drawn. That was the frustrating part. None of them was able to look at Donna and claim her as categorically their own. For a second, Michelle wondered whether there had been a third baby, whether Donna had been mixed with someone else's child, but she dismissed the idea. This was complicated enough as it was!

Now, though, there were decisions to make. Michelle had thought that Jeremy's solution of meeting to discuss things and not showing up if you weren't interested was a good idea when she'd first heard it. She assumed that she was invited, although Donna had been a little vague on the details. When you thought about it, though, the future of what happened to Donna, and she supposed Leonora too, was as much to do with her as anyone else, so why shouldn't she go?

The real question was, did she want to?

And what was she going to do about Dean? He had kicked off this whole charade with his loose tongue, but even though she could cheerfully kill him, she still thought that he should be given the chance to turn up at the art gallery and see what was said. It affected him as much as it did her, though it pained her to say so.

Her hand hovered over the telephone. She hadn't spoken to him since the night in the pub. She only had his phone number to use in emergencies to do with the kids. But this *was* an emergency to do with the kids.

She dialled the number, the receiver trembling in her hand. After three rings it was answered. There was a lot of background noise, some kind of party maybe, and the woman who answered had to shout to be heard.

'Merry Christmas!' she said as if she assumed that Michelle must be someone who merited this greeting, and it threw Michelle for a moment.

'Er, and to you. Is Dean there, please?'

'Dean!' the woman bellowed without moving her mouth from the phone so that Michelle's ear drum reverberated. 'Some woman on the phone for you.'

'Aye, aye,' said someone else, a man's voice. 'Who might this be, Deany-boy?'

'Who is it, babes?' asked a second woman who Michelle thought she recognised as Dean's new girlfriend. She felt herself bristle, as if Dean were still hers.

'Well, let me get to the phone and I'll find out,' she heard him say as he approached and then, 'hello?'

'Dean, it's me,' she said quickly. 'Wait. Don't put the phone down. Something's happened. Something important. I need to talk to you.'

'Well, I'm busy,' Dean replied shortly. 'It's Christmas and we've got some friends over. Won't it wait?'

It could wait a day or two, Michelle supposed, but she wanted to talk about it now. And she definitely didn't want to be second billing to these new friends of his.

'It's about Donna,' she tried again.

'Oh,' replied Dean.

Could she hear a tiny note of shame in the single syllable? She thought she might be able to and it was encouraging. She changed tack.

'I can hear that you're busy right now, but this is important. Could we meet for a drink tomorrow night and I'll fill you in?'

Her heart was pounding so hard that she could feel it in her head. She knew it was a ridiculous reaction. This wasn't a date she was trying to arrange. That boat had left the harbour and was sailing off into the deep blue yonder. Yet she couldn't seem to get her body to understand that.

Dean was quiet for a moment as he considered the proposal. In the background they seemed to be playing a drinking game, a low roar of voices building to a crescendo.

'Okay,' he said. 'I'll meet you in the Ring o' Bells at seven tomorrow.'

The pub was nowhere near where he lived now and Michelle took the suggestion and the fact that he would have to go out of his way as a kind of olive branch.

'That's great,' she said. 'Thanks.'

'Right. See you then,' he said abruptly and then he put the phone down.

Michelle replaced the receiver in its cradle. That hadn't gone quite how she'd imagined, but the result was better than she could have hoped for, especially if Dean was feeling a little bit guilty about his outburst before Christmas.

Now she just needed to work out how she wanted to play it, and to do that she had to know what she wanted to happen at the art gallery.

That was the tricky part.

63

Sylvie heard what Jeremy had said perfectly clearly but she didn't respond, didn't even look up at him.

He repeated himself, his voice calm but insistent. 'Sylvie? How come you didn't tell me that the woman had been here when she first turned up?'

How come indeed?

Sylvie sat and stared into her mug, wishing she was anywhere other than here and having to deal with the mess she had created. She had known that this would catch up with her eventually, but had she ever made a plan that she could pull out of the hat now that the moment was here? Of course not. She had simply entombed the memory of Michelle's visit in the darkest part of her mind and refused to think about it on the basis that it would go away.

But that wasn't good enough any more. She could feel Jeremy's eyes boring into her, searching for clues, desperate to understand. She was going to have to tell him the truth. She owed him that. She loved him, for goodness' sake. They were a team and always had been, except on this one solitary issue.

She swallowed and looked up, meeting his eyes with hers.

'I didn't tell you,' she began, 'because I couldn't bear to think about what she had said.'

His face softened a little as he attached meaning to her words.

'Oh Sylvie, darling. You mean, it was too big to handle on your own? Well, you didn't need to handle it. I was just here. We could have dealt with it together.'

Sylvie's heart plummeted. It would be so easy to let him run with this explanation. He seemed to be accepting her answer at face value without probing any more deeply into it. And it was true, as far as it went. She hadn't been able to think about the implications of what Michelle had said. But she suspected that Jeremy's interpretation of this was far from what she had meant.

But it would be the coward's way out, to allow him to carry on thinking like that. There had been enough hidden between them already. If the girl turning up on their doorstep was to be the catalyst for anything, let it be a clearing of the air, a telling of the truth so that at least moving forward they would all know precisely where they stood.

'It wasn't just that,' she continued, her voice barely above a whisper. 'I mean, it was that partly but also . . .'

Jeremy was looking at her expectantly. Could she do this? It was going to break his heart when she told him how she really felt, how she had felt since they had first discovered she was going to have a baby.

She started again. 'The thing is, Jeremy, I never wanted children. I mean, you knew that, didn't you? I told you right from the very start.'

Jeremy smiled fondly at her. 'You did,' he confirmed. 'You always said that. But then you changed your mind and we had Leonora.'

Sylvie held his gaze, trying to explain her meaning with her eyes. She could see his expression change as he realised that what he'd just said didn't match her feelings. Then his eyebrows came together, expressing his confusion without the need for words.

'I didn't change my mind,' she continued. 'I've never changed my mind.'

'But then, why . . . ?'

Sylvie looked up at the ceiling, no longer able to hold his gaze. She could feel tears forming in the corners of her eyes and she strained to prevent any more from appearing. Her crying wouldn't help anything. She took a deep breath and then blurted it all out before he could interrupt her.

'Because of Jo,' she said. 'I said I'd have a baby because of what happened to Jo. Your mother told me that it might help you with your grief. She was worried you might hurt yourself. You were so low for so very long. And I was worried too. So I did it for you. Not to replace Jo, of course, but to try and help you all with the pain of your loss.'

Jeremy's eyes were glistening now.

'Oh, my darling girl,' he began, his face a picture of compassion.

No, no, thought Sylvie. He hadn't understood. He was thinking that she had made this huge sacrifice for him, and she had, but that was still only half the story.

She touched him on his arm, feeling the need to make a physical connection to him as she made her confession.

'But I didn't want to,' she continued. 'I never changed my mind. Even when Leo was here I didn't want her. I just kept hoping that one day I would feel differently, that I would come to terms with being a mother. But I never did. And then it turned out that I was hopeless at being a mother on top of everything else. I did try, but I just couldn't do it. I kept waiting for some wave of maternal love to wash over me, but it never came. And then Leo was, well, she was Leo, and I thought the way she was turning out had to be my fault because I was such a terrible parent.'

Jeremy had stopped shaking his head in protest at her words. She could see that he was thinking about what she was saying, and wondering if it might be true. He would blame her now. He would finally see what she had always known. It was her fault. It was all her fault.

'And then, when the woman turned up on the doorstep telling me that Leo might not be ours after all, that was the final straw. The idea that I had been through it all for a baby that wasn't even your real child, your mother's real grandchild . . . well, I just couldn't deal with that. So I simply pretended that it had never happened.'

Jeremy put his hand up to stop her talking.

'Hang on,' he said. 'Hang on. You do know that this whole baby swap idea is ridiculous? It's a complete cock-and-bull story. I'm not saying that this Michelle woman didn't believe it at the time. Having a baby can do peculiar things to your mind. But you just have to take one look at Donna to see that she's nothing to do with us.'

A small flame of hope flickered into life in Sylvie's heart.

'Really?' she asked.

'Absolutely. I studied her hard when she was here and I would swear that we're not in any way related. And, looks aside, I'm sure you'd know, wouldn't you, if there was a biological tie? You'd feel it somehow, don't you think?'

You would, Sylvie knew that for certain.

'And as for all that other guff,' continued Jeremy, standing up and coming to put his arms around her shoulders, 'I know you never wanted children but you did it for me and my family. I've always known that and it's made me love you even more. You are not a terrible mother. Leonora is a difficult child but that has nothing to do with you or me. It's just how it is.'

Sylvie knew that she wasn't going to be able to hold her tears back for much longer. It was a relief to have things out in the open, for the secret that she had been carrying for over a decade to finally be told. But she wasn't out of the woods, not just yet.

She let Jeremy hold her for a little longer, enjoying feeling small and safe, but then she said, 'I don't think we should go to this meeting. I think we should let sleeping dogs lie.'

Jeremy released her and held her at arm's length so that he could properly focus on her face.

'Why?' he asked.

Why indeed? She was thinking fast.

'Well, if you're sure that there's nothing in it, then aren't we giving them some kind of false hope by turning up?'

'I don't see how?' replied Jeremy. 'If anything, I think it's quite the reverse. If we can show them that we don't think the girls were swapped, then that would let them put the whole thing to bed and move on.'

It was difficult to argue against that, but Sylvie tried.

'What about Leo?'

'What about her?'

'Well, we'd need to tell her.'

'Yes, probably,' agreed Jeremy, 'but if we're sure that there's nothing in it then what harm can that do? It's simply an entertaining story for her, nothing more. And I can't see her being bothered about coming to the meeting, can you?'

Sylvie wasn't so sure. There was little Leo enjoyed more than a good drama.

She had one last go.

'I really think that the greatest good would be achieved by us just forgetting about the whole thing,' she said. 'Let's not go. We could go out for the day instead, do something lovely.'

But she could see that she was on a hiding to nothing. Jeremy shook his head.

'No. As you sat on this whole situation for such a long time, I think it's my turn to make a decision, and I think we should try and straighten everything out for this Michelle woman so she can stop worrying about it.'

Sylvie knew she had lost. They were about to make a huge mistake, but there was absolutely nothing she could do to stop it happening.

64

Michelle got ready for her meeting with Dean with more care than the occasion merited. She didn't want to examine her motives too closely. She didn't need to. There was no mystery. She wanted to look nice for him. Every part of her knew that was wrong but she couldn't help herself. So she chose a top that made her look slim and spent time on her hair and make-up. She didn't want to come across as too done-up, though. Just enough that he might be reminded of what he'd found attractive about her in the first place.

When she was ready, she sat back and looked at herself in the mirror. She would do. There was no hiding the fact that she was no longer the girl that Dean had fallen in love with, but she wasn't doing too badly for a woman in her forties. The girlfriend was a good ten years younger than her, though. Michelle tried to dismiss the thought. No point thinking like that. She could hardly wind time back.

Donna was downstairs watching a Christmas quiz on the television. She looked up as Michelle walked in.

'You look nice,' she said. 'Going somewhere special?'

Michelle could lie but what would be the point?

'I'm going to meet your dad,' she replied. 'Tell him about what's been going on.'

'Oh,' said Donna, her face falling.

'I have to tell him,' Michelle pressed on. 'It's his right to know. And he might want to go to the meeting. I can't just not tell him about it.'

'I suppose not. It's just that I've not seen him since that night. Do you think I should come with you, talk about everything?'

That was exactly what Michelle didn't want.

She shook her head. 'No. I think me and your dad need to talk this through on our own. For today at least,' she added.

Donna seemed to accept that, her attention turning back to the television. Michelle thought she might look a little bit relieved.

'Well, I hope it goes okay,' she said, without looking round.

Michelle slipped into her coat and went out into the night. As she walked through the dark streets she tried to run through what she was proposing to say to Dean, but she couldn't get her thoughts to sit still in her head. There had been a time when she would have known exactly how he would have responded to anything, but she wasn't sure she still knew him that well. And on this issue she really couldn't second-guess him at all. Pretty much anything could happen.

She pushed open the heavy door and went into the pub. It was warm inside and the air was thick with cigarette smoke and the smell of beer. Dean was already there, sitting on his own at a table facing the door, a half-drunk pint on the table in front of him. That hadn't changed then, thought Michelle fondly. He never had liked the idea of her waiting in a pub on her own and always made sure that he got there before her. She smiled at him, waved her arm and then signalled that she was going to get a drink for herself.

Minutes later she settled down on the stool opposite him.

'Hi,' she began, hoping that her body language wasn't giving away her nerves. 'Nice Christmas?'

'Yeah, not bad,' he replied. 'You?'

'Much the same as last year,' she said. 'They just keep coming, don't they?'

'You're not wrong.'

She hated this awkwardness between them. When had it built up? How had she become uncomfortable in front of the man she had loved for most of her life?

'Listen,' she continued, determined to stay focused on the task in hand. 'Something's happened and I just need to talk it over with you. Is that okay?'

'I'm listening.'

Michelle took a deep breath. There was no way of beginning this conversation without referring to his outburst before Christmas, but she didn't want to set things off on the wrong foot before she'd even begun.

'You remember that night in here, just before Christmas?'

Dean rolled his eyes and gave her a lazy grin.

'Barely,' he said. 'I was pissed as a newt.'

Michelle relaxed a little. It would make it easier if he wasn't defensive. She avoided the temptation to agree with him on the state of his drunkenness.

'Our Donna had some questions after that. You can imagine.'

Dean nodded. He might even have looked a little sheepish, although Michelle couldn't be sure.

'I told her what had happened when she was born. And I told her about seeing the woman from the next bed up by the cathedral that time.'

She had to be careful. She had never told Dean that she had gone back to the house, had spoken to Sylvie. He had told her not to go and she had done it anyway.

'Okay,' he said, an air of caution entering his voice now.

'I showed her where the couple lived.'

'Not sure that was wise,' he chipped in.

Michelle felt an irritation rise up in her. What did he expect her to do when his actions had blasted Donna's life to pieces, leaving her to rebuild it?

'Well, that's what I did,' she said, not wanting to get caught up in the whys and wherefores. 'So, Donna, being Donna, went and knocked on the door.'

'Christ! And they let her in?'

Michelle nodded. 'The husband did at least. The woman wasn't there. So Donna tells him all about why she's there, what I'd said, and he listened to her. She said he was good about it.'

Dean was listening hard now too. She could see him leaning in towards her so that he didn't miss a word.

'And he came up with a proposal,' Michelle continued. 'He's suggesting that we all meet in the art gallery on Sunday to have a chat.'

'Funny place for a chat,' said Dean. 'The art gallery.'

'Well, they're artists I think. That's the kind of place they must hang out in. Anyway, the arrangement is that if you want to talk about what happened then you turn up. And if either side isn't there then the other will drop the whole thing and not mention it again.'

'Sides, is it?' asked Dean.

Michelle shook her head. 'No. I don't think so. It's not an argument or anything. Family then. If either family doesn't show up.'

Dean nodded and took a drink of his pint. He smacked his lips together to catch the froth from his beer. It was a gesture that Michelle had seen a thousand times before and her heart turned over.

'Right,' he said. 'I see.'

He blew his lips out, leaned back in his chair, let his eyes dance over the tobacco-stained ceiling.

'So. What do you think?' she prompted.

'About what?'

'About what I just said! Do you think we should go?'

'Am I even invited, given . . . everything?' he asked.

'Of course you are. You're still her dad even if we don't live together any more.'

This was a moot point, Michelle knew, but she hoped that Dean would step above it.

He fell quiet again. Michelle was tempted to fill the silence with more words but she resisted the urge. Even though it was killing her, she had to be patient. This was all new to him. He needed time to process what he had heard.

Eventually he said, 'What do you think we should do?'

Michelle rejoiced in his use of 'we' but she tried not to let it show.

'I think we should go,' she said. 'I think we owe that much to Donna, and she's keen.'

'What did Donna say about the bloke? Did she think he might be her real dad?'

Michelle shook her head. 'She said she couldn't tell. I suppose it might be different when she meets Sylvie. That's the woman.'

'It's a bit risky,' said Dean. 'What if we go and they don't turn up? That would be pretty hard on Donna.'

He was thinking like he was her dad, Michelle thought, caring about the fallout on her. She liked it.

'It is risky,' she agreed. 'But I think it might be worse if we don't go. Then she'll always wonder. At least if we turn up and they don't then it's something that she could never have controlled.'

Dean nodded. 'That's true enough,' he said. 'When is it, this meeting?'

'Sunday at two,' she said, suddenly worrying that he might not be able to make it and all this would have been in vain.

'I could do that,' he said. 'Question is, do you want me to?'

Michelle sighed involuntarily.

'God, yes please,' she said.

65

Sylvie had no way of getting in touch with Leo other than just turning up on her doorstep and hoping that she was in. She supposed she could have sent her a letter telling her daughter when she would arrive but that felt very formal.

It took two attempts. The first time she knocked at the boarded-up house, one of Leo's housemates opened the door and told Sylvie that Leo was out. Sylvie wasn't at all sure that she believed him; something about his expression suggested that he was covering for Leo, which made her wonder what her daughter might have done that required covering up. Maybe living in a squat just made you suspicious of everyone.

'I'm her mother,' she added in case the boy thought she was a policewoman, but he shook his head.

'Makes no difference who you are,' he said. 'She ain't here.'

Sylvie resisted the urge to correct his grammar and instead said, 'Could you tell her I popped by, please? I'll try again at the same time tomorrow.'

He closed the door, leaving Sylvie wondering whether he had heard what she'd said or intended to act upon it.

As good as her word, she turned up the following day and this time it was Leo herself who opened the door.

'Mum! Hi! This is a nice surprise.'

The message hadn't filtered through, then.

'I came yesterday but you were out,' Sylvie said.

'Actually, I know,' replied Leo, wrinkling her nose at her lie. 'Dessie said. Do you want to come in?'

Sylvie really didn't. It was hard enough knowing that Leo was living in this kind of place. She didn't need to see it again and really give her imagination something to play with.

'I have something I need to talk to you about,' she said, 'so we can either do that here or at a café somewhere.'

Leo craned her neck and looked up at the sky behind Sylvie. 'It's a nice day. Why don't we go for a walk?'

Sylvie tried not to look surprised. Since when did Leo suggest a walk as an activity of choice? She wasn't going to knock it though. It would be easier to have the conversation she needed to have if they were moving and looking straight ahead.

'That sounds great,' she said.

'Just let me get my coat,' said Leo, and disappeared back into the house.

A coat too? She really did seem to be growing up. Time was when she would have gone out in just what she was wearing and ignored the weather conditions.

Leo reappeared in a navy blue duffel coat that Sylvie didn't recognise, a yellow scarf twisted around her neck.

'Right. Let's go.'

She stepped out into the street, closing the door firmly behind her.

'How was your Christmas?' asked Sylvie as they headed down the pavement. 'Did the nut roast turn out okay?'

Leo grinned at her. 'It was disgusting,' she said. 'The top and bottom inch were charcoal and the bit in between was raw. We ended up making a "chuck it all in" curry instead.'

'Sounds fun,' said Sylvie, and it did. The 'go with the flow'-ness of it reminded her of their house in London where pretty much anything went, especially at Christmas. This train of thought led her smartly to Jo and the accident and then to . . .

'And how was Christmas in the house of misery?' asked Leo.

Sylvie pulled a face. 'Don't call it that, Leo. You know your dad finds Christmas hard after what happened to Auntie Jo. But actually, I was at Christine's this year. I left him to it.'

'Good for you, Mum,' replied Leo. 'Christine okay?'

'Yes. She's really well. It was great to see her.'

They reached the common, a large open area of grassland used for dog walking, football, fairs and anything else that needed space. It seemed quite busy, lots of children riding on new Christmas bicycles, some with their dads running behind holding on to wobbling saddles.

'That's sweet,' said Leo wryly, tipping her head at a particularly precarious pair.

Had Jeremy ever done that with her? Sylvie wondered. She didn't think so. She wasn't even sure that Leo could ride a bike.

'Actually, something odd happened when I was away at Christine's,' she began.

She could feel her palms becoming clammy even though her hands were cold. She wished with all her heart that she didn't have to have this conversation, but she could see no other option. Leo needed to know.

'Oh yes?' said Leo.

She was curious, interested even, which made Sylvie feel even more heinous than she already did. What she was about to reveal would rock Leo's life to its foundations.

'A girl about your age turned up at the house. She said that her mum believed you and her were mixed up at the hospital when you were both born.'

Sylvie paused, letting her words settle, but Leo seemed to have processed this already. Sylvie prepared herself for an explosion, but Leo remained preternaturally calm.

'So,' Leo said ponderously, her pace slowing as she thought about what was being said. 'She reckons she's your daughter, and I'm theirs?'

Sylvie swallowed. Leo always had been quick on the uptake even if her school record didn't always reflect that.

'Precisely,' she said.

'Shit. That's weird,' replied Leo. She kept staring straight ahead, her mouth turned down at the corners as she considered it.

They continued to walk. Sylvie was desperate to know what was going on in Leo's head but Leo was giving nothing away. Is that something she's learned from me, she wondered, keeping her emotions so well hidden?

Learned from me, or inherited from me?

Now that was a question.

It felt like an eternity before Leo spoke again.

'And what did Dad say?' she asked.

Yet again, her astute daughter had managed to home in on the very essence of the situation. Where had this maturity come from? Sylvie wondered. Was it a result of living on her own, or had it always been there but they had been so busy shouting that no one had noticed?

'I'll bet he was delighted at the idea that I might not be anything to do with him after all,' Leo continued, but now there was the tiniest crack in her voice.

Sylvie went to put an arm around her shoulder, and then thought better of it. The key to getting through this had to be to maintain the status quo.

'He thought no such thing,' she said instead. 'But he didn't want to send the girl away with a flea in her ear when she was clearly confused, so he suggested that we wait a week to let the idea settle, and then all meet up to talk about it. So, that's why I'm here. To catch up with your news, of course, but also to see if you want to be a part of it.'

Leo had stiffened, her body suddenly wound defensively tight. Sylvie could feel the tension coming off her as they walked.

'And if it's true?' Leo asked. 'Then what? You ship me off to this other lot without a backward glance?'

There was a bitterness in her voice that made Sylvie wince. Did Leo really think they would even consider doing that? But then could she, hand on heart, say that it hadn't crossed Jeremy's mind?

'No! Of course not,' she said quickly. 'Don't be silly. And anyway your father thinks it's all rubbish. He only suggested the meeting so that we can dismiss it and get back to normal. There's been no talk of swapping families. Heaven forbid!'

Leo suddenly looked very young, all the bravado of the girl who lived by herself at sixteen evaporated.

'And what do you think, Mum?' she asked. 'Do you think it might be true?'

The question Sylvie had been dreading. She replied before the words were barely out of Leo's mouth.

'No,' she said. 'I don't.' She hoped she sounded convincing. 'Will you come?' she asked quietly. 'To the meeting.'

She sensed a shifting in Leo. The vulnerability of a moment ago had gone and was replaced by the familiar cocksure carapace that usually enveloped her daughter.

'Too right,' she replied. 'If you think I'm going to miss out on this little showdown you've got another think coming. What did she look like anyway, this girl?' she continued. 'Could she be the long-lost daughter he's been dreaming of?'

'Please don't talk like that,' replied Sylvie. 'It's upsetting for everyone. But no. I'm not sure your dad thought that there was much truth in the story.'

'Couldn't resist having a poke at it though, just to see if it could breathe on its own?'

'I think he just wanted to help this other girl get it out of her system. It must be very disorientating, thinking that you don't belong somewhere.'

Leo raised her eyebrows. 'You don't say. So, when is this little gathering?'

'Sunday at two in the art gallery.'

'How very Dad. Well, you can count me in. I'll be right there to check out this freak show family.'

Sylvie opened her mouth to yet again tell Leo not to say things like that, but then she closed it again. What would be the point?

They walked on a little further and reached the children's play area.

'Fancy a go on the swings?' Leo asked, and veered off the path on to the tarmacked area without waiting for a reply.

Sylvie followed her. Leo made straight for the swings and then hopped on to one, starting herself going by pushing back with her legs and then working them hard until she was flying at the full height the chains would allow.

Sylvie got on the swing next to her. She couldn't remember the last time she'd been on one and she thought she might have forgotten how to make it move, but it turned out it was just muscle memory and as soon as her bottom hit the plastic seat her body knew exactly what to do. Soon she was swinging too, not as high as Leo, but it still felt fabulous.

'Funny old things, families,' said Leo as their swings passed one another.

Rarely had she said anything as true.

66

Sunday was upon them far more quickly than Michelle would have chosen. She had thought of nothing else but the meeting night and day, but still she had no clear idea in her head of what she wanted to do. And now time had run out and she wasn't much further forward than she had been before.

Why was she still so unsure? Michelle had spent the last sixteen years looking at her daughter and wondering who she really was. Admittedly, this had been happening less often in recent years. Sometimes weeks would go by without her questioning anything at all, but then Donna would say something that she didn't understand and Michelle's doubts would be thrust back to front and centre of her consciousness.

The whole mystery had trotted along at her ankles for years, getting underfoot at every turn. Yet here she was, facing the chance to finally get the answer, and she found that she was no longer certain she wanted to know. She had become used to the status quo. Donna might or might not be her biological daughter, but she realised she no longer cared. She was her daughter – that was all that mattered.

The idea that Sylvie might steal Donna away, leaving Michelle with the mysterious Leonora, filled Michelle with dread. She kept telling herself that it couldn't happen. Donna was a good kid.

She wouldn't just abandon the family she had always known for a bunch of strangers.

So, why put the opportunity to do so in her path? It was such a risky thing to do. What was the point if they were sure it wouldn't make a difference to how Donna thought? It was a perpetual loop that she couldn't break free from.

The two of them were watching an old James Bond movie, the one where Roger Moore seemed to twinkle his way out of a crocodile-infested pond. Michelle had seen the film so many times that she could probably quote huge chunks of the dialogue and yet still she watched, comforted by the familiarity of it.

Donna was flicking through the Christmas *TV Times* which was on its last legs now that it was New Year's Day.

'We should get this every week,' she said. 'Not just at Christmas. It's dead handy to see what's going to be on.'

Michelle shook her head. 'It's a Christmas tradition,' she said. 'Wouldn't be much of a treat if we had it all the time.'

Donna flicked back to the front cover and peered at the price. 'It's expensive too,' she said.

This was why she was Michelle's daughter. None of the other kids would have thought about that.

'Listen, Donna,' she began, hesitant to say what was on her mind but still determined to do it. 'We don't have to go on Sunday, to the art gallery. We could just walk away. I'm not sure how we'd reach any answers anyway, just by talking. Maybe it would be better to forget about the whole thing?'

Donna refolded the magazine so it was open at that day's listings and put it down next to her. She seemed to be thinking about what she was going to say next, her eyes focused on the middle distance. Michelle waited, knowing that it was always best not to interrupt when Donna was considering. Michelle's breath came shallow and quick.

It felt like an age before Donna spoke again.

'Do you remember when I was little,' she began, 'and I had Lucy?'

'Your invisible friend? Of course I remember.'

'Did you ever wonder why I had an invisible friend?'

Michelle didn't like the way this was going at all, but she had backed herself into a corner by asking the question in the first place so now she just had to follow it through.

'Well,' she said. 'There was quite a big gap between you and Damien, and he and the others used to leave you out a bit.'

Donna's face slid into a wry grin before becoming sombre again. 'They did, didn't they, the buggers. But that wasn't the reason. There were other kids my age around. I could have played with them, and there were people from my class at school. But I preferred Lucy.'

'You always did like your own company,' agreed Michelle.

'Still do. But back then, I had this feeling I was in the wrong place, that I didn't quite fit in. So I created Lucy so I had someone who got me.'

Michelle opened her mouth to object, but Donna kept speaking.

'It's not a bad thing,' she said quickly. 'And I'm not saying that I didn't belong here, just that I thought I didn't. It's quite common, kids who believe they're secretly adopted. It's a little fantasy that we play out in our head for fun.'

A fantasy that her daughter belonged to someone else? Had Michelle made such a bad job of being Donna's mother that she'd thought she was in the wrong family?

'Oh God, Donna. I . . .'

But again Donna silenced her, putting up a hand to stop her. 'Look. I know I'm different to the others. I'm quiet and I like reading and all that. But what I realise now is that that doesn't mean I don't belong. It just means that I'm my own person. And actually, we're all different. Tina isn't a tearaway like Carl was. Damien can be dead gentle, which the others aren't. And I'm brainy and like being on my own. That's just who I am.'

Michelle still wasn't sure where this was going, but she nodded anyway. The main thing here was that Donna felt supported.

'When I went up to their house I wanted answers. I'd only just found out what you told me and it was still crashing round my head looking for a place to live. But when I got there and met Jeremy it was like a massive anticlimax. Nothing felt familiar about him. Nothing at all. There was no buzz between us. He was like a total stranger. And that's when I worked it out. Of course I'm your kid. Yours and Dad's. So, you've got no reason to worry when we meet them. And I'm not about to run off with them and leave you. It's just not happening.'

Michelle gave her a weak smile. The relief was making her feel light-headed.

'Well, that's good,' she managed, hoping it sounded like the thought had never crossed her mind.

Donna reached across and gave her a quick hug.

'But I do think we need to put it to bed,' she continued. 'I've opened Pandora's box and I need to be the one to close it again. We just have to hope too much hasn't sneaked out already.'

Michelle had no idea what she was talking about, nor who Pandora was, but she decided just to go with it. 'Okay,' she said. 'And . . . ?'

'We go and we hear what they have to say and then we tell them that we don't believe that there was a swap. I mean, it's obvious when you look at us. I can't possibly be related to Jeremy. And then that will be an end to it.'

Michelle listened, and as she did she could feel all the questions that she had ever asked herself about Donna gradually ebb away.

Her daughter was right, as she usually was. They needed to grasp this nettle and then just drop it and trample it down into the grass.

'Okay,' Michelle replied. 'If that's what you want to do then that's fine by me.'

And the relief she felt was enormous.

67

Sylvie had always loved the art gallery. It was a tiny little affair when compared to the grand old dames of London where she used to hang out, but its eclectic collection of paintings, furniture and grandfather clocks had been a comfort to her over the years. She had a great affection for all the pieces in the collection, built up over hours of close examination. It had been a sanctuary of sorts, a place to escape to when life at home felt too difficult. The gallery had always been there for her, except on Christmas Day and New Year's Day each year, which was a shame as she would have cheerfully spent a Christmas or two in there if she could have done.

It was irritating, therefore, that Jeremy had chosen this special place as the venue for the forthcoming meeting. She feared that the gallery would be forever tainted by the event, that it would lose some, or maybe all, of its charm as a result.

But the arrangement had been made without her and, as none of them had any way of getting in touch with one another, there was nothing that she could do to change it.

'Did you say a particular room?' she asked Jeremy as they made their way down the cobbled street towards the gallery. 'To meet in, I mean.'

Jeremy shook his head. 'It was all such a shock that I didn't think of that,' he confessed. 'I just said the gallery. But I'm sure we'll find them, assuming they're there to be found. You've met the mother before and I'll recognise Donna. And who is going to be in on the Sunday after Christmas anyway, except us?'

Sylvie felt the nausea that had been building all morning rise up in her throat. She swallowed it back down.

'They might not come,' she said, realising as she said this just how much she hoped for this outcome, but Jeremy shook his head again.

'I can't see that happening,' he said. 'Donna was all fired up. Even if her parents don't want to be there, I'm sure she will be.'

The knot in Sylvie's stomach tightened.

'And Leonora said she wanted to come? That's what she said?' He looked at her questioningly.

She nodded. 'Not that that means much. Leonora will do as she pleases, as well we know.'

Sylvie wished with all her heart that she hadn't had to invite Leo, but there'd been no way round it as far as she could see. And they both knew that hell would freeze over before Leo missed something like this. The opportunity to disrupt was just too strong for her to resist.

They arrived at the art gallery, a squat stone-faced building sitting in a small sloping park a little down the hill from their house. As they walked up to the main doors, Sylvie grasped Jeremy's arm, holding him back.

'It's not too late,' she said, her voice uncharacteristically desperate. 'We could still change our minds?'

Jeremy stopped walking and turned to face her. He gave her a wide, confident smile. She assumed it was supposed to be reassuring but it just made her feel like shaking him.

'Look, Sylph. We're only going for Donna's sake,' he said. 'So she can get this out of her system. We both know there'll be nothing in it. Although,' he said, raising one eyebrow, 'can you imagine if it were true? Wouldn't that explain how difficult Leonora has been over the years?'

No, it wouldn't. Leonora was their child, their responsibility and just because she hadn't always matched up exactly to Jeremy's hopes didn't mean that it was anything to do with biology. It was far more likely to be a result of Sylvie's failure to engage properly as a mother.

How could she persuade him that it would be in everyone's best interests to leave well alone?

She had one last go.

'Jeremy, darling. I love you, you know I do. But I really think that we are about to make a huge mistake. It'll be awful for Leo to think that we're taking any part of this seriously. Let's catch her before she goes inside and go back home. This woman's story is a fantasy, born of her own demons, and there's no reason for us to get caught up in it.' She let her eyes trace his smiling face, imploring him with everything she had to change his mind.

But it was no good. Jeremy put his arms around her and pulled her into him. 'I understand what you're saying, Sylvie, but we've been over this. We'll hear them out for Donna's sake. Then we can just walk away.'

Sylvie's shoulders slumped. She knew she was defeated.

'Okay,' she said. 'If you're sure.'

68

The lights were on in the art gallery, but there was no sign of life as Jeremy pushed open the door and headed inside. The regular security guard was sitting at his station reading a Dick Francis novel and he looked up as he heard them approach, his face bursting into a smile when he saw who it was.

'Mrs F!' he said. 'How lovely to see you. Did you have a tip-top Christmas?'

'I did thank you, Frank, and I hope yours was lovely too,' Sylvie replied, trying to sound as natural as she could.

'It's always much of a muchness these days,' he said, 'but mustn't grumble.' He turned to look at Jeremy. 'I hope you don't mind me being so familiar with your wife, sir. It's just that my old tongue trips up over that posh surname of yours.'

Jeremy beamed at him in that way he had when he wanted someone to like him.

'I don't mind at all,' he said. 'It is a dreadful mouthful. Now, are we the only ones here today?' He looked around the ground floor that could be seen from where they were standing.

Frank nodded. 'Just you,' he said. 'Everyone else is at home watching crap on the telly and eating the dregs of the Quality Street. That's the strawberry creams in our house. Can't abide them.' He gave Sylvie a wink.

As they never had any Quality Street chocolates in their house, she had no idea how to reply so she just smiled. 'We'll just . . .' she said meaninglessly, and then pulled Jeremy away into the first room.

'You have a nice wander,' called Frank after them. 'I'll be right here if you need anything.'

'Where do you think we should go?' she asked Jeremy, whispering even once they were out of earshot. It was a big empty space and sound travelled easily.

Jeremy cast his eyes around. 'Upstairs, maybe?' he suggested.

'Will we hear them come in?' Sylvie asked. 'I'd hate for them to think we weren't here and just leave.' Or perhaps that might be the ideal solution, she thought but didn't say.

'Bound to hear them,' said Jeremy. 'This place echoes like a cave.'

They headed up, following the curve of the sweeping marble staircase. The ceiling was vaulted and covered in a lattice of plasterwork that always reminded Sylvie of the bottom of a boat. Classical statues of naked Romans were scattered at intervals, as if they were there to keep watch. They'll be in for a treat today, Sylvie thought.

She made straight for the collection of enamel snuff boxes at the back of the upstairs gallery. Each was beautifully decorated with intricate images of people and landscapes. Given her own style of art, it wasn't surprising that she was always drawn to these tiny masterpieces. Now she let her eyes roam over each picture, their familiarity spreading calm through her. Behind her Jeremy was pacing, the click of his heels reverberating around the space. She wanted to tell him to stand still, but she recognised that he too was nervous so she held her tongue and tried to block the sound out. Inside her chest her heartbeat aligned with his steps.

Her eyes flicked down to her watch. It was just before two. Her stomach lurched and she breathed in slowly through her mouth, trying to calm the nausea. It would be all right, she told herself. Everything was going to be all right.

She just wished she could believe that.

Her gaze settled on an oval box decorated with an image of a woman in a bonnet fussing over a baby in a wicker crib. Above them she could make out the words 'Parental Affection' painted in tiny dark lettering. Sylvie squeezed her eyes tightly shut. What were they doing here? Every instinct was telling her that this was wrong, that they should leave and forget all about it.

But then the main door opened downstairs. So they'd come. A couple of whispering female voices floated up the stairs towards them. It must be Donna and Michelle, she thought. Leo would never enter a room whispering.

They spoke briefly to Frank, and then she heard their tentative steps coming up the stairs. The temptation to make a bolt for it was so strong that Sylvie had to hold on to the wooden display case to stop herself from running. She didn't turn round. She didn't want to see them. Behind her she heard Jeremy's steps moving towards the staircase and then his voice, confident and cheerful, calling out to them.

'Hello, Donna,' he said. 'You decided to come. I'm so glad.'

'I said I would,' replied Donna.

Her voice sounded strained, wary as if she didn't like to be doubted. Part of Sylvie was desperate to turn round and look at her, but her nerve failed her. She stayed where she was, hidden by the gallery wall.

'You did indeed,' agreed Jeremy. 'And this must be Michelle? How very nice to meet you.'

'We met once before,' said Michelle.

Her local accent was more pronounced than Sylvie remembered, although accents always sounded stronger when you couldn't see the speaker.

'Of course, we did,' said Jeremy, 'although I'm ashamed to say that the meeting has completely slipped my memory. Well, it's nice to meet you again,' he added.

Sylvie couldn't hear Michelle's reply. Was she as nervous as Sylvie?

'And is your father coming, Donna?' Jeremy asked.

'Yes. But he's a bit late,' replied Donna. 'He said he'd definitely be here, though. That's right, isn't it, Mum?'

'Yeah. Should be here any minute,' said Michelle. Her voice was reed-thin with nerves.

'Our daughter Leonora is also late,' said Jeremy in a tone that suggested an accompanying eye roll, and Sylvie sent him a silent message begging him not to criticise Leo in front of these strangers. He must have heard her because he said nothing else.

'Has your wife not come?' Michelle asked.

Sylvie could picture her looking around the gallery and she knew that she could stay hidden no longer.

'She's around here somewhere,' said Jeremy jovially. 'Sylvie. Show yourself. Come and say hello.'

Sylvie stood where she was for another second and then, taking a deep breath to stop her head from spinning, she stepped out on to the landing.

Michelle was standing slightly in front of her daughter, protective. The lower part of her face and neck were wrapped in a thick scarf, but Sylvie could make out just enough to recognise the woman who had come to their door all those years before.

And then there was Donna. Or at least there was a second person standing next to Michelle. Sylvie couldn't bring herself to look at her. Instead she focused her gaze on the space just above Michelle's head and forced her mouth into a smile.

'Hello,' she said.

'Hello again,' said Michelle, her tone guarded, which wasn't surprising given Sylvie's behaviour the last time they'd met.

'Hi,' said Donna.

'I was just saying to Donna that I can't remember the last time I was in here. School trip in the juniors I think. God, isn't that rubbish?' Michelle looked at them to confirm that she was the philistine that she seemed to believe herself to be, but Jeremy shook his head.

'Not at all,' he said and then, dropping his voice, 'it's not a very good art gallery. There's very little here that merits a second visit.'

Sylvie wanted to step in to defend her beloved gallery, but she could see that would seem odd in the circumstances so she focused on maintaining her smile.

Before they had a chance to say anything else the door opened downstairs.

'And here's another person, but will it be Leonora or your husband?' quipped Jeremy, like some jovial game show host. 'I'm sorry, I don't know his name.' He looked to Michelle to fill in the details.

'Ex-husband,' she said. 'And it's Dean.'

'Chelle?' came a deep voice from downstairs. 'You in here?'

'Dean it is,' said Jeremy just as Michelle called, 'We're up here.'

They could hear Dean bounding up the stone stairs. It sounded as if he were taking them two at a time and seconds later he was there. He was wearing jeans and a battered jacket, a Nottingham Forest cap pulled down low on his head.

'All right,' he said, nodding at Jeremy and Sylvie in turn. 'I'm Dean.'

'Good afternoon,' replied Jeremy. 'Nice to meet you.'

He held out a hand to Dean and Dean shook it. He had working hands, Sylvie noticed, strong with large knuckles and several silvery scars telling tales of past adventures. There was engine oil under his nails. She was more used to paint than oil, and Jeremy's hands were less battered, but they both had working hands which made a connection of sorts between the two men.

'This is all a bit weird,' said Dean. 'It's not every day you meet the people who might have taken your kid by accident.'

'I don't think anyone took anyone, Dean,' hissed Michelle. 'It was a mistake, if it happened. No one's fault.'

'Except the moron at the hospital,' he said. 'I mean, how hard can it be to keep track of a few babies?'

'We're still waiting for Leonora, I'm afraid,' said Jeremy, wandering over to look out of a large window that gave out over the park. 'She's not always entirely reliable, so if she's not here in a couple of minutes then perhaps we should start without her.'

Start what, exactly? Sylvie thought, and from Dean's expression he thought much the same, but neither of them made any comment.

Donna wandered away from Michelle's side and went to look at a grandfather clock. The face was white with Roman numerals and a gold decorative background and the case was fashioned out of austere mahogany. It always reminded Sylvie a little of a coffin.

'That clock's wrong,' said Dean. 'Not much point in a clock that doesn't tell time.'

'But it's old, Dad,' replied Donna. 'That'll be why. It'll be made by a famous clockmaker or something.'

Sylvie knew exactly who had made the clock and when, but she didn't want to draw any attention to herself so she kept the details quietly in her head. Donna was a curious person. She liked that. Curiosity for its own sake was a gift few people were bestowed with.

Dean shrugged as if he thought a clock that didn't tell the time had no merit no matter how old it was.

'I'm not sure what I think about all this, to be honest,' he said. 'When Michelle first told me, I thought she'd gone mad. We'd only just brought our Donna home and I assumed she wasn't thinking straight because she was so knackered. And then after that I wondered . . .'

Michelle seemed to signal to him to be quiet, her eyes wide and eyebrows raised.

'Well, that doesn't matter now,' continued Dean, taking off his cap and rubbing his hand through his cropped hair. 'But I'm just not sure that hospitals make mistakes. It all seems a bit pie in the—'

He stopped talking mid-sentence.

'What?'

Jeremy was staring at him, open-mouthed.

Dean pulled a face at him. 'What's up, mate?' he asked. 'You got a problem?'

Jeremy still didn't speak.

But Sylvie knew exactly what was going on.

He is seeing what I saw all those years ago, she thought.

69

Michelle hadn't liked how things were going. She wasn't sure what she had been expecting to happen but it wasn't this, all skating around each other with no one taking a lead. She needed someone to take control, to give them a direction to follow, but knew that it couldn't be her. She hadn't a clue where to start.

Typically, Donna seemed to be distancing herself from the group, looking at the exhibits that pulled her further and further away from everyone else. That wasn't really a surprise, but Michelle wished her daughter would stay closer by. She wanted to be able to reach out and touch her, to claim her as her own in case the others tried to take her.

Dean was compensating for feeling like a fish out of water by being overly chatty, but he was coming across as a little bit aggressive which only emphasised how uncomfortable he must be. At least he hadn't said the art was crap, not yet at least.

Sylvie was barely engaging at all. She wasn't quite as catatonic as she had been when they first met, but it was obvious that she didn't want to be there, that this meeting was being driven by Jeremy. Michelle tried to examine her features without appearing to stare. Was Donna in there somewhere? She definitely couldn't see it, not in Jeremy either, and with each moment that passed she began to feel more secure. It must be obvious to the others that

Donna couldn't be Sylvie and Jeremy's daughter, so that should bring an end to it all. Thank God. She would finally be able to put the whole horrible nightmare behind her.

How long would that take? she wondered. They were going through the motions here, striking up polite but awkward conversation. There must come a point, though, when they all agreed that she'd been flogging a dead horse with this swapped baby theory. In fact, it was probably up to her to say so, seeing as it was her who had kicked that ball rolling all those years ago.

She was about to open her mouth to say that she'd obviously made a mistake and that maybe they could all just forget about it and go home when the gallery door opened again. This must be Leonora, Michelle thought. She'd better wait until she found them before she gave her little speech.

Then she noticed that Jeremy, all open and friendly a moment ago, had suddenly gone very quiet. Perhaps he was feeling a little intimidated by Dean. Dean was a big bloke and not afraid to call a spade a bloody shovel if called upon. Jeremy was an artist. His body was soft and bulged against his clothes, whereas Dean's torso was still solid. Jeremy would definitely come off worse in a fight, a fact that might just have occurred to him and might explain his sudden silence.

They heard Leonora speak to the security guard and then begin coming up the stairs. She was singing under her breath – 'Yeah, yeah, yeah . . .' Michelle recognised the Stereo MCs' hit as she began the next line.

'Anyone up here?' she called out as she reached the top of the stairs. 'Where's everybody hiding? I'm here for the big family reveal as instructed.'

And then she appeared in the room. She was wearing a blue duffel coat and her hair was dyed pink and cropped very short. Her nose was pierced and there were tiny silver rings dangling up the sides of her left ear.

Michelle went very cold. It was as if all the walls of the gallery had fallen away leaving her exposed on a chilly mountainside.

Leonora stood where she was and took in the scene.

'All right, Mum,' she said, nodding at Sylvie with a smile. 'Dad.'

Then her eyes tracked back to the rest of them. Michelle wasn't breathing. She seemed to have forgotten how. She felt Leonora's gaze pass over her, like the beam of a searchlight. Then she took in Donna, still standing a little back from the group, and kept moving.

And then she reached Dean.

Everything changed. It felt as if time had stopped ticking, leaving them frozen like a still from a film, the attention of all the characters caught by the same thing.

Dean was staring at Leonora, his jaw slack, his eyes wide. Michelle saw him swallow, bite his lip as he saw what she had seen.

Then Leonora put her hands on her hips.

'Well, fuck me!' she said, each word slow and clear.

There could be absolutely no doubt. Leonora was the double of Dean. Everything about them chimed. The shape of their heads, emphasised by their matching short haircuts, the angle of the cheekbones and jaw, the almond eyes with the slightly hooded lids, the bottom lip so much fuller than the top. There was no question about it. Leonora was Dean's daughter.

'Shit,' said Dean, running his hands through his hair. 'Shit. I never thought . . . I mean, I know you told me, but I never believed . . . never in a month of Sundays. I just thought . . . But you were right.' He turned to face Michelle. 'You were right, Chelle, all along. Shit. I don't know what . . .' His voice drifted off.

353

No one else spoke. Jeremy had gone very pale and looked as stunned as Dean. Sylvie was staring at the tiled floor as if she didn't want any part of it.

Then Donna started to mumble.

'No, no, no no no.'

The mumble turned into a moan and then a guttural wail that got louder and louder. The hollow sound reverberated around the room until it felt like it had replaced all the air and there was nothing to breathe. Michelle had never heard anything so haunted, so anguished as the noise that her baby girl was making. Every maternal instinct she had ever had was screaming at her. Her child needed her right now.

Before she could reach her, Donna dropped to the floor, her legs splayed beneath her, and then crumpled.

70

Then, almost as quickly as it had started up, Donna's wailing stopped. The gallery fell silent, the ticking of the grandfather clocks the only sound. Sylvie had always found their rhythmic ticking soothing, the constant soundtrack to her visits, but now the relentless beat felt sinister, as if the clocks were bearing down on her.

Donna was lying very still, unnaturally still, Sylvie thought. Drawn by an instinct that she didn't understand she took the few short steps towards her and dropped to her knees. She lifted the curtain of dark hair away from Donna's face. Her eyes were closed and it almost looked as if she were sleeping peacefully.

Was this her baby, the child that she should have had? Looking at her pale skin, the light dusting of freckles across her nose, the way her cheekbones cut away high and angular, Sylvie tried to work out what it was that she was feeling. Was it anything new? Did being confronted with the child that she had given birth to fill her with a hitherto undiscovered rush of maternal love?

No. It appeared not. She was curious about this new daughter, the one who might have shared their lives if things had turned out differently. She might even be interested in an exercise of compare and contrast between the two children, but as far as a sudden discovery of what it ought to feel like to be a mother, that was still missing. She felt nothing different. It didn't matter to her which of these two wonderful young women was her daughter. Her response, or lack of it, was exactly the same.

But just as Sylvie was processing this thought, she felt a hand on her back shoving her out of the way. It was Michelle, desperate to get to her child.

'Donna! Donna! Oh my God! What's wrong with her? Dean. What's happened to her?'

Michelle was on her knees now too, shaking Donna gently by the shoulder, trying to get her to respond. 'Donna, Donna, wake up, love!'

Sylvie could hear the panic rising in Michelle's voice.

'Dean. Dean. She's not coming round. I don't know what to do. Call an ambulance. Someone call an ambulance. Quick!'

Sylvie reached out with her hand to stroke Donna's cool cheek. If she touched her skin, would she feel their natural chemistry chime?

'Get off her,' screamed Michelle. 'What the hell are you doing? Are you crazy? Can't you see she needs help? Dean. Get her out of here.'

Dean was across the room in two bounds, placing himself between Sylvie and Donna so that Sylvie could no longer see her child, let alone touch her.

'Where's the ambulance?' Michelle screamed. 'Why isn't it here yet?'

Surely she knew that no one had called an ambulance yet? Sylvie didn't understand why she would say something so foolish.

'We don't need an ambulance. She's just fainted, that's all. And you lot pawing at her won't be helping. Let me see.'

Sylvie looked up to see who was talking, barely recognising the calm, authoritative voice. She was surprised to see that it was Leo. A flutter of pride moved inside her. Leo was taking control. Her daughter Leo.

Firmly Leo moved Michelle to one side and sat down next to Donna, who was still lying motionless.

'Donna, it's Leo here. Everything's all right. You've fainted but you're going to be fine. I'm just going to move you so you're safe. Is that okay?'

Leo worked with a focused confidence, manipulating Donna's arms and legs until she lay on one side supported by her hand. Sylvie could hear Michelle shouting but the sound blurred into the background and she wasn't interested in making out individual words. All Sylvie was concentrating on was the way Donna's hair fell across her face, how her ear peeped out where the hair parted, the line of her jaw. She remembered what she had seen when Michelle had come to her door, the echoing of Leo's features in the face of a stranger. She searched now for similar reflections in Donna's face, but they evaded her. Either they weren't there, or she wasn't destined to see them.

And then Donna stirred.

'What's going on?' she asked, her eyes still not fully opened, her voice drowsy as if she'd just woken up from a lengthy sleep.

'Oh Donna, oh my baby, thank God,' Michelle shouted. 'Dean, she's awake. Is she going to be all right? Donna, love, are you all right?'

Donna didn't seem to have much idea what was happening. She tried to lift her head but it seemed to require too much energy and it dropped back to rest on her arm.

Leo was there again, gently moving Michelle out of the way for a second time.

'Shall we give her some air?' she said. 'She's going to be completely fine. She just needs a bit of space.'

'Donna. Are you okay?' asked Dean. 'What's up with you?'

'I just felt a bit woozy,' replied Donna. 'I'll be okay. Just give me a minute.'

'I'm going to raise your feet, get your blood back to your head,' said Leo. 'Would you . . . ?'

She gestured to Dean to allow Donna's feet to rest in his lap. There was some reorganising of positions to facilitate this and after a moment or two Donna seemed to feel confident enough to sit up. Sylvie watched this other family moving together in a tight little knot with a common purpose. Was this how other families functioned, like this?

'Thanks,' Donna said to Leo. 'I feel dead stupid.'

'No worries.' Leo shrugged her thanks away, as if dealing with fainting people was something she did every day. Where had she learned what to do? Sylvie wondered.

'I'm so sorry,' Donna was saying to Michelle this time. 'God, so embarrassing to faint like that. And . . .'

And then Donna's expression changed, becoming darker and more guarded. Sylvie watched as her eyes flicked from Leo to Dean and then back again.

'And there you have it,' Donna said. Her voice sounded bitter now, the drowsiness of a moment ago evaporated. 'The truth just there for us all to see. Be careful what stones you turn over, eh?'

'Look, Donna,' Dean began. 'Just because . . .'

His eyes went from Donna to Michelle, desperate, pleading with her to help him, but Michelle was shaking her head, wanting him to stop talking.

'This doesn't change anything,' he tried again, but his tone was far from convincing.

Donna started to cry again, more controlled this time, without the raw pain of before. She tried to speak through her sobs. 'How can you say that? It changes everything. You're not my dad. You're her dad. It's obvious. You just have to look at the pair of you. So where does that leave me? Where do I fit?'

Her gaze switched to Michelle. Sylvie saw that Michelle was crying too. Tears streamed down her face but she made no effort to wipe them away, barely seemed to have noticed them.

'I am your mum,' Michelle said. 'I always have been and I always will be. In every way that matters, that is.'

Donna turned towards Sylvie then, and Sylvie swallowed hard. What was Donna expecting from her? Sylvie had no idea how she was expected to react.

But Donna didn't hold her gaze. She passed by Sylvie and settled back on Michelle.

'Oh, Mum,' she said, getting shakily to her knees and then her feet. 'I don't know what to do.'

'Come here, baby,' said Michelle, her arms open wide.

Donna ran into them and buried her face in Michelle's neck.

And at that point, Sylvie knew that nothing was going to change. It didn't matter what had happened in the past, what revelations had just come to pass. In every way that was important, Donna was Michelle's daughter and Leo was hers.

71

Michelle pulled Donna as close to her as she could. She couldn't bear as much as a hair's breadth to come between them. She wanted to absorb Donna into her own body, merge the two of them to form one being if necessary. Whatever it took to show Donna how loved she was, how safe Michelle would keep her, that was what she needed to do.

'It's okay,' she murmured into her hair as she rubbed her hand up and down Donna's back like she had done when she was a little girl. 'Everything's going to be okay, Donna. Don't you worry about anything.'

She could feel Donna still shuddering against her, but her sobbing was running out of energy, becoming more subdued. She continued to whisper reassurances.

'It's okay. You're safe.'

Over the top of Donna's head Michelle looked for Dean, found him staring at her, helpless. He still looked shell-shocked, face pale, eyes edgy and anxious. She signalled to him with her own eyes, trying to make sure that he was coping despite the messages his expression was sending her. She needed them both to be all right. She needed to make everything all right.

Dean returned her signal with a tight nod of his head. He wasn't important right now, he seemed to say. Focus on Donna.

'Well, this is a bit of a mess,' said Leonora.

Oh, God, Michelle thought. Leonora. Leonora who, as was now as apparent as the sunlight streaming in through the plate glass windows, was her daughter by blood. Leonora who she hadn't taken any notice of whatsoever. Leonora who was not on her radar in any way.

'Isn't it just,' agreed Jeremy. He exhaled, long and hard. 'I'm at a bit of a loss, to be perfectly truthful. Not really sure what I'm supposed to say.'

'I think we all feel a bit like that, mate,' said Dean, rubbing at the back of his neck with his hand. Jeremy gave him a grateful smile.

'So what happens now?' Jeremy asked. 'Now that we seem to have got to the bottom of the mystery?'

Michelle felt Donna stiffen next to her and she took her hand and squeezed it tightly.

'Time,' said Leonora. 'That's what happens now.'

Michelle considered Leonora for the first time. There were no signs of tears. The swagger she had arrived with seemed to have evaporated, but other than that she appeared unchanged. Was it the shock? Or was she really this self-composed?

This made Michelle remember how Leonora had dealt with Donna.

'I didn't say thank you,' she said. 'For what you did just now. You were so calm when we were all flapping about not knowing what to do.'

Leonora threw her half a smile, uncertain but grateful.

Jeremy cleared his throat. 'I have to say, that was a very impressive demonstration, Leo,' he said. 'I had no idea that you knew first aid.'

There was a reserve in the way that he spoke to her, as if she were an acquaintance rather than his daughter. It was odd, Michelle thought. But then hadn't Donna said that Leonora had moved out of home? Maybe relations were strained before this.

Leonora shrugged at her dad. 'Did a course,' she said. 'You never know when it might be useful.'

'You never do,' agreed Jeremy. And then, 'Well, well done.'

Leonora raised an eyebrow, the slightest hint of a smile flickering across her face.

'Listen,' she said, addressing them all. 'It's bloody stupid to be here when there's a perfectly good house with chairs and a kettle and everything just up the hill. Why don't we go there instead, and then we can have a chat about everything. Is that all right with you, Mum?'

Sylvie still hadn't spoken, Michelle realised. She was standing slightly away from the group, pale but very controlled. Was this why Leonora seemed so unruffled? Something she had learned from her mother?

At being addressed directly, Sylvie nodded but didn't speak.

'Right then,' Leonora continued, clearly happy with being the one in charge. 'Are you okay to walk, Donna? It's not far.'

'I'm fine,' replied Donna. 'Just mortified.'

She grinned at Leonora and Leonora winked back.

'Right then. Our house it is,' Jeremy said. 'We can all have a cup of tea. Or something stronger.'

'I definitely need a drink,' said Dean, shaking his head as if this were all beyond his comprehension.

'Yes,' replied Jeremy. 'Me too.'

They made their way back down the stairs, Donna leaning on one side of Michelle, more for comfort than for support, and Dean tucking in closely on the other. Jeremy took hold of Sylvie's hand.

Leonora struck out ahead and, Michelle noticed, didn't seem to need any of them.

72

They sat in a strange little group in Sylvie and Jeremy's sitting room. The room was pretty much as Michelle remembered it, clean but with a definite air of chaos about it. Over ten years on from her first visit, the bookshelves were now double-stacked and the piles of stuff on the floor were taller than they had been. There was more art on the walls too. She noticed a really nice painting of Steep Hill and one of a field of crops with the cathedral in the background. She wouldn't have minded those on her wall, not that she'd have been able to afford them.

Dean had been sticking to her side like glue ever since they'd left the art gallery and Michelle was grateful to have him there. They were working as a team again, for today at least. It felt like old times, natural, as it should be.

She caught him staring at Leo, and then, when he became aware that she was watching, he looked back at Michelle, shaking his head in disbelief. What was he thinking? Michelle wondered. Was he sorry that he hadn't believed her, that he had smashed their lives apart because he simply couldn't accept what she was telling him?

Not that that mattered now. That water had flowed under the bridge a very long time ago. What was important now was making sure that Donna was all right. Leonora too, of course, but Michelle was surprised by how little she felt for her. All her maternal instincts were gathering to protect Donna. There was nothing left over for the other girl.

Jeremy had taken charge, mustering drinks for everyone and making sure that they all had a seat. Now, though, the room fell into silence. No one wanted to be the first to speak, it seemed.

Michelle focused on them all in turn. Donna still looked seconds away from tears, her eyes glistening and her bottom lip gripped tightly between her teeth. Dean was tapping out an urgent rhythm on the arm of his chair with his fingers as if he was trying to send a coded message. And poor Jeremy, who kept leaping up to fetch some ice, or a coaster or a teaspoon for the sugar, was unable to settle at all.

Sylvie was very still. There was a calmness about her, a sense of resignation, and it occurred to Michelle that maybe she'd known all along. But if that was the case why on earth hadn't she done something about it when the girls were babies? The hospital would have taken far more notice if both mothers had claimed that a mistake had been made. Or later, when Michelle had tracked her down and turned up on their doorstep.

But for some reason that Michelle couldn't fathom, Sylvie had chosen to keep her mouth shut.

And then there was Leonora, the baby that should have been hers. Out of all of them, she was the only one who looked totally unfazed by it all. It was as if she was neither particularly surprised, nor terribly bothered which set of adults turned out to be her biological parents. Self-reliance radiated out of her. It was as if she had reached the conclusion that she didn't need any of them. Michelle found that she admired this attitude and even felt a strange sense of pride that her daughter – could she call her that? – was so very mature and independent.

Or maybe she'd got that wrong. Perhaps Leonora's attitude displayed a lack of care. Michelle hadn't seen her show any concern for Sylvie and Jeremy, who must be having a difficult time processing all this, just as she and Dean were. Yet their 'daughter' hadn't given them anything: no displays of affection, no regard for their well-being, nothing. Perhaps that quiet respect that Michelle had been developing for Leonora was actually misplaced.

Jeremy finally ran out of things to fetch, and sat down. The hush was all-consuming. Michelle thought of that expression about cutting through atmospheres. That was exactly how this felt. The air was heavy with anticipation and unspoken words, nobody wanting to go first. They were all just waiting for someone else to take the lead.

Then Donna spoke. Michelle's head whipped round to smile at her in case she needed help. Donna caught her eye, gave her a little smile. Her voice quavered a little, but it was loud enough for them all to hear.

'I started this,' she said. 'Well, Dad did actually, by letting something that I didn't know slip out.' She looked over at Dean. He twisted his mouth into an unconvincing smile and gave a little shrug. 'So, I feel responsible for making sure that we sort out a solution that works for everyone.'

Both Michelle and Jeremy interrupted her to say that she was in no way responsible for any of it, but she put her hand up to silence them both.

'I don't know what any of the rest of you think,' she continued. 'I barely know what I think myself. But there's one thing that today has made obvious.' She gestured to Leo and Dean. 'Mum was bang-on when she said she had the wrong baby. You just have to look at the two of them to know that Dad, I mean Dean, is Leo's dad.'

Heads nodded sadly. Michelle let out a long stuttering breath as if something was escaping from deep inside her.

'I've always been different to the rest of my family,' Donna continued. 'Not in a bad way. But it's been there all the same. Yet even though they didn't always get me, they've always loved me. Sometimes I felt as if I didn't belong, but I've always felt loved.'

Her voice broke and Michelle made to go and comfort her, but Dean put a restraining hand on her arm and held her back.

'I can't speak for you, Leo, but I've been brought up by good, kind people who have tried their very best for me all the way along . . .'

Michelle's throat began to thicken again and her eyes stung hot with tears as she listened.

'And as far as I'm concerned that makes them my parents. We can have all the tests in the world but it won't change a thing. Michelle and Dean are my mum and dad.'

Donna looked at Michelle sideways, as if to confirm that she had done the right thing by speaking, and Michelle threw her what she hoped was a supportive smile and a tiny nod to acknowledge how well she had done.

Michelle felt prouder of her than she ever had done before. She reached into her jeans pocket for a tissue and pulled out a straggly tail of loo roll instead. She didn't care. This was who she was. She blew her nose vigorously.

And then Leo began to speak.

'That's great, Donna. I'm chuffed that you're happy. I really am. Michelle and Dean seem like nice people. I'm not sure I want them as parents, though. No offence and all that.'

She gave Dean a cheeky grin and Dean winked at her, a subconscious gesture that Michelle had seen a thousand times before and knew came as naturally to him as breathing.

'But I have my own parents.'

Leo dropped her chin and eyed first Sylvie and then Jeremy through her eyelashes. It was hard to read her expression, but to Michelle it seemed to contain a playful warning and she wondered why.

'To be honest,' Leo continued, 'it sounds like you got the better end of the deal, Donna. My two' – she raised an eyebrow – 'well, what can I say? We haven't always seen exactly eye to eye, have we? Sylvie's done her best and actually, as mums go she's pretty cool. I don't know many people that would have put up with what I've thrown at her and stayed so calm. I'm thinking now that she was calm because she knew I wasn't anything to do with her, but no matter. She's been okay.'

Michelle looked at Sylvie but there was no suggestion of tears on her face. Either she was one cold fish or she had had years of practice at suppressing how she felt. Michelle couldn't be certain which it was, but Sylvie didn't strike her as unfeeling, so maybe it was the second.

'Now, Jeremy here has been different,' Leo continued, and the atmosphere switched again. Was she going to have a pop at the man who had raised her?

'I bet he jumped at the chance to arrange today's little fiasco, didn't he, Donna?' Leo asked.

Donna shrugged and then gave a tiny nod.

'Yeah, that'd be right, because you turning up gave him a chance to offload me on to someone else.'

Jeremy took a deep breath and pulled himself up so that he was sitting straight-backed in his chair.

'That's not fair,' he said. 'I thought no such—'

'Be quiet, Dad. You'll get your turn,' countered Leo. Jeremy opened his mouth to object, and then closed it again. 'I've always been a disappointment. I couldn't get anything right for you, or Grandma either for that matter. So in the end, I just gave up trying.

What was the point? I was never going to live up to the expectations that you had of me. You even named me after someone else. Right from the start you were setting me up to fail. But I haven't failed. Okay, I have no qualifications but what do they matter, really? I live by myself totally successfully. How many sixteen-year-olds can say that? I haven't asked you for anything. I can cook. I can fix stuff. I know what to do if you take an overdose, or choke on your own vomit. I can talk people down from the highest of high towers. And I am loved by people whose existence you're not even aware of. In every way that counts, I'm a successful person.'

Jeremy looked desperate to defend himself, but he stayed quiet as Leo continued. Michelle had to respect him for that.

'But none of that is the issue here. We have to decide what to do about this little mess. And, if I'm right, the law would say that we have to act in the best interests of the children. Oh, I know a bit about my rights now too, Dad. It's amazing what you can learn when you're interested. And what is in Donna and my best interests now that we're almost adults has to be what we want to happen.'

Michelle looked over at Sylvie but she still wasn't responding. Michelle didn't get how she could be so cool when Leo was being so honest, but she couldn't waste time thinking about that now. She turned back to Leo.

'So, I agree with Donna. For all their inadequacies, these two are my parents. I don't need any more. Once bitten, twice shy, eh?' She raised her eyebrows at Donna and Donna smiled back. 'I'm not saying let's cut off all communication and never see each other again. But I want to make it clear that I'm definitely not in the market for any more family.'

Leo shrugged. Michelle hardly dared breathe for fearing of fracturing the flimsy grip that they seemed to have on the situation. It felt like they were operating in a kind of airlock and that one wrong move could rob them all of the vital oxygen they needed to survive.

But something was washing through Michelle's veins like golden sunlight. Relief. They could have gone round the houses for hours and still ended up exactly where Leo had just put them. At least if they all walked away now then nothing more would be said that couldn't be unsaid; nobody would get hurt.

Then finally there was a response from Sylvie. Her face still impassive, she stood up, crossed to where Leo was sitting, dropped to her knees and rested her head in Leo's lap.

She didn't say a word.

SEVEN YEARS LATER

73

Leo sat and stared out over the Ngorongoro crater and caught her breath. The sun was just dropping to the horizon, casting the sky in a beautiful pink light. The plains beneath her were a hazy purple as the evening mists settled across them. Sometimes the mist reminded her of the fields of crops around Lincoln in the early morning, but the scale was so very different. The biggest field of oilseed rape was like a pocket handkerchief compared to the vastness of the crater.

She tried to catch the sunset every night, nipping away from her desk for a moment to watch, and she never grew tired of seeing it. Each one was different and magical in its own way. She had tried to capture them in photographs when she'd first arrived, desperate to share their beauty with her friends at home, but she'd given up pretty quickly. No photo could do justice to the majesty of East Africa.

She looked at her watch. Donna's plane would have landed a few hours ago. Leo pictured the tiny Arusha airport with its corrugated roof and open walls – a far cry from the European airports that Donna would be used to. Leo's colleague Simon had volunteered to make the four-hour drive to pick her up so that Leo could finish her duties and then they would have the whole weekend together before Leo had to return to work.

Standing up, she dragged herself away from the view and back to her desk in the hotel's reception to close down for the night. It was a little bit early, but the guests would just have to hang on to their questions until tomorrow.

As she came off the viewing terrace and turned the corner towards reception, her heart sank. Mrs Johnson was loitering by her desk, her head turning this way and that, seeming at once both irritated and anxious about Leo's apparent absence.

Leo painted on a friendly smile as she approached and called out brightly, 'Good evening, Mrs Johnson. Did you catch the sunset?'

Mrs Johnson looked perturbed and glanced out in the direction from which Leo had just come. 'No. I missed it because I was standing here waiting for you. It says here' – she pointed at a triangular cardboard sign on Leo's desk – 'that the office is manned until seven p.m.' She looked at her watch pointedly.

'Well, I'm here now,' replied Leo, broadening her smile. 'So, how can I help?'

Her smile seemed to weaken Mrs Johnson's determination to be angry with her, but Leo knew she still had some work to do to win her round. She had met clients like Mrs Johnson many times before. First trip to Africa and so very anxious about the unfamiliar dangers of the natural world, which she would endeavour to moderate by ensuring that everything else about her visit was entirely under her control. What guests like Mrs Johnson failed to grasp was that out there on the vast African plains, nature was entirely in charge. Humans made various feeble attempts to stamp their authority on things, but really the only way to survive was to surrender oneself and just to be swept along with the current. Unfortunately, Mrs Johnson had yet to fully appreciate this.

'I was walking past the Millers' room this evening,' she began, 'and their door was open. I couldn't help noticing that Mr Miller has laid out his clothes for tomorrow morning's safari and his trousers are black.' She nodded for emphasis at this important point and Leo raised her eyebrows as if she couldn't wait to hear where it was going, although she had heard the complaint a thousand times before.

'Now, it says quite clearly in our Safari Information pack that black clothing is ill advised because it attracts tsetse flies. We share a jeep with the Millers and I don't want to ride with them if their clothing is a beacon for dangerous insects. I have no intention of being infected with sleeping sickness just because he can't read the safety information.' Her voice had become higher and higher as she spoke, her anxiety radiating out of her like a neon glow.

Leo gave Mrs Johnson her most sympathetic smile. 'Please don't worry yourself, Mrs J. It's true that tsetse flies are attracted to darker colours but that doesn't mean that you will be bitten. I saw what you were wearing this morning and that was totally perfect.'

Mrs Johnson softened a little, pleased with the praise, and a tiny proud smile crept across her lips.

'We do make the suggestions about clothing colours,' Leo continued, 'because there is scientific evidence to support it. But the risks are very small. Typically only one American a year contracts the disease so you really mustn't worry. But if you like, I'll pop by the Millers' room now and have a quick word.'

Mrs Johnson almost swooned with relief. 'Oh, thank you, Leo. I'm so grateful. I was getting myself all worked up there.'

You don't say, thought Leo, but she smiled and said, 'All part of the service, ma'am,' in a fake American accent and gave a little bow.

Mrs Johnson shuffled away to go and get ready for dinner and Leo turned off her desk lamp and went to find the Millers. She would find a tactful way of mentioning the clothing issue without upsetting them. It was one of the things that made her so good at what she did, smoothing the waters, averting the storm.

74

Leo lay on top of her bed and drifted in and out of sleep. Even though she had been doing this job for years now, the early starts still took it out of her. Outside her window the savannah reverberated with the sounds of night: the insect chirps, distant bird calls, rumbling roars from a roaming pride of lions.

Saida the chambermaid had already been in with her hot water bottle and she rested her feet against it. She didn't think staff were supposed to get the same treatment as the guests, but Saida always said it was no trouble to just drop in with one as she passed by on her rounds. It was their little secret, she said, and Leo was grateful. It could get very cold once the sun dropped below the horizon.

She must have missed the first knock because what woke her was the sound of a voice at the door.

'Leo? Are you in there? It's me – Donna.'

Instantly awake, Leo bounced up from her bed and rushed to open the door. And there stood Donna, tired-looking and a little dusty from the journey, but beaming from ear to ear. Leo threw open her arms and pulled Donna into her.

'You made it! It's so good to see you.'

She squeezed her tightly, feeling Donna leaning into her. They stood like that for a long moment, Leo absorbing Donna's body heat, and then Leo pulled apart.

'A drink!' she announced. 'Come on. The bar should still be open.'

She led Donna out into the dark night, the sounds that drifted up from the crater louder outside. It was almost pitch-black, the only illumination coming from the low lighters that marked the path and the torches of the security guards that panned round in their direction as they walked.

'You okay there, Leo?' asked Peter, the guard most often stationed near her room.

'Right as ninepence,' replied Leo. 'Peter, meet Donna, my friend from England.'

Peter waved his torch up and down in acknowledgement.

'Hi, Donna from England. Welcome to Tanzania.'

'Hi,' replied Donna shyly.

Peter dropped the beam of his torch to show their route and they made their way to the hotel reception, it getting easier to see the closer they drew to the light.

'Why are there security men everywhere?' asked Donna anxiously once they were safe inside. 'Are we in danger of being kidnapped or something?' Her eyes darted over to the darkness beyond the plate-glass windows.

'No!' replied Leo with a laugh. 'Who'd come all the way out here to kidnap us? It's because of the wildlife. The buffalo have a tendency to wander into the grounds at night and you wouldn't want to meet one of those in the dark. They're massive with huge horns.'

Donna still looked a bit nervous.

'Don't worry. Peter and the team are very good at what they do. No one has been gored to death yet, as far as I know.'

She led Donna through the hotel to the bar. Fires blazed in the grates and some of the guests were wrapped up snugly in the tartan blankets. It was perfectly warm inside, but Leo knew that visitors enjoyed the idea of it being so cold at night when it was so hot in the day, and embraced all the trappings with enthusiasm.

She found them a table in a corner out of the way and gestured to Donna to sit. Nizar the barman waved to her and gave her a thumbs-up sign before starting to pour a beer for them both.

'This place is amazing,' said Donna, her head turning as she took everything in. 'I can't believe you actually live here.'

'Well, not here exactly,' replied Leo. 'This is just for the summer, but yes. It is pretty cool. So, tell me everything. What's the news from the home front?'

'Where to begin?' said Donna. 'I've got a new job. I'm teaching art history at the university in Nottingham now. It's a bit of a steep learning curve. There's loads of internal politics that I just don't get, but I'm just focusing on not upsetting anyone important for now. Tina had the twins last month. Twins! Still can't get my head round that.' She grinned at Leo, shaking her head in disbelief. 'So now she's got three boys under three. The fuss she makes you'd think she was the only woman ever to have more than one kid. But you know Tina. It's all about the drama with her, and there's plenty of that! They're cute though, when they're not crying.'

Leo nodded and smiled wistfully. Tina's boys would have been her nephews, if things had worked out differently. She couldn't help but feel a small tug in their direction, despite her determination to keep her distance emotionally.

'Did you know Sylvie had a picture accepted for the Royal Academy summer show?'

They always referred to their parents by their Christian names. It saved confusion. Leo shook her head.

'I saw a piece about her in the *Echo*,' Donna continued. 'It didn't say anything about Jeremy though. I assume he didn't. It was always Sylvie who had the talent, wasn't it? I still walk past the house sometimes, when I'm home. The new people repainted the front. It's a mossy green now. It looks nice.'

Leo wasn't interested in her old house or whatever colour it was painted, but she listened to the news as if it was all equally compelling.

'I saw them in London not that long ago. They've bought a loft apartment somewhere. Shoreditch, maybe? I didn't go to the apartment. We met in a restaurant. They seemed well. They send their love.'

Leo nodded again.

'And, get this for ridiculous, Michelle and Dean bought a static caravan in Mablethorpe. They go at the weekends. Carl and Tina take their kids over, drive Michelle mad getting sand all over the carpet.'

'Nah, she loves it really,' said Leo. 'What's it like, this caravan?'

This was what she really wanted to hear. The details about Michelle and Dean, the parents she never had. She didn't keep in touch with any of them except Donna, but even though she had moved as far away from them all as she could, she still found her mind drifting to what might have been from time to time. A caravan in Mablethorpe sounded like it could have been fun.

Donna chattered on about the caravan and how Michelle and Dean bickered over the smallest thing but always made up, and how Carl's new girlfriend was a vegan, which had confused everyone, and Leo listened, absorbing it all.

Eventually Donna gave an enormous yawn.

'God, I'm sorry,' she said. 'I'm falling asleep here. It's been a long couple of days.'

'Come on. Let's go back to the room and get you in bed,' said Leo.

There were only a few stragglers left in the bar now, and the fire had burned down to the embers. As they got to their feet, both yawning and stretching, Nizar came over to collect their empty glasses.

'Are you going to introduce me to your friend, Leo?' he asked.

Leo grinned at him. 'This is not just a friend,' she said. 'She's like my sister. We even have the same birthday.'

'Twins, then,' Nizar said.

Leo looked at Donna and took her hand in hers.

'Yeah,' she said. 'Something like that.'

ACKNOWLEDGEMENTS

When I was young, my mum told me the story of a girl she knew who had been swapped at birth with another baby. The story fascinated me then and has continued to do so ever since. In that real-life story, the children didn't look anything like the parents who had brought them up, but one of the families chose to ignore what was staring them in the face. When I came to write my story, I decided that I didn't want it to be obvious that there had been a swap. In fact, I didn't know myself whether Donna and Leonora had been muddled up until I wrote the scene in the art gallery. Such is the excitement of writing into the dark.

I do remember the summer of 1976 but not well enough to know about what went on in maternity wards. For that I needed some help, and via my friend Susan Saville, I was able to talk to Sheena Byrom, a midwife with forty years' experience whose book *Catching Babies* was a *Sunday Times* bestseller. My thanks go to Sheena who talked me through the practices in the 1970s and assured me that whilst baby swaps weren't an everyday occurrence, they happened more often than you might expect.

My family lived in Lincoln for a few years in the 1980s and so my thanks also go to my schoolfriends from there who shared their memories of the summer of 1976.

As ever, the creation of a book is a huge team effort, and I am thrilled to have the wonderful team at Amazon Publishing in my corner. Particular thanks go to Victoria Pepe, who always has my back. Thanks also to editor Caroline Hogg for her clear vision of what the book could be whilst also understanding what I needed to include to make it mine, and also to Gill Harvey who tirelessly points out my grammatical misdemeanours.

I want to also thank my husband John for his unerring love and support. This was our first 'empty nest' book and the house was spookily quiet as I wrote, which took some getting used to.

Finally, thanks to you for choosing this book from the very, very many available to you. I hope you enjoyed it and if you did, please consider leaving me a review or rating on Amazon which will help other readers to find and choose it too. If you are interested in me or my writing, head over to my website at https://imogenclark. com where you'll find links to all my social media pages.

I also write as Izzy Bromley so please visit https://izzybromley.com/ to discover more.

With very best wishes,

Imogen.

ABOUT THE AUTHOR

Photo © 2022 Carolyn Mendelsohn

Imogen Clark writes contemporary fiction about families and secrets. She has sold over a million copies of her books and has topped the Amazon Kindle chart eight times. *Where the Story Starts* was shortlisted in the UK for Contemporary Romantic Novel of the Year 2020.

After initially qualifying and working as a lawyer, Imogen left her legal career behind to care for her four children and then returned to her first love – books. She went back to university, studying English Literature part-time whilst the children were at school. It was a short step from there to writing novels.

Imogen's great love is travel and she is always planning her next adventure. She lives in Yorkshire. You can find out more about her by visiting her website https://imogenclark.com. She also writes as Izzy Bromley. Visit https://izzybromley.com/ to discover more.

Follow the Author on Amazon

If you enjoyed this book, follow Imogen Clark on Amazon to be notified when the author releases a new book!
To do this, please follow these instructions:

Desktop:

1) Search for the author's name on Amazon or in the Amazon App.
2) Click on the author's name to arrive on their Amazon page.
3) Click the 'Follow' button.

Mobile and Tablet:

1) Search for the author's name on Amazon or in the Amazon App.
2) Click on one of the author's books.
3) Click on the author's name to arrive on their Amazon page.
4) Click the 'Follow' button.

Kindle eReader and Kindle App:

If you enjoyed this book on a Kindle eReader or in the Kindle App, you will find the author 'Follow' button after the last page.